MO 2116

06 JUN 2016

CU00969059

C

Leeds Library and Information Service
24 hour renewals
http://www.leeds.gov.uk/librarycatalogue
or phone 0845 1207271
Overdue charges may apply

THE WHITE WORM

SAM SICILIANO

TITAN BOOKS

THE FURTHER ADVENTURES OF SHERLOCK HOLMES:
THE WHITE WORM
Print edition ISBN: 9781783295555
E-book edition ISBN: 9781783295562

Published by Titan Books
A division of Titan Publishing Group Ltd
144 Southwark Street, London SE1 0UP

First edition: February 2016
10 9 8 7 6 5 4 3 2 1

A CIP catalogue record for this title is available from the British Library.

Printed in the USA.

What did you think of this book? We love to hear from our readers.
Please email us at: readerfeedback@titanemail.com,
or write to Reader Feedback at the above address.

To receive advance information, news, competitions, and exclusive offers online, please sign up for the Titan newsletter on our website:
www.titanbooks.com

This one is for my father and my son.

Two of my three earlier Holmes novels derive from other works. *Angel of the Opera* is a retelling of the *Phantom of the Opera* with Sherlock Holmes, and it closely follows the plot of Leroux's novel. *The Grimswell Curse* is a sort of theme and variations on *The Hound of the Baskervilles*. In both cases, I could be sure that most readers· had at least some familiarity with my source material. However, this time around that is not the case.

Since Bram Stoker wrote a real masterpiece, *Dracula*, which can still scare modern readers, I wish I could say his last book *The Lair of the White Worm* is a lost treasure. Sadly, that is not the case. It's like a Victorian curiosity shop full of bizarre and kinky knick-knacks. The prose is overwrought, the characterization simple-minded, and there is a minor black African character whose lip-smacking, leering portrayal is beyond embarrassing. The fear of female sexuality also found in *Dracula* reaches new heights, and Freudians can have a field day. The femme-fatale villainess who is both a woman and a centuries-old gigantic white serpent is unintentionally comical, as is her final fate. There are two versions of the novel, both available as free ebook downloads: Stoker's original 1911 version makes a bit more sense than the posthumously released abridgement of 1925.

Despite its weaknesses, *The Lair of the White Worm* did inspire this latest book. However, it is certainly a much looser connection than with *The Angel of the Opera*. Certain of Stoker's characters made it into my story (but not the black African!), along with some Freudian undercurrents and a Gothic atmosphere. I also moved the story to Yorkshire for reasons that should be apparent by the conclusion. I hope my readers will enjoy the results.

One

Although it was April and the days had grown longer, the air seemed sodden and heavy that particular Monday evening. It was just after six. The sun would not set for another hour or so, but this perpetual twilight had begun mid-afternoon. Winter might be gone, but the stench and dark presence of coal smoke still hovered over London. As I went up the short stairway to my cousin's flat, I wished again for a good rain to cleanse the air. Where were the proverbial showers?

The indomitable Mrs. Hudson, short, plump and smiling, opened the door.

"How is he?" I asked.

She shook her head. "Not well at all. Perhaps you can reason with him, Doctor."

I went up another short flight of stairs, rapped lightly at the door, then opened it. I blinked twice and a pungent smoke filled my lungs, making me cough. "Good Lord," I murmured. Through the haze I could see my cousin seated at his favorite armchair wearing his faded purple dressing gown with his pipe in hand. I stepped closer, waving my fingers to try to part the noxious cloud. "This is unbelievably foul. If you are feeling unwell…"

Holmes shook his head. "There is little else to do. Allow me the luxury of my favored vice."

"Really, this is too much. This must be the cheapest possible shag. Certainly you can afford better."

Holmes turned to me, his dark brows knotting over the beak of his nose. "Henry, do not lecture me on the evils of tobacco-poisoning. I had enough of that from Watson."

"Well, he was right, you know."

"Nonsense. No one has ever proven…" He raised one hand to cover a sharp cough. "It has never…" A fusillade of coughs suddenly overwhelmed him, barking noises, and he bent over, setting down the pipe.

I shook my head, looked about, then went to the sideboard and poured brandy from a decanter. I handed him the glass, then took the pipe and found a nearby ashtray. I turned over the pipe and tapped it against the glass.

Holmes swallowed, shook his head wildly–"No, no!"–he shook his head again, then had another swallow of brandy. "You must not commit battery against a well-made pipe like that one. It must not be knocked about so rudely."

"Forgive me." I went to the bow window, unfastened the latch and opened it. "The air outside is hardly better, but at least it may clear the haze."

The coughing fit gradually came to an end. I seized my bag and dug around for my stethoscope. "Let me have a listen to your lungs."

"There is nothing wrong with my lungs."

I laughed sharply. "Come now, you need not remove your

dressing gown or shirt. Just undo a button or two."

His thin face seemed paler than usual as he stared up at me. I warmed the bell on my hand, then set it on his chest between two ribs. "Breathe in and out." I listened carefully. "I think you have only the beginnings of bronchitis. You definitely should abstain from tobacco for a few days."

"Henry, Watson's scolding about tobacco was one of the causes of the breach between us. If you also are going to start the same thing, our friendship cannot endure."

"And if you will not listen to me and if you drive me away, then perhaps I will take up my pen and publish something about our adventures together."

Holmes scowled fiercely, then he laughed. "Touché! Anything but that! One Watson is bad enough, but a second..." He shook his head. "No, it could not be endured."

"And I suppose you have not eaten since breakfast."

He had to think for a few seconds. "I suppose I have not."

"Let me have Mrs. Hudson bring you something—as well as a cup of tea. That will soothe your throat."

He shrugged slightly. "Oh, very well." He gave a long sigh. "It is good to see you, Henry. I was rather lost in my thoughts, too much so."

I stared closely at him. "Violet Wheelwright?"

The corners of his mouth rose very slightly. "Oh very good, Henry. Our association has aided your powers of deduction, but it must be very obvious indeed."

Violet Wheelwright had been at the center of a case that had ended tragically, and I knew Holmes admired her more than any other woman. It had been over a year since they had parted, but my wife Michelle and I still hoped that someday they might be reunited.

I spoke with Mrs. Hudson, poured Holmes a little more brandy, poured myself one, then sat at the nearby sofa. Holmes held the glass in his long, slender fingers and stared down at the liquid. "It is ennui, you know. Since the Grimswell Curse, there has been little to interest me."

"Dartmoor seemed to agree with you. I think you could do with a holiday, an outing. Some fresh air would do you good."

He shrugged. "I would prefer an interesting case to a holiday." He stared at me. "Perhaps now that you are here... You are good luck for me, Henry. Two of my most fascinating cases began when you were sitting on that very sofa and I was bemoaning the dismal state of crime—in just such circumstances as these, there came a rap at the door..."

A light rap did sound, and Mrs. Hudson appeared without tea or food. "Mr. Holmes—" A huge young man wearing a brown tweed Norfolk suit and cloth cap, valise in hand, strode into the room. Mrs. Hudson frowned. "A visitor to see you."

He must have been six and a half feet tall, and the hand clutching the hat brim was the largest I had ever seen. Beneath his curly black hair, his face was pale. His features recalled some classical statue, and he had the air of a young Adonis.

"Mr. Holmes, I must speak to you—you must help me."

Holmes glanced at me, one eyebrow rising briefly, then back at the youth. "Gladly, sir, although you must pardon this informal garment. I was not expecting visitors."

"It doesn't matter to me."

"Would you care for a brandy?" Holmes asked.

He shook his head. "No, no." His head seemed to freeze, and then he took in an enormous breath. Although he was obviously a gentleman, he had a chest worthy of a stevedore. "Yes—I mean *yes.*"

I stood up and went to the sideboard. The young man somehow managed to take the brandy from me without really seeing me.

"This is my cousin and friend, Dr. Henry Vernier."

The young man turned abruptly to me. He had striking, vivid blue eyes. "Oh, I beg your pardon, sir." He nodded. "Thank you for the brandy." He took a swallow, and half of it was gone. He looked at me again. "Not Dr. Watson?"

"No," Holmes and I said simultaneously.

Holmes gestured with a flourish at the sofa. "Do sit down, sir. And who, may I ask, do I have the pleasure of addressing?"

"Selton. Adam Selton."

"How do you do, Mr. Selton. And how was your train journey? A rushed departure, and then rather long and fatiguing, I fear. And you came straight from the station."

Selton's eyes widened. He glanced at me, then back at Holmes. "It's true—you can read minds!"

Holmes laughed. "Nonsense. You are wearing dress more suitable for the country than the city. You did not bother to shave this morning. Your suit has a wrinkled, battered look—as do you—and you are carrying a traveling valise. Even Henry must have noticed this."

I smiled slightly. "Of course." Actually I had noticed little save his youth and size.

Holmes sat back in the chair. "And I suppose this must involve a young lady."

Selton struck his knees with two enormous fists. "Yes! If you can't read minds, how could you possibly know that?"

Holmes smiled. "You must allow me my little secrets. Tell me about yourself and the young lady, Mr. Selton."

He shook his head. "It's all such a muddle. I don't know where to begin, exactly."

"Why not with her name, her particulars, and then something of your own family."

He nodded. "Yes, of course. Her name is Diana–Miss Diana Marsh. Her family is an old and established one in the north of Yorkshire near Whitby, a port on the North Sea. Their estate is called Diana's Grove. Her father and mother died of influenza three years ago. She was their only child. After her parents' deaths, she lived with her grandfather, who died last year. Her aunt, Lady Verr, who was recently widowed, has been staying with her for some six months. Diana is... is..." He did not seem to know where to begin. "She is quite tall, something which runs in the family, and she has long red hair and striking green eyes. She is very slender, although she has a woman's shape..." His eyes seemed to lose focus. "Most definitely a woman's shape." A hint of color appeared in his cheeks.

Holmes glanced at me. "The situation seems somewhat familiar, Henry, does it not?" I knew he must be thinking of Rose Grimswell. "Does the lady by any chance have a large fortune?"

"Fortune?" He seemed genuinely puzzled. "I don't know. I doubt it. The estate and her home, of course, but the dwelling is badly in need of repairs. Perhaps a few hundred a year, maybe a thousand, hardly anything."

Holmes's eyebrow rose again. "Most in London would not consider that a pittance–to the contrary. I take it you must be rather well situated yourself."

He shrugged. "Yes. Someday I shall inherit the family home and a large estate in Derbyshire even as my father did before me. We also have a townhouse in London and another house in Yorkshire. My father has always had a fondness for the seaside, and he bought the place near Whitby ten years ago; Lesser Hill, it is called. That was where I first met Diana–Miss Marsh. I am only a year older than she, and we soon became friends."

"And how old are you, Mr. Selton?"

"I turned twenty-one last month. Anyway, Diana was always the adventurous one, afraid of nothing, while I..." He looked up at us both. "Because I am so tall, people assume I must be fearless. I only wish that were true."

"A traditional English family of the landed gentry, and as you said, someday you will inherit your father's estate." Holmes smiled faintly at me. "There is no obvious motive to cause trouble for the Selton family, Henry, as there was last time. And what are your intentions toward Miss Marsh?"

His cheeks reddened again. "They are honorable, of course."

Holmes smiled somewhat ironically. "Certainly. And so would these honorable intentions have a matrimonial bent?"

It took him a second or two to figure that out, and then the blood did seem to pour into his face. I don't think I've ever seen a man flush in such a way before. "I... I..." His throat seemed constricted.

"I did not mean to distress you, Mr. Selton."

"I don't know. I *don't.*" His voice was anguished.

"You do seem fond of the young lady."

"Oh yes! But there are... complications." The blood receded as quickly as it had come, white replacing red. "For one thing, Father does not think she is suitable. He thinks someone with a title would be more appropriate, given all that we have to offer."

Holmes glanced briefly at the ceiling, then at me, then back to Selton. "I take it you are referring to the family estate and fortune?"

"Yes. Of course."

This last phrase made Holmes almost wince. "And you are—*of course*—willing to comply with your father's wishes?"

Selton's jaw stiffened. "No, not necessarily. I... I..."

Holmes raised his right hand, long fingers stretched upward toward the ceiling. "You need not elaborate. I understand. Thus far I cannot see the reason for your rushing all the way from Yorkshire to seek my services. Yours seem to be the usual trials and tribulations of youthful romance."

"I came, Mr. Holmes, because… because… because I am worried." And indeed, he was clearly uneasy.

"Explain yourself, sir."

"I have received the most remarkable letter and document about the Marsh family, and I do not know what to make of it. Surely it can only be nonsense, and yet why would someone even send me such a thing? I cannot imagine Miss Marsh has any enemies, but the document is so frightful, and…"

"Show me, Mr. Selton—show me." Holmes eagerly extended his hand, palm up.

Selton reached inside the voluminous side of his jacket and withdrew some folded papers. Holmes quickly scanned the first one and frowned. "Short and to the point." He handed the letter to me.

Mr. Adam Selton,

if you value your manhood, you would do well to flee from Diana Marsh and that cursed family while you still can. Have you never heard of the dark history of Diana's Grove and the Marsh family? If not, you may want to peruse the venerable document enclosed. The tale itself was passed down for generations before being transcribed some two or three centuries ago. Think well before you involve yourself with one who actually bears the name of this accursed place. Believe me, there are serpents who can assume a pleasing female shape.

A friend.

"Serpents?" I murmured.

Holmes unfolded the other pages. They appeared yellow with age, the edges brown and uneven. He took the first page between thumb and forefinger, rubbed back and forth, thoughtfully feeling the paper. He hesitated, then turned over the page and sniffed at it twice, loudly. He looked at me. "A good thing you opened the window, Henry, and allowed the smoke to dissipate. By the way, you might close it again before we all catch a chill."

I did so, then returned to my seat. Holmes thumbed through the pages. "This is rather lengthy. Might I read it aloud so as to share the contents with Henry?"

Selton still looked pale. "As you wish, Mr. Holmes."

"'This story has been passed down within our family for many generations, but I at last shall write down the terrible tale of Sir Michael Marsh and the White Worm.'"

"Worm?" I murmured.

Holmes's eyes glanced down the page. "Ah, yes, he means 'worm' in the archaic sense of serpent or dragon, not our current lowly earthworm." He continued reading.

During the reign of the Mercian kings, one knight became known above all others for his bravery and remarkable deeds, especially the defeat of several terrible serpents who terrified the countryside, slaughtering men and beasts. His last and greatest conquest was that of the worm who dwelt near the sea and the moors of Yorkshire. Though that land was beyond Mercia's boundaries, its people sent a delegation to the Mercian king, begging him to send help against the clever and powerful dragon. This dragon lived in a grove of oaks on a cliff alongside the sea, a place originally known as Diana's Grove, but now called lair of the White Worm. Sir Michael went willingly, accompanied by his favorite mastiff, a white stallion and his squire Alfred.

After a long weary journey, he came at last to the grove. He dismounted and had Alfred help him into his best armor, the plates gleaming silver under the sun, and then the two men knelt down. Sir Michael inverted his massive broadsword, raising its jeweled hilt as a cross while they prayed God to aid them in their combat against the foul creature. The knight remounted and proceeded up the hill, his sword and lance at his side.

As is often the case, a heavy fog from the sea had risen to cover the land, damp and cold, turning summer almost to winter. The cry of the distant gulls could be heard. The trees had their summer leaves, and the black trunks and greenery could be made out ahead, as well as some ghostly white figures. Wary, Sir Michael drew his sword and held the blade before him. His steed whinnied, uneasy, but the knight stroked his mane and spoke gently.

As they drew nearer, he could see a number of women, all wearing white robes, all wondrously beautiful and fair, but none could compare with their leader. Many had blond, auburn or pale-brown hair, but hers was like flames, lapping in a fiery halo around her wondrous face. Her eyes were green, a true green like emeralds, her lips a brilliant red. Unlike the others, she wore a white gown which left bare her long white slender arms and clung so tightly it showed her sinuous shape. Round her throat was a necklace of emeralds which rivaled her eyes.

Despite her great beauty, Sir Michael felt uneasy. He slowed his horse but kept his sword raised high. The mastiff snarled loudly and would have lunged for the woman, but Alfred managed to hold him back.

"What seek you, good knight? Ours is a humble place of worship, but my votaries and I welcome you. Would you break bread with us?"

"Of what worship do you speak? Do you believe in Jesus Christ, our Lord, who has redeemed us all through his death?"

The priestess smiled haughtily. "No, my lord. Ours is an older religion, one that once held sway over all of Britain. The Celts and their Druids knew us well, as did the Romans, some of whom made it this far. Our ancient faith is bound to the earth, the sky, the rocks and water, and the trees of this grove behind us. Still, we respect your faith, as we hope you will respect ours. Come, will you join us for supper?"

"I seek a dragon—a white worm—a creature of great size whom men, women and beasts all fear. Have you seen him?"

The priestess laughed heartily. "That old tale! There is no worm here, my lord, only us women. You, a knight with your great sword and lance, can have no fear of the likes of us. Come now." She held up her hand and turned her palm outward toward him, and its rosy flush shone like the setting sun. "Come join me."

Sir Michael glanced down at Alfred. His squire shook his head even as he struggled to restrain the mastiff.

The woman touched her hips with her beautiful hands, turning slightly even as she lowered her eyes and bowed. "I beg of you, my lord."

Sir Michael felt a sudden ache about his heart: he had no wife, and he had never seen so lovely a woman. He lowered his sword. "Very well."

The knight followed the women into the misty grove, the dark trunks writhing upward all about them, until they came at last to a stone dwelling of great age. The knight dismounted, and the priestess bade him remove his armor and be at ease. He would take off only his helmet, and he kept his sword sheathed at his side. They came into a great hall where a fire burned before a table set with a wondrous feast. The priestess poured wine from a flagon into two golden goblets, gave him one, then held up her own and drank to his health and long life. The knight had never tasted a wine so sweet and fragrant. He was ravenous and ate the roasted game and fine white bread offered him. The lady, however, partook of nothing, only sipped at her wine as she watched him through her half-closed green eyes.

After he had eaten his fill, a great weariness came over him. The lady led him to a bedchamber, and he lay down, still clad in his armor. She took up a harp and began a sweet song in an unknown tongue. The knight slept, but his dreams were terrible. He rose once and went to the window of the chamber. In the distance, amidst the trees, a green light glowed.

In the morning he discovered that the mastiff had disappeared. Alfred bade Sir Michael depart, but the lady stared at him, bidding him stay by her look alone. The knight removed his armor and wandered that day in the shadowy grove. Something unseen followed him through the trees.

Again he was served food at a great banquet and drank a wondrous wine. He went to the chamber, and the lady sang him asleep. His dreams were worse than the night before. Again he woke once and saw the green glow in the darkness. In the morning his stallion had vanished, and Alfred begged him to depart while they still could. The lady said nothing, but again her look spake more than words. A great weariness came over the knight. He slept most of the day, then came again to the banquet, but his appetite had left him. Still, he drank more of the wine. The lady sang him asleep, and his dreams were full of terror and rapture. He started up during the night and found himself naked. Again he went to the window and saw the green glow. The next morning Alfred could not be found.

The knight felt sick in spirit, and he wanted only to sleep, but instead he went into the grove. Wandering through the trees, he came at last to dark, ancient stones set round in a circle, and in the center was a black hole which, from the look of it, went to the center of the earth. From its depths came a greenish mist and a foul stench. The knight threw a stone into the pit, but never heard it land. His heart began to pound in his chest, and a great fear seized him.

He staggered away, went back to the dwelling and found his sword by the bedside. He knelt, raised up the hilt, and prayed to God as he had never prayed before. A certain calm came over him. He went to the evening feast, but ate little and would not touch the wine.

"Something troubles my lord," the lady said. Her green eyes stared from within the nimbus of her flaming tresses, and he noticed that her pupils were dark slits rather than circles.

He looked away and said, "It is only that I am weary."

She extended her hand. "Come, my lord." She led him to the bedchamber, and then somehow she removed her gown without using her hands, slipping free, shedding it like a skin to stand before him, naked and white. The knight could not tear his gaze from her. Her ruby lips parted, and she raised her arms. "Come, my lord. Come to me. Take me. I am yours."

The knight did not move, but she stepped forward and used her hands to rip his garments asunder. The knight managed, at last, to look away and saw the harp and his sword lying nearby. He turned and took up the harp. "You have sung to me so often, my fair one. Let me sing to you."

She folded her arms across her breasts and stood waiting. He began a song which was a prayer to Mary, the Mother of God. The lady staggered as if she had been struck, and then her mouth opened impossibly wide, revealing two enormous fangs. "Stop!" she hissed, but Sir Michael sang on, begging the Virgin Mother for aid.

The lady tried to clap her hands against her ears, but her fingers seemed to take root there, and her arms shrank away, as did her legs. Only her torso, her breasts and fair face remained as she assumed the shape of a great serpent, growing larger and ever larger. Her beauteous white skin hardened, scales forming, and her tail lashed about even as she rose up higher still. A great hiss burst from her distended jaw, and she struck at the knight.

He thrust forth the wooden harp, which she caught in her mouth, and then he seized his sword. Even as she struggled to free her teeth, he swung with both hands and severed her head with a single blow. With a great shriek, the head fell to the floor, even as a spout of green blood shot from the serpent body. The green eyes stared up balefully at the knight, slowly clouding over as her red hair lost its brilliance.

The ruby lips formed a cruel smile. "Your sons may be yours, but your daughters will be mine evermore." Her eyes closed, even as the headless snake's body toppled over.

The knight staggered forth, sword in hand. A few of the

women in white robes tried to stop him, but he struck them down as he fled. The wind howled in the trees, but he broke free of the grove at last and went downhill out of the mists. He made his way to a nearby village where he collapsed. A priest cared for him for several days, but it was only after he made his confession that he began to recover. Later that summer he returned to the grove, had the pit covered over, the ancient dwelling torn down and a splendid new home constructed. He had determined to live at the site of his greatest triumph.

Ever after those days, Sir Michael was a grave and unsmiling man. A year later he met a beautiful lady, married her, and brought her to his estate at Diana's Grove. They had several children, both girls and boys. Sir Michael always had the priest bless and baptize the girls straight away. Golden crosses hung on the walls of their bedchambers, and the knight went to Mass daily to pray on his knees for his daughters' safe keeping. They were all spared, but his descendants were not so lucky. Thus is it that whenever a girl is born into the Màrsh family, there is no rejoicing, but only fear for what the future may bring.

Holmes set the papers down. "Quite a tale, indeed." He set the tips of his fingers together and stared at Selton. "I can understand that you might find this troubling. All the same—do you actually see some connection between this tale and the family situation today?"

Selton's eyes rose, then fell. "I am not certain. I had heard references to the White Worm and Diana's Grove before, but I had never actually heard the whole story. Even as a child, I noticed some people were afraid to go near the place, especially at night, and more recently there have been... stories."

"What kind of stories?"

"About some giant... some giant white..."

"Snake?" I exclaimed, as he could not seem to finish. He nodded. I shook my head. "Oh, that is simply preposterous."

Holmes tapped his fingertips together twice, then lowered his hands. "Obviously Mr. Selton does not find it preposterous."

Selton thrust forth his jaw, then brought it back. "There is an elderly gentleman who lives near our Yorkshire home, Sir Nathaniel de Salis, and he knows the geography and geology, the animals and vegetation of the region. All of England is riddled with caves and caverns of great depth. Since we know that creatures of great size lived in ancient times, Sir Nathaniel speculates that some great beast might still linger in the depths of the earth. The pit mentioned in the story does exist, and it is frighteningly deep."

I shook my head. "Werewolves and vampires are nonsensical enough, but white dragons and beautiful damsels who are actually serpents?"

Selton thrust his jaw forward again but would not speak. Holmes watched him carefully. "You admire Miss Marsh, Mr. Selton."

He nodded. "I do."

"And yet, you fear all is not well with her. That she may have something of this... serpentine nature mentioned in the story."

Selton went paler still. I shook my head and leaned forward. "No, no–please! It is difficult enough with a woman, without introducing–"

Holmes stared sternly at me and shook his head. Selton wiped his hand across his brow and let his fingers rest in the thick tangle of black hair. "I don't know what to believe. As I said, it's all such a muddle."

Holmes sat back and crossed his legs, drummed at the chair arm. "Someone is trying to frighten you, that is clear enough. The emphasis, however, is peculiar. That reference in the letter to your manhood, for example."

Selton raised his head, opened his mouth, then seemed to freeze even as the blood again poured into his face. "For God's sake," I said, "what is it? What is wrong?" He shook his head, unable to speak. As a physician I had a sudden suspicion. "Has something made you question your manhood?"

Selton sat up, then almost leaped from the chair, even as he made two huge fists. "I'll not be insulted by the likes of you!" He whirled about and started for the door. Holmes and I both stood, and I shook my head.

"You are being ridiculous, Mr. Selton!" Holmes cried. "Stop—just stop! No one is doubting your manhood. Be reasonable. We want to help you. You are weary from your journey. Please come back."

Selton stood before the door, his massive back toward us, one hand on the knob. At last he let it go and turned toward us. His face was still bright red. "Forgive me. I am… oh, I am a hopeless fool."

Holmes picked up Selton's glass and went to the sideboard. "Have another brandy, sir, and compose yourself."

Selton dropped his valise and hat, then collapsed into the chair. "I am tired." He sipped the brandy. His flush faded more quickly this time.

Holmes reached for his pipe, but I sternly shook my head. He folded his arms and briefly paced about before returning to his chair. Selton's eyes were fixed on his knees, and his outburst seemed to have consumed the last of his energy. "Someone wants to frighten you off," Holmes murmured almost to himself. "Are there any other men who seem interested in the young lady?" He shook his head. Holmes drummed again at the chair arm. "Tell me about the aunt, Mr. Selton. You said she was recently widowed?"

"Yes."

"What happened to her husband?"

"It was a frightful suicide."

"Ah!" Holmes smiled. "Suicide is always a matter of interest, especially as it often introduces doubt."

"Doubt?" Selton asked.

"Murder often masquerades as suicide."

Selton shook his head. "Not in this case. The man blew his brains out in front of his doctor and his wife. There is no doubt there."

Holmes nodded. "Now that is rather extraordinary. Is it known why Lord—was it Verr, Lord Verr? Was it known why Lord Verr might kill himself?"

Selton lowered his eyes. "It seems obvious. He had lost his fortune and was heavily in debt. He also seemed to be going mad."

"Going mad." Holmes nodded thoughtfully, then smiled at me. "More and more interesting. And Lady Verr has moved in with her niece."

"Yes. It seemed the sensible thing for them both."

"And what is your opinion of Lady Verr?"

"My opinion?" Selton seemed genuinely puzzled. "Oh, she seems nice enough. She's a bit eccentric, but good-hearted, I suppose. She's very… very pretty." Again some hint of color in his cheeks. "But of course, she is old."

"How old?" Holmes asked.

Selton thought for a while. "In her late thirties, possibly even forty." I laughed outright, while even Holmes smiled. "What is wrong?"

"Many would not characterize forty as old," Holmes said. "And does Miss Marsh like her aunt?"

"Oh yes, I think so. She appreciates all that she has done for her."

Holmes nodded. "Does this aunt have any suitors?"

"Not really."

"But you seem to consider someone a possibility."

"There is a recent arrival from abroad, a Mr. Edgar Caswall. He has returned to reclaim the long-empty family castle, Castra Regis. He is known as the wealthiest man in that part of Yorkshire."

"How convenient for a woman left penniless by a suicidal husband."

Holmes's comment didn't seem to register with Selton. He put one hand over his mouth and stifled a yawn.

"You are tired, Mr. Selton. We must allow you to get some rest. This has been an interesting conversation, but what exactly would you like me to do?"

"I want you to come to Yorkshire with me and help find out what's behind it all. I can pay you well for your help."

"Indeed? What do you propose?"

"I shall pay you ten pounds a day while you are assisting me, and another two hundred when I consider the case satisfactorily resolved. I can write you a check for two hundred pounds immediately."

My eyes opened wide. That was a formidable sum. Holmes nodded. "That is more than enough, Mr. Selton. And what would you consider satisfactory resolution? If I could tell you who sent you that letter and why, would that suffice?"

Selton's brow was furrowed. "I don't know. Probably."

Holmes sighed. "Tempting. All the same, I am not sure I am currently at liberty–"

"To decline," I said. "He will certainly accept. Your offer is more than generous. And I–" it came out before I had time for reflection "–I will accompany him." Holmes stared at me in disbelief. "The air of Yorkshire is just what you need. We were just now speaking of a–" I realized "holiday" was not the word to use. "Of some time in the country, some work outside the noxious air of London, and this is just the thing."

Selton smiled at me, then turned to Holmes, and his smile faltered.

"If only you would come, Mr. Holmes. If the money is not enough…"

"As Henry said, it is more than generous, Mr. Selton. Tell me, sir, have you spoken to Miss Marsh about this letter?"

"Of course not!"

"How, then, would we explain my presence in Yorkshire?"

Selton opened his mouth, then closed it, brow furrowed. "I don't know."

"We can simply say you are there for rest and recuperation," I said, "which would be true enough."

Holmes nodded. "Perhaps, although that might not be entirely convincing. Mr. Selton, you mentioned some local stories and rumors. How serious is this? Does anyone actually claim to have seen something?"

Selton still looked worried. "Yes. Some have seen a greenish glow in the woods at night… and even a white apparition."

Holmes nodded. "Then we can also say I have been asked by someone in the local village to look into the matter. Which village is closest to Diana's Grove?"

"Micklethorpe."

"Excellent. Someone from Micklethorpe has engaged me, and he recommended I stay nearby, with you. Be here at eight o'clock sharp in the morning, Mr. Selton, and we shall take the eight-thirty express train north."

Selton drew in a great breath which seemed to go on and on, swelling his chest. "Oh thank you, Mr. Holmes–thank you!" He downed the last of the brandy, then stood. He turned to me. "And thank you, Dr. Vernier." His crushing parting grip was exactly what might have been expected from someone his size, and after the door was closed, I shook my hand a few times, trying to regain feeling.

"Will you really come with us to Yorkshire, Henry?"

"Yes, for a while, anyway. You know I cannot bear to be away from Michelle for long."

"I wish she could come, too. With Miss Marsh and Lady Verr—and the distraught Mr. Selton—I suspect her feminine knowledge of the emotions would be useful."

"I'm sure it would, but she is busy as ever. Even as my practice withers, hers grows. Still, I shall try to persuade her. She could certainly do with a holiday, too."

Holmes shook his head and returned to his chair. "Somehow I do not think this will be a holiday. Oh, the story is preposterous enough, as you noted, and I doubt we will find a great white serpent lurking in Yorkshire. All the same, as I have often noted, human evil is far worse than anything found in the natural world. The most fearsome monsters are those which assume human shape—and frequently a pleasing one, at that." He raised the first page of the document which Selton had left behind. "This is an obvious forgery, but it did require time and effort."

"How can you tell it is a forgery?"

He shook his head. "This is a common enough paper of good quality which can be purchased at any shop in London. The brownish yellow tint comes from tea."

"Tea!" I said with a laugh.

"The sheets were dipped in tea, then allowed to dry. However, a faint odor remains. No doubt the edges were charred by a flame. As I said, it would have taken time, but it is a rather amateurish effort. The story, on the other hand, is a tour-de-force. I recall some Romantic poem about a lamia, a snake who assumed the form of a beautiful woman. The lamia came from Greek mythology, but closer to home there was the Lambton Worm which terrorized the countryside before a knight slew it. That tale is the most likely source of this document, although the beautiful and seductive maiden is an addition. It also owes much to the romantic poets and to Tennyson's Arthurian *Idlylls of the King.*"

"Why would someone go to all that trouble? Poor Selton. He is certainly an odd duck."

"He is only young, Henry, and way out of his depth. Whoever is playing with him is far, far beyond his league. Tell me, though–and in this I must defer to you–despite all that blushing, I suspect that Mr. Selton may have had more of a relationship with this young woman than he admits."

I felt my brow crease. "Carnal relations?"

Holmes nodded. "Exactly."

I shook my head. "I do not think so."

Mrs. Hudson arrived at last with a tray bearing tea and a sandwich for Holmes, which she sat next to his chair. Holmes poured himself tea from the porcelain teapot. "You are certainly more knowledgeable in this area than I. What do you make of Selton?"

"Might I have another brandy?" I poured myself some, then resumed my place on the sofa. "I have had male patients come to me because they were unable to consummate their relationship with their spouse. Young men, recently married, are the most desperate. Young girls are not the only ones to go to the marriage bed woefully ignorant and unprepared. The men hope I will have some magical pill or potion. There is none, and mostly what they need is time and reassurance. Another variation is when a youth has been presented with a prostitute by his supposed friends or a parent, and…"

"A parent?" Holmes exclaimed.

I nodded. "Yes, a parent–a father, to be precise. They want to get the young man started, to make him into a man. With a sensitive youth, it is not all mechanics and blind lust. Without some feeling or strong physical attraction, it is simply impossible. Such an introduction is a cruel trick to play on a vulnerable nature. It can take its toll for years afterward. I suspect that may be the case with Selton."

Holmes nodded. "I am glad I asked for your counsel." A faint, rather bitter smile pulled at his lips. "This is where your knowledge is clearly superior to mine. Given his youth, his bewilderment and nervousness, your appraisal strikes me as the correct one."

"I wonder what the young lady is like. And the aunt."

Holmes nodded slightly. "Snakes, of course. White snakes."

My eyes widened, and then Holmes laughed. "We shall see soon enough."

I lay holding Michelle close to me, my breath gradually slowing, almost ready to dream.

"You do well at ardent farewells, my dear," she murmured.

I caressed her hip. "So do you."

"I didn't think I had it in me. It has been such a long day. But if you are to go traipsing off to Yorkshire tomorrow with Sherlock to bask idly in the sun..."

"I would like that, but it certainly didn't turn out that way last time. I just hope it doesn't become a nightmare, as happened at Dartmoor. I have never been so glad to see you in my life as when you appeared that morning. Even under the best of circumstances, you know I don't like being apart from you. Are you certain you can't get away for a few days' holiday?"

She sighed softly. "I wish I could, but now is not a good time."

"It is never a good time with you."

She kissed my shoulder. "Oh Henry, you know I would like to come. Don't sulk."

I squeezed her hand tightly, then turned onto my back. "Promise me, though..." I frowned into the darkness.

"Promise you what?"

"If something happens like last time—if I really need you—that you will come."

She rose up on one elbow and kissed me gently. "Of course I promise you."

"Thank you."

Two

With his copious knowledge of the train schedules, Holmes had found us an early express train to York. Late that afternoon we transferred to the train for Whitby. The weather had been almost fair for the first part of our journey, blue sky showing, the sun intermittently lighting up the rolling greenery of the English countryside. However, as we traveled north from York into the vast desolation of the moors, the sky darkened and the heavens opened, a deluge of biblical proportions commencing.

Staring through the glass of our first-class compartment and the sheets of rain, we could hardly make out the landscape: only an impression of gently curving earth with blurs of brown which must have been the yet-unflowering heather, then occasional dark clumps of trees. Along a green hillside were the white figures of sheep. The train descended through a narrow valley as we approached the town of Whitby.

Selton's valet Evans was waiting for us at the station, a tall lanky figure in black overcoat and black bowler hat, luckily with umbrellas in hand. We walked through the pouring rain to a rustic-looking wagonette. I sat staring grimly at Selton through the drips pouring off my umbrella, even as the wagonette rumbled uphill along a narrow street. Holmes had begun to cough again.

I shook my head. "Spring sunshine? This is worse than London."

"Come now, Henry," Holmes said. "The air may be liquid, but it is cleaner."

The rain muted the colors of the red roofs, and we could not really make out the piers or much more than the vast amorphous gray of the sea. Once atop the hill, we passed the famous abbey, its dark stone remnants and arched windows framing the turbulent gray sky. A cold steady wind from the sea blew the tall green grass sideways and rippled the gray waters of a pond. A few cows grazed nearby. The wind picked up as we headed on to the moorlands.

"How far is it?" I asked, almost shouting to be heard over the downpour.

"About an hour," Selton replied. He sat in the seat facing us holding a big black umbrella, while Evans was up front holding the reins.

The ride was a rough one. The open wagonette was obviously not built for comfort and had no springs; the road was uneven and ill kept. By the time we came through a mass of black tree trunks to discover a dark stone house obscured by the rain, I was wet and miserable. My umbrella had blocked rain from overhead, but the wind had blown it almost sideways. Twice the wind was so fierce I had nearly lost it, a fate horrible to even contemplate! Four windows glowed with yellow light, and once we had passed through the entranceway, shedding our wet hats and coats, a hall with its welcoming fireplace awaited us. Huge orange flames leaped and twisted about two massive limbs of dark wood.

"Oh Lord," I murmured. "It has been a long day."

Beside me, Holmes had stretched out his long, thin fingers, warming them. "It has indeed."

Selton joined us. "What would you like to drink, gentlemen? A whisky and soda, brandy, sherry?"

Evans soon complied with our requests, and I held up a snifter of genuine cognac, letting the firelight illuminate its amber depths, then took a big sip. "I do feel almost human again." I wiggled my toes, which were damp. My fine London shoes were not made for the Yorkshire moors.

Holmes sipped at his sherry. "If I am not mistaken, this is a genuine Amontillado."

Selton nodded. By the firelight I could see the fine texture, the curving woolen threads, of his brown tweed jacket, and so close to me, I was again aware of his sheer size. I am slightly over six feet tall, but I still found his height and brawny bulk imposing. If he had been a violent or quarrelsome man, he would have been intimidating, but my impression after a day's journey together was that he was a gentle soul, albeit something of a lost one.

"You must be hungry, gentlemen. I know I am. They are getting supper ready. It's nothing fancy, hardly London fare, more of a thick stew, which I prefer in the country."

"It sounds wonderful," I said.

Evans stepped forward with a piece of paper folded on a tray. He had a thin face, his blond hair parted in the middle. "I forgot to tell you, sir. This telegram came earlier."

Selton unfolded the paper and read. His forehead creased. "Oh da–" He bit off the word, shaking his head in annoyance. He crumpled the paper and threw it into the flames.

Holmes and I looked at one another, then he spoke. "Is anything wrong, Mr. Selton?"

Selton's jaw was thrust forward as he shook his head. "No, no, it is only... My parents are coming up from London. I thought they were staying in town for the entire season and that I would be... A little solitude is agreeable sometimes. I don't know why they would be coming now of all times. Unless..." His forehead creased again. "How could they possibly know?"

"'Know?'" I asked.

"Know that I have engaged Mr. Holmes's services."

"Why would that matter to them?" I asked.

Selton almost scowled, even as his massive shoulders rose in a shrug.

Dinner revived us all. Mrs. Childes, the combination cook and housekeeper, was obviously a local, a plump, smiling woman with brawny forearms and a distinct Yorkshire accent. She set a huge platter of stew on the table and filled our bowls. Happily, for me anyway, it was not the expected mutton, but beef, cooked tender in a dark, rich gravy along with potatoes, carrots and leeks. She also served us a wondrous claret, and after my earlier cognac and a second glass of the dark-red wine with its perfect lingering aftertaste, *longueur en bouche* as the French put it, all seemed right with the world. And I had made it through the meal without once thinking about Michelle.

Selton lifted a second bottle and made to pour me more, but I covered my glass with my hand. "No, thank you. It was superb, but I have had enough."

He glanced at Holmes, poured for him, then filled his own glass. "It's nice to be away from London. I always like it here. Especially when..." His eyes took on a certain wariness, but then he shrugged. "I like being here alone, with no one to bother me about duties and society and... all of that."

"And you don't mind all the rain?" I asked.

"No. This time of year, it comes and goes. Besides, I've got a good broad-brimmed hat, a macintosh, some Wellingtons to keep my feet dry, and a good stout stick. If you have the proper clothes, the rain is no bother. I've walked for miles in a downpour."

I shrugged. "That would help, but I hope the sun does appear during our stay."

Selton sipped his wine. "It will, Dr. Vernier, perhaps even tomorrow. No telling at night what the next day will bring, especially in spring. That I've learned."

"Either way," Holmes said, "rain or shine, tomorrow we must visit Diana's Grove first thing in the morning."

"Certainly, Mr. Holmes."

"How far is it?" I asked.

"About forty-five minutes' walk."

Holmes made a slow circle with his wine glass, regarding the glowing reddish color. "And you mentioned others whom I shall want to visit. The older gentleman, the one who speculated so freely on the nature of antediluvian monsters..."

"Sir Nathaniel de Salis. His house, Doom Tower, is about the same distance as Diana's Grove, but down the coast in the opposite direction. Yes, you must meet him. He is an expert on the Yorkshire moors, their history, their geology, their flora and fauna."

Holmes sipped the wine. "In that case, you must certainly have consulted with him about the letter and the document."

Selton stroked his chin, then nodded at last.

"And what did he advise?"

"He thought my idea of seeking you out was a good one."

"And what did he think of the tale of the White Worm?"

"As I told you before, he does consider it possible that such a creature might have survived through the millennia, and if it has, it may have developed great intelligence."

Holmes's smile was a brief grimace. "And what of the notion that the Marsh family might have been somehow cursed by the worm?"

Selton stirred in his chair, obviously uneasy. Although I understood Holmes's need to question Selton, it seemed almost cruel when the young man had finally relaxed. "He does not believe in curses or ghosts or the like, but he said there are..." Selton frowned slightly, searching for the words, "psychic manifestations which cross generations... perhaps even common memories. The mind and the will can play curious tricks."

Holmes's gray eyes were faintly amused. "That cannot be disputed. I shall look forward to meeting this worthy gentleman. And finally, the wealthy prodigal bachelor who has returned, where might his castle be found?"

"To the west, on one of the highest points on the moors. And I must warn you, Mr. Holmes, he is very odd."

"In what way?"

"The Caswalls are descended from ancient Roman stock, and they have always been known for being proud and hot-tempered. Fights and disputes within the family were common, thus his lengthy voyages. His father died a year or two ago, and Mr. Caswall decided to come home to Castra Regis at last. Anyway, he believes in... in mesmerism, Spiritualism, and all that sort of thing. He thinks those with a strong will can control weaker beings. His travels in the East have also convinced him that certain men have the power to levitate, to go into trances and stop their hearts, all that sort of mumbo jumbo."

Holmes laughed. "You are more skeptical, I take it? You mentioned he might be a suitor of Lady Verr, Miss Marsh's aunt."

Selton frowned again and was silent for a long while. "I think it may be more the other way round. He has several thousand a year."

"So the aunt has a certain pecuniary interest. And what of Miss Marsh? Does money interest her?"

Selton sat straight up and set both hands flat on the tablecloth. "Not at all—not at all!"

"Calm yourself, Mr. Selton. I was only asking you a question. I take it... Perhaps your father considers her a greedy fortune-seeker?"

Selton almost winced, then nodded. "But it's not true—I swear it isn't! Money has never interested her. She loves the moors and the sea and the wind and the sky. She's not like those London *girls* who only care about silks and dresses and snubbing one another, and all of that nonsense!"

Holmes nodded. "The fact that she has remained in Yorkshire for so many years and not gone to the city supports what you say."

"Father does not know her—he does not know her at all."

I put my hand over my mouth, struggling with a yawn. Selton reached into his jacket pocket to withdraw a massive gold watch. "It is late, nearly ten, and you must be tired. I'll have Evans show you to your rooms."

We all stood, and soon Evans, candle in hand, led us up a narrow staircase. The door to Holmes's bedchamber was directly opposite mine. My room was rather spartan, though the ancient, dark-oak bed was unusually complex, a kind of cabinet built against the wall and its window. If one chose, there were doors which could be closed to shut out the rest of the room. I yawned again, then quickly undressed and put on my night shirt. Once I had lain down, I could hear the wind rattle the window and the rain drumming against the glass.

I suddenly remembered where I had read about such a bed: Emily Brontë's *Wuthering Heights*. The narrator had started the night in a similar room on the Yorkshire moors, only to be visited by Catherine

Linton's ghost who begged to come inside. I had last remembered the novel when I was at Grimswell Hall on Dartmoor, a similar setting. "No ghosts appeared then, and none will appear now," I told myself. All the same, I missed Michelle. One of the privileges of marriage I most valued was having her sleeping beside me during the night, near enough to touch.

I was too weary for reflection and quickly fell asleep. Blurry gray landscapes slipped by, fields and woods, small villages, and the sounds of wind and lashing rain wove themselves in and out of my dreams. The abbey stood on its hill, black against a moonlit sky, and some huge white thing slithered round and hid behind the dark stones. *No, no.* Gradually the storm abated, and my sleep grew less restless.

When I awoke, it took me a moment to recall where I was. It was quiet, far more quiet than ever possible in London, but then I heard the distant cawing of crows. I sighed, then sat up and set my elbow on the window ledge. The sky was a clear cloudless blue. I found my watch. It was nearly seven, and the sun would have risen before five. I dressed, putting on an informal gray tweed walking suit and black lace-up walking boots, then went downstairs.

Holmes and Selton were already up. The usual enormous country breakfast laid out in silver trays, much of which would be wasted, was lacking. Instead, Selton asked me if a rasher of bacon and some scrambled eggs would suit me, and Mrs. Childes soon brought me a plate. After I had eaten, we lingered over coffee.

"When are your mother and father expected?" Holmes asked.

"Tomorrow or the next day." Selton had a face that seemed incapable of deceit, his every emotion obvious. He was not happy they were coming. "I hope my father does not try to make trouble with you, Mr. Holmes. It's my money, after all, and I may spend it as I wish. You will… you will support me, won't you?"

Holmes nodded. "I certainly shall, Mr. Selton. You may count on that. It is peaceful here at Lesser Hill. The house might sleep twenty, but I take it that just now it is only you, Evans, Mrs. Childes, and the housemaid?"

"Her name is Anne. Yes. I have no need of more servants."

"Although I suspect your parents will not be alone."

"Oh no, there will of course be my father's valet, my mother's maid, a different and much worse cook, the family butler, and two more housemaids."

I laughed. "They travel in state, do they?"

Selton nodded grimly and set down his cup. "Let me show you round a little, and then we can start for Diana's Grove. Do you mind walking or would you rather take the wagonette?"

"I would love to walk," I said, and Holmes nodded.

We went out the front door. The trees, set in a kind of miniature park, looked completely different in daylight. Their dark limbs were covered with moss and lichens, and the leaves, which were just beginning to bud, were small and yellow-green. We could hear the distant murmur of the sea, and as we went round the house, the sound grew louder. Before us was a grassy slope, a wet shining green under the vast blue sky, and the murmur became more a roar. The sharp cries of gulls rose over the sound of the sea, and I saw two of them circle upward. We followed a small path to the top of the rise.

"Good Lord," I murmured.

The earth dipped downward, the green grass swept flat by the wind, and about twenty yards away was a drop, and then the deep blue-green sea extending out to the distant horizon. To the left and north, the coast curved inward and round to a distant hill covered in trees, the white limestone cliffs along the way falling a good hundred feet to a beach of gray shingle. The tide must have come in, and the waves washed all white and foaming across the pebbles, left them black and glistening as the sea withdrew. To the south, the grass-covered earth curved round again, with more cliffs visible, and rose to another hill, this one even higher and barren. Upon it, a gray square tower rose above a stone dwelling.

The sun felt warm, but the light wind coming off the sea was cold. I could only imagine what it must have been like during the storm the night before. In a real maelstrom, one could probably not even stand at this scenic point.

Holmes was wearing an informal brown tweed suit, and the brim of his walking hat shaded his eyes. He held a gnarled walking stick, a blackthorn, nothing like his usual London one with its brass head, and he pointed its tip toward the north. "That must be Diana's Grove." He turned to the south. "And that Doom Tower."

"Exactly so, Mr. Holmes."

"Is there a way down to the beach?"

"There is. A small rocky path which winds down along the cliffs."

I could not repress a shiver, and Holmes smiled.

Selton was puzzled. "What is it?" he asked.

"Henry suffers from vertigo," Holmes said. "He does not care for heights."

"That's a shame. The beach is well worth a visit. I like to watch the waves come in and out and hear the ocean and the gulls."

Holmes nodded, smiling. "So do I."

Selton looked genuinely concerned. "There is another path down from Diana's Grove. It's not so steep and goes through the trees. I think perhaps you could manage it."

I smiled. "Thank you. You are very kind."

Holmes set his stick against his shoulder and turned toward Diana's Grove. "Shall we be on our way?"

It was a beautiful morning. The path didn't amount to much. Luckily for me, it mostly avoided the sheer cliffs. To our left, inland, we could see the earth rising upward to a distant hill, upon which perched a castle that must have an even more spectacular view. Lower down were green fields and some scattered woods, higher up was the bleaker moorland, topped with brown heather. In late summer when it bloomed, all would be awash with pinks and purples, but now the moors looked desolate as the dark sea and the rocky cliffs. A gull soared out past the edge, cried out twice, then swung inward, rising higher before it began flapping toward the distant hill inland.

None of us felt like conversation. For the first time, Selton seemed truly comfortable, at home and in his element. The awkwardness and unease which hovered about him in London and in the train compartment had vanished. He was a giant of a man, but impossibly, he seemed to have grown even larger. His stride was enormous. He would get ahead of us, then politely slow down again. I was a fast walker, but I don't think I could have kept up with him if he were truly in a hurry.

At the edge of Diana's Grove, on a sheltered inland knoll, stood an enormous oak, the massive trunk easily ten feet across, with a swollen bulbous node another two or three feet wide about six feet up. Half the tree was budding, while the other half appeared almost dead. All the branches were black and twisted. We stopped to admire it.

"That tree must be a century old at least," I said.

Selton nodded. "They say it is two or three hundred years old."

"Amazing. It has such character." Holmes shook his head and started forward.

Something reddish-brown flashed across the path, swirled sideways past the trunk and vanished round the other side. Another sprang on to the path, stopped, then regarded us warily. The red squirrel had splendid tufted ears and a huge puffy tail. Its nose twitched at us, even as it shook its tail. It looked toward the tree, then back again.

"Look at the size of that thing," I said. "I've never seen such a large one."

The squirrel bounded to the side and ran around the tree. The first squirrel popped its head out, then each made a quick circuit round the trunk. They went up the side, the big one chasing the other, who went flying off one limb onto another tree without slowing in the least. The big one followed, and then they both gamboled off into the woods, their red tails waving.

"Hide and seek," Selton said.

I smiled. "Or perhaps some mating ritual."

Selton gave me a hard stare, obviously finding my reflection distasteful. He started forward into the woods. Though many of the trees were still bare, the leaves were not completely out, but it was dimmer and quieter, the ocean sound muted. The shade about us felt cold. Growing amidst the tree trunks were sparse clumps of green grass and various ferns, some with large shaggy yellowish fronds. On the black and white rocks grew brilliant mosses of different shades of green, brown and red. Selton strode ahead of us, and we could hear him taking in great long breaths, then easing the air out.

Someone sprang out before us, a radiant-looking, young, red-headed woman all in blue who raised a long white finger to her lips, silently shushing Holmes and me. She lowered her hand even as her smile grew. She rose up on her toes, then whirled about and rushed toward Selton. "*Surprise!*" she shouted.

He stopped and swung round. His stern face slowly eased into a smile. "Wanted to startle me, did you?" She was tall, but in his coarse woolen jacket and hat with its wide brim, he had nearly a foot over her.

"I did startle you—admit it!"

"I heard you coming. You made too much noise."

"You didn't—you didn't. I could tell. Natty Bumppo or Chingachgook could have done no better. You were surprised!"

His smile grew. "All right, I was surprised."

"You deserve it! You left without saying goodbye or telling me when you might return or anything! I was—I was worried!"

"I'm sorry, but it was—it was business."

"Promise you won't do it again—don't go without telling me."

"Diana…"

"*Promise.*"

"Oh, very well, I promise." He gave us an embarrassed glance.

She had had her back to us, but now she turned. "And who are these gentlemen?"

"They are… come up from London to stay with me." He bit warily at his lower lip. "Mr. Sherlock Holmes and Dr. Henry Vernier."

She gave us a slight curtsey. "Pleased to meet you, sirs." Clearly she had never heard of Sherlock Holmes.

Her smile was somewhat lopsided because of a dimple on her right cheek, but unrestrained and exuberant. She had another dimple, a permanent one, in the center of her chin. A swirling tangle of red hair surrounded her thin white face and spilled down on to her shoulders. She wore a practical sort of heavy woolen skirt and jacket for the outdoors, which were, nevertheless, as I have mentioned, a brilliant blue. I could not help but think of Michelle—this might be her cousin, or even younger sister. They had the same pale complexion and fiery hair. And also like Michelle, I could tell she did not believe in corsets. (I fear I have an eye for such things.) However, Miss Marsh was much younger, more slender still, without yet a woman's fullness, and her eyes were an amazing green, rather than blue. But as Selton had remarked, she did have a woman's shape, even without the corset.

She was not wearing gloves; nor was Selton. She suddenly reached out and took his enormous hand between her white, slender fingers and clasped it tightly. "Oh, Adam—I'm so glad to see you again!"

I gave my head a slight shake. I didn't know if Selton really cared for her, but she was certainly smitten. He did seem to bask in the glow of her approval.

She glanced at us. "It's too early for tea or lunch, but I can show you round Diana's Grove. And you must meet Aunt Arabella." She swung back round and grasped Selton's upper arm, directing him forward. "What was this business? What's so important, anyway, that you had to just disappear like that?"

"Diana..." he rumbled. "Business, as I said. Confidential. I..."

"Oh, all right—just don't do it again. Promise me."

The path wound through the trees, but we came at last to a wider, graveled road, ten feet across, which seemed to be a formal entryway for carriages. The two young people turned to follow it. Miss Marsh was still talking rapidly, but I could not make out all the words. Once her hand slipped down furtively to give his hand a quick squeeze, then rose again to grasp his arm just above the elbow. I glanced at Holmes. A faint smile tugged at his lips. They made me feel centuries old, but they were rather endearing.

We passed another side path leading into the trees. Holmes raised his stick. "Miss Marsh, where does that path lead?"

"That? Oh, it goes north to a clearing with some ancient standing stones overlooking the sea. There's also a big hole in the ground."

"Hole in the ground?" I asked.

"Actually, I think the pit is supposed to be boarded up. They say the Celts sacrificed people there. Mummy and Papa used to tell me scary stories and forbade me to go there because it was unsafe for a child. Grandpa didn't say much, but he never went there himself." She turned, resumed walking, and we all followed.

The road curved and rose, and before us through the slender tree trunks we could see the huge shape of the house, no doubt constructed of the local limestone which had weathered to black, white and gray over the years. Three rows of elaborate arched windows were on either side of the entrance, and the roof had gothic-style abutments and jutting spires. As we came closer, we could see that several window panes were cracked, one was even missing, and the slate tiles along one side of the roof seemed broken.

The road ended in a grassy clearing round the house. Holmes was just ahead of me, looking to and fro as he walked, but he came to a sudden halt, his eyes fixed to the right. I turned that way. "Lord!" I exclaimed.

Two long forms slithered rapidly round each other in the grass, a darker one and a lighter one, both marked with a vivid zigzag pattern, their scales glistening in the sun. "Blasted vermin," Selton said. He stepped forward, raising his stick like a cudgel.

"Wait!" Holmes cried, seizing his wrist.

The two snakes retreated incredibly fast, vanishing into the woods. "Why did you stop me?" Selton exclaimed. "Those were adders! They are poisonous. Can't have them lurking about."

"They will not attack people unless greatly provoked. I have a certain fondness for reptiles and spiders, although I know many people have a revulsion to them. Perhaps that fear is instinctual, but it can be overcome by reflection and familiarity with the animals. After all, they form a part of the great web of the natural world and provide a useful function. Those adders help to keep vermin like rats and mice in check."

Selton shook his head, still scowling.

"Bravo, sir–bravo." A woman stood before the entranceway, and she clapped her hands together in mock applause. "I have never heard it put more sensibly."

We walked forward toward the towering doors. Carved in stone just overhead was a knight in the process of cutting off a serpentine dragon's head, the relief badly weathered. The woman had to be the aunt. Her silken gown with its elaborate white and ivory pattern showed off her slender waist (*she* was a believer in corsets), but it would have been more suitable for a London townhouse than the Yorkshire countryside. Her hair was the same shade of red as her niece's, but tightly bound up, thus showing off her slender white neck and face. Her nose was slight and turned up (another similarity), her mouth full. I suspected she also had green eyes, but I could not tell because her gold-framed spectacles had octagonal lenses of green glass.

Green had been a popular color for lenses when I was a child, but had fallen out of favor, replaced by blue. As a physician, I was familiar with the arguments for blue, green, gray or orange lenses, but I thought that clear glass, which was now most common, worked as well as anything. Lady Verr was a beautiful woman (as she clearly knew), but the spectacles did give her an oddly antiquated look. About her throat was a splendid golden necklace with three large emeralds at the center. She descended two stone steps, one of which had crumbled at the end, and approached us. Tight white leather gloves covered her long, slender fingers.

"How good to see you, Adam. And who are these two gentlemen? I am especially interested in this defender of the serpentine race."

Selton looked wary again. "He is Mr. Sherlock Holmes, and this is–"

"Dr. Watson!" she exclaimed.

I shook my head. "No. I am Dr. Henry Vernier, Mr. Holmes's cousin."

Her forehead knotted up. "But you are not in the stories."

Holmes smiled. "Madam, they are, after all, only stories. Dr. Watson and I are not quite so close as he has portrayed. In fact, Henry is my preferred companion."

"This is Lady Verr," Selton said.

She lifted her copious skirts with her right hand, bowing gracefully. As she swung round, I realized she was wearing a full bustle under the white dress, the most outlandish of fashions which had finally–thankfully!–gone out of style in the last year or two. Michelle had an absolute horror of these grotesque contraptions of metal abutting the posterior: they make women resemble centaurs, completely destroying their natural shape.

Miss Marsh's smooth perfect forehead had been creased during our exchange, obviously puzzled. Her aunt noticed her expression. "Have you not heard of Mr. Sherlock Holmes, Diana?"

"Indeed, I have not."

"He is a consulting detective, the most famous in England, whose adventures have been recounted in several volumes by Dr. John Watson."

"With a certain amount of embellishment and distortion," Holmes said.

Lady Verr stared at him. "And what mystery, what conspiracy, brings the celebrated Sherlock Holmes to the wilds of Yorkshire? We have no ghostly hounds here, Mr. Holmes."

Holmes smiled faintly. "Mostly I am here for my health." He glanced at me.

"He has been working too hard, and the wretched smoky air of

London disagrees with his lungs. I prescribed a holiday in the country."

Lady Verr shook her head. "Come now, there must be more to it than that to lure him here."

"There is another matter which hardly qualifies itself as a true case. I have heard rumors about a certain legendary White Worm reappearing in the neighborhood. Someone in Micklethorpe actually wrote to me, and, ridiculous though it seems, I thought I might look into the matter."

"*Worm?*" Miss Marsh seemed confounded.

"Come now, Diana," Lady Verr said. "You've heard the tales about how our great-great-great-grandfather several generations back slew a wicked dragon. Worm, as Mr. Holmes uses the word, means dragon or snake." She turned again to Holmes. "And where do you expect to find this beast, Mr. Holmes? Here at Diana's Grove in her old lair?" She laughed.

"I doubt it will be that simple, Lady Verr. I must admit to a certain skepticism."

She nodded. "Ah yes, I remember that aspect of your character."

Holmes looked irritated, which was generally the case when someone indicated they knew about him from having read Watson's stories.

"Well, I concur with you, Mr. Holmes. There is a contingent of locals who claim to have seen this creature—and old Sir Nathaniel is convinced the beast has reappeared—but it seems nonsensical to me."

Miss Marsh shook her head. "I have not heard of such a thing."

"All the better, Diana dearest. I didn't want to pass on such silliness."

Miss Marsh was staring at Selton. "Have you heard these stories, Adam?" He nodded. "And why didn't you tell me about them?"

"I didn't want to worry you."

"*Worry me?*" She could not seem to comprehend his words.

Lady Verr was staring at Holmes. The tiny octagonal lenses shrank her eyes and hid their true color. "I suspect, Mr. Holmes—or rather, I somehow know—that you are a naturalist at heart."

"How could you know that?" Selton asked.

She smiled. "Elementary, my dear Selton! Anyone who cared enough about two adders to rescue them from a brute's stick must be a naturalist. How is that for reasoning, Mr. Holmes?" He bowed his head slightly. "As such, you must know what these two snakes were doing." My eyebrows came together, and Lady Verr laughed at my expression. "And I also can tell that the good doctor is *not* a naturalist. This was not some mating behavior, Dr. Vernier, but only the Darwinian struggle for survival, the battle between males for supremacy. Male snakes will writhe about one another and sometimes strike. The loser retreats, and to the winner goes the female and the prize of immortality by way of serpentine progeny."

I stared at her in disbelief, and she laughed again. "No, not a naturalist at all! Anyway, Mr. Holmes, I have no white worms in my collection, but I have quite a collection of dead beetles and living reptiles. The prize is a Burmese python, now well over six feet long."

"Have you?" Holmes exclaimed eagerly.

Selton shook his head angrily. "This is madness, just madness."

Lady Verr stepped forward to touch him lightly on the arm. He quickly jerked backwards. "Come now, Adam—don't be ridiculous. I have had Delilah for several years, and she is harmless, so long as you are not a small mammal."

I frowned slightly. "You actually feed it…"

"Rabbits, Dr. Vernier. It is all over very quickly, and watching a snake actually swallow its prey whole—remarkable."

I shook my head, repressing a shudder. "I fear my sentiments are more like Mr. Selton's."

"Well you need not see Delilah, but come inside for a few moments. Diana and I shall give you a tour of the old family pile. Oh, it may have lost some of its splendor of yesteryear, but it is our home, after all." We started up the steps. A very tall woman in a black dress, obviously a servant, had come outside. Her hair and eyes were dark; she looked Italian or Spanish.

"While I'm showing them around, Diana, put on something more appropriate for a lady. This female gamekeeper attire is hardly fitting for our guests."

"But…"

"Go on now—Angela can help you select something suitable. I'm sure Adam will find you more attractive when you are garbed as a woman."

Miss Marsh shook her head, her irritation obvious. Selton's cheek had reddened at the mere mention of his name. Once we had stepped into the hall, Miss Marsh and the maid headed for a stairway. Their footsteps echoed slightly off the distant stone ceiling. Sunlight streamed into the hall from the windows, but it was much colder and damper inside. A coal fire off to the side could not warm the center of the room. The heavy rug might have been splendid once, but its reds and purples had faded almost to gray. Massive battered chairs and a sofa seemed puny in so large a space.

Lady Verr swung her long arm and fingers round, twisting them slightly in the process. "The great hall at Diana's Grove dates to the Tudor era."

"And what of the ruins nearby?" Holmes asked.

"Oh, some of the stones go back to Celtic times and earlier. The site was used for rituals and sacrifices by the Druids and, before that, by the Neolithic dwellers on the moor."

Holmes stared at her closely. "And were these offerings for the White Worm?"

"Doubtless. The sacrificial creatures must have been slaughtered, then thrown into the pit. Traditionally the foul odor coming from its depths was attributed to the beast, but there is a more obvious explanation."

"What's that?" I asked.

"Animals now and then must fall into the pit and die. The smell of decomposing flesh can last for days. At any rate, I will gladly show you the site another time, should you wish, but for now, let us see some high points of this splendid example of Tudor architecture."

The house might have been a beauty at one time, but now seemed only dark, gloomy and cold. Also, if it appeared that way on a bright sunny day, I could imagine what it must be like in the midst of a rainstorm or a winter blizzard. A gallery above the hall had paintings of notable members of the Marsh family, including a fantastical one of Sir Michael with the expired dragon at his side.

One large room had been dedicated to Lady Verr's beetle collection: the stacks of wooden boxes with glass covers were piled high. On their ends small cards in metal frames had inked notes on the specimens. Her favorite was a collection of "rhinoceros beetles", enormous horned monstrosities, so large and ferocious-looking they were unbelievable.

Lady Verr noticed me restraining a shudder, and she smiled again. "No, definitely not a naturalist. A shame you cannot appreciate them." Holmes, of course, found them fascinating. "Did you know beetles are the most common of all insects, Dr. Vernier? That is why I chose to collect them. My deceased husband–God rest his soul– was a diplomat, and we spent nearly twenty years traveling abroad. Everywhere you go, there are beetles. It is never too cold, too hot, too dry, too wet. In almost any place on earth, you will find some type of beetle. There are those who argue that God must have favored beetles, since he made so many of them."

I could tell that Selton felt exactly as I did about such reflections. She wanted to show us the python, but Selton and I demurred. She opened an oaken door, loosing upon us a blast of warm air and a rank zoo-house smell. We waited in the gallery while she and Holmes went inside.

"You were right," I said. "She is rather eccentric." Selton rolled his eyes upward without speaking. "Attractive enough, though," I murmured. Selton's brow furrowed, then he looked away.

Holmes came out first. "You really should have a look, Henry. It is a remarkable specimen. The bathtub is a clever touch. The Burmese python does like water, and since it obviously must be confined, this allows it a more natural habitat."

I smiled ever so slightly and shook my head.

"Well, we must find Diana, and I know I am boring Mr. Selton and Dr. Vernier frightfully. I have some other snakes and a few lizards, including an iguana, which you might like to see another time, Mr. Holmes."

"I would be delighted."

We walked along the gallery and started down the stairs. Selton was ahead of me, but he stopped abruptly, and I almost walked into him. Below us was Miss Marsh, transformed, to say the least. A few feet behind her stood the maid in black. Diana had been spared a bustle, but she wore a pale-green silk dress with voluminous skirts and the fashionable "gigot" sleeves which puffed out at the shoulders and tapered at the forearms. Her red hair had been bound up and given some semblance of order. Now her pale white neck and face appeared even more slender than those of her aunt. As we descended, she stepped forward, awkwardly–because of pointed-toed shoes with high heels and all those skirts, no doubt. I realized abruptly that she must have put on a corset–which was ridiculous! Why submit a slender young woman to such an unnecessary constraint?

"Well, Adam, I think you are pleased with the results, are you not?"

Selton's cheeks began to redden again.

"Are you not?" Lady Verr repeated.

Selton seemed in the midst of a great struggle. "She... she... looks very well."

Miss Marsh's mouth pulled sideways in a partial smile, away from the cheek with the dimple, and she gave a slight shrug.

Lady Verr shook her head. "Hopeless, hopeless. The young are not trained as we were. Proper dress, proper manners. It is such a battle." She glanced at the maid. "Well done, Angela. *Molto bene.* Well, the hall was never comfortable, even in its prime, but there is a drawing room. Perhaps you might care for some tea. Or, as it is nearly noon, you might join us for lunch."

Holmes bowed slightly. "That is gracious of you, Lady Verr, but we have another appointment this afternoon. Perhaps next time."

"Well, you cannot rush off quite so quickly, especially with Diana in all her finery. Have some tea and biscuits before you leave. I know it is completely the wrong time, but..."

Holmes bowed again. "Gladly, madam."

The drawing room was the nicest room we had seen, and a coal fire kept it pleasantly warm. The plush leather chairs and sofa were quite comfortable. A bank of windows let in the sunlight. We were on the opposite side of the house from the entrance, and you could see the green lawn and the vast expanse of the sea. A few puffy white clouds had appeared amidst the blue sky. Because of her bustle, Lady Verr sat perched forward and upright on an upholstered Napoleon-style backless window bench, which had elaborately curving sides of ebony wood. She did most of the talking, although Holmes and

I politely chimed in on occasion. We were served tea by the stocky housekeeper with a practical, down-to-earth look. The tall Italian maid in her black dress stood in the corner waiting attentively, her arms crossed, her eyes fixed on Lady Verr.

You could tell Selton was trying not to stare, but his eyes kept returning to Miss Marsh. Her expression was oddly vacant. She did look lovely in the dress. I had wondered earlier about his feelings for the young lady, but they were now obvious–he was also smitten.

We rose at last to leave, and the ladies accompanied us to the front doorway. "You must come again, Mr. Holmes. It is so agreeable to find someone with shared interests in the neighborhood! You have no idea... Sir Nathaniel is a naturalist, it is true, but he is past seventy years old and can be..." She gave a long sigh. "To say 'tiresome' would be cruel. No, not exactly that. And should you or Adam grow weary of one another's company, for whatever reason, you and Dr. Vernier are welcome to stay at Diana's Grove."

Selton stared at her as if she were completely mad, but Holmes nodded. "That is very kind of you, Lady Verr. I may well take you up on that offer." He put on his rough wool walking hat.

Miss Marsh extended her arms, stretching her hands before her, palms up. "Oh, let me come along with you–part of the way, at least!" She gave Selton a stunning smile.

Lady Verr shook her head. "What are you thinking? You cannot go gallivanting about the forest in that dress! You'll soil it at best, tear it at worst."

Miss Marsh frowned. "I didn't want to put it on in the first place–I didn't!"

"Diana, you are a young lady, and you need to dress like one."

Miss Marsh shook her head. Her face had begun to pale. "Oh this–this damned dress–this damned... !" She clutched at her belly.

"Diana! What on earth is the matter with you? *Please.* There are gentlemen present!"

"Oh pardon me," she moaned.

I recognized the symptoms and stepped quickly forward, seizing her arm. "You must sit down."

Her eyes stared at me but went suddenly blank. She staggered. "I don't... feel well."

"Diana!" Selton exclaimed.

"She will be perfectly all right. Sherlock, her other arm if you please."

Selton seemed paralyzed. Sherlock and I half led, half dragged her back inside and set her on the sofa. I turned to the maid. "You have laced her up far too tightly–loosen her corset immediately! The poor girl cannot breathe."

The maid scowled. Lady Verr stepped forward. "Oh dear. The hazards of being a lady. We are still experimenting, you know. I shall see to it."

Lady Verr was a beautiful woman and her smile was bounteous, but I had had quite enough of her for one day. "Make sure you do." I made for the door.

"Good day, madam," Holmes said. We stepped out into the bright sunlight.

"Idiots," I murmured.

Selton was waiting for us. He stared at me, his anxiety evident. "What is it? Will she be all right?"

"There is no danger. She..."

"What is it? You must tell me! Is it the worm's curse? I must know!"

"Her corset was far too tight. She could not breathe."

Selton stared at me, eyes widening, then he took a step back even as the blood rushed into his face.

"Oh, Lord!" I exclaimed. I started down the road.

"Henry!" Holmes was just behind me. "Henry!"

I turned at last. "What?"

His lips flicked upwards at the corners. He glanced back in Selton's direction. "Be patient. He may look like a giant of a man, but it is only an illusion. Inside… Neither one of them is much more than a child. Can you not remember any occasions of youthful anguish and embarrassment?"

I drew my breath in slowly, and a particularly horrific experience that had taken place when I was fifteen popped suddenly into my head. It was something I had not recalled for years, something I would have gladly kept buried. "Yes. You are right. Forgive me."

"I admit his obtuseness can be tiresome."

"As can Lady Verr's chattering. She is… not to my taste."

Holmes shrugged. "How odd, since she does resemble Michelle."

I stared at him. "She does not!"

"Come now, Henry. I'll grant you that Lady Verr is not quite so tall, nor does Michelle wear spectacles, but their general appearance…"

I shook my head vehemently. "Perhaps in the most superficial ways, but if you spend more than five minutes with them—not in the least. And Michelle has never in her life worn a bustle!"

He laughed. "And Miss Marsh? Is she more to your liking?"

"What is this inquisition?"

"Is she?"

"Well, yes."

Holmes nodded. "How interesting."

Three

❧

"What a pleasure, what a great honor, to meet Mr. Sherlock Holmes and..." Sir Nathaniel's enthusiasm wavered. "And Dr. Vernier."

Lady Verr had indicated he was in his seventies, and Sir Nathaniel de Salis looked it, although he was clearly in good health. He was slightly stooped with a rounded belly, and the light from the window shone on the curving dome of his bald crown. However, the thick old-fashioned mutton-chop sideburns which came to his jawline and the bushy eyebrows were compensation. Both were salt-and-pepper-colored. Although we were in the country, he wore a double-breasted blue-black frock coat which fell to his knees, the satin lapels and the wool looking a little worn.

Adam Selton held the brim of his hat with his massive fingers. "Now that you have met Mr. Holmes, perhaps I could... I don't think I am really needed here. Would you mind if I left you?"

"But, Adam!" exclaimed Sir Nathaniel, "surely after having climbed all the stairs to my tower, you will linger a while?"

"I would like to, sir, but I wish to see… I must know if Miss Marsh is better."

Sir Nathaniel beamed and nodded, winking at Holmes and me. "Ah, so it has something to do with Miss Marsh! That is understandable."

"She almost fainted this morning."

"Be off with you, then. But first." He grasped Selton's arm above the elbow, not even half covering its circumference. "I must tell you gentlemen what a fine, fine lad this is! Alas, I have no children of my own, but if I did, I could wish for none better than young Mr. Selton. His character is of the highest, exemplary in every way, and he has always been most kind to a lonely old man—most kind! He's as fine a specimen of good, sturdy, English manhood as could ever be found."

Selton smiled. "You are exaggerating, Sir Nathaniel."

"Not at all, my boy—not at all. Off with you then. You may entrust the celebrated Mr. Holmes and his companion to my company."

I shook my head. "Diana's Grove is a long way to walk."

Selton shrugged. "Not at all. On my own, I can do it in a little over an hour." It had taken the three of us forty-five minutes to return from Diana's Grove to Lesser Hill, and the trek to Doom Tower after lunch had been another forty-five. "I'll be back by supper." He nodded, then started down the winding stone staircase.

Sir Nathaniel turned and gestured with his hands at the cases filled with books of all sizes. "As you can see, gentlemen, this is my library." The shelves stood across from an enormous desk of black oak littered with papers and open volumes. Above it, a bank of weathered, rather dirty windows faced the North Sea. The sun spilled yellow light across the cluttered surface. "I spend much of my day here. Ascending and descending make for my daily constitutional, so to speak. My one major addition to Doom Tower, adding a privy just there–" he pointed at a new-looking door in the corner "–was the wisest ever. Although if I had forgone it, I might be less stout." He laughed at his joke. "I do still walk a great deal in the countryside, but I have a fondness for the table and for a good port."

Holmes strolled over to the bookshelves. "I hear you are a naturalist, Sir Nathaniel."

"Yes, I have tried to familiarize myself with all the flora, fauna, geological and geographic features of this part of Yorkshire, as well as the history and prehistory of its occupants, going back to Neolithic times. I had a career as a diplomat–the Queen rewarded me for my services with a knighthood–but now that I am retired I spend my days entrenched in my studies." He sounded faintly forlorn.

Holmes nodded, then walked with his hands in his pockets toward the desk and looked down at a large, open volume. "So the Celts interest you? May I?" Sir Nathaniel nodded, and Holmes turned the page. "Their Druids, too, I see."

"We know so little about them."

Holmes nodded. "Little more than what Caesar related. He claimed they practiced human sacrifice by burning their victims in giant figures made of straw."

"Nonsense!" Sir Nathaniel exclaimed, his goodwill momentarily vanishing. "Caesar was not objective, not at all! He was writing propaganda, nothing more."

"You do not think they practiced human sacrifice?"

The old man shrugged. "We simply do not know. But I doubt they burned their victims in straw dummies."

"I hear, too, you have some ideas about the story of the White Worm and that note which Mr. Selton received."

Sir Nathaniel shook his head. "A black business that, and the worm…" An odd look appeared in his eyes, and he half smiled. "Yes, I have my theories about the beast, theories which may seem fantastical but which are based on scientific fact." A gold chain hung between his waistcoat pockets, and he withdrew his watch. "But before we discuss that, now might be the best time to go aloft and have a look around the neighborhood. The sun is past its zenith, and the winds are not too bad." He pointed at a flag, a Union Jack, which hung outside from a pole near the windows; it stirred lightly in the breeze.

He started for the corner and another door next to the privy. I hesitated, then took a single step. "Perhaps I shall just wait here for the two of you."

Sir Nathaniel gave me a pained and incredulous look. "But we have one of the best views in the neighborhood! Caswall's Castra Regis is higher, it is true, but he cannot see so far south."

"My cousin suffers from vertigo, Sir Nathaniel. Perhaps it would be best if he remained behind."

"No, no—there is a good stout stone wall round the whole top, massive stone, massive, and most well mortared. No chance of it breaking off, none, and no chance of a body tumbling over—much too high, the wall—even young Selton would be safe. And you needn't come too close to the wall if you wish, yes? Have some courage, man! You'll not regret it."

I found this speech mildly annoying, but also amusing. "Very well. But I can't promise I shall actually walk up to the wall."

The old man shook his two fists in gleeful emphasis. "Agreed! Come then, gentlemen." Next to the door was a shelf, on it a weathered black top hat and a brass telescope. He put on the hat, then took the telescope, opened the door and started up the stairs.

As we climbed, the sound of the wind and the sea grew, and we came out, luckily for me, several feet from the perimeter wall. The wind swept in from the sea, still very cool, but the sun overhead was warm on my face. It must have been around sixty degrees, which seemed a heat wave after our recent wretched London weather and yesterday's dreary ride in the downpour. I closed my eyes and savored the warmth.

"It is very nice up here," I said.

"Come, Mr. Holmes. The view from the south is interesting. You cannot quite see Whitby from here, because of a hill and valley which obscure the town."

I put my hands in my pockets and slowly turned, reassuring myself about how far I was from those nice sturdy walls of gray limestone. Sir Nathaniel held his black top hat firmly in place with his left hand, while his right grasped the telescope. I turned back toward the sea and took a few steps forward. I could see the dark blue-green waters touching the long expanse of the paler horizon. Seaward were a few clouds, while inland were none. I turned further round. To the west was the hill and a rocky summit where I could make out the gray shape of Caswall's castle. Above was clear blue sky and...

I blinked my eyes, frowned, then blinked my eyes again. An odd brown splotch still showed off to the right of the hill, suspended in the sky. I wondered if it was only some blot on my eye, but it would not go away. "What on earth," I murmured. "Sir Nathaniel?" They turned toward me, and I raised my hand. "Perhaps I am imagining it, but no—there is something in the sky there north of the hill, a brown spot."

Sir Nathaniel came closer, hand still holding his hat down. Suddenly he grinned, revealing yellowish teeth. "No, you're not imagining anything, Dr. Vernier. Can you guess what it is?"

"I certainly cannot."

"Have a look then. See if this helps." He handed me the telescope.

I opened the telescope to its full extent, then raised it. The blue sky danced in a circle, a brown shape showing, disappearing, and then

I had it–brown, with two great yellow eyes with black pupils and a fierce beak. "Good Lord! That's impossible. It cannot be a bird!"

Sir Nathaniel laughed in delight. Holmes extended his hand. "May I have a look, Henry?" He took the telescope, stared for a while, then shook his head. "It is a kite, is it not?"

"A kite!" I exclaimed.

Sir Nathaniel laughed again. "Very good, Mr. Holmes."

"A grown man is flying kites?" I asked. "Which are made to look like giant birds?"

"Not just any bird," Holmes said. "Although a clumsy representation, it is a hawk."

"Why on earth would he be doing that?"

Sir Nathaniel briefly rolled his eyes upward. The slivers of his brown irises were almost as dark as the swollen pupils in the sunlight, both contrasting with his bushy silvery eyebrows. "He's trying to scare off birds. Gulls, and especially doves. He doesn't like doves."

"Does that actually work?" I asked.

The old man shrugged. "He thinks it does."

I shook my head again, reflecting that the local inhabitants of this corner of Yorkshire were an odd lot.

We lingered a while, Sir Nathaniel pointing out all the local sights to Holmes. I gradually took a few steps closer to the wall. It felt good being outside, and for the first time in weeks, in months, I felt actually warm. A few yards out a white gull hovered in the air, watching me, then with a cry swept in toward us.

"No!" cried Sir Nathaniel. "Off with you, beggar! Nothing for you here." He looked at us. "Had your fill, gentlemen? Won't actually go to the wall, Dr. Vernier? Very well, let us go in, then." He clutched the railing tightly as he descended. Once we were back in the library, he set his hat on the shelf, then the telescope. "If it is not raining, I try to go out at least once a day. The view is splendid. Of course, even on the bad days, I can sit at my desk and stare out at the sea. My stove keeps me warm enough, although I don't need it on a day like this." He sank down into a chair of wood and leather, gestured at a chesterfield sofa of dark leather. "Have a seat, gentlemen. Perhaps a little later we might go down for tea."

Holmes and I sank into the opposite ends of the sofa. I covered a yawn with my hand. All the fresh air and walking had made me sleepy. Holmes let the long fingers of his right hand dangle off the sofa arm. I could not recall when he had last seemed so relaxed. The couch was angled to the northeast, and we had a good view of the sea through the windows.

"I envy you your aerie, Sir Nathaniel," Holmes said.

"It is pleasant enough after the bustle and activity of the great capitals, but sometimes I do wish I had married. I always meant to, yes? It just never seemed to happen, and now I am an old bachelor far too set in my ways to submit to any woman."

Holmes stared closely at him. "Even someone like Lady Verr?"

Sir Nathaniel laughed. "Oh, she is a beautiful and charming lady, but I am truly old enough to be her father. I must admit…" His face seemed to color ever so slightly. "I first met her and Lord Verr some twenty years ago in London. They had just married, and my first thought was that Verr was a lucky devil indeed. I'm not quite such an old fool to dream of marriage, but I have one major failing to help keep any such idle fantasies in check."

"What might that be?" Holmes asked.

"The lady is seeking a fortune, and I have very little money, Mr. Holmes, a pittance only. Doom Tower is my family home, but there is little land of any value attached to it. My sister lived here until her death, and then the old house steward Mitchell and his wife maintained it until I returned. There is an entail, and the estate cannot, of course, be sold. When I die, it will go back to the Crown, and that will be the end of the de Salis line. No, the lady needs to find someone wealthy like Caswall to satisfy all her feminine wants and vanities. It is natural enough, yes? Besides, I am some thirty-five years older than either her or Caswall. I admire Lady Verr greatly, but I am not so foolish as to covet her for my wife. No, no, I shall be a bachelor until the day I die."

"How long ago exactly did Lord Verr die?"

"It has not been even a year, not quite. Terrible business that, simply terrible. I talked to him briefly on two occasions after they returned to Yorkshire. He was much changed. Clearly his mind was going. Dr. Thorpe was actually with them when he blew his brains out, and Lady Verr had to witness the whole thing! You'd think the fellow would have wanted to spare his wife such a dreadful spectacle, but then he was lost in his fantasies."

"What were these fantasies?"

"He had become insanely jealous, raving to her and the doctor about her supposed infidelities."

Holmes put his fingertips together. "And is it quite certain these were only fantasies?"

Sir Nathaniel stared at him closely. "Of course it is certain! She is a lady after all, and even if one were to doubt it... There is simply no one suitable in the neighborhood! No one unsuitable either, yes? Caswall had not yet returned at the time. Her only male servant Hamswell is nearly fifty and quite ugly. She is hardly the type of woman to take up with some farmer or common laborer. There are simply no viable candidates. No, Verr's mind was lost, consumed, by mere fantasy."

"Do you know this Dr. Thorpe?"

"Very well. He is my own physician, and a man only some fifteen years younger than myself. He has dwelt in Micklethorpe and been the local physician for thirty years. His character is absolutely unimpeachable."

Holmes nodded. "I see. Sad how a person can be obsessed by mere thoughts. Well, enough of so unpleasant a topic. Perhaps we could discuss that which brought us here: the White Worm of Diana's Grove."

Sir Nathaniel's smile became almost ferocious. "Ah, now there's a topic more to my liking!" He sank back into his chair. "We are, I think we can agree, all men of science and men of reason, are we not?" This seemed a sort of examination question, so Holmes and I both nodded. "Therefore we must agree to approach this topic with an open mind, yes?" Again we nodded rather mechanically.

"Let us begin, then, by noting the discovery in our century of the dinosaurs. I was at Oxford in the forties when Owen first named the creatures. We were all fascinated, but this was nothing compared to the impact of the displays at the Crystal Palace in 1854! Who would have ever imagined that giant reptiles had inhabited the earth eons before man, that we were relative newcomers compared to these monstrous beasts? This revelation opened up a new window to the past, to times after the dawn of creation when nature operated on a gargantuan scale. Given these monstrous lizards, who can argue that an enormous serpent like the White Worm may not have also arisen? All such animals belong to the first geologic age—the great birth and growth of the world, when natural forces ran riot, when the struggle for existence was so savage that no vitality which was not founded in a gigantic form could have even a possibility of survival. And if enormous lizards were possible—were an actuality—why not serpents, yes?

"Even now, we know that giant creatures thrive in our oceans: there are our leviathans, the great whales, and giant squids who battle them in the black depths of the seas. I have no doubt that sea serpents exist, and if at sea, why could they not have their cousins on land? England has always been full of deep caves and watery depths; these abysses would be the natural home to such monsters. Perhaps, too, there are creatures equally at ease on land and in the sea, a great serpentine sort of amphibian. That would explain why a site like Diana's Grove so near to the ocean might be home to the worm. In the depths of that pit there may lie caves which empty into the sea, as well as tunnels weaving inland. Can we not admit, then, the possibility that a creature like the White Worm exists?"

His musings were a kind of rhetorical tour-de-force which swept you along, but I still could not bring myself to make the leap he demanded. "I think we may agree to that," Holmes said. He glanced at me, and I could see that he was not convinced either.

"There are also extreme differences in lifespans. Some men die in their twenties, others live past a hundred. Nature has spawned every sort of conceivable oddity. Certainly it is possible that some of these creatures could live longer than others. And with age, could not something like intelligence develop? An intelligence rather cold and reptilian compared to our own, but intelligence all the same, yes? And could not this intelligence continue to grow and grow as the centuries passed?"

Holmes nodded thoughtfully. "Such a creature might exist, but if it was active—if it was feeding—it could not keep itself hidden for long."

"That is true. That is why there is talk now. Cattle and sheep have disappeared from the moors. People have seen strange things at night in the local woods."

"What things?" I asked.

"White forms and green lights. Two green lights."

"Eyes, I suppose."

"You need not take that tone, Dr. Vernier," he said sternly. "We agreed to a free and open discussion without preconceptions, yes?"

I nodded. "Forgive me."

"You seem to be arguing, Sir Nathaniel," Holmes said, "that this beast has been long dormant and has only recently reappeared."

"That is indeed my theory."

"And how do you account for this dormancy?"

"Think about it, Mr. Holmes. We know that amphibians can hibernate for long periods of time. There are certain toads that live in deserts and burrow into the mud during the brief rainy season, then go dormant for ten or twenty years. Only when the rains return years later does the water bring them back to life. This is a being of great size and, I suspect, of great cunning. Why could it not also go dormant for many years, possibly even centuries? Only now has something finally resurrected it."

"What might that be?" Holmes asked.

He shrugged. "Hard to say. Perhaps... perhaps it went dormant because of hunger, and somehow it was fed again. We know that snakes can go for long periods of time between feedings. All things with the worm, all aspects, would seem to involve measurements on a colossal scale."

Holmes nodded, even as the fingers of his right hand drummed at the sofa arm. "Most interesting, Sir Nathaniel. Your speculations show... a clever mind. You are truly a naturalist extraordinaire."

Sir Nathaniel beamed, taking this appraisal at face value, but I doubted its sincerity.

"I can admit the possibility of such a creature, but what would be the connection to the Marsh family, especially its women?"

Sir Nathaniel actually scowled. "There, alas, I am on shakier ground. As I have told you, I am a confirmed bachelor. Oh, I have spoken and even flirted with women over the years in various social settings, but the female sex remains a mystery to me."

Holmes's smile this time was clearly the real thing. "I fear I am equally at sea on that topic, Sir Nathaniel." He turned to me. "We do have an expert present, however."

I shook my head. "Being married does not make me an expert on women, even though I may know one of them well."

"One is infinitely greater than zero." Holmes turned again to Sir Nathaniel. "I suspect, however, that you have also speculated about this subject, especially since Mr. Selton showed you the letter and the supposed manuscript."

Sir Nathaniel's brow knotted. "'Supposed'?"

"The document is a forgery. It was recently created."

"All the same, someone wrote down what was already known. That tale about Sir Michael and the White Worm is an old one, as is the association with Diana's Grove."

"And was the worm always female, with the ability to assume a beautiful woman's shape?"

"Yes." The old man smiled. "Which is hardly surprising. The link between women and serpents is truly ancient, as is the idea of the woman as temptress. Take the story of Eve, for example. There are also the so called 'lamias' in Greek myth, beings akin to succubae or vampires, who would slowly consume the vital essence of men. Keats wrote of 'La Belle Dame Sans Merci', who drained the life of a young knight."

"An association to which the letter seems to refer." Sir Nathaniel looked puzzled, and Holmes went on. "'If you value your manhood', the letter warned."

Sir Nathaniel nodded appreciatively. "Ah yes, exactly so."

"And was this warning about the daughters of Sir Michael also in the original story?"

Sir Nathaniel opened his mouth, frowning, then shut his mouth briefly to reflect. "I am not certain, but I believe so. Lady Verr certainly knows about a curse which can fall upon the Marsh women."

"Does she? And what exactly is the nature of this curse?"

"Various forms of madness or melancholy, I believe. Some of the Marsh women have so despaired that they have hurled themselves into the pit near the sea."

I opened my mouth to pronounce this preposterous, but Holmes gave me a brief warning look.

"Lady Verr said her great-aunt or great-great-aunt was one such unfortunate. There is also an interesting variation of the story which further connects the worm and the Marsh women."

Holmes leaned forward slightly, setting his hands on his knees. "Yes?"

"In one version, Sir Michael marries one of the former votaries of the grove, a red-headed woman like the worm herself. Thus the family has links both to Christianity by way of Sir Michael and to some earlier pagan cult, Celtic, or perhaps even pre-Celtic by way of his wife. And who knows for how many centuries—millennia even— religious rituals dedicated to the worm may have been carried out at Diana's Grove?"

A grim comical smile pulled briefly at Holmes's mouth, vanishing at once. "What are you thinking?" I asked.

"Well, this whole story of sacrifices and people hurling themselves into the pit does provide simple motivation for our gigantic specimen: *food.*"

I shook my head in dismay, but Sir Nathaniel nodded eagerly.

"I have thought the same thing myself! This beast may go dormant from time to time—she may sleep or hibernate—but eventually hunger wakes her, and she returns to the surface!"

"Come now!" I exclaimed. "Do we really know this snake is female?"

"The stories all agree on that point."

Holmes gazed at me and nodded. "We may take its being female as a working hypothesis."

I shook my head again. "I'd prefer that it remains an 'it'."

"And what of Miss Marsh?" Holmes asked. "Do you see any signs of the curse manifesting itself in her?"

Sir Nathaniel shook his head firmly. "Not in the least. She is much too vain and silly."

"Vain?" I asked.

He nodded. "Is not her pursuit of Adam Selton the height of vanity? Oh, I humor him, but his true friends cannot help reflecting on the unsuitability of the young lady."

I realized I was frowning. "Unsuitable in what way?"

"Her lack of either wealth or a title."

A sharp laugh slipped free from my mouth.

Sir Nathaniel looked severe. "What is so amusing?"

"Everyone seems to acknowledge that Lady Verr is after a rich husband. You said so yourself, but you did not fault her for it."

He shook his head twice, his face reddening. "It's not the same thing at all."

"How is it not the same?"

"Lady Verr has a title now. Her husband was a baron. She has traveled in the highest circles. She is a mature woman."

"Oh I see," I replied sarcastically. "That makes it perfectly all right, then." Sir Nathaniel didn't seem to know how to take this.

"Has the young lady ever shown any signs of a melancholy disposition?" Holmes asked.

Sir Nathaniel shook his head. "Not that I am aware. From what I have seen she is a complete flibbertigibbet."

Holmes shook his head. "She must have a more serious side. She has lost both her parents and her grandfather in the last few years. Especially given her isolation here, it must have been hard to bear."

The old man shrugged. "I suppose that is true. She is lucky to have a fine lady like Arabella to look after her now."

Sir Nathaniel wanted us to stay for tea, but Holmes told him we had business in the village. Micklethorpe was just over the hill from Doom Tower, only fifteen minutes' walk the old man assured us.

As Holmes and I started down a gravel path winding through a grassy slope below the gray stone manor house, I shook my head. "There was a certain rational semblance to what he said, but you cannot have taken all that gibberish seriously?"

Holmes smiled at me, the hand with the stick rising and falling in time to his pace. "You were not convinced by all his scientific reasoning?"

"I am no naturalist, as we all agree, but I don't think he is a genuine scientist either."

"As you noted, there is a certain logic to his conclusions, but he makes some erroneous and gargantuan leaps to get there. For example, the likeliest candidate for the mythical sea serpents of legend is nothing like a snake, not a reptile at all, but a fish, the oarfish. Fish and reptiles are not the same at all, so to see some sort of brotherhood—or sisterhood—between the sea serpent and his white worm, is false. We also know that no animal can live for centuries—none. To assume that great size means longer life is another fallacy. He is certainly sincere, but all the same... The great French mathematician Laplace once said, '*Le poids de la preuve pour une affirmation extraordinaire doit être proportionnel à son degré d'étrangeté.'*

Holmes's French was quite good, but he had not passed much of his youth in France, as I had. I could hear his accent. "'The weight of proof for an extraordinary claim must be proportional to its degree of strangeness.'" I nodded. "In other words, extraordinary claims require... extraordinary proofs."

Holmes nodded. "Exactly, Henry, exactly. By the way, you must restrain that knight errant aspect of your character when we are around the old gentleman." I gave him a puzzled glance. "Your rushing to Miss Marsh's defense."

"He is maddening! He condemns her for wanting Selton and assumes her motivation is greed, but with Lady Verr all is forgiven, all is excused."

Holmes laughed. "Exactly so. A beautiful woman like her levels Sir Nathaniel's massive walls of reason and rationality with a single smile."

I shook my head. "That's almost poetic! And quite apt. They say love is blind, and that certainly applies in his case, although perhaps it is more infatuation."

"Yes, Henry, it does apply."

There was a rustic wooden sign with "Micklethorpe" carved in it pointing to a path on our left. Holmes turned onto that path. "What exactly is our business in Micklethorpe, anyway?"

"Truly grave and serious business, Henry. We must find a pub."

I laughed. "You had me there. I thought you were serious. A glass of beer does sound wonderful after all this fresh air and walking."

"I was serious, Henry–it is not mere thirst. Libraries and books are not the only places where one can conduct useful research."

Micklethorpe was one of those extraordinarily picturesque and quaint English villages. It had the requisite worn gray old church with a steeple and a nearby ancient graveyard, a few stone cottages with slate roofs, a small shop with a window for the post office and telegraph, and of course, a public house, the White Swan, which looked as if it had stood there with its wooden sign since the days of Robin Hood.

After the bright sun on the moors, the interior of the pub seemed like a cave. Massive oaken beams crossed the ceiling, and everywhere was dark, aged, rough-hewn wood. The publican was stout and ruddy-faced, his appearance indicating a fondness for his brew. He wore a white apron and was smoking a clay pipe when we entered. He filled two heavy glasses with beer and set them on the gray slate counter.

Holmes raised his glass and took a drink. "Excellent, excellent, sir. I have not tasted better in the countryside."

The publican had placed his pipe stem between his teeth, and he gave a slight nod.

"My friend and myself are visiting Mr. Selton at Lesser Hill. Perhaps you know Mr. Selton?"

The publican nodded again. "All right, he is. No airs like so many from the town." His eyes had a certain warning look with this pronouncement.

"We are taking in all the local scenery and estates. Perhaps you can help settle a dispute between my friend and myself." He turned toward me.

"What dispute?"

"We are considering a night-time visit to Diana's Grove and its ancient sacrificial site by the sea. I argue that in these enlightened times, one need not worry about ghosts or malevolent spirits, or any influence from the past, while my friend says it would be best to stay away from such a place after dark."

Three creases appeared in the publican's forehead, and he drew slowly on the pipe.

"Well, sir, what would you advise?"

"Do as your friend says."

"Indeed? What can there possibly be to fear?"

The publican shrugged and did not speak.

"Nasty things," someone muttered. We turned and saw a little man in rough garb sitting at a nearby table.

"Nasty things?" Holmes took his glass and sat down across from the man. I joined him. "What sort of nasty things?"

"Never you mind." The man took a big swallow of some dark ale. He looked to be about forty, his hair cut short, not by a barber, and he hadn't shaved in several days. "I knows what I knows. First a calf gone, then a cow. It's near wiped me out. I don't know what I'll do."

"Surely you cannot imagine something in Diana's Grove had anything to do with your cattle disappearing?"

"Can't I?" He laughed dully.

"I would think cattle could wander off and be lost."

"You don't know much about farming, do you, squire?"

"I suppose not. Perhaps something attacked them, a wolf for example."

The man laughed again. "No wolves here, not in two or three hundred years."

"Perhaps feral dogs, then. And were neither of these animals seen again? No bones or other remnants?"

The man had black eyebrows and eyes; he scowled, then smiled bitterly.

"What is it, man?"

"It don't make no sense. None at all." He stared down at his beer, shaking his head. "It couldn't have been."

"You've piqued my curiosity, sir," Holmes said. "What couldn't have been?"

"A fisherman told me, old Ned told me, he saw her floating out at sea."

Holmes seemed genuinely surprised. "Someone saw your cow floating in the sea?"

"Yes, just off the coast near here, a-bobbin' and a-floatin', all bloated and swollen and... half eaten, big bites out of 'er."

Holmes shook his head. "How could he possibly know it was your cow?"

"She was a Highland breed with a curly black coat, the only one in the county. He could see the black and her horns."

Holmes tapped at the table. "Incredible. And... he did not consider fishing her out of the sea and bringing her ashore?"

The man laughed in earnest. "Are you barmy? Why ever would he do that? Cow's far too heavy, and why would you want to bother with the carcass? Can't eat such a cow, not after a few days in the ocean and all the guts still insider her. Most of them, anyway. Better the fish have her."

I felt sick to my stomach and took a big swallow of beer. "This makes no sense," I said.

"When did the cattle first begin to go missing?" Holmes asked.

Again the man scowled. "'Twas last October or so, just before the first snows. Old Farley up north of the grove lost one."

"And sheep have gone missing too?"

He nodded. "Aye." He stared at Holmes. He had obviously been drinking for quite a while. "For a city fellow, you're awful interested in livestock."

"I still don't see why you think Diana's Grove has anything to do with this."

"Light there at night, green light shining through the trees and the mists. Not natural, not natural at all."

"Perhaps it was only someone with a lantern."

"No green lanterns round here." He rose awkwardly to his feet, steadying himself with one hand on the table, then went to the counter. "Another, Ted."

The publican shook his head. "You've had enough."

"I'll be the judge of that!"

"No. You've had enough. Go home and have your supper."

"So my business isn't good enough for you! I'll go elsewhere, I swear I'll go elsewhere." He slammed down the glass, turned and lurched toward the doorway.

The publican stared warily at Holmes. "You ask too many questions, mister."

We finished our beer and rose to leave. A large man with a reddish beard sat in the corner near the door. He gave us a hard stare. Outside, we blinked our eyes at the bright light, then started back along the path to Doom Tower. The sun was lower in the sky now to the west.

I shook my head. "I had so hoped this would be a pleasant holiday in the country and nothing more, but I don't think it is going to turn out that way."

"No," Holmes said. "I don't think so either."

"That was truly a bizarre story–the cow floating out at sea! That must be a mistake." Holmes only shrugged. "How could the cow get out there in the first place?"

"Perhaps someone threw her from the cliffs."

"But half eaten? And wouldn't she have simply washed ashore? This is all very odd, and Sir Nathaniel's lunatic speculations... With the case of the Grimswell Curse, there was an obvious motive–Rose's great fortune, over four hundred thousand pounds. But Miss Marsh and her aunt have almost nothing. Could... could there possibly be some factual basis to this story about the worm?"

Holmes glanced at me from under the brim of his walking hat. "You know my thoughts on ghosts, phantasms, werewolves, vampires and all such kin. I have never encountered any true otherworldly manifestation—only men. And women. I think this will turn out the same."

"But if cattle and sheep have gone missing, and people are seeing odd things at night in Diana's Grove, someone must have gone to a great deal of trouble."

"Yes, a great deal."

"But why? Again, where is the motive?"

"We shall have to wait and see, Henry. I have some ideas, but they are only ideas, idle conjecture, at this point. One must resist the temptation to speculate too soon. We have not even rounded out our cast of *dramatis personae.* Tomorrow we shall meet Mr. Edgar Caswall. I must admit to a certain anticipation."

I shook my head. "I suspect he is the craziest of the bunch, and that is saying something."

We had come up a rise, and the sea appeared before us, the waters a dark deep blue, glistening, quivering, but almost flat, awash with yellow highlights from the sun. We paused to take in the view.

"A cow out bobbing and floating, half eaten." Holmes laughed softly. "Remarkable."

That evening after supper, Holmes and I went outside to see the sunset from the ridge at Lesser Hill. Selton remained inside. Perhaps even he was weary from all the walking he had done! After ironically asking my permission, Holmes slowly smoked a single cigarette as the orange disk slipped below the hills to the west. The clouds went pink and orange, and the waters of the sea took on a brilliant glow, reflecting the dappled sky upon their rippling surface. It was cool, but we were dressed warmly, and the evening was truly spectacular. The sky darkened, a few stars gradually appearing. Neither of us seemed in a hurry to go in.

Holmes finally sighed, turned to the left, then laughed softly and shook his head. "Nicely done."

"What are you talking about?"

"Look there, toward Diana's Grove."

I could see the dark shape that was the woods beside the sea. "I don't see anything."

"Give it a moment."

A green light suddenly lit up the grove, a spot of glowing color against the darkness. "What on earth?"

"I think that is supposed to be our worm."

"Are you serious?"

"You heard people speak of the mysterious green light. You have now witnessed it yourself. There is your proof the monster exists."

"I don't find any of this very amusing. Where can that light be coming from?"

"You don't think it is the serpent's glowing eyes?"

"No!"

"Neither do I. It probably is some type of lantern, an enormous one, with a lens of green glass."

"But who would do such a thing?"

"Again, Henry, we shall have to wait and see. Let's go back inside. It's getting cold."

I shook my head. "The stars will be truly spectacular in another hour or two."

"Yes. We must come back outside and have a look." A brief smile pulled at his lips. "Perhaps the worm itself will appear."

We opened the door and went through the entryway into the main sitting room. Evans strode toward us. He wore a well-cut woolen suit and long overcoat, and carried a bowler hat of lustrous black felt. Compared to his master, he was quite lanky, his face thin with high cheekbones. He had that typical fair but ruddy English complexion, his blond hair parted neatly on one side, the pomade obvious. His pale-blue eyes matched his coloring, but they had an air of calculation.

"Ah! Going out for the evening?" Holmes said.

Evans nodded. "Splendid night for it. The moon will light the way to Micklethorpe and the Swan. Time for a pint or two with some local chums."

Holmes nodded, but Evans lingered, hat in hand. He was staring expectantly at Holmes, who glanced at me, then smiled faintly. "How long have you worked for Mr. Selton?" Holmes asked.

"Nearly four years, sir. And if I may say so, no one knows him better than me."

Holmes nodded again. "Yes, a valet often knows his master well. He is privy to his secrets, to the emotional storms and various tribulations. Sometimes the valet becomes a confidant."

Evans smiled. "Funny you should say that, sir. Truly, I am very close to Mr. Selton. He is my employer, and I know my place, but all the same... He tells me things. I know all about him. And Miss Marsh as well."

"I'm sure you do."

"I hate to see him troubled so, and everyone has heard about the famous Sherlock Holmes. I know you want to help him. Still, I'm not sure as how... Well, I'd be happy to talk with you, Mr. Holmes, but all the same..."

"You might want some compensation."

Evans looked relieved. "Compensation? Well, if you insist…"

"And if I do not insist?"

Evans looked worried, the mask of amiability briefly slipping.

"Don't worry, Evans, you shall have your compensation. I can oblige you with a few pounds for certain facts."

"And I shall only give them to you because I know you have the master's best interests at heart!"

"I certainly do."

"I hope you do not think…" Evans tried to look embarrassed, but I was not convinced. "It's just that a valet does not make a great deal of money, and I have an old mother that needs my aid."

"Indeed? Mr. Selton seems very generous."

"So he is, to an extent, but all the same…"

"He must be generous. Those boots of yours were not cheap, were they? It is unusual for a valet to have custom-made shoes. And your suit and overcoat… How agreeable that you can support your elderly mother and still dress so impressively."

A slow flush appeared on Evans's cheeks. "I had to save a long time, and these are my best, not the usual thing by far. Surely it is no crime to want to dress well? I'll wager your shoes are custom-made too. I don't want to be a valet all my life, Mr. Holmes. I have aspirations. I want to better meself. Is that wrong?"

"Certainly not. Well, we mustn't keep you, Evans. The Swan awaits. I am certain we can work out some compensation and have a little chat in the next day or two. You do know something about Miss Marsh as well?"

Evans looked a little wary. "I do, sir."

"Excellent. Our talk may save me a great deal of effort. Well worth the expense! Have a good evening, then. Given your sartorial splendor, I must say I suspect one of your chums at the Swan may be a lady."

Evans quickly shook his head. "No ladies, sir. I just always likes to look my best." He put on his hat and quickly walked away.

I shook my head. "What an odious character. I think we had better warn Selton that his valet is not trustworthy."

Holmes shrugged. "Perhaps. Or we might leave well enough alone. This certainly explains a thing or two."

Four

The next morning, Thursday, Holmes and I made the long trek uphill to Edgar Caswall's Castra Regis. Selton had mentioned that Caswall seemed to have taken an odd dislike to him and that we might do better alone. As we walked, the gray-white mists hanging over the green fields around us gradually dissolved, revealing clear, blue sky and the summit above with its gray-brown moorlands. When we reached the weathered castle at last, the climb up its tower stairs took even longer and was more exhausting than that of the day before. As we neared the top, the elderly servant behind us began gasping.

We came out at last into the open air. Holmes walked forward to the wall. "Good Lord," he murmured. "What a view. Henry, you must see this. The wall is even taller and thicker than at Doom Tower."

I smiled weakly and shook my head.

"Stay back a foot or two if you must, but have a look."

I warily advanced, stopped three feet away, advanced another foot. He was right. Below us was rolling countryside divided up into an uneven patchwork of green squares by the hedge rows, the darker green of solitary trees or groves, then the gray stone and finally the expanse of blue-green sea. The castle was the highest point for miles around, but to our left was a rocky ridge and a continuation of the dusky brown moorland which would be spectacular when the heather flowered in summer.

Holmes had set his right hand flat on the thick, rough-stone surface. He shook his head. "Incredible." He looked left, then right, then stepped back and turned, his eyes fixed on the heavens. His left hand held his tweed hat, and the sunlight shone on his damp black hair and glistening forehead. His gray eyes briefly caught mine, even as he smiled and nodded faintly. "Look up there, Henry."

I turned. Far off in the distance, set against the brilliant blue sky, hung the brown bird-shaped kite with its hawk face, those yellow piercing eyes and beak. Some kind of tattered-looking tail hung from it, but we could not make out the string. We had noticed the kite during our journey.

On the other side of the tower, near a wall a good ten yards away, stood a man in a black cloak with his back to us. From an elaborate sort of winch with a wooden handle came a taut silver wire, glowing faintly in the sun, briefly visible before it vanished into the heavens in the direction of the kite.

"Wire," I said. "I suppose that guarantees that he cannot lose his kite."

Holmes nodded. "Exactly."

The old servant in his black frock coat had one hand over his chest, his face still red, even though he had managed to catch his breath. "I shall introduce you to the master, sirs." He staggered forward, taking small steps, in the direction of the man. "*Sir. Sir,*" he croaked. "Mr. Caswall?"

The man swung around. His arms were folded against his chest, but his face—and especially his eyes—were a shock: harsh, arrogant, edgy, extreme. The eyes were that dark brown often called black, and his eyebrows dipped slightly over his aquiline nose, hardly thinning, the effect being of one thick black line drawn across his face. The wind had further tousled his mane of curly black hair, and his thick lips had a sneering sort of smile. I don't generally believe much can be made of first impressions, but he looked so disturbing, I knew something must be wrong with him. The family was supposed to be of ancient Roman stock, and he had a face which would have fitted any of the mad emperors who followed Augustus.

"These gentlemen have come to pay their respects, sir."

Caswall nodded imperiously. "Welcome to Castra Regis, gentlemen. Welcome to my tower."

Holmes nodded. "I am Sherlock Holmes. Perhaps you have heard of me. And this is…"

Caswall lowered his arms and stared at me. "Dr. Watson. Yes, of course. So it must be."

"I'm sorry, but I am Dr. Henry Vernier."

"Nonsense—don't try to lie to me, John! It will not work. It is you. Of course it is Watson." He stepped forward and grasped my arm fiercely. Surprisingly, given the power and vigor of his countenance, he was not a very tall man, a good six inches shorter than I. "You must give up Holmes for good. You have found a new and better subject. You will become my amanuensis, my Boswell."

I stared at him in disbelief. "Indeed?" was all that I could manage.

His face was inches from mine, more than uncomfortably close.

"Yes, John. I will tell you all my secrets, and you will write them down and make me and my marvels known to the world."

I nodded, smiling nervously, then pried his fingers lose and took two steps back.

"Your time has come and gone, Mr. Holmes. You had your day in the sun with the English public, but now a new and greater hero will take your place."

Holmes's mouth pulled into a one-sided smile, even as one black eyebrow rose. "I yield my place most willingly, sir."

"That's noble of you. You are wise to bow to the inevitable."

I swallowed nervously. "That's quite a kite you have there. I see that you must enjoy playing with your kite and…"

"Playing?" His black eyes opened so wide the whites showed around them. "Playing! I do not play. I commune with the heavens." He looked around warily, although it was obvious enough that only Holmes, I and the servant were present.

From a wooden shelf below the winch, he withdrew a thin metal disk some six inches across. He took some crayon or grease pencil and wrote in large letters: ZEUS = TARANIS = CASWALL. "A simple equation." The disk had a hole in the center, and a split which he could open up to get the hole into the wire. He slid the disk a way up the wire, then let go. It drooped for a minute, then the wind caught it and sent it flapping like some weird bird up the wire; it hesitated, then flew again. We all watched as it rose upward into the sky. "These runners are not truly necessary, of course, but they facilitate things."

I smiled warily at Holmes, murmured softly, "Taranis?"

"The Celtic version of Zeus," he replied, then more loudly: "Quite remarkable, Mr. Caswall. I see you have come up with a clever solution for direct communication with the heavens. And the hawk shape of your kite?"

He shook his head angrily. "All the wretched white birds—gulls and especially doves. Crows and ravens are my brothers, but insipid white doves all cooing and shitting everywhere! The kite keeps them at bay."

Holmes nodded. "Another clever solution. You have certainly made your mark in the neighborhood since your return to Yorkshire. How long exactly has it been?"

"About seven months. I arrived the day of the autumn equinox, the exact point of balance between the light and the dark."

Holmes nodded. "Ingenious. And you have settled in so well. We are just visiting this corner of Yorkshire and thought we would call."

He stared at me. "But Watson must remain."

"Yes, I can see that now," Holmes said. "However, we have some business nearby to which we must attend before he can stay." I tried to smile, but some of my dismay must have showed.

"In the interim I shall make some notes for him." Caswall seized a pair of binoculars from the shelf and gazed up at the kite. "The message is almost there."

"Do you know your neighbors well? We were thinking of visiting some of the notable estates, such as Diana's Grove."

Caswall nodded. "Arabella's home. Yes, the house—and she—are worth a visit. The embodiment of female charms and voluptuousness." He raised his right hand toward the heavens. "This is my domain." He suddenly strode across the stone floor to the opposite wall, then pointed down toward the thick green grove of trees and the gray house. "And that is hers. The sky for me, the earth for her. To each his dominion."

"Quite sensible. And you must know Miss Marsh as well, Diana Marsh."

If Caswall's smile had had a certain sneering quality, now it changed to more of a leer. "Yes, I know the young virgin. She is ripe for the picking."

Holmes's eyes briefly went hard, but he quickly recovered. "I have heard rumors–I hope I am not being too forward–of a possible matrimonial union between you and Lady Verr."

Caswall shrugged. "Perhaps, perhaps. But only if she proves worthy. Only if she shows that she appreciates my powers and can assist me in my great endeavors."

I was still uneasy about his earlier words. "I suppose then she'll come here and Miss Marsh can remain at Diana's Grove. Perhaps…" He was staring at me as if I were mad. "Perhaps she will marry someone near her own age."

Caswall raised his head high and shook it three times. "No, no– impossible. Impossible. She must first learn submission."

I could not hide my disgust. "I think not! I'll wager that she'll marry Adam Selton."

Caswall's eyes shot open again in that extreme way, even as he clenched both fists. "Selton–Selton! That great lumbering oaf, that… yokel! She could not possibly choose a clod of mortal clay over the divine."

Holmes nodded, his mouth locked in a grimace of a smile. "I see. And do you know Sir Nathaniel de Salis?"

"I do. He is a wise and worthy gentleman. We spend an occasional evening together discussing both the natural world and the heavenly one that lies just beyond our mortal ken."

"I suspect there can be few who would appeal to you in Micklethorpe or Whitby."

"No one, Mr. Holmes. Foolish stupid mortals grubbing for money and slaving at the land or fishing the waters. What can such worms teach one such as I? I was not sure at first about returning to Yorkshire, I who had traveled the great globe, who had seen the wonders of the pyramids, the glories of Greece and Rome, the dark depths of Africa and the Indian continent, but I realize now that I came because this is my true home–here, high in the sky, amidst the clouds and the elements of the air. Here atop Castra Regis, I am truly lord and master!"

I tried to restrain a shudder. I had seen occasional cases of lunacy, but rarely one so pronounced, so extreme. How could someone like Lady Verr possibly consider marrying him? No amount of money was worth that.

"And have you heard the local tales of the White Worm, Mr. Caswall?"

"Certainly. The worm is Lady Verr's creature. It lives in the pit at the grove." He spoke as if it were the most natural thing in the world.

"And is it… a dragon or merely some great serpent?"

He shrugged. "The beast is female, as in the old tale. As a female, she is vain, sensual, stupid and very, very dangerous–only not to me. To you, without a doubt, but not to me. My male powers protect me. As for you, do not go near the pit at night. That is when the worm likely comes forth. And for God's sake–do not commit foul blasphemy!–do not worship a *mere worm*." This last was said with the greatest possible contempt.

I glanced at Holmes. "Had we better not be leaving?"

Caswall clapped a hand on my shoulder. "But you will return soon, yes, John?"

I nodded. "Of course."

"Before you go, you might like to see my museum. Two large chambers hold my most treasured objects. One room is filled with lethal weapons: tomahawks and clubs of the American Indians, Chinese high pinders, Afghan double-edged scimitars made to cut a body in two, ghost daggers from Tibet, the terrible kukri of the Ghourki in India, assassins' weapons from Spain and India, to name a few. The other room contains my animal specimens: stuffed serpents of every variety, giant insects from the tropics, fish and crustaceans covered with weird spikes, dried octopuses, and, preserved in bottles, various embryos and…"

"Fascinating," Holmes said. "Unfortunately, we are rather rushed today. We shall return another time when we can linger and truly savor your collection."

Caswall seemed genuinely disappointed. "Very well. I hope it will be soon. I suppose…" He pulled out another silver disk. "There are many messages to be sent, and I must track their progress. The heavens may seem adamantine and immovable, but it requires a strong will to maintain that fixed order." He scrawled something on the disk, then fitted it onto the wire.

"Well, we shall leave you to your most essential work, Mr. Caswall." Holmes started for the doorway, and I quickly followed. Behind us we briefly heard the buzzing noise of the disk beginning its journey.

It was only after we had made the long descent and the old servant had closed the massive castle doors behind us, that I finally spoke. "My God, Sherlock–I have never seen such a case before! It is not subtle in the least. He is completely raving mad."

Holmes nodded. "Truly he is, Henry. You could see that immediately in his eyes."

"And would Lady Verr actually consider marrying him?"

Holmes's smile was brief. "It would obviously not be a marriage of love. The lady has a strong will. I think she might be a match for him."

I shook my head. "And the way he talked about Miss Marsh– disgusting. If I were a relation of hers, I would not let him anywhere near her."

Holmes nodded grimly. "I agree with you there. He is all sickness and corruption, while she is all innocence."

I smiled. "Perhaps not *all* innocence."

He frowned slightly. "And what do you mean by that?"

"She is clearly in love with Selton, and I don't think her feelings are merely platonic."

Holmes shrugged. "I suppose not."

We had started down the path. On either side were long, brown grasses, gray stone covered with moss and lichens, and dull, gray-brown heather bushes. A stunted tree thrust itself free from crevices in the rocks, but the top branches were black and withered, no doubt blasted by lightning. I felt the cool steady wind on my face.

As we walked, I slowly regained my composure, so much so that I could say, "And will you be sorry to lose me?"

Holmes had his blackthorn stick in his right hand. He turned to stare at me, the brim of his tweed hat shadowing his eyes. "Lose you?"

"Yes. I must soon return to help Mr. Caswall write his divine book."

Holmes laughed. "It will be a sad day, Watson, a very sad day, when you must leave me."

We arrived back at Lesser Hill shortly after noon to discover a fancy brougham and a pair of grays before the house. Selton introduced us to his parents who had just arrived: Mr. Richard Selton and Mrs. Ann Selton. In an odd reversal, the lady turned out to be the larger, a sturdy woman a good six feet tall with a pinched, unhappy face. Mr. Selton was half a foot shorter, somewhat stout, but with massive shoulders, arms and hands. His dark-brown hair was thin on top, but his enormous mustache hid his upper lip and curved down half an inch on either side. He had the same blue eyes as his son, eyes which regarded us warily.

Much to Adam's discomfort, the elder Selton demanded to speak with Holmes alone. Holmes insisted that I be included and affirmed my trustworthiness. Selton grudgingly nodded, then led us to a small over-decorated sitting room filled with furniture. He did not ask us to sit down, but immediately folded his arms. "Whatever my son is paying you, I shall double it if you can end his absurd infatuation with Diana once and for all."

Holmes had also folded his arms. His black hair shone faintly, still damp from our long walk, and his face had some red-brown color to it. "Paying me?"

"Come, come, Mr. Holmes. I know why you are here: some ridiculous letter about white worms and curses on the Marsh daughters. Clever enough, but obviously from someone who, in pretending to drive him away, wishes to bring them together."

Holmes gave a sharp laugh. "Do they now? After careful consideration, I came to the opposite conclusion. I think someone wants to separate them."

Mr. Selton frowned. "If that were truly the case... Well, regardless, I want you to do whatever you can to make him see the unsuitability of the lady. What has he offered to pay you, anyway?"

"Twenty pounds a day; two hundred when the case is resolved to his satisfaction."

Selton's eyes widened, even as he seemed to freeze. Gradually his mouth pulled into an ugly smile. "If you think you can name any preposterous sum and that I shall believe you..."

"Sir, I am not in the habit of lying to try to raise my fees. You asked what your son had offered me, and I have told you."

Selton's smile faded, and he shook his head. "The boy is crazy. He has no understanding of money." He swallowed hard. "Very well, then. I said I would double his offer, and I shall. Forty pounds a day, and... four hundred upon... satisfaction." Saying such words aloud obviously pained him.

"I'm sorry, Mr. Selton, but as you know, I have already been engaged."

Selton stared at him hard. "Are you serious?"

"Absolutely serious."

He shook his head. "Impossible! This is insolence."

Holmes gave a brusque laugh. "Insolence? Hardly. My services are not up for auction to the highest bidder. Your son has employed me, and I shall do my utmost on his behalf."

Selton was still shaking his head. "I cannot believe it. I cannot. Do you have any children, Mr. Holmes? No? I sometimes think... it is just as well. There is generally more frustration and anger in fatherhood than satisfaction. That and... disappointment. Can you not understand? Miss Marsh simply will not do."

"Why not?" I asked.

He stared at me in disbelief. Obviously he had thought I was to be a silent observer, not a participant. "Because she has nothing to offer. She is also quite plain and... What are you smirking at, sir?"

"Obviously you must not care for redheads, but as I am married to one, my opinion differs."

"Oh, this is ridiculous. Miss Marsh is a nitwit full of foolish and romantic ideas. From the first day they met, even as children, she has involved him in her ridiculous games. I recall, even when he was thirteen or fourteen, they were still playing hide-and-seek in the woods and assuming some silly names. She was Natty something, and he Chin–Chin–Chin–"

"Chingachgook," Holmes said. "He was the Indian companion of the woodsman Natty Bumppo in Fenimore Cooper's *Last of the Mohicans.*"

"See–that's exactly what I mean! Creeping about in the woods and playing Red Indians instead of cricket, rugby or football with other young men! No wonder..." A worried look showed briefly in his eyes. "Anyway, Adam is far too young to be thinking of marriage. He is barely twenty-one. I was twenty-eight when I married, a much more reasonable age for a man."

"Mr. Selton, you may feel at liberty to discuss the young lady and her qualifications, but I do not. Besides, she is not the center of my investigations. By the way, I suppose Evans must have told you about your son's trip to London to summon me."

Selton seemed to take half a step back, half opened, then closed his mouth.

"No, you needn't bother trying to deny it. Evans is the obvious suspect."

"Why should I deny it?"

I shook my head. "You hired your son's valet to spy on him?"

"I have my son's best interests at heart, Dr. Vernier!"

Holmes stared closely at him. "Do you indeed, Mr. Selton?"

"Of course I do. Why are you looking at me that way?"

Holmes glanced at me, then back at Selton. "And did you actually procure for him the services of a prostitute?"

Selton stared at him for a second or two, then clenched his fists even as the blood poured into his face. "You cannot..." He turned to me. "Spying—you dared speak of spying! You are the spies!" He turned again to Holmes. "How much did you pay the dirty little whore? She promised she'd keep her mouth shut! I swear I shall make her pay for this—she will be sorry—she will be sorry."

Holmes shook his head. "Do not be ridiculous, Mr. Selton. No one has spied on you."

"Then how could you possibly know such a thing!"

"It was a guess on my part," I said.

He turned to me. "*You?*"

"I am a physician, Mr. Selton. I have seen such things before."

The blood began to seep away from Selton's face almost as fast as it appeared. "What things, Dr. Vernier?"

"Difficulties with… women."

"Then you… you know about my son's condition."

I laughed softly. "Condition? I doubt anything is physically wrong with him. He was only… afraid, which is quite common. The sexual act is not merely biology, Mr. Selton."

Selton was deathly pale now. "You dare to speak to me this way?"

"What way? I am sure you meant well, but…"

"You have both insulted me in every possible way. This is insufferable, absolutely insufferable. I want you gone. I want you both out from under my roof within the hour. Take your things and go. At once!" His voice rose to a roar for this last.

Holmes nodded. "As you wish, Mr. Selton. As you wish."

He went back into the hallway, and I followed. "But we just got here!" I said. "Where will we go? The inn at Micklethorpe?"

Holmes shook his head. "No."

"Where then? Not back to London."

Holmes glanced at me, his gray eyes faintly amused. "Diana's Grove."

"You're joking?"

"As you may recall, Lady Verr invited us to visit should we or Mr. Selton grow weary of one another. Well, it is a different Mr. Selton, but he is already weary of our company."

Adam was waiting for us at the end of the hallway. His pallor somehow emphasized the classical nature of his features, the high cheekbones, the firmly carved jaw, the full lips and straight nose. "Was that my father shouting just now?"

"It was," Holmes said.

"Oh, damnation. He must know. How could he have found out?"

"I suggest you start looking for another valet."

"Oh no—not Evans! But he has been with me for over three years. I trusted him."

"Unwisely, I fear. I would like to speak with him before we leave."

"Leave? Where are you going?"

"To Diana's Grove to determine if Lady Verr's hospitable offer was genuine. Your father insists we leave his house at once."

"This is my house too!"

Holmes gripped his arm. "That is kind of you, Mr. Selton, but do not fear. I can continue to work in your interest at Diana's Grove. In some respects, it may turn out to be advantageous."

"He cannot throw you out."

"It is just the excuse I need. And where is Evans?"

Selton was frowning. "He wasn't in his room, and there is no sign of him about the grounds. Perhaps I'll walk to Micklethorpe and see if he is still there. He went to the Swan last night, and he has a weakness for malt. He may have drunk so much he could not walk home."

Holmes's brow creased, his eyes fixed on Selton. "Let us hope that is the case. In the meantime, Henry and I will be off to Diana's Grove to see if the Marsh ladies will shelter two such reprobates."

"Are you sure, Mr. Holmes? Perhaps I can make my father see reason. It is not—a gentleman does not drive people from his home on a whim."

Holmes smiled gently. "And you are a gentleman, Mr. Selton. Truly you are. All the same, I have my reasons for wanting to stay at Diana's Grove. It may help me get to the bottom of this case more quickly."

"All right. Do you want to walk or...? Blast it, there's no one to drive the wagonette! I can do it, or you could borrow it, if you prefer."

"We shall just walk over after we have a bite to eat. We must make certain of our welcome. If we do not return by three or four o'clock, then you might bring the wagonette over with our bags. That will also give us a chance to talk further. If we are to leave Lesser Hill, we must arrange a daily meeting elsewhere."

Selton slowly drew in his breath; his chest was so large the inhalation lasted a long while. "As you wish, Mr. Holmes." He turned away, then turned again to us. "I must apologize for my father's rudeness."

"The fault is not yours, sir. Come Henry, let us pack our things."

Selton glanced at me and shook his head. "What must you think of me and my family."

After packing, Holmes and I went to the kitchen, and Mrs. Childes prepared us some ham and cheese sandwiches laden with mustard. Holmes put them and two bottles of cider into a knapsack, and we were soon on our way. We stopped to eat atop a grassy knoll with a superb view of the sea. I, of course, sat well back from the edge. The tide was in, and we could hear the rhythm of the waves sweeping in against the cliffs below. Several big white gulls with their yellow beaks and feet had landed nearby and stood watching us with rapt attention.

Holmes finished his sandwich and took a last swallow of cider. He lay back, put both hands behind his head and closed his eyes, basking in the warm sunlight. His face gradually relaxed, losing its usual fierce alertness and energy. He spoke softly. "Coming to Yorkshire was an excellent idea, Henry. The weather has certainly been ideal."

I drank some cider; it had a cool, sharp, tangy taste. "I hope…"

"What do you hope?"

"I hope we do not regret the decision. Young Selton is a good-hearted decent fellow, but his neighbors… 'Eccentric' is far too mild, especially in the case of Caswall."

"So you do not believe in the idyllic nature of the country with its noble squires and hearty farmers, those emblematic figures of our sceptered isle? Watson makes up so much in his stories, but there was one where he quoted me quite accurately. The lowest and vilest alleys in London do not present a more dreadful record of sin than does the smiling and beautiful countryside. The houses are isolated, the people ignorant, and deeds of hellish cruelty can go on unchecked for years and years."

I shook my head. "After our visit to Caswall and the encounter with Selton *père*, I was already feeling troubled. Must you completely ruin this peaceful setting?"

He opened his eyes, blinking at the bright sun, and the corners of his mouth rose ever so slightly. "Forgive me, Henry. My profession always preoccupies me." He took in a deep breath then brought his hands round as he sat up. "Sickness and disease are always troubling, but sickness of the mind… Caswall had the same effect on me. One wonders how much is heredity, or whether if sometime somehow he had done something slightly different, he might have been another man. Was it one thing he did, one turn he took, that led him off the path for good?" He gazed out at the sea. "You are right. Melancholy reflections for such a peaceful scene."

We both sat quietly for a while. At last Holmes took the brown tweed walking hat and put it on. He seized his blackthorn stick and stood. "We must not keep the ladies waiting."

"If we must stay there, just… just do not ask me to watch her wretched python swallow a rabbit!"

He laughed. "I promise, Henry. All the same, there is no malice in the python. It is only hungry. The rabbit is merely… a ham sandwich."

I was actually sweating by the time we reached the trees of the grove. The temperature must have been well into the sixties, but it dropped dramatically in the shade. We again followed the same narrow footpath through the woods to the entry road. We reached the clearing and the house at last, and Holmes used the big brass knocker.

The stocky housekeeper who had brought us tea the day before appeared in the doorway. She looked obviously uncomfortable in her formal apparel–white lacy apron, matching white cap and black dress.

"Might I speak with Lady Verr and Miss Marsh?" Holmes asked.

She opened her mouth, closed it, looked left, looked right. "I... I... I'm not..." Her cheeks reddened dramatically.

"Is something the matter?" Holmes asked.

"Yes," she murmured, then shook her head. "I mean, no. I mean..." She suddenly went bright red. "You'd best talk to Angela. I'll fetch her." She fled, her hands clenched into fists.

"What was that all about?" I asked.

Holmes's brow had furrowed, and he smiled warily. "I do not know."

We waited impossibly long, but at last Angela came walking toward us. She wore a maid's black formal dress with white collar and cuffs, but one clearly better made than that of the parlor maid. She was quite tall, only an inch or two shorter than Michelle. Her black hair was bound up tightly, a few curls spilling onto her forehead, and she had the classical features of some Greek or Roman statue. Her skin was not white like that of the Marsh women or ruddy like that of the other maid, but an olive-tinted brown. If Selton was Adonis, this was some Venus, a type one might see even now on the streets of Rome or Naples.

"Lady Verr and Mees Marsh take-a the sunshine on the terrace. They see you now."

We followed her across the great hall, down a brief corridor, and then she opened two large french doors. After the dim interior, even the doorway was enough to make me squint. I stepped outside, looked around the stone terrace and saw two naked women, all white with red hair, sitting on some black wrought iron chairs. One woman was wearing octagonal green spectacles, and the other moaned, bent over and desperately tried to cover her breasts with one arm, her hips with the other. Her limbs and her feet were long, pale and bony. Lady Verr smiled graciously, her much larger breasts with the pink areolas proudly thrust forward. "Good day, gentlemen."

I jerked my head to the side. Holmes had seized my arm in a grip of iron, his gray eyes frantic. "Good Lord," he moaned. He had turned to go back inside, and I was ready to follow.

"Wait, Mr. Holmes—wait, if you please."

He paused in the doorway, and I could hear his breath coming and going.

"We are merely sunbathing in that most natural state of man—or woman. I hope you are not so puritanical as to be disturbed by the human body in all its splendor, as first created by God, without all the wretched deceitful layers of clothing. I was once such a prude, but my travels on the Continent have opened my eyes."

"My eyes are open enough," Holmes murmured so that only I could hear him.

"On the Continent they understand that the body is an object of beauty and wonder not meant to be always hidden away. Especially in Italy, monumental nudes in bronze or marble abound, visible in nearly every public square. The hot-blooded Latins have a much healthier attitude than the dreary frigid English. They know there is nothing wicked about the body! And indeed, in shedding all our cumbersome layers of smothering vestments, can we not regain some small portion of the primal innocence of our first parents in the garden of Eden? The Italians also comprehend the beneficial effects of the sun's rays as an aid to health and beauty."

Holmes drew in his breath slowly, stood upright. He was still staring into the house. "The climate there is much warmer."

I heard a sound between a laugh and a sob. "Oh Lord," said Miss Marsh. "Oh, no, no."

"Diana, must you carry on so? You would think… Anyway, won't you gentlemen please join us? You would be welcome to assume the natural state as well, but I suspect you are not yet ready for that. Nevertheless, you might remove your woolen jackets and sit with us for a while."

"Is everyone in this corner of Yorkshire absolutely crazy?" I exclaimed.

"Crazy, Dr. Vernier? Of course not. Can we not all act like mature human beings? Can we not see past our narrow prejudices and primitive taboos? Certainly there is nothing innately wicked about the naked human body. Come, have a seat. Surely, Mr. Holmes, you cannot be afraid of two mere women?" This last had a playful taunting tone.

Holmes swung around. "I suppose we must join you, madam, especially as I have a favor to ask of you."

"Sherlock?" I moaned.

He looked at me, his brows diving inward. "You are a married man," he whispered. "This should be easy for you."

"Are you mad?" I whispered back. "I am not married to either of these two!"

"We cannot let her drive us away with her oddities. We must stay."

"I'm ready to pack up and go back to London!"

Lady Verr laughed softly. "Come, come, gentlemen, it is not polite to whisper. Will you join us or not?"

"Oh, no, no." Miss Marsh was obviously agonized.

"Certainly, Lady Verr, although—call it prudery if you wish—but I would say rather 'distraction'—that is, I do not wish to be distracted." Holmes started in their direction, his head firmly twisted to the right in the direction of the sea.

"This is absurd," I said.

I took a quick look—both were still quite naked, although Miss Marsh was in contortions to hide herself, while her aunt sat with her legs crossed, one white knee just over the other, completely unperturbed. Both had let down their long red hair so that it spilled onto their shoulders, probably in keeping with the *au naturel* theme. I looked away, very much aware of the conflict in my nature. I was a married man, much in love with my wife, quite satisfied with her, aware that looking at naked women could only create trouble and unfulfillable longings—and yet, and yet...

Sherlock resolutely took an iron chair and twisted it so it faced in the opposite direction from them. He sat down with his back to the ladies.

"What is this favor, Mr. Holmes?" Lady Verr did have incredible sangfroid—from the tone of her voice, one would never in a million years imagine she had no clothes on.

"Mr. Selton's parents have come up from town, and I'm afraid there is no longer room for us at Lesser Hill. I was wondering if we might take you up on your kind offer to let us stay at Diana's Grove?"

"Certainly, Mr. Holmes! Certainly! You are more than welcome. Stay as long as you wish. You can see my collection in detail, and tomorrow is the day we must feed Delilah a rabbit. I know you will find it interesting. It will be wonderful to have someone of your intellectual capacity and brilliance with whom to converse. And you, too, Dr. Vernier—you are more than welcome to stay."

I frowned and turned to stare at her, focusing my eyes on those green spectacles and trying to ignore her breasts. *You have seen naked women before—and one in particular who is more than her equal!* I tried to notice her long red hair, her face, anything but her body, and I also tried to ignore Diana. I did catch a glimpse of her scarlet face. Perhaps that was what gave me courage.

"How long have you been out here?" I asked.

"Only a quarter of an hour or so."

"You had better not stay out much longer. Your skin is very fair. You will sunburn badly."

She shrugged. "What is a little sunburn? The skin must be toughened up."

"Sunburn is no joking matter for redheads. It's bad enough if it's just the face, but..." I shook my head. I had never had a patient, male or female, who had sunburned their entire body.

"Thank you for your consideration, Dr. Vernier, but I have partaken of the sun's rays in this way before. No great harm came of it. Please do sit down."

I walked over to Holmes and jerked an iron chair outward toward the ocean.

"Oh, I want to go in." Miss Marsh sounded near tears.

"Don't be ridiculous, Diana. We are all settled at last. Anyway, Mr. Holmes, so you are going to stay with us for a while? You say Mr. Selton's parents have arrived. Still, Lesser Hill is large enough; I would have thought it could accommodate you all." Her voice was faintly ironic.

"I must admit, Lady Verr, that his father, Mr. Richard Selton, does not seem to care much for consulting detectives."

"Well, his loss is our gain."

"Do you think you will take tea inside this afternoon, madam, or out here on the terrace?"

"The terrace, of course, Mr. Holmes. Such fine weather must not be wasted."

I drummed my fingers on the cold metal arm of the chair and stared at the sea. Holmes had his back to them, while my chair was actually facing them, although turned outward. He might find this vaguely amusing, but I hadn't the patience for it—nor for Lady Verr. Something clacked, clacked again, a short burst of sound. I frowned slightly. The sound repeated itself. I turned. Diana's desperate eyes briefly caught mine, those slivers of green around pupils swollen huge and black in the sun. I realized immediately what it was. She made the same involuntary sound; her teeth were chattering.

"All right—enough is enough." I stood up, took off my coat, and walked round toward Miss Marsh, trying not to exactly look at her. "You are freezing—put this on." She turned, and I slipped my coat over her shoulders. She immediately stood and seized the lapels, pulled it awkwardly round her, then her long slender white arm came out and drew it closer, wrapping it more tightly, hiding her torso. I could see the gooseflesh sprouted on the rounded curve of her shoulder. She gave me a look of such gratitude that I knew I had made a friend forever. "Oh, thank you." Her eyes were full of tears.

Again I shook my head. "Come on, let's go inside." She quickly stood up.

"Dr. Vernier, you must not yield to her every whim."

"Lady Verr—as I said—enough is enough!" My voice had risen. "She will either fry or catch pneumonia out here! Come on," I said more gently.

I set my hand on her shoulder and led her toward the doorway. Holmes gave me an appreciative nod. The maid, Angela, had been standing by the doorway watching, unsmiling and enigmatic, as seemed to be usual for her. Diana and I went down the corridor and came into the hall.

She stared up at me again, her right cheek streaked with tears. "Thank you so much. I could not bear it—I simply could not." Her voice broke.

I smiled. "It was certainly uncomfortable for everyone, but no harm is done. You may as well go and get dressed."

She nodded. "Thank you." Another fit of shivering came over her, her teeth clenching. "I'm so cold."

I looked about and saw a sideboard. "Wait a moment." I went over, poured some brandy and took the glass to her.

She downed it in a single swallow, coughed once, then again. I took back the glass. The yellow light from the big windows was enough to reveal the green in her eyes. "I won't forget this."

I smiled. "I'm sure you will not. And I won't either. Go on, get some warm clothes on and then come back."

She nodded. Her thin, white legs and bare feet almost seemed to glow beneath the rough, dark tweed of my jacket as she quickly went up the stairs. I shook my head again, then returned to the sideboard and poured myself a large brandy. "They are all complete lunatics around here," I muttered.

The housekeeper approached me warily. "Did... did...?"

"You might have warned us."

She blushed again, opened her mouth, closed it, and shook her head. "How could I?"

I shrugged. "I suppose you have a point. Has she done this before? Lady Verr. The... on the terrace?"

"She talked of it yesterday, but this is the first time. For this. Still, it's... typical." She shook her head. "I must hold my tongue, but..." She stared closely at me. "You gave Diana yer coat?" I nodded. Her hand shot out and grasped my wrist. "Bless you, sir." She shook her head, then quickly left the room. Her appraisal of the situation clearly matched my own.

I was not yet ready to face the naked Lady Verr again, so I stood sipping the brandy. A few minutes later I heard a slight noise on the stairs and saw Miss Marsh descending. Seeing me, some color came again to her cheeks, but she smiled. She had on the same bright blue woolen skirt and short jacket as when I had first seen her the day before. My tweed jacket lay folded across her left forearm.

"Still here?" she asked.

"I'm fortifying myself." I raised my glass. "Once more unto the breach, dear friends, once more!"

She laughed. "Or close the wall up with our English dead!"

I stared at her. "You know it, then?"

"Oh yes. Shakespeare's *Henry the Fifth*. I read a great deal, Dr. Vernier. There isn't much else to do around here, especially in the winter." She handed me my jacket. "Here. And thank you, again."

"You're most welcome." I put it back on. Obviously neither of us wanted to discuss the earlier situation—or to walk out onto the terrace. "Perhaps I can convince Lady Verr to come back inside for tea time."

She nodded. "I hope so."

I pulled out my watch. "Mr. Selton is likely to show up soon with our bags in the wagonette."

Her eyes grew large with horror, and she clutched desperately at my wrist. "You can't let him... he mustn't..."

"He will knock at the front door first, and you can waylay him." I was half joking, but she looked very worried. "I shall see what I can do."

I went back down the corridor and out onto the terrace. This time, of course, the element of shock and surprise was missing. I nodded at Holmes, then glanced at Lady Verr. I frowned at what I saw: her skin was turning bright red. Holmes was tapping at the chair arm. "Ah Henry, at last! Join us, please. We were discussing Sir Nathaniel's ideas about a gigantic serpent surviving into modern times."

I remained standing and folded my arms. "Lady Verr, you are clearly starting to sunburn. Please humor me in my capacity as a physician, and go indoors. I truly am worried that you will make yourself ill. Again, a bad sunburn for a redhead is no joking matter."

She gave a great sigh, scratched at her nose, then set her hand on her bare thigh. "Dr. Vernier, as I have told you…"

"Please. Humor me. In this case I promise you I have your best interests at heart."

She sighed, and I briefly looked out at the sea away from her breasts. "Oh very well, Dr. Vernier. I do feel a trifle warm." She looked at the woman in the doorway. "Angela, if you please."

The maid walked over and set a long, green velvet cloak over her mistress's shoulders. It went nicely with her spectacles, both contrasting with her red hair. Holmes had warily half turned in the chair. Now he stood up with a great sigh of relief. "We must continue our discussion indoors, Lady Verr."

"So we shall, Mr. Holmes. First, however, I must slip into something more suitable."

We went down the corridor and into the hall. Diana was standing talking to Adam Selton, her back to us. Selton's forehead creased warily, his head half turning. A green cloak is hardly typical indoor dress, and Lady Verr was barefoot. "Ah, good day, Adam!" Lady Verr exclaimed. She slipped her hand and part of her bare arm out in greeting. A variety of emotions showed in Miss Marsh's face, even as she went scarlet. Lady Verr went up the stairs followed by Angela.

I gestured toward the sideboard and spoke to Holmes. "There is brandy there."

"Thank you, Henry." He strode quickly in that direction.

Selton was staring at me in the oddest way. You could see the wheels turning, but of course, he would not ask the obvious. Miss Marsh could not face him, and her eyes were a mute appeal. I started toward them. "Well, we are here to stay, Mr. Selton, as you see."

"Good," he murmured. It was almost more of a question.

"And you have brought all our things? Excellent. Thank you so much."

Holmes had downed the brandy in one swallow. Now he walked toward us, his left hand smoothing back his long, black hair. He managed a smile. "Mr. Selton, we must speak briefly. Outside, I think." He stared at Diana. "Miss Marsh, you look…" He realized he was approaching dangerous ground. "That shade of blue suits you very well. I'm sure we both agree that Henry is the hero of the hour. Watson could never have managed half so well!"

Five

During the remainder of that first day at Diana's Grove, Holmes was clearly the object of a charm offensive by Lady Verr. Luckily, after she came inside, the campaign proceeded with her fully clothed. Perhaps it was Holmes's fame, or perhaps her isolation in the country with no one but a male lunatic or her young niece nearby had made her desperate for company. Her beauty, wit and intelligence were on full display. She was quite a conversationalist. I, however, was only marginally included. Possibly I was in disgrace for bringing Miss Marsh inside or for insisting that she herself come in out of the sun. As a result, I ended up spending more time talking to the young lady than her aunt.

Miss Marsh was rather shy, especially after all that had happened, but she soon warmed up. While Holmes and Lady Verr discussed the great capitals of Europe, and then matters biological and scientific, we talked about books. She was a great reader and her two favorites, naturally enough, were *Wuthering Heights* and *Jane Eyre*, which both had scenes involving the grandeur of the Yorkshire Moors.

At one point she stared closely at me, hesitated with her lower lip between her teeth, then spoke. "Do you believe in destiny, Dr. Vernier?"

"What type of destiny?"

"Destiny in… love, like that between Heathcliff and Catherine. They were meant to be together, to be one, and it was their separation that ultimately destroyed them both."

I nodded. "You have read the novel rather carefully, I see."

"I didn't understand it all the first two times I read it." She was still watching me. "Do you?"

I smiled. "Yes, I suppose I do believe in destiny, but it is rarely so grand or melodramatic. When you have been with someone for a while and when you truly love one another, as my wife and I do, it is hard to imagine an existence without the other person. It does seem like it was somehow meant to be—it cannot be mere coincidence or blind luck."

She smiled at me, the dimple on the right side appearing. "I am glad to hear it!"

I knew she was thinking of Adam Selton. He was a lucky man. I could not be exactly objective because she reminded me so much of Michelle—again, she might have been her younger sister. She had a natural vivacity and charm so different from the artifice of her aunt.

Holmes and I had adjoining bedrooms on the second floor. During the night I heard the murmur of the ocean, a peaceful sound. When I came down at about eight thirty to the breakfast room, Holmes and Miss Marsh were there, but not Lady Verr. Diana told us that her aunt rarely appeared much before noon. She typically labored in the library or in the chambers holding her insect collections or her living reptiles until two or three in the morning.

The housekeeper had on her black dress, but not the lacy white apron or cap. Yesterday she had had a weary sullen air which made her look older, but that morning she appeared quite cheerful. She looked to be in her forties. The enthusiasm of her smile surprised me.

"Good morning, Dr. Vernier! Would you like coffee and some breakfast?"

"Yes, please."

"Will porridge do, or shall I have cook fix some eggs and bacon?"

Holmes and Diana both had empty china bowls before them. "Porridge sounds delicious."

She nodded and went toward the kitchen. "What is her name?" I asked.

"Mrs. Troughton," Diana said. "Mrs. Mary Troughton."

"And has she been with you long?"

"Yes, since I was ten or so—about ten years, then." She hesitated. "I am glad—I am glad she is still here—and I only hope... Oh, she must stay!"

Holmes sipped at his coffee, his gray eyes peering closely at the young lady over the blue and white rim. He had on another woolen Norfolk jacket, this one a gray herringbone tweed with matching knickerbocker trousers, a gray shirt and black necktie. "You sound as if you fear she may depart."

"She would never go willingly."

"But your aunt might drive her away?"

Miss Marsh opened her mouth, closed it, then nodded, her youthful white brow creased.

"When she moved in, she must have brought her own servants, her maid Angela, no doubt, and Hamswell?" Diana nodded again. Her mouth had formed a taut, grim line.

Hamswell had helped serve dinner the night before. A large, portly man of about fifty, he had a boxer's nose and a bushy brown beard. Sir Nathaniel had pronounced him "quite ugly," which was perhaps a little strong, although he could never be called handsome. It certainly seemed impossible that he could be the secret lover who had driven Lord Verr mad with jealousy.

"Aunt Arabella said we could not afford so many servants, that we must make some economies."

"And which of your servants were given notice?"

Diana sighed. This was obviously painful. "Garth, the butler. Old Carter, who was the gardener and groundskeeper. Eleanor, who was first my mother's maid, and then my own. And my governess, Miss Guin—dearest Sarah, who had become my best friend and who…" Her eyes suddenly overflowed with tears. She put her hand over them and turned away. "Pardon me."

Holmes glanced at me, clearly aggrieved, then at her. "My dear Miss Marsh—forgive me! I did not mean to probe at so grievous a subject."

She shook her head, not trusting herself to speak. One hand still over her eyes, she used the other to raise her cup to her lips. She set down the cup and slowly drew in her breath. I had withdrawn a fresh handkerchief from my pocket. "Here."

She took it and dabbed at her eyes. "Sometimes…" She clenched her teeth briefly and shook her head. "Everyone is gone—everyone."

I recalled Sir Nathaniel calling her a flibbertigibbet and Selton's father, a nitwit. Neither had any understanding of the young lady. Mrs. Troughton entered with my porridge and coffee on a silver tray. She frowned fiercely at the sight of her mistress in tears and set down the tray. She glanced first at me, then at Holmes. My actions from the day before had put me in her good graces, but Holmes was still suspect. "What's wrong? Who has upset her?"

"We were discussing the paucity of servants," Holmes said. "The fault is mine. I certainly had no intention of disturbing her."

His sincere contrition soothed the lady. "Poor duck." She gently touched Miss Marsh on the cheek with her big hand. "You've still me left with you, praise the Lord." She set the porridge and a small jar of cream before me, then poured more coffee into our cups from a china pot.

"As your aunt will likely not appear anytime soon," Holmes said, "perhaps you might join us in a stroll. Mr. Selton told us there is an easy way down to the beach near here."

She swallowed once, then smiled weakly. "Gladly, Mr. Holmes. I love to go there. It is my favorite spot." She hesitated. "Adam and I often meet there, or... There is a point halfway between Lesser Hill and Diana's Grove where an enormous rock juts out over the crashing surf."

"Ah yes, he told me about that place. We plan to meet there occasionally."

She stared closely at him. "Has Adam engaged your services, Mr. Holmes?" He did not answer. "I shall not tell my aunt."

Holmes inhaled slowly through his nostrils. "He has, Miss Marsh."

"But why?"

He shook his head. "I am not at liberty to tell you. You must ask Mr. Selton. He has his reasons, which are perhaps best left private at this point."

"I hate secrets—I hate them! Why must there be mysteries and... and distrust, especially between those who love one another!" Although this was only a rhetorical question, it was delivered with heartfelt sincerity.

Holmes shook his head. "I do not know, Miss Marsh."

She sipped her coffee but said nothing, her eyes glistening again.

When we began our walk, a mist still hung out over the sea to the east, the air and water both grayish-white. The curl of the incoming waves had a muted bottle-green color. Gradually the mists dissolved, the sea taking on a deep bluish-green, the undulating waves creating dips of black and white. The tide was out, and the shingle near the foaming water was almost black, glistening. Further in, the dry pebbles were a pale gray. A few gnarled pieces of wood were scattered here and there, and the sun still in the east shone on the sheer gray-white limestone cliffs.

Miss Marsh stopped once and carefully selected a few stones. She turned out to be one of those enviable mortals who can hurl stones and make them skip, a talent I completely lack. Holmes proved to be almost her equal. They were a rather comical sight, this young lady in blue with her wide-brimmed hat and he, in his gray tweeds, England's preeminent consulting detective, throwing stones out toward the smoother waters and watching them, hit, bounce, hit again, before they finally sank.

When we returned to the house Lady Verr was waiting. I saw at once that my warnings about sunbathing had been prescient. She smiled and tried to make light of it, but her face was bright red and dry-looking, much worse than the evening before, and she moved very stiffly. Her rear might have been spared because she was seated on the chair (or had it been grilled by the wrought iron?), but the front of her must all have been burned. I knew the mere touch of her clothes must be painful on her skin, but happily she was wearing some today! I suggested that a cool bath with tea and water, or perhaps even milk, might help. She was surprisingly gracious, probably because she felt so wretched. I had noticed that Diana's face had only a hint of redness—I had brought her indoors just in time.

Holmes mentioned that he had business in Micklethorpe. Apparently the household still possessed a single aged horse and a primitive carriage, a dog-cart, and Lady Verr offered to have Hamswell drive us. Holmes, however, said he preferred to walk. Thus we set out, yet again, on foot. This was our third day in Yorkshire, and the fresh air and exercise had truly rejuvenated my cousin. He had also cut back on tobacco. He had smoked a few cigarettes the evening before with Lady Verr, but noticing my stern look, he had limited the quantity.

It was over an hour's walk, and he was rather taciturn. I suspected that he was mulling over all that we had seen during our brief stay and especially those he had referred to as our *dramatis personae.* A truly bizarre bunch they were! Even young Selton and Miss Marsh were odd, although in a much more appealing way than their seniors.

When we neared the village, Holmes spoke at last. "What would be an obvious reason for your wishing to see your professional counterpart in the village?" I stared at him. "I mean Dr. Thorpe. What would be an excuse for us to call upon him?"

"Well, given the size and the location of Micklethorpe, he can hardly be the equivalent of a specialized Harley Street physician who charges several guineas for a visit. Many modern doctors like Michelle and me have training both in medicine and surgery, but I suspect he assumes all three traditional roles and acts as physician, surgeon and apothecary. You are supposed to be resting and recuperating here. Perhaps we could ask him for a revitalizing tonic. Without a doubt, he will have several, but for heaven's sake, we must quickly dispose of it! Patent medicines are—at best—without effect."

"Excellent, Henry, a perfect excuse!"

"But why do you wish to see him?"

"It will be obvious soon enough."

We found the good doctor at home in an aged stone cottage. His sitting room also served as consultation room and dispensary. Along one wall were shelves lined with bottles and jars of every shape and color, each with a label on them. Dr. Thorpe was a tall, thin man of about sixty wearing a dark-gray jacket and waistcoat with a golden watch chain dangling between its pockets. His face below his forehead was browned, with an obvious line, and I did not need to be Sherlock Holmes to realize he must wear a hat when he traveled about the countryside making calls on horseback. His hair still had a little brown showing round his ears, but his mustache was completely white. He gazed at us through thick rectangular spectacles as I told him of Holmes's malady, then set down his clay pipe and stood up.

"I have just the thing, Dr. Vernier." He hesitated, staring at Holmes. "Not suffering from any male weaknesses, are we? Lack of desire, lack of vitality, that sort of thing?" Holmes shook his head resolutely. "So, something for general vitality. Yes, I have just the thing." He took down two small bottles and a brown glass vial. "I shall just mix some for you. Three drops morning and evening, and in a few days you will be a new man."

Holmes nodded. "I believe you know the lady with whom we are staying."

"Indeed? Who might that be?"

"Lady Verr."

Doubtless this was a test, and it had a dramatic effect. The doctor quickly set down the bottles, put one hand on the big table and gave a great sigh. "Of course I know her—of course! Good heavens, I shall never forget… You must have heard of the tragedy?"

"Her husband's suicide?" Holmes asked.

He nodded. "Dear me, yes. A ghastly business. Just last year. Never in all my years…" He had gone pale.

"Perhaps you should sit down for a moment, Dr. Thorpe," I said.

"No, no, I shall be fine, but—perhaps a drop of sherry—for medicinal purposes. It is late afternoon, nearly time. Perhaps you gentlemen would join me for a glass before I finish my preparation?"

We nodded, and he went to a table where he poured some sherry into three small glasses. He handed one to each of us, then took his own and gestured at a sofa of worn purple velvet. "Have a seat, if you please." He sat in a nearby chair and took a big sip. "Lord and Lady Verr. Such nobility, such breeding–they had everything! Yet, what did it matter? A ghastly nightmare indeed."

I had sat and took a sip of sherry. It was horribly sweet, something I would never willingly choose. Holmes swallowed some, and I could tell he felt the same. "I have heard you were actually there," Holmes said.

"So I was, Mr. Holmes. So I was."

"And he used a revolver?"

"So he did." Thorpe had gone paler still and took a big swallow of sherry. "I suppose it's odd that... But I was never trained as a surgeon, after all. Oh, I have picked up enough of it over the years to manage. One must do what one must do, but the simple fact is that I have always been troubled by the sight of blood. And to actually see a living, breathing human being shoot himself!" He shuddered. "Blowing one's brains out is not merely a description, gentlemen."

I grimaced slightly. "I know what you mean, Dr. Thorpe. I was trained in both medicine and surgery, but I still have little stomach for the latter. My wife, on the other hand–she is also a doctor–absolutely nothing bothers her."

He stared at me incredulously. "Your wife is a doctor? I had heard rumors. It is actually possible, then?"

"Yes. And she is a very good doctor."

He shook his head. "Amazing. We live in strange times."

"So you saw the whole thing?" Holmes asked.

"I did. I had visited him once before. He was weary and listless, but he had no fever, and his pulse was normal. He had little use for doctors, but his wife was concerned for his health. The second time, she warned me that he seemed irrational, that he was obsessed with the idea she was unfaithful, that she had a lover. She swore to me before God that she had been true to him, and I believe her, gentlemen. She was not an adulteress. No, it's impossible to even imagine."

"How long were you with him before he shot himself?"

The directness of the question made Thorpe wince. "Not long. Five minutes at most. It went as she predicted. He cursed her with every imprecation for betraying him and making him a laughing stock. I tried to tell him he was mistaken, and briefly I feared he would turn on me. However, she upbraided him and told him I was only trying to help bring him to his senses. 'Why must you torment us both so!' she sobbed. I thought this must bring him round, but he only laughed and called her devil and..." His words trailed away.

"And?" Holmes asked.

The doctor was lost in thought, his forehead scrunched up. "'Worse than whore.' He actually said that–that even a harlot was better than her." He shook his head. "Forgive me for saying such filth, even if I am only echoing what I heard."

Holmes had leaned forward, his eyes gleaming with a familiar intensity. "Not at all, Dr. Thorpe. Did he say anything else? Did he say anything about her lover?"

"Not... not exactly. He did say something about a 'black-haired devil,' yes, and later 'swarthy demon.' But at that point he no longer seemed sane."

"Did anything in particular actually seem to make him shoot himself?"

Thorpe was still frowning and staring into space. "His lady... She had begun to weep. She told him he would drive both of them mad. Then... then... she seemed to rally. She smiled at him, she actually smiled at him, and begged him to be done with it all. 'End this,' she said. 'End it. One way or another. It cannot go on this way.' He stared at her, then seized the revolver—I was in terror, Mr. Holmes—I thought he was going to shoot us both. Instead he put the barrel against his forehead and pressed the trigger." He shook his head wildly. "You cannot imagine how loud a pistol shot is in a small room. It was unbearable!" He finished his sherry, then stood. "I must have another."

Holmes sat back, even as he tapped his fingertips together twice. "I am sorry to bring back such painful memories, Dr. Thorpe. One last question. Where was the revolver when you entered the room?"

"Oh, it was lying on his desk. I noticed it immediately. I thought of trying to grab it, but I am an old man, and I knew Lord Verr would be much quicker. Also, he might take such an action the wrong way."

"Well, certainly you could not have prevented the tragedy. Clearly he was insane."

Thorpe nodded. "Exactly, Mr. Holmes."

Holmes sipped the sherry, his distaste for it obvious to me. "I suppose, given your many years in the neighborhood, that you must be well acquainted with the Marsh family?"

"Yes, of course." He sighed. "There again—truly, the family seems cursed." Holmes glanced at me, one eyebrow rising. "Robert and his lady, both taken down in their prime by the influenza, just a little over three years ago. I have never seen anything sadder. Miss Diana left only with the grandfather, with Herbert. Diana was quite ill herself, but the old man nursed her back to health. Somehow he alone had completely escaped the influenza, but two years later his heart gave out, and poor Diana was left all alone. How lucky that her aunt has returned to take care of her! They can comfort each other for their losses."

Holmes nodded thoughtfully. "And where was Lady Verr during all these illnesses, Dr. Thorpe?"

"She had spent the last ten years on the Continent, mostly in Italy I believe. Lord Verr was a diplomat, but apparently the Crown decided to dispense with his services."

"And Lady Verr never came home to visit?"

"No."

"Even during her father's last illness?"

"No. His death was something of a surprise. Oh, he was old and had problems with his heart, but there is never any telling how long someone may actually last." He glanced at me. "You must have noticed that, Dr. Vernier."

I nodded. "Indeed I have."

"So Lady Verr returned shortly after her father's death?"

"Yes, it was last spring. They leased a home between here and Whitby."

"Odd," Holmes said. "Why did they not go to Diana's Grove?"

Dr. Thorpe nodded. "Ah, that was because Lady Verr did not want her niece to have to endure her husband's mad ravings. She told me as much."

"Lord Verr was a baron. I wonder, too, that they did not go to his estate in Lincolnshire."

"Hard times, Mr. Holmes! Hard times. They had leased the family home, and he was hopelessly in debt. I am certain that also contributed to his melancholia."

"You seem to know a great deal about the family—and especially Lady Verr."

A slight flush appeared in his cheeks. "With all her troubles, the lady needed someone in whom to confide. I was only too happy to provide a sympathetic ear. She is a lovely and charming woman, Mr. Holmes."

Holmes nodded, his face carefully neutral. "Indeed she is."

"I first knew her when…" He laughed. "Arabella was about ten, and Robert was thirteen. He was the serious one, and she was something of a little devil. Has she told you about her beetle collection, Mr. Holmes? Ah, well, she probably did not tell you that her hobby began at the age of ten! Her brother tried to stop her—he did not like the idea of trapping and killing insects, but she outwitted him. I remember visiting the family one time when Robert had the croup, and she insisted on showing me her butterflies." He shook his head, glancing at me. "Women doctors, incredible! Lady Verr would have made an excellent one."

I smiled and nodded, even though I thought he was absolutely wrong. Michelle and Arabella might superficially resemble each other on the outside, but the inside was another matter entirely.

"And you must also know Miss Diana Marsh quite well," Holmes added.

Thorpe nodded, his look rather wistful. "So I do. A sweet, lovely girl." He shook his head sadly. "But so many losses at such a young age! I think the saddest sight I have ever seen was Diana and her grandfather at her mother and father's funeral. Neither of them wept. They were long past that, positively numb and exhausted with grief. Life has not been kind to her."

I nodded. "I hope her luck changes."

Thorpe smiled. "But it has—it certainly has!" My face must have shown my puzzlement, because he explained: "Her aunt, Dr. Vernier—her aunt. The situation is ideal for them both. They are no longer alone." He finished his second glass of sherry and stood resolutely. "Well, I must see to your tonic, Mr. Holmes."

Holmes also stood. "One last thing, Dr. Thorpe. Would you happen to know the name of the Marsh family solicitor? Someone in Whitby, I would assume."

"Yes, yes–Fitch and Fitch, it is. The father, Cedric, is about my age; the son, Gerald, twenty-five years his junior."

We soon stepped outside, Holmes in possession of a small bottle wrapped in brown paper. Once we were well away from the cottage I seized Holmes's arm. "You do not believe–surely this is nothing like the Grimswell case? Lady Verr cannot possibly have murdered her brother, his wife or her father?"

Holmes shrugged. "No, I think not, but I wanted to rule it out. Murder by influenza seems unlikely at best, and she was out of the country. The same would be true regarding her father's death."

"But her husband?"

"Obviously he shot himself, but... '*But*'–aye, there's the word. My profession as a consulting detective has exposed me to the darkest and most sordid side of human nature, so much so that my prejudice is always for the worst. Thus, all my instincts tell me there must be a lover, but it is as Sir Nathaniel said–there are no viable candidates, none. Also, if that were the case, she would hardly have gone to live at Diana's Grove, where a suspicious male in the household would be so noticeable. No, I may have to accept that there is no lover– although I do not have to like it."

He said this last as if annoyed, and I laughed. "Furious because there is no lurking Lothario! Yes, your profession has ruined you."

He shrugged. "We shall see. And now we have another visit to pay, Henry–to the local vicar."

"*The local vicar?*"

The Reverend, Mr. Tobias Sloap, lived with his wife in a cottage next to the church and its cemetery. She was plump and petite, he a towering beanstalk with long white hands and the trained smile of the professional clergyman. "Mr. Sherlock Holmes? Incredible! Incredible! And to what, in heaven's name, do we owe the honor of this visit?" He turned to his wife. "Annabelle, bring a glass of sherry for the gentlemen and myself!"

Holmes and I forced ourselves to smile. Soon we were sitting in a perfect little parlor with doilies scattered here and there, small painted figurines, and a plaque celebrating the Queen's golden jubilee hung on the wall. The sherry was sweet, but not quite so wretched as Dr. Thorpe's. I hoped we wouldn't be calling on anyone else! The only decent sherry in the neighborhood seemed to be at Lesser Hill, which was currently off limits.

We briefly discussed the weather and the idyllic countryside, but then Holmes got to the point. "Vicar, I have heard something about cattle and sheep mysteriously disappearing from the moors."

Sloap's face lit up. "Have you, now! It is indeed a frequent topic of conversation among my flock."

"Is it? It had occurred to me... Remnants and ruins of the Celts are common in Britain. Diana's Grove, where we are staying has a celebrated history going back even before the Romans and the Celts. Perhaps you know its alternative name?"

Sloap nodded, smiling. "The lair of the White Worm."

"Would you know...? Are you familiar with a group called the Ancient Order of Druids?"

"Certainly, I am, Mr. Holmes. There was a lodge at Oxford when I was at Christ Church. I had friends who were members."

"It is quite popular in London, too, although there are now two competing lodges. However, they are, as you must know, only fraternal societies. They actually forbid any discussion of religion at their meetings."

I smiled. "A civilized notion."

"However," Holmes continued, "there are other groups which have actually tried to revive the ancient Celtic religion, a difficult task, since so little is known about that religion or its Druids. Wales has been a strong center of such activity."

Sloap nodded. "Yes."

Holmes hesitated only an instant. "And would you know, Vicar, if any such groups are active in your parish?"

Sloap smiled and nodded. "There is one, indeed, Mr. Holmes. It is supposed to be a grand secret, but I know something about it. One of my parishioners has been an intermittent participant, and he keeps me informed of their activities."

Holmes stared closely at him. "You surprise me, sir."

Sloap shrugged. "I am a shepherd, a keeper of souls. It is my business to know such things."

"And does this local manifestation also involve the so-called White Worm, a great serpent or dragon?"

"Yes."

"I have heard that people have seen green lights or even gigantic white shapes in the grove."

"That is also true." He shook his head. "I do not find such reports credible. If there is any truth to it, I would suspect some prankster with a lantern or two and some green glass."

"How long has this been going on?"

"Well, the local farmers have always been a superstitious lot, although they don't realize how far back their superstitions go. However, this particular manifestation began only last year. Three animals disappeared last autumn, in October and November, a sort of prelude. Of course, the weather in the heart of winter is so dreadful many animals and most people stay indoors most of the time. However, the livestock disappearances resumed with greater frequency early in March."

"Let me mention a few names. Tell me if they might be involved. Edgar Caswall."

Sloap shook his head. "No, no—he is his own favorite divinity."

I smiled faintly. "You noticed that, did you?"

"A single visit when he moved into the neighborhood sufficed. The man is addled."

"Lady Verr. Miss Diana Marsh. Mr. Adam Selton. Sir Nathaniel de Salis."

Sloap nodded. "Yes. Sir Nathaniel participates in their ceremonies."

Holmes sat back and shook his head. "Does he! How interesting. And this group—I suppose they meet at night at Diana's Grove. They must wear white robes, march with torches in a procession, then sacrifice a beast."

Sloap nodded. "Exactly, Mr. Holmes. Ridiculous, isn't it, in this day and age? I have tried to ignore it, but finally, the Sunday before last, I gave a sermon on the evils of paganism."

"Do you have any idea who might be behind all this?"

"I do not. There is a red-haired high priestess who conducts the ceremonies. She is clearly in charge, but my parishioner did not recognize her. He is a sociable chap who knows everyone, so this priestess must be a stranger or someone who rarely goes out in public."

Holmes frowned. "Red-headed? But not Lady Verr—or her niece?"

I shook my head. "It cannot be Miss Marsh. That is impossible."

"No," Sloap said. "My parishioner would have recognized either of them. The Marsh family has a certain historical notoriety. The Marsh 'daughters' are obvious suspects, but those two are not involved."

Holmes tapped impatiently at a doily pinned to the end of the sofa arm. "All the same…" He shook his head. "I agree with you, Vicar. How can supposedly civilized people of the nineteenth century bring themselves to put on white robes, march over to a local grove and slaughter farm animals? One would hope we were long past such nonsense. I suppose the ceremonies correspond with... the phases of the moon, or..."

"Very good, Mr. Holmes!" Sloap exclaimed.

Holmes rubbed at his chin. "The solstices and the equinoxes would be significant as well. Summer, autumn, winter, spring." His brow furrowed. "And certain other ancient traditional dates–such as 1 May, May Day. It's only about a week away now. It is still commemorated with festivities."

"Dancing round the maypole," I said.

"There is something planned for May Day," the vicar said. "Something special."

"What might that be?"

"I do not know, Mr. Holmes. However, my source tells me the priestess has told them they must truly dedicate themselves to the worm and the goddess it represents once and for all if they wish to participate."

"This does seem nonsensical," I said.

Holmes tapped again at the sofa arm, savagely this time. "Do you think they would go so far as human sacrifice, Vicar?"

At this, Sloap, who was sipping his sherry, choked, gasped, and then coughed wildly. He took another swallow of sherry. It was a minute or two before he recovered. "I don't know, Mr. Holmes! Dear Lord, I never imagined... Cattle and sheep are bad enough. These people are only playing a game. It is common enough, this desire to dress up in special clothing, to light torches and chant, to participate in ancient rituals and mumbo jumbo about gods and goddesses."

I reflected that he might also be speaking of the Roman Catholic or high Anglican Church.

"I cannot believe they would be a party to such a thing," Sloap said. "They could not be so wicked!"

"I wish I shared your confidence, Vicar. People are easily led astray, especially in groups." He frowned thoughtfully. "Do they sacrifice the animals with a knife or…?"

Sloap shook his head grimly. "No. They push them into the pit. I could forgive the slaughter if it were quick, but such cruelty! No, no, that is what makes it all more than just some game of charades."

Holmes nodded. "Yes." He sipped his sherry, winced once at the taste, then glanced at the vicar, who was luckily preoccupied. Holmes held his breath for an instant, then swallowed the last of it. "This has been very helpful. Henry and I shall be staying at Diana's Grove for a few days. If you should hear anything more—especially about May Day—please send for me at once."

"Of course, Mr. Holmes. I feel more comfortable just knowing you are at hand."

"How long have you been at Micklethorpe, Vicar?"

"I am starting my third year."

"So you did not bury Miss Marsh's parents?"

"No, only her grandfather." He shook his head. "Poor girl. I wish I could do more. When someone is swallowed up in darkness, it is hard to even imagine the light."

"Lady Verr is not a churchgoer, I suspect."

Sloap shook his head sternly. "No, even though I have twice invited her. Each time she has assured me she will come, but she has yet to set her foot in this church. Earlier, her absence at her father's funeral was conspicuous."

"I heard that he died quite suddenly."

"That is true. But she has never, to my knowledge, even visited his grave—unlike Miss Marsh, who stops by frequently."

"Everyone seems to find Lady Verr charming and beautiful."

"She is that, Mr. Holmes. Nevertheless, I am not sure that she is… *good*."

Holmes smiled. "You are a perceptive man, Vicar."

"I try to be. Would you care for more sherry?"

I bounded to my feet even faster than Holmes, but he spoke first. "No, no, excellent though it is—we must be on our way."

We stepped outside. The sun was much lower in the sky, its bright light with a yellowish cast. I shook my head. "This is becoming truly bizarre."

"I said you had been good luck for me, Henry. This is indeed the third remarkable case which has begun with you nearby and a knock on the door at Baker Street."

I shook my head. "At least no one has died so far while we are on this case."

Holmes laughed grimly.

"Oh no! What are you thinking?"

"Have you forgotten that Evans has gone missing?"

I felt a brief quiver of fear square in my chest, a sensation I had not felt since our visit to Dartmoor. "Oh, dear Lord."

We were on the tiny cobblestone road which wound through the village. Holmes took a few steps, then turned toward the graveyard. A huge elm rose amidst the scattered crosses, the rectangular and rounded tombstones. Its bright green new leaves contrasted with the dark grass and with the aged gray stone often blotched by patches of dark lichens.

"Let us have a look," Holmes said. He walked slowly forward, gazing at the various headstones, noting the names and dates. I saw a small stone for a child who had lived only two years, a simple sort of tragedy which I always found inexplicable. The newer stones were elaborately carved with curving crosses and flowers, while others were simple rough-shaped slabs with only worn chiseled names and dates. The oldest I saw was from the seventeenth century. In the shade of the elm, the air was cool and faintly damp with a wet, earthy smell.

"Here we are." Holmes extended his stick toward a new-looking headstone, its reddish tint typical of the local sandstone. He took off his hat, then eased his breath slowly out.

On it was "in loving memory" and the names Robert Marsh and Jane Marsh, along with their dates of birth and death. Both had died in their forties. Next to it was another stone, gray and more worn, with the names Herbert Marsh and Rebecca Marsh. The grandfather had lived over twenty years longer than his wife. I sighed softly. Perhaps it was my profession that made me think about mortality, but even the idea that I might live that much longer than Michelle was unbearable.

"The Marsh family is well represented here." Holmes's mouth tightened, then he raised his stick and swept a half-circle in the air, encompassing much of the cemetery. "This is what it is all about, Henry."

"What do you mean?"

"These are the stakes, the ultimate stakes, for which I play. It isn't always that way, thank God, but often enough, if I lose, my clients end up underground, leaving me with the worst possible remorse."

"We all make mistakes."

"Yes, but we do not all make fatal mistakes. That, however, is occasionally my lot. A visit like this reminds me of my responsibilities."

I shook my head. "You cannot solve all the crimes in the world."

"No, but I can take responsibility for those in which I blunder badly." His mouth was stiff, his eyes fixed on the gravestones. "Which is... all too often."

I shook my head. "You mustn't think that way—you mustn't."

He said nothing for a long while. Finally he put his hat back on and smiled wearily. "It is a reminder, all the same. I do not want Miss Marsh or Mr. Selton to end up here—at least not for many decades.

No, I want them in *there*." He raised his stick to point to the rough stone wall of the church with its tall, narrow windows.

"So do I." My smile faded. "You do think this is another dark case."

He nodded. "I do. This business with the worm and Druids and all that has a faintly comical air, as if we were dealing with some twisted prankster. But I fear there is more to it than that. However, enough moody reflections. I will quote Gray's *Elegy*, which I always recall in a setting like this—'the paths of glory lead but to the grave'—and then we must lift up our spirits and be on our way."

Once we were back in the sunlight, I shivered slightly. "I am glad we are above ground."

"Yes, Henry." He gave a soft laugh. "For now, anyway."

We stopped briefly at Lesser Hill. Evans had not returned, nor had anyone seen him the night before in the village.

Six

Before dinner, Lady Verr insisted on showing us her reptile and amphibian collection. Delilah, the Burmese python, was the grand attraction. If you could get past the fact she was a giant snake (which I could not), she was rather beautiful. Her scaly skin had an elaborate pattern of dark brown on tan, with black and yellow highlights. Lady Verr had other creatures in her collection: a lizard that she called a "bearded dragon", bright red and yellow, his "beard" spiky frills under his chin; a big turtle with a brownish-yellow shell that was divided up into lumpy squares about two inches wide; and a grotesque-looking green-and-black toad, his eyes perched like big marbles atop his skull. The room was kept warm with a constant coal fire, and it had a rank, disgusting, animal smell. There was also a glass terrarium full of enormous beetles who were destined to become the other animals' main course at future meals. Rabbits and mice were also raised in a nearby room.

Although I found the animals repulsive and the whole notion

of keeping such a menagerie frightful, I managed to feign some enthusiasm. It did make me appreciate our cat, Victoria, all the more! Arabella obviously enjoyed picking up the creatures and touching their leathery or slimy skin, but I preferred a warm-blooded animal with lustrous fur. Holmes seemed genuinely interested, and I hoped this was not giving him ideas. I could only imagine how Mrs. Hudson might react to a pet reptile! They had had a long battle over a spider that had spun its web on one corner of his desk; in the end, the arachnid had died a peaceful death of age or some spider illness.

A good dinner along with three glasses of excellent claret helped me to forget the zoo. Hamswell again served us. A big burly type with balding pate and bushy brown beard, he did look odd in his black tail coat, white bow tie and white gloves, almost comical. As he ladled out the soup, I also noticed his enormous hands and thick fingers. Of course, having a male servant as opposed to a woman wait at the dinner table was a mark of higher class and status, something which would doubtlessly concern Lady Verr. Hamswell was assisted by Mrs. Troughton, now wearing her lacy white apron and cap with her black dress. There seemed to be a certain froideur between the two of them. Moreover, she always had a certain cold hard edge whenever Lady Verr was around.

Arabella was again monopolizing Holmes, so I chatted with Diana. She seemed to enjoy my company, but in her own shy way. I realized she must have had very little contact with any men besides her father and Adam Selton. She was amazed to hear that Michelle was a physician and had many questions. She was also interested in our courtship and marriage, but the little I told her obviously did not fit with her romantic ideas. Michelle and I had both been older and wary. However, our reluctance was soon consumed in the roaring fires of passion. Of course, I could not tell Diana that.

We had gone to the drawing room, and she held the stem of a small glass of port in her long, white fingers. Her hands were thinner and bonier than Michelle's, although almost as large. Her knuckles stood out, and below them were faint blue veins, then the darker blue silken cuffs. Both she and her aunt had obviously taken considerable care with their dinner attire. Diana was in a sky-blue dress with the popular mutton-leg sleeves, her red hair worn up and emphasizing her long slender neck. Arabella wore an ivory-white dress set off by the same spectacular emerald necklace which matched her spectacle lenses and two tiny emerald earrings. She had, however, dispensed with the bustle, which meant she could sink back into the depths of the sofa. Her face had grown redder throughout the day, and by tomorrow I knew the skin of her nose would begin peeling.

Diana sipped the brilliant ruby liquid, then lowered the glass. Her perfect brow was creased, her green eyes fixed on me. "Does one know, Dr. Vernier? Did you know? Was it always obvious that she was the one?"

I smiled faintly. "No, I'm afraid not."

She sighed, obviously disappointed.

"It took us both a while, but there came a time when I did know, when I was certain at last."

"What happened? What changed?"

Again, this was a loaded question, one I could not answer directly, especially since Arabella had paused and was listening as well. "Well, I... It was a brief separation that made me realize how much she had come to mean to me. I went to Paris with Sherlock on a case, and I missed her terribly."

Diana's brow was creased, her eyes fixed on me with the utmost concentration. "Yes?"

I shrugged. "People are different. Michelle and I were cautious.

We had had some unfortunate experiences earlier."

"Unfortunate experiences? What do you mean?"

"Romantic entanglements which did not work out. Ones that ended badly, to put it more plainly."

"Oh, I see." She drew in her breath slowly. "I'm not by nature cautious. But... but Adam is." She looked worried. "Sometimes I just do not understand him. I think–I know he likes me–but I just don't know if..." Her words trickled away into silence.

Arabella leaned over to grasp her wrist and squeeze it. "We will come up with a campaign to conquer him, you will see! Men never know what they truly want. It is up to the woman to make them understand. But really, it does not help to be so fixated on one person! My dear, I do hope it works out for you, but at your age, you must never make any man the be-all and end-all of your affections."

Her niece said nothing, but her eyes began to glisten.

Arabella shook her head. "No, no–don't do that. How can we talk intelligently about these matters if you cannot...?"

Diana clenched her fists, her discomfort obvious. "I don't want to talk about it–I don't!"

"But nothing will ever be resolved if we cannot discuss things in a rational manner."

I could see that the young lady was becoming upset. "Miss Marsh," I said, "he does care about you. I know he does. You must be patient with him."

She swallowed once, the corners of her mouth flickering upward, even as her skin seemed to glow. "Does he?"

Holmes had been listening, and he nodded. "He does, Miss Marsh. Henry is correct. Mr. Selton has certain difficulties which are preoccupying him, but you are clearly much in his thoughts."

She opened her mouth, closed it, said, "Good." She was clearly so moved she did not trust herself to say anything more. She smiled at Holmes, then at me, and again I had the same feeling as the day before when she looked up at me after I had put my coat over her naked shoulders: I had made a friend for life. I smiled back and thought how ridiculously young she was, how messy and complicated and dreadful affairs of the heart were, even under the best of circumstances, even when everything ultimately ended well.

Lady Verr sighed softly. "When I first saw him, I knew Cyril was the man for me. He was rich, charming and handsome, but he hardly noticed me. The next time we met I wore a gown which showed off my shoulders and a certain décolletage. That caught his attention, and it did not wane for many years. I loved him very much. We had our good times together. However, he gradually became someone completely different from the man I married—in the end, he was truly a monster, albeit a pitiable one. And his appearance—he also declined physically, becoming increasingly corpulent. There are never any guarantees, my dear. People change, often for the worse."

Miss Marsh resolutely shook her head. "I will not change. I will always…" She realized she could not actually say aloud that she loved him. "I will not change, I swear it."

Arabella shook her head. "You cannot stop time. Everything changes. Everyone changes. Nothing stays the same."

"Some things do."

Arabella shrugged. "Yes, but human emotions are the most volatile of elements. Still, my own situation has undoubtedly prejudiced me to expect the worst. Adam Selton could hardly turn out so badly as Cyril." She turned to Holmes. "You are quiet, sir. Have you ever been consumed by the flames of amour, or is Sherlock Holmes too sensible, too rational, to be ensnared by a mere woman?"

Holmes stared coolly at her. "You may wish to share the intimate details of your life with strangers, madam. I do not."

"Ah, touché indeed! However, I suspect if you were truly that rational misogynist portrayed by Dr. Watson, you would not hesitate to proclaim it proudly. Your response makes me suspect the worst."

"You may speculate to your heart's content."

She laughed. "Spoilsport! Very well, no more such questions."

Before we retired to our rooms, Lady Verr insisted on showing us the library. The large room on the second floor had a certain masculine air, a dark table and chairs with padded leather seats, shelves of dark-stained wood lined with books. On half of the shelves were novels, both serious works and those which were mere entertainment: Walter Scott, Dickens, Trollope, the Brontës, and George Eliot were well represented, but also Wilkie Collins and H. Rider Haggard. One title by Haggard caught my eye, and I pulled it out: *She.* I shook my head and slid it back.

"You do not care for Rider Haggard?" Arabella asked.

"No–and especially not this particular novel. I did read it, heaven knows why."

"Quasi-divine eternal females whose beauty instantly bewitches all men are not to your taste?" Her voice had a lilting taunting quality, and behind her green spectacles her eyes were playful.

"I fear not."

"And you, Mr. Holmes?"

"I have little time to waste reading idle fantastical fiction."

She stared closely at him. "But you read it–admit you read it!"

He sighed. "I did. Utterly ridiculous from beginning to end."

I looked at Diana. "Have you read it?"

She shook her head. "I had to stop halfway through. There was so much death, all those ancient corpses in the caves of Kôr." Her shoulders rose in an involuntary shiver. "It gave me nightmares."

Arabella shook her head. "You are too sensitive, my dear. It was only a story, all those corpses merely plot embellishments, so to speak."

The bookshelves were all crammed to their fullest, and crates with more books were on the floor. The other half of the library consisted of much thicker, taller volumes on natural history, geography, science, exotic lands and peoples. Arabella gestured toward the shelves with her long, slender fingers. "I have incorporated my own library into Robert's. My tastes were always quite different from his."

Holmes glanced down at a large volume on the table. He turned it toward the lamp, then flipped to the title page. "*Marine Animals of the British Isles.* So you have also a taste for aquatic biology, Lady Verr?"

"Oh yes. I only wish I had the money to create a giant aquarium and raise exotic fish. I am thinking of at least getting some goldfish. I also have grand plans for a pond on the grounds which I shall stock with koi."

Holmes nodded. "There is nothing more tranquil than watching brightly colored koi gliding about in a pond. That is the central feature of many grand conservatories." He turned a few pages. "This looks very interesting."

"Feel free to sample our library at will while you are at Diana's Grove, Mr. Holmes." She glanced at me. "You, too, Dr. Vernier. That is why I wished to show it to you."

Diana said nothing, but her thin, reddish eyebrows were creased inward just above her nose, her eyes troubled.

"Thank you, Lady Verr." Holmes turned to Diana. "And thank you, Miss Marsh. I appreciate your hospitality, and in fact, I believe I shall take you up on your offer just now and have a look at this particular volume before I retire for the evening."

We said our good nights, and I went down the hallway to my room. I sat in a large leather chair and stared at the coal glowing on the fireplace grate. The company of the two beautiful redheads had merely reminded me how much I missed my own special one. This was my fourth night away from London, and I would have given anything to have Michelle lying in that large comfortable bed waiting for me.

The day had also left me troubled, our visits with Dr. Thorpe and the Reverend Sloap disquieting. I tried, too, to tell myself that Evans had probably just taken the money from Selton senior and headed for London, but I did not believe it. This was too much like the Grimswell case. There, a footman had gone missing and had been discovered with his throat ripped open a day later in a wood. If Evans's body showed up, I would certainly telegraph to Michelle and ask her to come. I was already sorely tempted. Given all the eccentricity bordering on insanity, I missed her stable, down-to-earth good sense. And of course, it was not just her mind or her personality I missed! Men went off on safaris, expeditions or hunting trips all the time, leaving their wives for weeks or months, but they were made of sterner stuff than me. I always felt incomplete without Michelle nearby.

I was still gazing at the fireplace when Holmes came into the room. He opened his mouth, but I quickly said, "Don't say it—don't say, 'Amorous thoughts, Henry'. You know I hate it when you do that!"

He laughed. "I did not intend to say any such thing. You have given yourself away, although it would not be hard to deduce."

"No, it wouldn't."

He stared at the fire. "Would you allow me the luxury of a single cigarette, Henry?"

I sighed. "Oh, very well. You have earned one, I suppose."

He took a poker, got it hot on the glowing coal, then used it to light the cigarette. He exhaled a cloud of smoke. "The case is progressing nicely."

"Is it really?"

"I have most of the salient facts. On Monday I shall go to Whitby to speak with the family solicitor."

I found myself frowning. "Do you suspect there may be more of a fortune than we have been led to believe?"

"I do not."

"What then?"

The corners of his lips rose. "Do you know the story of the three bears, Henry?"

"*What?*"

He laughed. "Goldilocks and the three bears. Do you know it or not?"

"Of course I do, but I cannot see any possible relevance."

"No? Remember that the first porridge was too hot, the second too cold, and the third just right? I suspect that I shall find that the family income is 'just right,' so to speak."

"I don't understand."

"Think about it for a while. Perhaps it will come to you."

"I hate mysteries," I snarled. "I do hate them."

"You must relax, Henry, and enjoy this peaceful interlude. I fear it will not last long."

"Is Lady Verr going to throw us out, then, so she can resume nude sunbathing?"

He laughed. "You are in rare form. No, we need not fear that. Tell me, what have you noticed about Lady Verr and Miss Marsh thus far in our stay?" I gave him a curious look. "What is the nature of their relationship?"

I shrugged. "Lady Verr does seem fond of her niece, although…"

"Although?"

"She is rather domineering."

"Exactly, Henry—exactly. Think about what has happened here. Lady Verr has moved into the house and simply taken over. She has dismissed many of the older servants. She has commandeered many of the rooms and half the library. She even drags her niece out onto the terrace naked, although the girl is obviously horrified and unwilling. It is a relationship based on total domination—and on Miss Marsh's willingness to accept it."

I frowned. "Yes, it is. Perhaps... That has been bothering me, although I couldn't exactly put my finger on it."

"It became obvious within a few minutes of meeting Lady Verr that she is a woman who could never be subjugated, who could never play second fiddle to anyone. She knows only too well that she is beautiful, witty and charming, and she uses these attributes against men with the utmost skill. Sir Nathaniel and Dr. Thorpe are positively bedazzled by her."

"Odd," I said. "I can understand it, but... she does almost nothing for me."

"Both Sir Nathaniel and Dr. Thorpe are old bachelors. Little wonder they are putty in her hands. Then, too, you are relatively immune. Your association with Michelle has... inoculated you!" He smiled at this mock-medical metaphor. "Unlike so many of her sex, she is honest, true and absolutely good-hearted. She has made those females who deal in artifice, flattery, vanity and cruelty distasteful to you."

I smiled faintly. "She is a paragon—I won't argue with you. Though I'm hardly objective."

"But I am, Henry, and I can see it, too."

I stared closely at him. "And yet... you seem inoculated as well."

He nodded. "I am, Henry. In my case, the higher centers of reason are firmly in control."

"Caswall seemed somewhat ambivalent toward her. He hardly seems to be madly in love."

"When two titanic egos meet, neither one is going to simply shrivel up and yield to the other."

"You are full of interesting observations and metaphors this evening," I said. "In the end, perhaps the best thing would be for Lady Verr to marry Caswall and go to Castra Regis, leaving Miss Marsh in peace."

"And yet, Caswall is the wildest of wild cards. Reason and deduction cannot predict what a madman will do. I suspect that for once Lady Verr has met her match. He will not exactly outwit her— but she will not have her way, either."

I shook my head. "Poor Diana."

"Poor Diana indeed." He snuffed out his cigarette butt on the stones of the fireplace, then hurled it onto the grate. "Tomorrow should be interesting. I am looking forward to it."

I frowned. "Why do I feel worried? Where are we going?"

"To the heart of Diana's Grove, Henry, the ancient sacrificial site overlooking the sea."

"So long as you understand you won't get me anywhere near that pit!"

"You are safe, Henry. Selton is going to join us, and he is bringing some rope."

"Rope?"

"Yes. For my descent into the pit itself."

The next morning, Saturday, a cold white mist had settled over everything, hiding the sea and even cloaking the dark trunks and limbs of the trees. I didn't think this boded well for our expedition, but Holmes seemed confident it might clear. We spent a quiet morning in the library with Diana. Holmes was still interested in the volume on sea animals. Twice, he closed the book, put his hands on either side, supporting it upright, then let it fall open.

"What are you doing?" I asked.

"Just an experiment. Finding the most well-read pages."

I shrugged and tried to read the latest issue of *The Lancet*, which I had brought with me, but under the best of circumstances I find medical journals hard going. We left around eleven, before Arabella appeared. Diana watched rather forlornly as we departed. Holmes had told her we had further business in Micklethorpe, a harmless enough lie.

We went down the main road, then turned at last to follow the narrow path into the trees. The mist was very cold, and with the sun gone, the woods were transformed. The colors were all muted: the dark green leaves of yews and holly trees, the black trunks of ancient oaks, brighter green ferns sprouting everywhere amidst the grass and the large stones splotched with lichens or mosses. I was grateful for the path—one could be lost in an instant in this damp gloom. I was also wondering where in the woods the adders might live. Worse yet, it actually began to drizzle. I could only imagine how miserable it would be in a downpour like that one on the night we first arrived in Yorkshire. Holmes was actually humming some air from a Gilbert and Sullivan opera.

"You said it would clear," I muttered reproachfully.

"And so it will, Henry, so it will. Perhaps not for another week..." I groaned at that, and he laughed. "But I believe it will clear sooner than that."

The path curved and twisted, rose and fell, finally opened up before us. Seven tall gray-white stones stood before a wall of white fog, and the gently sloping ground was all small rocks and green grass. A single giant blasted oak stood to one side of the clearing, black and leafless with broken limbs, obviously centuries old. Holmes stared out at where the sea must be: we heard the low rumble of the waves coming and going, and the cries of gulls. As if on command, the mists stirred faintly, grew more tenuous overhead, even as a faint swath of blue appeared.

Holmes nodded. "Definitely sooner." He withdrew his watch from his waistcoat pocket. "Selton should be here any moment now."

Near the summit of the grassy slope were several ridges of gray-white limestone, bare and glistening with moisture. Holmes and I started round and saw, amidst the long grass, a jagged opening which resembled some enormous mouth with lips of rock. On one side were the yellow-green fronds of a fern, the plant plunging into the gap. The rock along the other was gray-white on top, limestone, but within a few inches it became reddish-brown sandstone. Holmes promptly walked up to the very edge, but I stayed well back.

"Miss Marsh was wrong about the pit's being boarded up. There is not even a warning sign. The opening approximates an oval of about five by eight feet." He held the handle of his stick tightly as he leaned over and peered down. "What a stench! It would certainly dissuade most people from coming this close. The bottom cannot be seen. There is a small ledge, and... That must be the source of the smell, some small decomposing animal. The opening narrows, becoming more rounded even as it curves slightly to one side. Yes, one could easily imagine a giant white worm slithering up from down there."

I shook my head. "You needn't have said that."

"The beaches along this part of the coast abound with fossils of primitive sea animals from millions of years ago, and those standing stones go back to at least Neolithic times, millennia ago. One can imagine generations of men and women trudging to this sight to worship or sacrifice, to stare out at the sea by day or up at the stars by night. Yes, looking into this abyss, one can comprehend Sir Nathaniel's willingness to believe an ancient beast from the dawn of time lives on, dwelling deep in the bowels of the earth."

"Do you actually think that might be possible?"

Holmes turned to smile at me, even as he shook his head. "I do not." He leaned forward slightly.

"For God's sake—be careful!"

"I am always careful." He suddenly knelt down, stretched himself out prone on the ground, then thrust his head forward over the opening, turning slightly. "Ah, as I suspected. I can hear the sea. Dimly, but there is definitely a connection. This is not just a hole into the ground." He looked about, found a small stone and dropped it into the pit. A few seconds later he spoke. "I heard it strike something, then, possibly a splash. If so, it was far down." He turned to me. "Why not have a look, Henry?"

"What?"

"The hole is not large, and it soon slopes downward into blackness. If you lie on the ground, surely you cannot feel vertigo."

I inhaled very slowly. "I suppose not."

"After all, it is not some sheer cliff where one can see the rocks a hundred feet below."

"But you said it stinks. And is there actually anything interesting to see?"

Holmes shrugged one shoulder awkwardly, since he was lying down. "Well, actually not. A small ledge some six or seven feet down, as I mentioned, and layers of different-colored rock. I wish I knew more about geology. I can also see some moss-like vegetation about ten feet down which probably marks the high-water point of the sea."

"Dr. Vernier?"

I turned to see Adam Selton approaching. He had a big coil of rope over one shoulder, a knapsack in hand. He wore heavy tweed trousers, jacket and a cloth cap.

Holmes rose up off the ground. "Ah there you are, right on time." He glanced at me. "The tide will be at its lowest in about fifteen minutes. I checked my copy of the local tide tables before I arranged our rendezvous. That will allow me to go as far down as possible."

I shook my head. "It sounds exceedingly foolhardy to me."

"We shall secure the rope to that tree there. As you know, Henry, I am something of an alpinist. There is a technique I learned, which the Germans call *Abseilen*, that allows a gradual descent down sheer cliffs. In this case, there will doubtless be footholds along the way, too, should I wish to rest."

"And just how are you going to see?"

"It is not truly essential that I see, but Mr. Selton also has some long cord. He will gradually lower a dark lantern just at my command. It will proceed ahead of me, so it cannot possibly strike me on the head."

I smiled. "That shows wise caution on your part. And how exactly are you going to get back up? Surely you don't think you can pull yourself all the way up."

"I might be able to, but we will go the safer route. You and Mr. Selton will hoist me up."

I shook my head. "You have thought of everything, but my opinion remains unchanged—this venture is extremely foolhardy. And is it really necessary? What do you hope to discover?"

"Perhaps some gigantic worm droppings." I did not find this amusing, but Holmes gave a great bark of laughter. "Look at the bright side, Henry. My lungs are vastly improved. A week ago I would not have been up to this, but now I feel quite fit."

Selton had listened to this conversation with a furrowed brow. Holmes turned to him. "Let me have a look at the rope." Selton took it off his shoulder, and Holmes set it on the ground, then took up a length of it. "Excellent, premier quality indeed. I had him purchase this in Whitby, Henry. It is a port town, and ships are always in need of various lengths of good sturdy rope."

"How long is that?" I asked.

"One hundred and twenty feet," Selton replied.

"Good Lord." I shook my head. "You would actually go down that far?"

Holmes smiled again. "No, no, only about one hundred feet. There will be about twenty feet between here and the tree trunk. Well, we must get started. The tide will be at its lowest in another fifteen minutes or so."

It was with some dismay that I watched his final preparations. I could think of nothing more terrifying than what he was about to do. He wrapped the rope round the oak trunk, then tied some ingenious knot. Next he withdrew a dark lantern from his own knapsack, the standard variety used by policemen, and lit it. A cord was fastened to the ring on top, and then Selton lowered it into the opening.

"Let it out very slowly. If it catches on anything, you may need to raise and lower it gently. You can also try moving it to the side." He took the end of the rope and fastened a double knot about six feet from the end. "This will be my warning that I am nearing the end of my rope. One danger with this technique is to simply run out of rope as you descend, and so plunge to your death."

He unwound the rope and dropped it down into the pit. "This is my favorite hat, and I could not bear to lose it. However, I have a substitute I could easily part with." He tossed the brown hat with the wide brim to the side, and his swept-back black hair and prominent forehead glistened in the light. The mists were dissolving, the blue more prominent. He knelt beside the knapsack and withdrew another hat, a classic deerstalker with the two brims which Sidney Paget had so immortalized in his illustrations of Watson's stories. Never in all the years I had known him, had I actually seen Holmes wear such a hat!

At last he took the rope, looped it from between his legs around and up over the opposite shoulder, then back around his neck, such that it formed two loops. His hands were protected by thin leather gloves, and his sturdy black lace-up boots had thick rubber soles. He tugged at the rope, then slowly began to back into the opening, letting it out, so to speak, by putting one hand a few inches below the other.

I felt a certain constriction of dread in my chest. "Sherlock—are you absolutely certain you want to do this?"

"Yes. And you might help by lying there and listening for my voice. I will keep you up to date on my progress, and you can tell Selton when it is time to lower the lantern." He glanced a last time at the rope. "Notice that I have it supported on dirt at the edge, not rock. It would be hard to wear through a rope of such thickness and quality, but it is safest not to take chances. I am not totally insane, Henry, despite what you may think." He started again to lower himself.

I got down, then cautiously inched forward on my knees and elbows until my head was thrust over the edge of the pit. I lay flat. "What a stink!" I exclaimed.

Already Holmes had descended to the ledge. "I shall just get rid of these remains for you, Henry. It looks like a dead rabbit." He kicked with one foot at what was left, knocking it into the pit. The smell immediately abated. Below him I could see the rocky walls and the glow of light from the lantern.

"Lower the lantern," he said.

Selton let it out until Holmes said, "Stop," and I repeated his command. Holmes then eased himself down, using his free leg and foot to keep himself off the wall. Thus he proceeded, as we followed a regular routine.

He commented on what he was seeing in between requests to raise or lower the lantern, and the narrow passage seemed to act as a natural amplifier. "Clearly most of this shaft is a tidal area. Sea mosses and vegetation are on the walls... Ah, here is a starfish... Now I have found an outcrop of mussels. A pity there's no way to bring some back for supper... The sound of the sea is getting louder... The lantern is caught on a rock. Best take it a little to the left. Ah, very good! I can hardly see the opening above me now. I must be getting near the end of the rope. Let the lantern down a little more—stop, stop! I can actually see the water now. It is only a few feet away."

"Shouldn't you come up?" I shouted.

"Give me a few minutes more, Henry. Ah yes, incredible—incredible! Pull the lantern up a way. I want it far above me now. I shall tell you when to stop." Next to me, I could see the cord move as Selton did so. "That's good. There is light down here, Henry! The cavern must open to the sea, and the light has made it back this far. The water is lapping at bare rock only two or three feet below me. I wonder how deep it actually is. If only I could explore further!"

"Don't you dare try! Haven't you found out enough?"

"Yes, I suppose so. It is curiously beautiful down here, all dim, with water splashing about. The cavern opens up to one side, but upon one wall are fixed various sea animals and plants."

"Let us pull you up. You have been down there a long time."

"Give me another minute or two. I am not uncomfortable."

Well, I am, I thought.

"All right, I suppose all good things must come to an end. Lower the lantern again, very slowly so it does not hit me on the way down. I want it below me so I don't have to worry about striking it on the way up. Good—very good. I am tying it about my waist. Now you and Selton can pull me out. Don't worry about the lantern. I will be in darkness part of the time, but I shall use my feet to keep myself from striking the side. Hoist away whenever you are ready."

I crept carefully back from the edge, then rose to my feet. Above, the sky was a clear blue, and yellow light had spilled onto the gray-white limestone outcrops and onto the thick green grass. Beyond the huge stones now was the blue-green expanse of the sea and the azure of the sky.

"Let's get him up," I said.

We both had on gloves, and we began to heave away at the rope, soon settling into a regular rhythm. It was easy enough work for two, especially given Selton's huge muscular arms.

After a few moments, we heard Holmes cry, "That's enough—I am almost there. I shall pull myself out the last few feet." We held the rope fast, and he soon appeared at the edge, then used his hands and arms to hoist himself up. One leg came up, then he staggered forward and sprawled onto the ground.

We dropped the rope, and I went to him. He raised one hand and smiled. "I am perfectly well, Henry, only a little dizzy—and rather stiff. I would, however, like to stand again on terra firma." I extended my hand, and he grasped it, then slowly stood. I felt a brief tremor as he caught his balance. He drew in his breath. "That is better. I enjoyed it, but it is a relief to be above ground. It is also good to see the sun." He rubbed at the back of his right leg with his hand. "I may have a rope burn here from my abseiling. Nothing serious, however."

I shook my head. "I am always amazed at the differences between people, how what is torture to one is amusement to another. Was that descent truly necessary?"

"It was, Henry. I have learned a great deal. To begin with, we have ruled out once and for all the possibility that it could be the 'lair' of some great prehistoric serpent. It is not a nearly bottomless hole plunging to subterranean depths where some huge beast lurks between those interludes when it rises to terrorize the neighborhood. The waters of the sea cave are down about ninety feet during low tide. I pulled up the rope when I was nearest the bottom, and only about ten feet remained. The cavern opens out on one side to the sea. I could not tell how far back in the other direction it goes. It must twist and turn, as does the shaft itself, varying pressure in such a way that the water rises dramatically during a high tide, within ten feet or so of the top. I'm sure, too, if one took a boat and went around these cliffs at low tide, the cave entrance would be visible."

I shrugged. "That's interesting, but hardly earth-shaking."

"Perhaps not, but I think it may explain a great deal."

"It does?"

He smiled. "Yes." He turned to Selton. "Thank you for your assistance, Mr. Selton. You have been a great help. It is too early to reveal much, but I can say that I am making progress in my inquiries–good progress."

"I am glad to hear it, Mr. Holmes."

"And tell me–I suspect there is still no news of Evans? He has not reappeared?"

"He has not."

Holmes shook his head. "Hardly a surprise, unfortunately. I doubt we shall see him again. If we do, one may find the uncertainty preferable."

"What are you talking about?" I asked.

Holmes smiled grimly. "'Sufficient unto the day is the evil thereof,'

Henry." He turned to Selton again. "I don't know about you two gentlemen, but my exercise has made me ravenous. The good Mrs. Troughton had the cook prepare us a picnic lunch. Here we have an excellent sunny spot with a view. Let us eat!"

We were soon sitting on a flat rock well back from the cliff edge. The sea was relatively calm, no white caps showing on its deep-blue surface, and a faint salty breeze came from that direction. A crow had perched atop the old oak, and it cawed loudly, triggering an answering cry from somewhere in the woods. The setting was so completely different from London with its crowds, noise and squalor, that it might have been another world–or perhaps a prehistoric one, still untouched by man. Of course, realistically, someone had shaped those stones, brought them here and stood them upright, but the rock had long since melded into the natural setting. Certainly one might well imagine primitive creatures lurking in those dense woods.

Holmes quickly devoured two bites of a sandwich, then drew in his breath. "This is delicious–lobster salad, I believe, the crustacean no doubt hauled from the local waters. Is yours the same thing, Henry?"

"It is, and you are right. It is very good, much better than anything I've had in London."

"And you, Mr. Selton?"

"I have ham. Lobster salad would be wasted on me. I must admit–" he smiled, his expression self-mocking "–I've always found lobsters frightening-looking. Too much like big insects for my taste."

Holmes had switched the deerstalker for his favored brown hat, and its brim shaded his eyes from the bright sun. "I suspect you would not care for Lady Verr's zoo."

Selton shook his head. "She has asked several times if she could show her collection to me, and I have always declined."

"And she accepted that?" I asked.

"She did taunt me once. Said something about 'a big strong man.'" He shrugged. "I've had to put up with worse."

Holmes looked thoughtfully at him. It was hard to imagine that this embodiment of physical perfection, someone so strong and handsome, could have ever been an object of mockery.

Selton stared out at the ocean, then back at Holmes. "At school. I was always miserable, it seemed. That was one reason I looked forward to summers so much. And to seeing Diana." His entire face seemed to soften, to lose its wary edge, even as his eyes stared into the distance.

"She has had some very hard times," I said. "I suspect your friendship has meant a great deal."

"I tried to help her, Dr. Vernier—I tried so hard, but what could I do? What can you say to someone who suddenly loses both her father and mother? I could not mouth empty platitudes I do not believe." He shook his head angrily. "Oh, I just don't know—I wish there was some answer to all these mysteries. I came home from school when they died. I didn't tell my mother and father because they would have never understood, but of course they found out. She was glad to see me, even if I did start her crying again." He stared out at the ocean. "I know it helped. And last year, when her grandfather died, I came again, and I stayed for two weeks. Again, my father didn't like that, but he never likes anything I do, anyway."

I stared at him thoughtfully. At last he frowned. "Why are you looking at me that way?"

"You do love her, don't you?"

He slowly drew in his breath. "Yes. Of course I do."

"And she loves you."

He shook his head sadly. "It doesn't matter."

I stared incredulously at him. "Of course it matters. What is wrong?"

He shook his head fiercely this time. "I don't want to talk about it." He tore off a huge bite of sandwich and chewed savagely, even as his eyes filled with tears.

Holmes and I exchanged a glance. For once, he appeared as puzzled as me.

Seven

On Sunday morning Holmes, Diana and I went to the service at the Micklethorpe church. Arabella had admitted the night before that she was not much of a churchgoer; moreover, the mere idea of being up and abroad well before noon was abhorrent to her. Holmes drove the battered old dog-cart, a two-wheeled model, while Diana and I sat side by side, our backs to his. The aged cob plodded along the rough, winding path. A fine drizzle and fog like the morning before obscured the landscape.

Mr. Sloap gave a fairly decent sermon, although his speaking style was rather grandiloquent for my taste. Perhaps time in Yorkshire away from Oxford would gradually ameliorate his formality. We sat at the back on stiff, hard pews, and we could see Adam Selton and his family up near the front. Afterward, the vicar greeted us warmly outside the church. He seemed genuinely pleased to see Diana.

She smiled at him, then stepped to the side and turned toward the tombstones. Her eyes grew sad, even though her smile lingered. She wore white leather gloves, and her right hand lay loosely over her left. Her woolen hat was related to a man's bowler, but was bright blue and had a few feathers, practical enough for Yorkshire. The mists overhead were again dissolving as noon approached, a yellow cast showing on the trees, grass and lichen-splattered stone.

When Selton stepped out of the church, his eyes immediately found her. His huge hands tightened about the brim of his hat held before him, and he started forward. Diana's whole face took on a radiant glow, her smile much more unrestrained and exuberant than his. She certainly was not one of those women who, either by nature or by intent, could conceal their true feelings. Her face was an open book.

She stepped away from us, and he went over to speak with her. His parents had just come out of the church, and his father briefly rolled his eyes upward when he saw them together. He glanced at Holmes, and his face stiffened. Mrs. Selton looked stern and worn down, but expressionless. No face could be more different from Miss Marsh's than hers.

Mr. Selton *père* approached us. "Good day, Mr. Holmes, Dr. Vernier." He glanced about, making sure his son was not in earshot. "Sir, perhaps I was rather hasty the other day. Surely you can understand why I was dismayed." He also looked around to make certain his wife was not in hearing range. "It appeared that you had been investigating my most intimate affairs."

Holmes nodded. "Given the circumstances, your reaction was understandable, sir."

Selton gave a long sigh. "I don't suppose there is any possibility of your changing your mind about working for me?"

"No, I fear not."

"Well, perhaps that is to your credit. We shall be leaving this afternoon. Should you... should you wish to resume your stay at Lesser Hill, you may do so."

"That is generous of you, Mr. Selton, but I prefer to remain where I am. I think it may help me to resolve the case more quickly."

"Perhaps. But you should not necessarily believe everything you hear at Diana's Grove. You said you think someone wants to separate my son and Miss Marsh, but I still think the opposite is more likely. This seems a ploy to bring them together."

Holmes shook his head. "I don't think so. Someone wants to frighten off your son."

"Frighten him? How could these fairy tales about monstrous worms and family curses frighten anyone?"

Holmes shrugged. "He was already wary of the female sex."

Selton rolled his eyes again and shook his head. "I don't understand him. I do not. Although I have told him… My estate is entailed, and as eldest son, he cannot be disinherited. However, I have warned him that he would be completely cut off financially should he marry Diana Marsh. He would be penniless until my death."

I looked at him and shook my head. "Are you blind? Look at them together. And Miss Marsh—he could have no more devoted wife than her. She loves him desperately. And you would cut him off?"

Selton's face reddened. He looked for an instant like a dog who was about to bite, but his eyes were anguished. "Damn it! I don't exactly know what I would do. You can hardly expect me to encourage such a match."

"You must admit he could do far worse."

He shrugged. "I suppose so. There is no point in discussing this further. It will only create ill will. I must be going."

"Before you do," Holmes said, "might I ask about something which does not involve Miss Marsh? Your son obviously has a somewhat melancholy disposition. I suspect that has been the case for many years."

Selton smiled ironically. "Very good, Mr. Holmes. You are certainly right about that."

"He seems to have had an especially hard time at school."

Selton shook his head twice. "Yes, yes, which is inexplicable to me. It is a very good school–I went there myself–and it cost a small fortune. I could understand some difficulties the first year in adapting to being away from home and living with other boys, but it was always the same with him. He was miserable. And how someone his size could allow himself to be bullied or intimidated... Yes, inexplicable, inexplicable."

The corners of Holmes's mouth rose. "Human behavior is frequently inexplicable, Mr. Selton. If we always acted in our best interests, life would be much easier. Thank you and good day."

Selton nodded, then turned. His wife took his arm.

"I don't understand Adam Selton," I said. "I wonder what else might be going on, or I wonder if something is wrong with him, physically or mentally."

"We have two mysteries to solve, Henry, and in the end, the business with the worm is likely to be easier of the two. Mysteries involving the heart, the emotions, can be irresolvable. The truth is difficult to determine for others and even for ourselves. Things are rarely what they seem, and confirmation is often impossible."

I smiled. "Yes, it can be difficult with affairs of the heart, especially at the beginning, but you exaggerate. People resolve such mysteries all the time, and they are happily married in the end. My own story is proof of that."

He shrugged. "I think you may be the exception, not the rule. Novels often end triumphantly in marriages, but we never see what follows. In real life, marriage is as likely to lead to a life of misery as to happiness."

I laughed. "No, I think that is overstating it. Your profession prejudices you."

"I suppose that is true, but each of us is influenced by his own situation. Unhappy people are the ones who most often come to Baker Street."

Adam and Diana were still talking. He had clearly relaxed. He was smiling in a way which I could not recall, and she looked as if she were teasing him about something.

Holmes laughed softly. "We must give them a few moments, Henry."

"Yes," I said. "It is good to see them happy, without the dark clouds hovering about them."

Holmes shook his head. "The clouds are still there, even if we cannot see them."

Luckily the fair weather lasted until we reached Diana's Grove, but then the heavens opened. The dog-cart had started along the path into the trees when a wind swept through, shaking the leaves and branches, and then the rain poured down. We were close enough that it made little sense to stop to get out umbrellas, but by the time we reached the barn, we were drenched. I did take out an umbrella and sheltered Diana as we strode back to the house.

Holmes took off his hat, shook it once, twice, before he stepped inside. "No more outdoor treks today, Henry. I'm glad we had time for our little exploration yesterday."

After lunch, we all went to the library. Holmes pulled out another volume on the marine life of the British Isles. Diana was reading Eliot's *Middlemarch*, a favorite book of my own, although I found the idealistic physician Dr. Lydgate dragged down by his vain, silly wife to be a sad character indeed. In general, too, the book seemed to illustrate Holmes's observations about bad marriages all too well. Lady Verr had pulled out a massive tome on beetles of the world, but she seemed more interested in getting Holmes's attention than in reading.

The maid Angela, dressed all in black, sat in the far corner working on some embroidery in a hoop. Occasionally she would raise her dark eyes to gaze at her mistress. Her mouth was large and sensual, her lips a natural red, and any normal man would at some point have fantasies about kissing her. However, that mouth was contradicted by her general coolness and hauteur.

Around mid-afternoon Lady Verr left to feed the reptiles, begging Holmes to join her. He said he would do so shortly. Once she was gone, he stood, raised his arms and stretched. The pouring rain streaked the panes of the great bank of windows. He advanced toward them, but stopped before Angela, who frowned slightly, although her gaze was fixed on the fabric.

"Have you been with Lady Verr long, madam? You must have joined her in Italy."

She raised her eyes. "I no speaka the English."

"No? Perhaps Lady Verr speaks Italian. Still, if it has been many years, I suspect you must understand English quite well."

She shrugged. "*Assai, signore.*"

"*Parlo Italiano un poco,*" Holmes said.

"*Veramente?*"

"Perhaps sometime we might have a little chat."

She shrugged again, then lowered her eyes and returned to her needlework.

Holmes looked at me, the right side of his mouth pulling upward. "Want to come along, Henry? I do not think Delilah will be eating today."

I grimaced slightly. "No thank you. I would like to stretch my legs."

Diana set down her book. "So would I."

"I suspect you are not interested in feeding time at the zoo either," Holmes said.

She shook her head. "I am not."

We walked down the corridor to the gallery overlooking the hall. Holmes went down the stairs, while Diana and I started along the gallery. I glanced up at the paintings, but she seemed uninterested, perhaps because she knew them by heart. The clouds and rain left the hall itself dim and cold, the fire going against the distant wall a feeble thing.

"You seemed happy to see Mr. Selton this morning," I said.

She smiled and nodded.

"And he seemed happy to see you."

"Yes, he was. You do think he cares for me, Dr. Vernier?"

"I do."

"Oh, I hope so." She was quiet for a while. I stared up at some redheaded Marsh nobleman with a frilly, Elizabethan-style round collar. "I wonder… Sometimes he acts so oddly. I wish I knew. I wish… Dr. Vernier, do you think…?"

"Do I think what?"

She had turned to look down at the hall, then her eyes shifted back to me, her discomfort obvious. "Never mind."

"We have known each other only a short while, but you can trust me, Miss Marsh. I would like to help if I can."

The green of her eyes was lost in the huge dark pupils, and her red eyebrows had come together, creating two vertical creases. "Would you truly?"

"Yes."

"Sometimes… sometimes it is almost as if he is afraid of me, Dr. Vernier. How can that be?"

Her voice was so anguished that I touched her arm lightly and shook my head. "It is not really you that he fears. I think perhaps he is afraid of himself–or, rather, for himself."

"I don't understand."

I scratched at my jaw and wished Michelle were here to have this conversation. "Everyone thinks–or women often think–that men are always confident and brave. They do not understand that men can also be afraid and awkward and unsure, especially when it comes to matters of love."

Her eyes were fixed on mine. "'Matters of love.'" She nodded. "But–but I wasn't afraid–but that would explain it."

"Explain what?"

She didn't exactly seem to hear me. "And we were doing so well." It was almost a whisper.

"What are you talking about?"

The flush appeared first on her cheeks and spread. "Oh I cannot tell you–I cannot."

I shook my head. "Nothing you say will greatly astonish me. I am also not one eager to lay down judgment or give lectures on morality." She smiled at this. "I suspect..." It was more than suspicion, the only question was how far things had gone. "Tell me."

She drew in a breath. "I was kissing him."

I nodded. "And at first he was very eager," I said, "but then he seemed... afraid of you."

Her flush began to fade. "How can you know these things?"

I smiled. "It is not such a mystery. You mustn't take it personally. He is only... I suspect he had a bad experience once with a woman, perhaps a woman who wasn't exactly his choice."

"How could that happen?"

"Perhaps... perhaps some friends dragged him off to a tavern and tried to get him to… to kiss the barmaid, and perhaps, naturally enough, since she didn't mean anything to him, he became uneasy. And now he is afraid that history is repeating itself every time he gets intimate even with someone he cares about." A tortured rendition, but I certainly couldn't reveal everything.

"Is that really possible?"

"Yes–yes, I assure you it is. I am a physician, and I have seen similar things before."

She suddenly looked stricken. "But is there a cure?"

I again touched her arm lightly. "Yes. Absolutely. The cure is time, and real affection, the genuine thing. Even when people care about one another, it can still take a while to truly become comfortable with each other."

She shook her head. "It is so hard to understand. I'm not a child, Dr. Vernier, and what I feel for Adam is… I don't think it can be wrong." Again those huge black pupils were fixed on me.

"It is not."

"He is so big and strong and handsome, and his arms… It seems impossible that he could be afraid."

"But you must know him well enough to understand that it *is* possible. Hasn't he spoken to you about his school and how unhappy he was there? The smaller boys had no difficulty tormenting him." I smiled. "And he finds lobsters frightening."

She smiled. "I know. And insects of every variety–especially beetles. He tries to hide it, but it is obvious. I've teased him about it often enough."

"Well, then. You know the old story about the elephant being afraid of the mouse. Size has nothing to do with it."

"Oh, I feel so much better!"

I laughed. "Good. Be patient with him. If it… happens again, do not act disappointed or angry, and above all, don't reproach or criticize him."

"I could never do that!"

"Good. Play it by ear, as they say. These things come and go. If he sees that you are not upset, if you are kind to him, then his mood may change again equally quickly."

"Yes, yes. There is something else." Again her cheeks slowly flushed. "You do not think...? A man and a woman..."

"What is it?"

"Aunt Arabella said... She said I should simply..." She could not bring herself to say it.

"Offer yourself to him?"

She nodded, still flushed. "She says then he will do whatever I want. Then he will marry me."

I smiled ironically. "Did she also tell you that it worked for her?"

Her eyebrows rose, even as she gave a quick nod.

"And what do you think of this strategy?"

"Oh, I don't know—I don't know. It must be wrong, but sometimes I think if we could only be together, everything would be all right."

"Laws and morality and convention can seem stifling and nonsensical, but they exist for a reason. Women have the most to lose. However, in this case, it's simply a bad idea because he is not ready. If you throw yourself at him, you are likely to frighten him all the more."

She nodded. "Yes, I see that."

"Someday, however, things will change, and then you may have to decide. Waiting until marriage is generally a good idea." Michelle and I had certainly not waited, but then we had been older and experienced. "All the same, marriage is only a kind of... contract. What is important is the bond between two people, the love and the

commitment they make to each other. That is the most important
thing. A marriage without that is worthless."

"Yes," she whispered. She drew in her breath slowly. The flush had
begun to fade. She glanced down at the gallery, then looked at me
again. Her left hand reached out to grasp mine and squeezed tightly.
"Thank you so much, Dr. Vernier–*thank you*. There has been no one
to talk to–not really. I have felt alone for so long. It seems forever
now. I thought it would be better with Aunt Arabella here, but it…
it has not. She does not understand, not really, and she is so… so
condescending. You do not treat me like a child."

I shook my head, smiling. "You are not a child."

"No." She released my hand. "I must return to my book. I have
troubled you long enough."

"It is no trouble."

She smiled at me, then turned and quickly walked away, her long,
straight arms swinging at her sides, her fists some six inches from
her hips.

"Thank *you*," I murmured. I shook my head, rather moved. Twice
before I had thought to myself, half mockingly, that I had a friend
for life in Diana. Now I knew that was true. All the same… I don't
often talk to myself, but I actually said, "Damn it, Michelle–I need
you here!" I was out of my depth. All the same, this was definitely
not Sherlock's territory.

This was the second case with him where I seemed to have
become the confidant of a beautiful young woman. While this might
be flattering, it also made me restless–especially with Michelle
absent. Other than Sherlock, I had few male friends, and I had
always seemed to prefer the company of women to men. I walked
along the gallery for a while, then returned to my room and wrote
Michelle a lengthy letter, briefly presenting our cast of characters. I

ended by telling her how much I missed her and how helpful it would be to have her at Diana's Grove.

The afternoon dragged on and dinner was a welcome break. The cook had again outdone herself with a joint of well-cooked pork, the fat crisp and crackling. An excellent white Burgundy accompanied the meal, a pleasant change after the claret of the last few days. Lady Verr had resumed her charm offensive, including me as well as Holmes this evening. Miss Marsh was quiet and often raised her hand to her mouth, stifling yawns. Dessert was an excellent apple cake.

When we had finished, Arabella dabbed at her lips with her fine linen napkin. "Shall we go to the sitting room and have some port?"

Diana shook her head. "I'm rather tired. I did not sleep well last night. I think I shall go to my room."

"As you wish, my dear. I hope you have a better night."

We had all stood. Diana bowed slightly, as did Holmes and I. Her eyes caught mine. "Good night, Dr. Vernier."

"Good night."

We left the dining room and started for the nearby drawing room. Diana turned toward the stairway. Lady Verr had taken my arm with her left hand, Holmes's arm with her right. "You have made a conquest, Dr. Vernier."

"What are you talking about?" I did nothing to hide my annoyance.

She laughed softly. "Diana is clearly taken with you."

"That's ridiculous—Adam Selton is the object of her affections."

"All the same, it's a pity you are married. Some competition would be helpful. Nothing like a rival to drive a man to action. It is generous of you to offer her so much of your attention."

"Generosity has nothing to do with it—she is a charming young woman."

"My! I see this cuts both ways."

"Please—don't be silly."

"You are *gallante*, Dr. Vernier. I didn't mean to offend you. In Cyril's circle, I grew accustomed to a certain amount of harmless flirtation, even amongst married people. It is more common on the Continent than in England. And you, Mr. Holmes, you are silent. Do you also find Diana to be a charming young woman?"

"I find all the Marsh women quite charming."

Arabella laughed, then let go of our arms and clapped her hands together. "Bravo, Mr. Holmes—bravo, indeed! Very well done. You would do very well in diplomatic circles."

We went into the drawing room. A wood fire blazed in the grate, and two lamps were lit, illuminating the dark wood and leather furniture. Hamswell stood by the sideboard, clad formally in his black tail coat with white shirt, waistcoat and bow tie. Somehow a rough-hewn, stout man like him with a bushy beard looked faintly ridiculous in such garb. His massive fingers also looked ready to burst free of the white gloves. He offered Arabella a glass, then said gravely, "Would you gentlemen care for the port as well?" We nodded, and he raised the bottle to pour.

"Hamswell, Mr. Holmes is going to Whitby first thing tomorrow morning. You shall drive him."

"Very well, madam."

Holmes shook his head. "If you have other work for him, I can certainly drive myself, as I did this morning."

"There was only room for three in the dog-cart, or I would not have allowed such a thing. You must let him take you. Besides, he also has some business of mine to attend to in Whitby."

Holmes took his glass of port. "Very well, madam. Thank you. It is most kind."

"Not at all."

Holmes sat down at the far end of the sofa, and Arabella promptly sat in the middle. I took the big armchair. We all sipped our wine. The wood in the fireplace crackled and popped, throwing out an ember which landed on the hearth rug.

"A fire is truly agreeable on such a foul night." Arabella turned to me. Her eyes were shrunken and obscured by the green lenses of her spectacles. Her nose was still red from the sunburn, her skin peeling there in earnest. "I hope, Dr. Vernier, that you understand that you were being teased. I certainly was not questioning your fidelity to your wife." I shrugged. "I still hope we may meet her soon. You spoke of some possibility that she might join us."

"It is possible." I suspected it was becoming more possible all the time.

"Then I should have Mr. Holmes all to myself."

Holmes smiled politely, but I noticed certain subtle signs of annoyance.

"You told me, Mr. Holmes, you did not care to share details of your personal life with strangers. However, since Dr. Watson has already written of the adventure, perhaps you could at least comment on Irene Adler. Is she *the* woman?"

Holmes inhaled through his nostrils. "She is most definitely not *the* woman. Watson's story is ridiculous on the surface of it–would I be smitten by a woman of so brief an acquaintance, merely because she bested me on one occasion?"

"I found it credible."

"Well, it is not–it is fiction."

"Well, if she is not *the* woman, then who is?"

Holmes smiled. "My reply of the other evening still holds true."

Arabella laughed, a high rippling sound. "I should not have tried so obvious a ruse. I am convinced there is someone. I can tell, however, that you really are something of a misogynist, Mr. Holmes. I don't think Watson erred in that case."

Holmes only shrugged, but I said, "That isn't true."

She turned to me. "Isn't it?"

Holmes frowned. "No," I said. "He only dislikes women who behave stupidly. That hardly makes him a misogynist. You would have to put me in that category too."

She grinned wickedly. "So your wife never behaves stupidly?"

"No–hardly as often as I do."

Again she clapped her hands together. "Bravo to you, too, Dr. Vernier. I wish I had had such a husband. But you must admit, that sometimes men *want* women to behave stupidly. You cannot deny–" her lips twitched upward "–men find nothing so dangerous as an intelligent woman."

I shrugged. "There is something to what you say."

"And you, Mr. Holmes–do you fear an intelligent woman?"

"Not in the least. Intelligence is a virtue. Nothing is more tiresome than a truly stupid woman. Intelligence only becomes reprehensible when combined with greed, vanity, cruelty, jealousy, ambition, or their like."

A smile lingered on her beautiful mouth, then she glanced mockingly at me for an instant. "I suppose there is something to what you say." She sipped at her port, then cupped the bowl with her long, elegant fingers. "All the same, as men, you cannot truly understand. You are used to being in charge of your life, used to doing as you please. We women have no such freedom. We must fend for ourselves with all the constraints that society puts upon us." She looked at me again. "You should understand that, Dr. Vernier. It cannot have been easy for your wife to become a doctor. That must have been a battle."

"It was, but she persevered."

"Then you should admire perseverance."

"I do, when it is combined with a noble goal. If the end is something base or venal, it counts for nothing."

She shook her head. "All the same, I think you hold women to a higher standard than men. Ambition or greed are often seen as virtues in them."

"Not by me," I replied.

She turned to Holmes. "You cannot deny, I think, that you are ambitious, Mr. Holmes?"

"No. But it is as Henry said–ambition for a worthy end is admirable. My ambition, my greatest ambition, has always been to seek out evil, wherever it may lie, and eradicate it."

She laughed softly. "*Evil.* You think evil is so clearly defined? That one can always and absolutely tell the difference between right and wrong, good and evil?"

Holmes opened his mouth, clearly intending to say yes, then seemed to falter. His eyes shifted to mine. I knew he was thinking of Violet Wheelwright. "Not always," he said.

"Not even Sherlock Holmes, consulting detective extraordinaire?"

He shook his head. "Not even he–not always. But often it is very clear."

She laughed. "Remind me not to make an enemy of you, Mr. Holmes. Still, I think you are both being hard on women. My sex certainly does not have a monopoly on stupidity. If you had traveled in my circles in Europe and attended as many dinner parties as I have… Sometimes I would look around the room and wonder if there was a single man who had more than an ounce of brains–besides Cyril, that is. That is why I so enjoy your company, Mr. Holmes. And yours, too, Dr. Vernier. You both actually know something about biology and science. An intelligent conversation is possible–and it is a delight."

Holmes nodded. "It is indeed. And certainly we can agree with your last observation–stupidity is also widespread among men."

"Especially when it comes to women," I murmured spontaneously. Arabella laughed. "You are wicked, Dr. Vernier!"

Holmes left shortly after breakfast, and oddly enough, Arabella came down at ten. I could not understand this until Mrs. Troughton announced that Edgar Caswall was at the door. We were all in the library. Arabella rose. "Diana, dear," she said. "You must come down. I am certain he will want to see you, too."

"In a moment," Diana said.

"Well, don't be too long."

As soon as Arabella was gone, Diana stood up and set her white hands on the dark wood of the table. "Oh, Dr. Vernier–will you please come down with me?"

"I can't say I am very eager to see Edgar Caswall either." However, one look at her face had showed me this was more than annoyance. Her face was very pale, her green eyes fearful. "But I shall come."

"Oh good. I don't like him–and he can be so strange."

"He is rather mad, I'm afraid."

Diana shook her head. "Aunt Arabella says he is only half mad, and that all the interesting people are half mad."

"More than half by far, in his case."

"He looks at me so strangely. I don't like it. I will feel better if you are nearby. Only Aunt Arabella says we must humor him."

I shrugged. "Very well." It had also occurred to me that it was probably not a coincidence this visit was happening while Holmes was away.

Miss Marsh and I slowly went down the broad stairway that led to the great hall. Caswall had just come striding into the hall. He again wore a black velvet cloak, glistening with moisture from being out of doors, and the hood was thrown back to reveal his dramatic features, the black curly hair, the black mono-eyebrow, the aquiline nose and those mad black eyes. They caught fire at the sight of Diana, taking in her face and shape in a frankly lewd way. He and Arabella were both inches shorter than Diana, who was tall, five foot eight or more.

"Edgar, I think you have met—" Arabella began.

"Watson and I know each other, don't we, John?" Caswall said.

"Oh yes."

"He will be joining me soon to work on my biography."

Arabella's brow furrowed above the green octagonal lenses. "I see."

Caswall's hands rose to unfasten the cords of his cloak—he had thick black hair below the knuckles—then he removed it with a flourish, whirling it about slightly. He wore a black velvet frock coat of a style I had not seen before, black trousers and long black cavalry-style boots. He threw the cloak at a nearby chair, then turned and walked resolutely toward the distant fireplace. Mrs. Troughton's mouth was straight and fixed, her face rigidly expressionless. She took the cloak and walked away. The two women and I walked toward the fireplace, Diana lingering behind me.

The tall bank of windows along the outer wall let in the gray light, which illuminated the limestone slabs of the floor and the faded carpet. The stone casements were arched on top, each window made up of many panes of blurry, ancient glass. The rain had ended during the night, replaced by white mists. I was already tired of the cold fog and wanted the sunshine to return. Caswall reached the fireplace, turned and folded his arms dramatically, then stared at Diana.

"How are you, Edgar?" Arabella asked.

He did not even seem to hear her. Diana turned toward me, seeking reassurance. "How is your kite, Mr. Caswall?" I asked.

"The rains were so bad yesterday we had to haul it down. I am hopeful that it will fly again this afternoon when I return." He had not taken his eyes off Diana. A furrow had appeared above his nose on either side.

"And so you think the sun will return?"

"I do." His gaze was fixed on Diana in a most inappropriate way.

I tried to stand in front of her, but he moved forward at this, which caused her to walk around me and come nearer. She was obviously trying to hide behind me, and he was determined not to allow this.

"Mr. Caswall, what are you doing?" I asked.

"It needn't concern you."

"But if I am to be your biographer…"

His eyes shifted briefly to mine. "Are you familiar with Mesmer and mesmerism, John?"

"Only vaguely."

"Mesmer was the genius who discovered animal magnetism. Some men—an elect few—possess powers of mind and will which allow them to control others at a distance. This is a rare and terrible gift."

I nodded. More insanity. "And you think you possess such powers?"

"I know I do. My will is very strong. It cannot be resisted." His eyes were fixed on Diana again. His face was slightly flushed, his thick upper lip curving in something between a sneer and a smile. "Especially by the weaker sex."

Arabella had a fixed smile on her lips, and she stood behind him just to his side. "Perhaps we might go to the sitting room, Edgar. It is much more comfortable there."

"No."

"I wish you wouldn't do that," Diana said.

This made Caswall's face strain even more, and his right hand with fingers open made an arc through the air. "Mesmer had to lay his hands upon people, and he often used actual magnets. His disciple Lombarghi dispensed with these techniques. They are superfluous for the superior mind. My grandfather studied with Lombarghi in Paris in the 1820s. He left a trunk filled with his journals and certain instruments of power. I recently discovered this trunk and have been poring over its contents. I am very near complete mastery of Mesmer's secrets."

I nodded. I didn't know whether it was better to try to keep him talking or not. "And I suppose this power gives you complete control over another?"

"It does. When applied with maximum force it is irresistible, especially for the female sex."

"So the goal is submission?"

"Exactly, John." Through what seemed to be a herculean effort, he raised one eyebrow.

I heard a hiss of breath behind me. I turned. Diana had clapped her hand over her mouth. Her eyes were rather wild, then she made an odd coughing sound which was clearly a suppressed laugh.

Caswall made another swipe at the air with his right hand. This caused a flutter of nervous laughter from Diana. "Oh, don't!"

Caswall motioned behind himself with his left hand, waving it at Lady Verr. "Assist me, Arabella—*join me.*"

"Edgar…" She stepped closer to him.

Diana put both her hands over her mouth. "Oh, stop it—just stop it." She laughed in earnest, but with a hysterical edge.

"That's quite enough, Mr. Caswall," I said, "quite enough!"

Caswall contorted his face in a manner which made even me want to laugh, and it produced a shriek of laughter from Diana.

"You cannot resist me—you cannot!"

Diana laughed in earnest. "Oh—that face."

"Obey—obey!" Caswall shouted, which brought on another paroxysm of laughter.

I took Diana by the arm. "I think you need a brandy."

She looked at me. "Do you?" This seemed to trigger another laughing fit.

"Come on." I led her toward the sideboard.

Caswall realized he had failed. He whirled and raised his arm with outstretched fingers toward Arabella. "You—you have betrayed me!"

Arabella folded her arms and shook her head wearily. "Don't be ridiculous, Edgar."

"Ridiculous? *I?* I cannot be ridiculous. You promised me you would help. I am the lord of the sky, you the goddess of the earth and fecundity. You claimed your powers were as great as mine, and so they must be! How else could I have failed? You have turned against me! You made her laugh at me!"

"I did not!"

"You did!"

"Edgar, you are behaving stupidly."

"Foul harlot!" He burst into a string of obscenities and expressions directed at Lady Verr, which, luckily, I was sure Diana would not fully understand.

Arabella, however, clearly did. "Edgar, I think perhaps you should leave."

"So I shall, treacherous traitor! You have betrayed me, and you shall pay the price. A Caswall never forgets. You—you foul worm! I will destroy you, filthy slut, even as your ancestor destroyed the

White Worm, only this time your lair itself shall be no more!"

"Oh Lord, Edgar—be reasonable for once. Just stop this nonsense. You know that I care for you, dearest."

This brought on a renewed stream of obscenities. Arabella shook her head. "I shall get your cloak. We shall talk again when you have come to your senses." She started for the door, and Caswall followed her still screaming curses and threats.

Diana stopped laughing, moaned, then gasped and started over again. I poured a brandy from the decanter on the sideboard. "Drink this all at once." She did so, and it made her gasp. "Turn sideways." She did, and I slapped her hard on the back, between the shoulder blades. "It will be all right now. He's gone, I think." She swallowed once, then took a long, deep breath. I poured more brandy. "Now sip it very slowly. It's all right to laugh if you want." She moaned, then giggled.

I poured myself a brandy and tossed it down. "Lord, he is totally batty."

Diana sipped the brandy and gradually calmed down, although an occasional snicker slipped out.

Soon Arabella came striding across the hall. Her tight white dress showed off her spectacular emerald necklace and her sinuously shapely figure. The green spectacles hid her eyes, but her mouth and jaw were tense. I poured another brandy and handed it to her. She downed it in a great gulp, then slammed the glass onto the sideboard. She glared at Diana. "You might have humored him!"

This made her niece laugh once, then moan.

"Don't laugh—" Lady Verr began.

"Humor him?" I exclaimed. "He is completely mad! What was she supposed to do? Faint? Tear off her dress? Go bug-eyed? What?"

"You needn't take that tone of voice, Dr. Vernier."

"Forgive me, but raving lunatics tend to unsettle me."

She drew in her breath, then eased it out slowly. "They tend to unsettle us all."

"Would you really consider marrying him?"

Now she turned her glare on me. "Don't you dare judge me, Dr. Vernier." She walked away toward the fire.

I glanced at Diana. "Do you feel better?"

"Yes. Thank God you are here."

"Miss Marsh...?" I realized her aunt would hear my question. I shook my head. "Later." I started slowly toward Arabella.

"Perhaps... perhaps if I give him a few days," she said. "All may not be lost. One must hope..." Another weary sigh, then she turned. "Forgive me, Dr. Vernier. I was also upset."

"With good reason."

"We shall not speak of this further." Her voice had an imperious tone. "He did behave badly. I am going to feed the reptiles." She bowed slightly and then started across the hall toward the stairs.

The light coming through the windows had brightened and changed color; the mists were clearing. I turned to Diana. "Let's go for a walk."

She nodded fiercely. "Yes. Let's."

"I'll meet you at the front door in five minutes."

Blue sky showed overhead now, and the cool air had a fresh, clean smell impossible in London. We went down the steps and walked onto the path. A big rock stood in sunshine, and as I half expected, an adder lay beside it, sunning itself, its zigzag-patterned scales glistening. It seemed at one with the setting, a part of nature, and since I had expected its presence, I did not feel the sudden panicky stab of surprise. Certainly the snake was far less disturbing than Edgar Caswall.

We walked at a brisk clip down the road for a long while, and neither of us said a word. At last we paused to catch our breath. "Feel better?" I asked.

She nodded. She stared at me, and in the swath of sunlight I saw her pupils had shrunk, showing flecked green irises. She had on a blue wool hat with a big floppy brim to protect her from the sun. Her lips pulled into a smile, the dimple appearing on one side briefly, but her expression was pained. "I still don't know whether I want to laugh or cry."

"Neither—he's not worth it."

We began to walk more slowly. I heard a chattering noise and saw one of the red squirrels with the tufted ears in a tree. "Diana, I shall be frank with you. Have you ever thought of asking your aunt to simply pack up and leave?"

Her shoulders rose briefly. "I have thought of it. But I could not do it."

"Why not?"

"Where would she go? She has no money, nothing. She is my aunt, after all, my only living relative. I cannot turn her away."

I said nothing for a while. "Did she ever actually ask you if she could move into your home?"

Diana was quiet for a few seconds. "I don't exactly remember."

"I think that means no."

"I suspect you are right. She talked about all the advantages for us both, how ideal it would be."

"And has it worked out as you hoped?"

She didn't answer for a long time. "No," she said. I turned to look at her. Tears were running down her cheeks.

"Oh, I'm sorry."

"It is—it is so awful. My mother should be here—and my father—not her—not her."

"Don't cry—I'm sorry. Do you have a handkerchief?"

She nodded, then pulled it out of her pocket. "I want—I want Adam—I want him—I want him so badly. Is that wrong?"

"No, of course it isn't." I set my hand on her shoulder, and she turned and almost crashed into me. If I were a smaller man she would have knocked me over. She hid her face in my shoulder, sobbing. She was almost Michelle's height, but while Michelle was muscular and sturdy, she was slender and bony. I patted her back awkwardly. "You mustn't give up. I know it is hard. I have to go to Micklethorpe, but you can see Adam. He'll be at Lesser Hill."

"But his father *hates* me!"

"His parents left yesterday. He will be alone. You can talk to him, perhaps stay while I go on to Micklethorpe. It's going to be a beautiful day. You can walk down to the beach together."

She nodded without speaking, then slowly drew back and dabbed at her eyes with a handkerchief. She drew in a breath, then eased it out slowly as she squared her shoulders. "Another 'thank you' hardly seems enough after all you have done for me in the last few days."

"I am only glad I was here to help."

"So am I." A faint involuntary shudder made her clench her teeth for an instant. "So am I."

Eight

Adam Selton was at Lesser Hill, and he was as glad to see Diana as she was to see him. I managed to get a moment alone with him and told him briefly what had happened with Caswall. His face darkened, and he said a single vulgar word. "Be kind to her," I whispered. Soon I set out for Micklethorpe.

I went directly to the telegraph window and composed a short note begging Michelle to come as soon as possible. *This is a dark business*, I wrote, and explained how Diana needed a woman's help. I also mentioned that no bodies had yet appeared, but hinted that could change, as a man had gone missing.

Afterwards, I went to the White Swan for a late lunch. The ruddy stout publican seemed to remember me from our last visit when Holmes had asked so many questions. He held the stem of his clay pipe between his teeth, his eyes wary. He filled a glass with beer, and a few minutes later a plate was set on the table before me: a slice of ham, two large wedges of different cheese, and some rustic bread.

I sipped the beer, then put the ham on the bread and had a bite.

Certainly Michelle would heed my appeal. It was Monday afternoon. She could be here tomorrow. The last week without her had dragged along, and now things seemed to be spiraling downward. Holmes had been exuberant when he had come out of the pit yesterday. He must have some suspicions about what was going on, but as usual, it all seemed a hopeless muddle to me.

"Mind if I join yuh, squire?" said some gruff voice.

I looked up and saw Holmes's thin face with the hawk nose and piercing eyes. I gave a soft laugh. "I certainly didn't recognize your voice."

"That was my intention."

"Where is Hamswell?"

"On his way back to Diana's Grove. The weather had turned so pleasant I thought I would stop here for lunch, then walk back on my own. I had hoped to develop some friendly rapport with Mr. Hamswell during our journey, but he did his utmost to reveal as little as possible about himself, Lady Verr or his former master. Oh, he did answer a few direct questions, but I learned nothing new. He had his guard up the entire time. He has been with Lady Verr a dozen years, about the same length of time as her maid Angela."

"We had a bizarre morning."

"Indeed?"

A barmaid brought Holmes a plate of food and a glass of beer, and I told him all about Caswall's disastrous visit and Diana's reaction. Afterwards, he was silent for a few seconds, then took a drink and set his glass on the table. "It is a very good thing you remained behind, Henry. I do not like to imagine exactly what might have happened had you not been there. However, I suspect Lady Verr will not abandon her pursuit of Caswall."

"No, I don't think she will either. She obviously is aware of his deranged oddities, so she was not surprised. She seemed to think a brief separation might make him more amenable to her charms, or so I gathered."

Holmes nodded. "Good. It is best she still has her hopes for a union with Mr. Caswall."

"Why?"

"Let's just say it keeps her content with the status quo."

I shook my head. "More mysteries. Oh, and I just sent Michelle a telegram, begging her to come."

"Excellent, Henry–excellent! It should reach her before your letter, which I posted this morning. Her female perspective would be most useful at this point. Perhaps the two of you can untangle this whole business between Adam Selton and Diana Marsh. That is certainly *not* my province."

"And what did you find out in Whitby?"

"That my suspicions were correct. Miss Marsh's income is just right." I must have appeared confused, for he explained. "As with Goldilocks and the bears. Besides owning the estate, she receives nine hundred pounds a year."

"Not to be sniffed at," I said. "Only the most successful doctors on Harley Street earn that much."

"Selton senior must make five or ten times that. I told the solicitor, Mr. Fitch senior, that I was assisting Miss Marsh and was concerned about her well-being. He was most obliging. Robert Marsh's will is, of course, a public document, and he let me examine it at some length. Marsh left everything first to his wife, then to his daughter in a very straightforward way. There is no entail on the estate, so Miss Marsh may inherit it. Of course, were she to marry Adam Selton, it would become his–a pittance, however, compared to what he will inherit from his father. I also asked if Miss Marsh had made a will of her own. He said she had. He could not show it to me, but said it was a standard sort of will for a young lady, with the usual clauses."

"So, she has no great fortune."

"No. I also took the opportunity to visit the local constabulary and talk with its chief. He had heard something about a Druid-type group in the vicinity, but he did not realize how far things had gone. Nor had he connected the disappearance of cattle and sheep to these worshipers. I asked him if he could arrange to have a couple of his best men at the ready, should I need their assistance if I felt something criminal was about to occur, and he agreed to arrange it. My reputation is sometimes useful."

"I don't like any of this," I murmured. "This is definitely not turning out to be a simple holiday in the wilds of Yorkshire."

We ate silently for a while. I downed the last of my beer and noticed the publican watching me sullenly. "I suppose he's one of the pagan followers," I said. "Oh, let's get out of here, Sherlock. It's too fine a day to be inside."

He nodded, then swallowed the last of his beer and set down the heavy glass. "I would like to stop at Doom Tower. We have not spoken to Sir Nathaniel since the vicar's revelations. I am certain the old man knows a great deal more than he let on before."

Doom Tower was only about a fifteen-minute walk. The elderly servant greeted us, slowly plodded away, and returned several minutes later. His master was indisposed, not feeling well, but hoped to be better the next day. He wondered if we might join him for dinner around six. Holmes accepted the invitation, and then we set out for Lesser Hill.

The weather was glorious again, and the path often wound along the top of the cliffs. The sea was at our right, the sound of the waves coming in and out, and the countryside to our left. The wind never seemed still along this part of the coast. We could hear its soft murmur in the tall grasses, which stood upright, quivering in the constant breeze. Occasionally we passed green fields where a few cows or sheep grazed. This land was hardly as harsh or barren as the upper moors along the wind-swept ridges covered with brown grass or bracken. We passed briefly through a small shaded wood, crossing a stone bridge over a dappled stream that bubbled and gurgled as it flowed down toward the sea. The sun coming through the trees made their leaves a study in chiaroscuro: the white-yellow light illuminating the tops, the bottoms all dark shadow. The walk did relax me. All the turmoil and lunacy of human society were briefly set aside.

We reached Lesser Hill and found Diana still with Adam in a small drawing room. Her face was faintly flushed, and she was much happier than when I had left. One look at Selton, however, showed that something was amiss. "Mr. Holmes, Dr. Vernier, I need to speak with you." He turned. "Diana, could you give us a moment alone."

She frowned. "Why?"

"Something… has come up. I need to speak to Mr. Holmes in private."

"Must we have secrets between us?" Her voice was pained.

He shook his head. "They are not secrets, exactly, but… And yes, there must always be some secrets, even toward those who are dear to us."

Her hands made fists. She looked at me. "Dr. Vernier, do you think that is true? Do you and your wife have secrets between you?"

I grimaced slightly, annoyed at being dragged into the battle, but then I considered the question. "Yes, I'm afraid we do."

"How can that be?"

"There are always things we don't want to share with others, especially when they have to do with our own weaknesses and stupidities. These can be embarrassing and incomprehensible even to us, but to reveal them to another... No, some things must remain secret."

My answer obviously disappointed her. "Please, Diana," Selton said. "It won't take long."

"Oh, very well." She stood, imperiously, then swept from the room, closing the door behind her rather hard.

Selton walked over to a writing table and pulled out a sheet of paper. "This letter came this afternoon while we were walking on the beach."

Holmes picked up the paper, held it before him with his long, slender fingers as he read. He nodded, then handed it to me.

Adam Selton,

Sherlock Holmes cannot save you from one of the cursed Marsh daughters. He cannot begin to understand what you are up against. He will only watch, powerless, as you hurtle toward your doom. Send him away and escape while you still can— return to Derbyshire or London—or suffer the consequences. There are worse things, even, than what happened to your servant. Sometimes death is a blessing. A man is not a man after a succubus or vampire has finished draining the life fluids from him, but only an empty, half-dead husk. The process has already begun. Diana Marsh is not what she appears to be.

A friend

I shook my head. "Some friend."

"Do you have the envelope?" Holmes asked. Selton showed it to him. "Posted from Whitby, which tells us little."

Selton looked rather pale. "What exactly is a succubus?"

"A female demon or evil spirit," Holmes said, "one who often appears in dreams to tempt and seduce men."

"Sexual activity with them is supposed to gradually drain the vital essence from a man." I shook my head. "A ridiculous notion."

Selton seemed to have briefly stopped breathing. At last he said, "Could there possibly be any truth to such ideas?"

"Absolutely not." I shook my head. "Someone is trying to frighten you."

His lips formed a brief bitter smile. "I'm afraid it's working."

"It's only natural," I said. "Someone seems to know your weaknesses only too well."

"But how?"

Holmes's gray eyes had a fierce glare. "There are no supernatural forces at work here, Mr. Selton—I can promise you that. This is only some cruel and demented person."

Selton slowly drew in his breath. He seemed reassured.

Soon we started back for Diana's Grove. Selton went with us as far as the grove itself and the enormous oak tree at its outskirts, then touched lightly on the arm and said farewell. We had walked into the woods a short way when she spoke.

"It was about the letter, wasn't it?"

Holmes smiled faintly. "Yes. His distress must have been obvious."

"So it was. What's going on, Mr. Holmes? Can't you tell me?"

"As I said before, you must ask Mr. Selton." This response obviously disappointed her. "However, this much should also be obvious. Someone is trying to frighten Mr. Selton, and in doing so, to separate the two of you."

She frowned fiercely. "His father—it must be his father."

Holmes shook his head. "I think not."

"But then... I don't understand."

Holmes was watching her closely. "Sir Nathaniel also considers you unsuitable as a prospective bride for Selton."

"Sir Nathaniel!" She gave a sharp laugh. "He doesn't even know me. How can he presume to judge my fitness?"

Holmes hesitated. "Edgar Caswall seems to have an unnatural fascination for you."

She stopped walking abruptly, her face going pale. "Oh, no, no." She shook her head savagely. "He–he couldn't–I..." She swallowed. "I love Diana's Grove and Yorkshire–it is my home–but I would give it all up and flee rather than have anything to do with him."

"It will not come to that," I said. "We will not allow it."

She nodded. "Thank God."

Her outburst had troubled Holmes. "I did not mean to alarm you. Henry is correct. We shall protect you from Caswall."

She smiled wanly. "Thank you. It is good to have friends. Although..." Her forehead creased, and she was lost in thought for a second. "Mr. Holmes, I can also pay you for your services if need be. I would gladly hire you."

Holmes smiled and shook his head. "That is generous of you, Miss Marsh, but it will not be necessary. I am certain that Mr. Selton's interests and yours coincide. In serving him, I serve you."

"I hope that is true. Mr. Holmes, you and Dr. Vernier–he has been so very kind to me–and you... Oh, I am so embarrassed! I hope someday you can forgive me."

"Forgive you, Miss Marsh? What on earth for?"

She bit at her lower lip. "For... for not knowing who you were. Aunt Arabella explained that *everyone* knows about Sherlock Holmes."

Holmes halted briefly, then a loud laugh slipped out. Diana stared at him in alarm. He coughed once, then laughed again. "My dear young lady, you could not have presented yourself in any better light! Not knowing me—coming to me with, so to speak, a blank slate—is the greatest compliment you could ever pay me! Half of England thinks they know me intimately because of Watson's wretched stories. You can make your own judgment, for better or worse, about my character."

She laughed. "I am so happy to hear that! And I already understand that your reputation is well deserved indeed."

When we came into the great hall, Arabella strode forward wearing her emerald necklace and another splendid white silk dress. She greeted us warmly. Clearly Caswall's morning visit was to be forgotten—it had never happened! Dinner was the best one yet, the main course being a roast lamb. No one did scintillation better than Arabella: she smiled, she laughed, she showed off her splendid teeth and her long neck, her beautiful white hands moved about in a graceful dance to accompany her witty comments and amusing anecdotes. Somehow even the octagonal green lenses of her spectacles added to her appeal. It was quite a performance.

I was half-dazzled myself. Holmes was also unusually charming, but I knew him well enough to see that he too was "inoculated" against Arabella, as he had once said. Little wonder Sir Nathaniel or Dr. Thorpe were utterly infatuated with her. Most men, even married ones, would probably find her irresistible, but in the end, she was too theatrical for my taste. Although she must be in her late thirties, her beauty was almost completely intact. I wondered what she would do in another ten or twenty years. Nothing was worse than an aged beauty still trying to play the part of the ingénue. Perhaps she wanted Caswall's money so she could dispense with the act. But had she behaved this way for so long that it had become automatic? Could she not stop?

Diana appeared weary and preoccupied. Obviously she had not forgotten about Caswall or what Holmes had told her in the woods. That was just as well–it would have been hard for her to get a word in edgewise.

The next morning was clear and sunny, the mists nowhere to be seen. Holmes told me he needed to see Caswall again, a prospect which filled me with dread. I begged that we might postpone the visit a day or two. Holmes said he might simply go alone, but Caswall seemed so crazy that I would not hear of it. In the end, Holmes agreed to a postponement. We were having dinner with Sir Nathaniel that evening. I was determined not to stay too late at Doom Tower because Michelle might arrive.

After all the excitement of yesterday morning, I longed for a plain, uneventful sort of day. My hopes were soon shattered. Adam Selton came into the library, his face deadly pale, his big hands tightly clutching the brim of his hat. Diana set down her book and walked quickly to him.

"What is it, Adam? What's wrong?"

He was staring at Holmes and me. "A body has been found, out at sea. It may be Evans. Dr. Thorpe has the body."

"As I suspected." Holmes nodded, then slowly stood. "I must have a look."

I was feeling the dread, as usual, square in my chest. "Must you?" I had seen one or two drowned dead bodies, but not close up. I was a doctor, but one who dealt with living bodies, not corpses. Of course, as part of my medical training, I had helped dissect cadavers, but I had never overcome a certain squeamishness. I had merely learned to hide it.

"Yes, Henry."

I slowly stood. "Very well."

"How could this happen?" Diana asked. "How could he have fallen into the sea?"

"Perhaps he fell from one of the cliffs when the tide was high," Arabella said. "What a terrible tragedy."

Holmes's lips drew back into a mirthless smile, but he said nothing.

"I brought the wagonette," Selton said.

Once we had stepped outside, Holmes spoke to Selton. "Did they mention the state of the body? By any chance was it… half eaten?"

Selton froze for a second, his blue eyes all awash with fear. He nodded. "How could you know that?"

"It was not difficult."

"Mr. Holmes, they may want me—they may want me to identify…" He could not finish.

"That should not be necessary, Mr. Selton. I believe I can identify him."

Selton drove the wagonette, but no one had anything to say. The mere thought of our destination ruined the beautiful blue sky and grand vistas for me. At last we reached the cobbled street of the village and drove up to Dr. Thorpe's cottage. The good doctor greeted us effusively, but he looked as distraught as Selton and me.

"I have sent for the chief constable from Whitby, Mr. Holmes. He should be here within an hour."

"And where is the body?"

Thorpe actually flinched. His face was pale, looked almost as washed out as his white hair and mustache. "It's in the garden—in the shed. I did little more than verify his death, but the smell alone would have vouchsafed that. What a horror, gentlemen—what a horror! I have seen drowned men before. They are generally bloated and horribly disfigured, as is this one, but never in such a state!"

"What state?" Holmes asked.

"Huge chunks taken out of him, Mr. Holmes! Dear Lord, it's as if some giant beast had feasted upon him."

"It must have been fish," I said.

Thorpe shook his head wildly. "I have seen bodies nibbled upon by fish. That is common if they have been in the water a week or two, but it was nothing like this. Only a shark or some other monster would have a jaw large enough to do such damage, and there are no sharks in these waters, Dr. Vernier! Once, only once, I have heard of a shark in the Channel waters, but that was twenty years ago. Never here–*never*." He paused to draw in his breath, and his thick white eyebrows came together. "I wonder... I have never had sherry before lunch, but perhaps in an exceptional case such as this..."

"Do you have any brandy? That might be better. For medicinal purposes."

"Brandy? Yes, of course I have brandy. Very astute, Dr. Vernier. And would you gentlemen care to join me?"

I shook my head. "Perhaps a little later." I tried to persuade myself I could do this.

Holmes touched my arm lightly. "I can take care of this by myself, Henry."

"No, I shall come with you. At least to the shed."

Selton seemed both unwilling and unable to speak. He opened and closed his mouth twice. "Must I... must I...?"

"The chief constable will insist you identify him," Thorpe said. "I assure you."

"I doubt that will be necessary," Holmes said. "If the head is intact. He had a mole below his left ear, and the earlobe itself was split. I also happened to notice his dress, the cut of his suit and his boots especially. Neither would be common around here. Was he clothed, by the way?" Thorpe nodded. Holmes turned to me. His gray eyes were grave but without fear. "Shall we have a look, Henry?"

"Yes. Let's get it over with."

Thorpe smiled weakly. "Can't miss the shed. On the left. I had them set him on the floor. The smell was already terrible, but once a body is out of the water for a few hours it becomes... I shall just have that brandy, and you must join me, Mr. Selton. You seem to have as great a need as I do."

Holmes and I went outside. I tried to reassure myself. Doctors do, of course, have to regard dead bodies all the time, but I felt about them as I felt about blood. It was reassuring to see that Thorpe was even more squeamish than I. An elm kept the back of the cottage in shade and sheltered the small wooden shack. Holmes did not hesitate, but went straight to the door and pulled it open. He stepped inside, while I lingered in the doorway.

The smell was incredible, a ghastly mixture of fishiness, sea water and general putrefaction. The body lay on a pallet covered by a heavy tan tarp. Holmes knelt down and pulled it away. One quick look was enough. "My God." I turned away and thrust my head outside, drew in several long slow breaths. "I did not think... it could be so bad."

"I have never seen anything like it." I could tell Holmes had knelt down. "The right ear and part of the neck have been bitten away, but luckily the left is intact. I see the mole, and yes, although the earlobe is greatly swollen, here is the cleft. If you were not looking for it, you would never see it. Also, this is definitely the same boot I noticed the other evening, no cheap mass-produced item, but one made by a cordwainer. It is in the latest style popular among gentlemen in London. Selton clearly paid no attention to Evans's wardrobe, or he would have known he had another source of income."

Thank heavens he was still mostly clothed, so you could not see all the dead flesh. The face was grayish green and bloated, unrecognizable, part of it gone on one side. Other pieces had been torn away, at the upper hip, the shoulder, the clothing ripped apart. One foot was gone entirely, only shredded black wool and a shard of bone remaining. I had taken that much in at a single glance, and I wanted to see no more.

"These bites... They are indeed remarkable. Dr. Thorpe was right. This was not your common fish. The jaw is long and almost pointed. I expect it must be ten or twelve inches across. Are you sure, Henry, you would not care to have a look? No, I think not. You can just step outside if you wish."

"I am fine right here." I had braced my right hand against the door jamb.

"Let me just have a look at the back of his head and neck." I heard him moving the body. "Blast it, his coat is in the way. I shall just use my knife to cut it open." A ripping sound. "His neck seems untouched. *There*–ah, yes. Exactly what one might expect. Let me use my knife again to remove some of his hair. It's difficult to tell with all the swelling, but I am certain there is a contusion, a lump and bruise. He was struck on the back of the head. I doubt the blow killed him, but it allowed them to throw him into the pit."

Small black specks began to dance before my vision, obscuring the stones of the doctor's cottage. I slid down until I was sitting, still facing out of the shed. I leaned over and took deep slow breaths.

"Henry–*Henry*." Holmes's face was beside me, those gray eyes and that beak of a nose. I noticed that he had cut his cheek shaving that morning.

"Forgive me," I murmured. "I thought I was doing all right, but you said... *the pit.*" I shuddered. "Someone threw him into the pit."

"I am certain of it. At high tide, when the water was almost to the top."

I moaned. "And then his body was washed out to sea. And something took large bites out of him. Or did something take large bites out of him first? Before he went into the water?"

Holmes squeezed my arm tightly. "Easy, Henry. Easy. The bites were afterward, when he was in the water."

I took a long slow breath. "Yes, of course. He was drowned, already dead, and some monstrous fish ate at him. But why? Why was he killed?"

"Because he knew too much. He was not only working for Selton senior, but for someone else. He would gladly sell information to anyone willing to pay. We saw that. I suspect he may have decided to try a bit of blackmail, threatening to reveal this person to the celebrated detective, Sherlock Holmes. That was most unwise. He should have realized he was disposable. Of course, he must have foolishly assumed that his employer was not capable of murder." He shook his head. "A nice touch, this. The neighborhood was already awash with rumors and talk because of the missing livestock. This will cause a sensation. Come on, Henry. A couple more deep breaths, and then let's get you back to the doctor's. You have earned your brandy."

I slowly rose, my back to the shed. Holmes closed the door. "It's over and done with, Henry. Given my business with the crime of London, I have seen many a body dredged from the Thames, but never anything quite that ghastly."

I walked slowly. The further from the shed we were, the better I felt. "And yet you did not collapse. I feel such a weakling sometimes. Michelle would not have flinched."

"Henry, the world is full of brutal men with no feelings or sensitivity. That does not make them superior."

"How could you stand it?"

"Many years of experience have blunted my emotions. Then too, I feel not so much fear or dread as..."

"As what?"

"As sadness, Henry, a simple sadness at how cruel life can sometimes be. Evans may have been weak and corrupt, but no one deserves to die the way he did." He paused before the door. "By the way, say nothing about the pit to Selton or the doctor."

We went inside and found the two men seated on the sofa sipping brandy. Holmes went to the decanter, poured out some and handed me the glass. I took a big swallow, then coughed once. "Wouldn't you like some?"

He shook his head, then turned to the men on the couch. "It was Evans. There can be no doubt."

Selton seemed to freeze briefly, then raised his glass and drained it. "I cannot believe it. It was him. And he is dead. He is truly dead." Holmes nodded. Selton shook his head. "He was with me for over three years, ever since I left school. I saw him nearly every day. And now he is gone." He closed his eyes tightly, clenching his teeth. When he opened his eyes, they had filled with tears. "I cannot believe..." He put his right hand over his face. "I thought... I thought he was a... friend."

Holmes shrugged. "Perhaps he was. There are many agreeable scoundrels. Your father may have convinced him that he had your best interests at heart."

Selton stood up. "I... I want to be alone—I want to walk." His face clearly showed his struggle with grief. He set down his glass and strode across the room.

Holmes came forward and touched him lightly on the arm. "Walk, then. Go to Diana's Grove and tell Miss Marsh and Lady Verr. They will want to know. We shall return your wagonette to Lesser Hill."

He nodded, then went outside. I took another swallow of brandy. Dr. Thorpe shook his head. "The poor lad has such a tender heart. Of course, they say people who live in glass houses should not cast stones. But that wasn't really a stone, was it? I find as I grow older, I have less and less stomach for my profession. I have some money set aside. Perhaps it is time to take down my shingle and give away my elixirs."

Holmes smiled. "Break your staff and drown your book several fathoms deep into the sea? You must not let a single extraordinary episode like this make you rush to conclusions, Dr. Thorpe. You are not likely to see another such sight in your lifetime." He glanced at me, his eyes faintly angry. "I shall see to that."

The chief constable from Whitby soon arrived along with one of his men. Mr. Pratt was a small man wearing a black suit and bowler; he had an enormous bushy black mustache which dominated his small, delicate face. He immediately demonstrated his strong constitution in viewing the body, but his deputy was not made of such stern stuff. The man ended up retching outside the shed. Holmes revealed something of his suspicions to Pratt, but asked if he might keep it quiet for a while. Pratt agreed, but warned there would be an coroner's inquiry in a week or two, and that it must come out then. He and his deputy drove off with the body in the back of their cart.

I went down the street and sent Michelle a brief telegram: "Gruesome body found, come at once." I hoped it would be gratuitous because she was already on her way.

* * *

Dinner at Sir Nathaniel de Salis's was pleasant enough. His old cook served a splendid prime rib of beef, and the claret was truly first-rate. The old man had the same sort of easy charm as Arabella, which must have come from being in diplomatic circles. However, he tended to become long-winded and tendentious, and his frequent interjections of "yes?" grew tiresome. During the meal, we avoided the topics of concern, and he regaled us with stories about his career abroad and observations upon the peculiarities of other nationalities.

We lingered at the table until about seven, then trudged slowly up the winding stairway for port and cigars atop his tower. Given the enormous meal, Sir Nathaniel made frequent stops to catch his breath. Just behind us was the old servant, Mitchell, wheezing and carrying a bottle of port. We came out into the huge room with its bookshelves and the bank of windows facing the sea. The sun was low in the sky to the west, at the back of the tower where we could not see it. The light streaming in the windows had a deep yellow-orange cast. I gladly sank into the huge chesterfield. Holmes took the other end, Sir Nathaniel his favorite chair.

Still wheezing slightly, Mitchell poured port into three small glasses on the sideboard, set them on a silver tray, then plodded first to his master, then to Holmes and to me. He soon followed with a box filled with cigars. Holmes took one, but I declined.

Holmes put the eight-inch cigar under his nose. "Ah, a genuine Havana, if I am not mistaken."

"Yes, Mr. Holmes, a weakness of mine." Sir Nathaniel had withdrawn a cutter from his pocket and neatly nipped off the end. He gestured to the servant, who struck a match to light the cigar. Mitchell then took the cutter to Holmes, waited, then lit his cigar as well.

Holmes drew in slowly, savored the smoke a bit, then exhaled a fragrant cloud. "Truly superb. I can honestly say I have never had better."

"You flatter me, Mr. Holmes. I don't allow myself many luxuries any longer, but this is the one exception which, as they say, proves the rule."

Holmes withdrew his pocket watch. "It will be dark soon. The sun sets at about seven thirty."

Sir Nathaniel's mouth twisted to one side in an odd smile. "I may have something to show you, gentlemen, something which will make your visit well worthwhile."

"It would have been worth it because of the excellent dinner, this port and this cigar, Sir Nathaniel. We need no other reward."

My brow had furrowed. "What exactly are you going to show us?"

"If it does occur—and there are no guarantees—it must be a surprise. We shall want to go outside after the sun has set."

Holmes nodded. "I suspect it may have something to do with the White Worm."

Sir Nathaniel gave a sharp laugh. "Very good indeed, Mr. Holmes."

"While we wait, I have a few questions for you, Sir Nathaniel. I hope you will be willing to answer them."

"I believe in frankness, sir. Fire away, as they say."

Holmes nodded, exhaled another cloud of smoke. "This really is very good." He tapped the ash into a big glass ashtray next to the sofa arm. "Very well, Sir Nathaniel. I have heard that you are part of a band of worshipers trying to revive the ancient Celtic religion of the Druids, a group which has been sacrificing animals at Diana's Grove."

The old man nodded thoughtfully. "Very good again, Mr. Holmes. I suspected I could not have any secrets from you. Your description, however, is somewhat misleading. I attend these ceremonies, but not as a true worshiper. I am agnostic on all matters religious, although I must admit I find the Druids and ancient Celts much more appealing than the sniveling Christians of today with their crucified god."

"If you are not a believer, why do you participate?" Holmes asked.

Sir Nathaniel laughed. "Come now, Mr. Holmes! Surely that is obvious."

Holmes nodded. "Yes, I suppose it is. You are interested, above all, in the White Worm. You may not believe in Celtic gods and goddesses, but you do believe that some ancient gigantic serpent lives on deep within the earth. These rites may bring him to the surface."

"*Her*, Mr. Holmes–*her* to the surface."

"May bring *her* to the surface where you might observe her."

"Yes. Exactly. And..." His eyes had taken on an odd luster. "It has happened. We have succeeded."

I said nothing, but reflected that he must be almost as crazy as Caswall. Sir Nathaniel grinned ironically at me. "I am not mad, Dr. Vernier. As I hope you will soon see."

I shook my head. "Grown men and women throwing poor dumb animals into a pit."

He laughed. "Come now, Dr. Vernier! Do you not eat those poor dumb animals? You seemed to enjoy the roast beef this evening. How do you think that animal met its end?"

"It wasn't drowned."

"The animals are mostly not drowned either."

"Of course they are."

"No, the worm gets them."

I shook my head. "This is hopeless."

Holmes had been listening thoughtfully to this exchange. "I suppose you have heard the cries of the dying animals. And you may have even... seen something."

Sir Nathaniel's eyes still had an odd intensity. "Yes."

"Possibly... possibly a smaller version." He shrugged. "An infant."

Sir Nathaniel laughed again, then shook his head. "Remarkable, Mr. Holmes–remarkable! Even the stories they tell about you do not do you justice."

I was staring at Holmes. "Sherlock...?"

"You are a naturalist, Sir Nathaniel, a scientist. It is hardly surprising that you would do almost anything to see a remarkable creature like the worm, a prehistoric beast who has somehow lived for millennia."

"Yes, Mr. Holmes–*yes*. It is the opportunity of a lifetime. And if the discovery of fossilized dinosaurs created a stir, think of this! It would be the discovery of the century. A living fossil resurrected! A colossus, a being of a size and intelligence unimaginable to us puny mortals of today, yes? It must be intelligent. What if we could communicate with it? What could it tell us!"

"Yes, your reasoning makes perfect sense," Holmes said. "This whole business started last autumn, I believe. Was Lady Verr involved? Is she the mistress of ceremonies?"

The old man shook his head once. "No, absolutely not." He laughed, exhaling smoke. "I must admit it is a relief to see that you do not know everything, that you have no preternatural powers."

"But there is a high priestess. A redhead."

"Yes. Her name is Corchen." This last made him smile.

"Corchen? That is... some Celtic goddess, I believe. Something to do with... Yes, of course, a snake goddess."

"A hit, Mr. Holmes! A palpable hit!"

"Then that is certainly not her real name, but only an assumed one. Who is she? A member of the local community, or someone new–someone you had not seen before."

"The latter."

"So she just appeared. Out of nowhere."

He laughed. "It does seem that way. I almost suspect... Lady Verr and I had a long discussion about the White Worm and all the legends, as well as the Celts and their history at Diana's Grove. I had related my thoughts on the possibility that such a creature could have survived into our own times. The Welsh efforts to revive the Celtic religion also came up. It was only two weeks later that I received a letter from Corchen asking if I would help her to create a local Druidic religion based on the worship of a great serpent. She came to see me a few days later."

Holmes's brow had furrowed. "Describe her."

"She does somewhat resemble Lady Verr, only a taller specimen. She is fair-skinned, but her hair is even redder, wild and unkempt. She visited me shortly after dark, and insisted we talk outside. She was wearing white woolen robes. Her English has some strange accent, a slight one, which was tantalizingly familiar, but which I could not quite identify. We arranged for a first meeting at the grove on the night of the full moon. I knew some people who might be interested. I spoke to them, they in turn spoke to others. We were ten at our first gathering, but our number has since grown to about thirty-five."

I shook my head. "Incredible."

"So it is, Dr. Vernier, although you seem to find it reprehensible."

"And was it Corchen who suggested the animal sacrifices?" Holmes asked.

"Yes."

"And was...? Were there any other strangers at that first meeting, people you did not know?"

"Yes. Corchen's acolyte. She has never spoken. I do not even know her name. She is another beautiful woman, but a brunette with long flowing hair, dark-complexioned, as if she were Spanish or Italian."

Holmes abruptly leaned forward. "Do you know Lady Verr's maid, Angela?"

"Yes, of course. I have been to Diana's Grove many times and noticed her waiting in attendance."

"Could this acolyte have been Angela?"

He laughed. "No, no, Mr. Holmes! Their faces are not at all the same, and the acolyte is too short. Angela is a giantess. Forget about Lady Verr. I do suspect she may have some connection with Corchen—even that is only a wild guess, but she herself has not participated in our rites. Then, too, I did later mention a possible Druidic revival to Lady Verr to see if she might be interested. She told me the idea of meeting in the grove after dark for religious ceremonies and sacrifices struck her as barbaric nonsense."

For once Arabella and I agreed on something.

"Perhaps," Sir Nathaniel continued, "perhaps Lady Verr knows Corchen and mentioned my interest to her. That would explain why Corchen then wrote to me."

"So Corchen determines when the ceremonies will take place. But I suspect you notify the others."

"Frequently she tells us the time of the next meeting, but if there are any changes, she writes to me, and I write to a few others, who in turn have their own contacts."

Holmes sat back in the sofa, resting his elbow on the arm, the cigar held loosely between two fingers. "Things would have been in hiatus during the height of winter, but once the snows lower down were gone, it resumed. And who provides the animals?"

For the first time, Sir Nathaniel seemed uneasy. "Some of our members... fetch them."

Holmes merely smiled, but I said, "They steal them, you mean."

Sir Nathaniel frowned, but nodded. "You understand I can give you no names, other than that of Corchen."

Holmes nodded. "Yes, and that is obviously not her real name."

Sir Nathaniel glared at me. "What are a few animals compared to a discovery of this magnitude?"

Holmes nodded. "Yes, yes, it all makes perfect sense." He glanced briefly at me, and I knew that he thought that it only made perfect sense if the worm existed, but it–*she*–did not. "I can certainly understand your position. However, I have heard some talk of the possibility of a human sacrifice."

Sir Nathaniel frowned. "It is only talk. I do not think... She has been vague."

"And what would you do if a human sacrifice were proposed?"

"I... I don't know."

"For God's sake," I moaned.

"I hope it doesn't come to that, but we... we know so little about the beast, about its dietary requirements and the like. I cannot believe... Surely it cannot require living prey? We might be able to satisfy her with those who have already died."

I simply stared at him, unable to believe what I was hearing.

"Once one is dead, what does it matter, Dr. Vernier? Being devoured by a prehistoric beast would be a far more magnificent end than rotting in a common pauper's grave, would it not?"

Holmes put the cigar in his mouth, then clapped his hands together twice, nodding. He took out the cigar and exhaled. "I agree. I would certainly prefer such an end to moldering away in a coffin under the earth."

Sir Nathaniel smiled. "Exactly, sir–exactly!"

Holmes glanced at the windows. "The sun has certainly set. Is it time to go outside?"

De Salis tapped his cigar against the ashtray, knocking off a huge ash. "Indeed it is. The evening should be beautiful. The moon is approaching full, and when it rises there will be considerable light."

Sir Nathaniel stood. He was wearing the same slightly worn, blue-black frock coat as on our first visit. He went to the doorway and took his battered top hat from its shelf, put it on, then opened the door and started up the steps.

When we came outside, the wind from the sea was cool on my face. Overhead was the vast expanse of dark sky, a few stars already strikingly bright. Holmes and Sir Nathaniel went toward the wall overlooking the sea. I naturally held back, not wanting to trigger my vertigo. The water was still faintly luminous from the faded sky, the long line of the horizon clearly visible. I heard the continuing crescendo and diminuendo of the surf below. I thrust my hands in my pockets. The day had been pleasantly warm, but once the sun was down, it grew cold quickly, especially given the damp air and the nearness of the ocean.

"A beautiful evening indeed," Holmes said.

"It is," Sir Nathaniel replied. "Sometime, perhaps you might spend the night at Doom Tower and come up here in the morning for the sunrise. It is spectacular over the sea, especially when there are a few clouds."

"Is this what you wanted to show us?" My voice reflected my puzzlement.

"No. That would be to the north." The old man turned and started off to our left. Holmes and I followed, although I still stayed well back from the wall. He paused after swinging some forty-five degrees round the tower's circular wall. "Do you see that second dark area, just there to the north along the sea? That smaller patch is the park before Lesser Hill, but the far larger one is the wood round Diana's

Grove. The house itself is hidden by the trees."

"I see it," Holmes said.

"Let us watch for a while." Sir Nathaniel leaned slightly sideways as he set one elbow on the wall. He began to hum softly to himself.

Holmes slipped one hand into his jacket pocket and stood silently. I drew in my breath and gazed again up at the sky, trying to forget about how far above the ground we must be. Again I remarked the striking difference between the night sky of London and the Yorkshire countryside. The sky was darker, contrasting dramatically with the brilliant stars, and even now with some residual light left inland to the west, far more stars were visible. The brightest were magnitudes brighter than in London with its gas lamps and smoky air.

"What an evening," Holmes said. "Someday, when I have enough of crime and my profession, I shall retire to the country where I can see the heavens like this every night."

Sir Nathaniel laughed. "It is enviable on a night like this, but you forget how frequently the clouds obscure the stars, and rain or snow fall. It is far too cold to come outside much of the year, too."

"You can always look at the sea from your aerie below."

Sir Nathaniel laughed again. "You needn't try to convince me, Mr. Holmes. I live here because I love this country, and… Ah! *Ah!* You see?" He had stood upright and set both hands on the wall.

I could not see past them, but Holmes also stood up straight. "What is it?" I asked.

"Very interesting," Holmes said. "Come closer, just to my right. You see how formidable the wall is. Have a look at Diana's Grove."

I stepped nearer. The wall was high and sturdy, and so long as I did not look down… I followed the still faintly shimmering sweep of the sea to the north and saw a swaying white shape, faintly luminous, slowly rising out of the dark woods. It rose higher and higher, stopped suddenly. It moved again: one vivid green light appeared, then another—two glowing green eyes in that white head. It bobbed slightly, then turned. Green beams streamed from the eyes.

Holmes laughed softly. "Oh, well done."

"Dear God," I murmured. I rested both hands on the wall, my fingers clutching at the cold stone. An odd shiver worked its way up my back. "It cannot be—it cannot."

The old man laughed. "Do you still think the worm is nonsense, Dr. Vernier?"

"But its eyes! You are the naturalist—how can they shine that way?"

"They must have adapted over the millennia to allow it to prowl through the depths of the earth."

The worm hovered for a few seconds, then slowly sank down. "It's impossible," I moaned, but almost immediately, it rose up, perhaps a little to the left of where it had just been. The two green beams swept from right to left as if it were searching the grove for something. It rose even higher this time. Given the height of the trees, it would have to be well over fifty feet high.

My mind was at war with itself—the rational part battling the instinctual. Hypothesis after hypothesis rose up, all of them conflicting with the more visceral responses of my body, which was alarmed, even at this distance. For once, even my vertigo was forgotten.

I grasped Holmes's arm. "For God's sake—what is that thing?"

"Are you blind, man?" de Salis exclaimed. "That is *her*! Behold the great White Worm in all her glory!"

Holmes spoke very softly, for my ears only. "It is a fake, Henry—a fraud."

I sighed. A part of me had already figured that out, but the other part was tremendously relieved.

"When did the worm first appear?" Holmes asked.

"About a month ago. Corchen somehow knows when she will come forth out of the pit."

"And how often have you seen it?"

"This is the fourth time, and it is generally just after dark. The last time she was moving about for almost two hours. Now do you understand? Eventually she must come forth during the ceremony, the mother herself. Imagine being able to see her up close!"

"Yes, yes." Holmes nodded. "If you'll forgive me, Sir Nathaniel, we must say farewell. I want to have a closer look."

The old man shrugged. "Have a try, although she will certainly see you coming and return to her lair. That was what happened when I tried walking over to the grove on one occasion."

"All the same, I should like to try." He glanced at me. "Henry?"

I followed as he rushed down the short stairway, and then the much longer one winding round down the tower. Holmes quickly hitched the horse to the dog-cart, then we set off back toward the grove, sitting side by side.

The swollen gibbous moon had risen, giving us enough light to make our way on the open moor. Holmes tried to hasten the old horse, but he was obviously not capable of much speed, which was well, given the darkness. As the cart rumbled and jounced along, the cold damp air on my face, I stared up at the writhing white form of the worm set against the dark sky. It grew larger, even as more and more stars were appearing. Its green eyes would sweep round like some lighthouse top. Occasionally the worm would sink down, a dim green glow still showing, then it slowly rose up again.

We had nearly reached the trees of the grove when it sank down for the last time, and the green was suddenly extinguished. "Blast it!" Holmes exclaimed. He pulled the reins, drawing the horse to a stop.

"No use rushing now. I need to light the lamps, anyway, before we enter the woods."

"You think it's gone?"

"Yes. They knew how long it would take me to get here from Doom Tower." He laughed softly. "I thought nothing could ever top the glowing Baskerville hound, but the White Worm is the clear victor!"

Nine

Holmes had just lit the second lamp when we heard a woman shout, "Henry!"

I turned, started down the path, then began to run. She shouted my name again. Under the moonlight I saw her and a huge man who must be Adam Selton. She started toward me. I put my arms around her, she did the same, and we embraced one another fiercely. Few women were as strong as Michelle. She wore a woolen traveling suit and a practical hat.

"Thank God you've come," I said.

"Is that how you greet your wife?" she said.

Our lips met, and the kiss quickly dispensed with formalities and became the kind best pursued behind locked doors. I was grateful for the darkness, but since Holmes and Selton were nearby, I soon drew away.

She touched my cheek with her big hand. "That's more like it."

"I am glad to see you."

"And I you." She looked up at the sky. "It's so beautiful here. Look at the stars–you can see the Milky Way."

Despite the moonlight, you could see the cloudy white band of stars overhead. "Yes." Suddenly I frowned. "But what are you doing *here*? Walking in the darkness?"

"My driver from Whitby took one look at that ridiculous apparition rising over the trees and would go no further. He dropped me off at Lesser Hill. I was determined to continue on to the grove, and Mr. Selton kindly insisted on accompanying me. He thought it would be best to go on foot, as we would be less likely to be seen."

I shook my head. "How could you do something so foolhardy?"

She laughed. "Mr. Selton felt much the same way." She picked up her medical bag, which she had dropped, opened it, and withdrew a long-barreled revolver. "However, things sounded sufficiently grave in your last telegram that I came prepared."

"So you were going to shoot the giant serpent?"

"Don't be ridiculous, Henry. Whatever that was, it was not a giant serpent."

Holmes laughed and stepped nearer. "Bravo, Michelle. I knew you could not be fooled."

I shook my head. "Unlike your idiot of a husband."

Selton had approached closer once we had stopped kissing. "That was not a serpent?"

"Most assuredly not," Holmes said. "It was a clever fake."

"Are you certain of that, Mr. Holmes?" Selton asked. "Absolutely certain?"

"I am."

"Thank God for that."

I could tell from the tone of his voice that he had been badly frightened. I suppose I came next in gullibility, while Michelle and Holmes were completely unruffled. I reflected again on the cruel trick fate had played upon me. How I wished I had been born with some small fraction of Michelle's sangfroid!

"I suppose your bags are back at Lesser Hill," Holmes said. "Would you like me to take you back for them?"

"Absolutely not. I have had more than enough of carriages and trains for one day. It can wait until tomorrow."

Holmes nodded. "One of the Marsh ladies will doubtlessly be willing to lend you a nightgown."

In the moonlight I could see her smile up at me. She squeezed my hand tightly. "That won't be necessary." Her voice was almost a whisper. I squeezed her hand back.

"What did you say?" Holmes asked.

"Oh, I mean, yes–of course," she said. "I am certain they will."

Selton had folded his brawny arms. "Whatever that thing was, are you sure that it is gone? That it is safe?"

Holmes nodded. "Yes, and besides, you can see that Dr. Doudet Vernier is armed."

"Very well. I'll be heading back to Lesser Hill then."

Selton turned, but Michelle reached out and seized his wrist. He turned again, and I could see his eyes opened wide, his lips parted. "Thank you for accompanying me, Mr. Selton."

He shook his head once. "I couldn't let you go wandering off in the dark with that thing over the grove."

"I know you thought I was quite crazy, but you came all the same. Again, thank you."

He nodded. "You're welcome, ma'am–I mean, Dr. Vernier–I mean Dr. Doudet... Vernier...?"

Michelle laughed. "It is complicated, is it not? Ma'am will do."

"Very well... Ma'am."

She laughed. "That was not so very hard, was it? Good night, then."

He nodded, turned and strode away. Michelle laughed softly. "Poor fellow. I don't know what frightens him most—giant white serpents or women."

I shook my head. "Given his nature, that was genuinely brave of him. And I can certainly understand his questioning your sanity. By the way, could you please put the revolver back in the bag now?"

She did so. Holmes stepped up into the driver's seat. I helped Michelle up, then started up myself. Holmes turned slightly toward us. "Say nothing of what we saw to anyone in the house. Even if anyone were out of doors, I doubt they would have been able to see anything through the trees." He shook his head. "Pity. In the darkness, it would be a waste of time to try to find anyone in the woods. They are probably gone by now, and even if not, they could see an approaching lantern's light from afar."

"Why bother with a lantern? I'm sure Michelle would be glad to stumble around the forest with you looking for lunatics in the utter blackness. However, please drop me off first."

Holmes laughed, and Michelle shook her head. "You need not take that tone."

"Yes, yes," I said. Soon we were on our way, our backs to Holmes. The carriage jounced slightly, and the lamps on either side lit up the woods, illuminating lichen-spotted trunks and the saw-toothed leaves of ferns.

I had put my arm around Michelle. "I am glad to see you, you know. You won't have received my telegram from today." I told her about Evans' body.

She shook her head. "How horrible, my poor darling. Another dark business."

We soon reached the house. Holmes stopped before the door. "I shall see to the horse, then join you. Sorry, old fellow," he said to the animal, "I'm afraid we pushed you to your limits this evening. I suspected it would be futile, but I had to try."

I used the knocker on the front door, and soon Mrs. Troughton ushered us inside. I introduced Michelle to the housekeeper. She curtsied politely, then said, "Miss Marsh and Lady Verr are in the sitting room."

"We'd best get all the introductions over with," I said.

Michelle sighed. "Oh, Henry—must we?" We had started up the stairs alone. She seized my arm, looked about, then quickly kissed me.

"We shall make them brief—very brief."

Diana and Arabella were playing cards at a small table, a lamp illuminating the cribbage board, while the flames flickered about a massive log in the fireplace. Angela sat in a chair near the fireplace working on her embroidery. Arabella set down her cards and stood up, smiling. As usual, she was in an elegant white silk dress, complete with emerald necklace. Her green spectacles sat low on her nose, and she stared up at Michelle, who was four or five inches taller than she. Her smile faltered briefly, her brows coming inward.

"At last—Dr. Doudet Vernier. I must admit, you are not exactly what I expected."

Michelle stared at her. "How so?"

"You are statuesque and quite stunning. I suppose I took the well-trodden path and assumed, foolishly, that a woman doctor must be rather plain. I do know better. What a pleasure to have you at Diana's Grove as our guest."

"You must forgive me for arriving so suddenly and with no warning."

"Not at all—not at all. We have been expecting you. We have heard so much about you!" She set her hand lightly on Michelle's forearm and gave a gentle squeeze. "It will be a pleasure to have a woman of beauty and intelligence in the house. I hope reptiles are more to your taste than your husband's."

"Reptiles?" Michelle's eyes shifted to mine, then back to Arabella.

"Yes, yes. I have a few pets–a boa constrictor, some lizards and a turtle. Surely a medical doctor cannot be afraid of snakes?"

Michelle smiled. "Not this one, anyway."

"And would you care to see Delilah swallow her weekly rabbit tomorrow?"

Michelle shrugged. "I suppose so."

Arabella gave her arm another squeeze. "I know we shall be friends, great friends! We have so much in common. We might be sisters–the three of us." She turned to encompass Diana in her gaze.

Her niece had stood as well. She looked rather pale, but at the mention of "a woman of beauty and intelligence" a faint flush had appeared at her cheeks. Her eyes were fixed on her aunt and Michelle, but they shifted to me. She smiled weakly.

"Michelle," I said, "this is Miss Marsh, Diana–I mean Miss Diana Marsh."

Diana stared at me. "You may certainly call me Diana, should you wish, Dr. Vernier."

Michelle stepped forward and touched her arm. Slender and slightly awkward, Diana still seemed a girl, while Michelle with her fuller figure and easy confidence was clearly a woman. "I hope when you know me better, I too might have that privilege."

Diana smiled at her.

"Why don't we dispense with the stuffy British formalities, and all use first names?" Arabella said. "I can dispense with the 'lady' if you can both let the 'doctor' go. After all, Dr. Vernier–Henry–has been here nearly an entire week. Oh, I know that Mr. Holmes simply must be Mr. Holmes, but for the rest of us, won't first names do?"

Michelle and I both hesitated, then nodded.

"Excellent!"

Diana shook her head. "I… I simply would not feel comfortable with that."

Arabella's eyes rolled upward. "Oh Diana!"

Michelle stared at her. "Whatever you wish, my dear. Perhaps in a few days it may seem less imposing."

Diana nodded. "Thank you."

"Michelle is rather tired after her long journey," I said. "Tomorrow you will have the opportunity to become better acquainted."

Michelle nodded, smiling. Her eyes shifted briefly, and I realized she had noticed Angela sitting by the fireplace in a chair, scrupulously doing her best to ignore us.

"Is there anything you need? Are you hungry, are you thirsty, are you…?"

"No, no, I just want to get straight to bed." Her eyes briefly shifted to mine. "It has been a long day."

"Yes, certainly. Since we have been expecting you, Mrs. Troughton has prepared a room, only two doors down from Henry's."

Michelle gave her an incredulous stare.

"How thoughtful," I said. "To the left or the right?"

"To the left."

"Excellent, well, good night, then."

The door opened and Holmes stepped into the room. "Good evening. I see introductions have been made." He noticed the cards and the board on the table. "Ah, a game of cribbage in progress."

Arabella nodded. "An idle game, but I had not played in a long time. I suggested it to Diana, and we began just after dinner."

Holmes smiled faintly. "You have been occupied all evening long, I suppose. Might I join you?"

"Certainly, Mr. Holmes. We can begin again–and you will not abandon us like the doctors!" She laughed.

Michelle and I soon fled. Diana gave me a sad parting smile. Michelle shook her head as we started down the hall. "The girl has excellent taste in men, I fear. She seems quite taken with you, Henry."

I shook my head. "Don't you start that too."

"Given the aunt, I can certainly understand why."

"You did not care for the aunt?"

"Not particularly. She has… I am always uneasy with people, male or female, who have both beauty and a certain easy natural charm. That charm always seems to have an element of artifice. I never feel I can take them at face value."

"The poor girl has been buffeted about so. I have helped her out of some difficulties."

"Little wonder she likes you. I suspect she thinks you will ignore her now that I have arrived."

"I would not ignore her!"

"I know that, but she does not. By the way, who was that rather striking woman on the chair? Italian, is she not?"

"Yes, that was Angela, Arabella's maid. Lady Verr and her husband spent many years in Italy."

"Well, she does not exactly resemble a maid. A certain spirit shows in those black eyes, as well as a sense of irony. Although… at one point she seemed almost angry."

I shrugged. "I'm afraid I hardly noticed her."

"That's not like you, Henry! Anyway, you must tell me all about Miss Marsh and Mr. Selton and their difficulties, and bring me up to date about the whole business with the White Worm and pagan believers. Afterwards."

"Afterwards?"

"Afterwards," she said.

"By the way, it's not too late—we could go back and ask them for a nightgown."

She laughed and struck my shoulder with her fist. "Nightgowns! As I said—that won't be necessary, not tonight. But you must promise to keep me warm."

"I promise. But wait—you will be in your room—and I shall be in mine."

She tapped my shoulder lightly again. "Oh yes, of course. And you will be wearing your woolen night shirt and night cap."

"Yes."

She stopped, pushed me against the wall, and then kissed me. It went on a long while, my hands feeling the length of her, all the curves. At last I had to catch my breath. "No nightgowns. Let's simply find the room with the largest bed."

"I'm glad you still fancy me, Henry. It's been only about a week, but it has felt like forever."

"That it has. And I don't 'fancy you'—I love you." I caressed her face with my hand, touched her neck with my lips, then her ear. "Still, I fear I'm being selfish."

"Selfish?"

"To want you here when it may well prove dangerous. Very dangerous."

"You know my thoughts on that—if there is to be danger, let us risk it together."

"I do feel I could face almost anything with you at my side."

"Enough talk, Henry—let's find that largest bed."

Afterwards, truly exhausted, I lay feeling Michelle all long and smooth and warm alongside me. We talked briefly, and I told her what Holmes had discovered about our various *dramatis personae,* the White Worm and the druid worshipers. Soon I fell asleep, a very black, deep sort of sleep. Eventually, though, I found myself on the moor again, the bright moonlight glistening on the heath and grass. I was walking as fast as I could, and soon I broke into a run. Finally I came to the edge of a cliff. The moon shone on the black waters of the sea. I turned to face my pursuer.

The worm really was a serpent, a great white one with its scales forming an elaborate pattern like Delilah's. Its emerald eyes glowed. Something was caught in its mouth. It swayed before me, then let its burden drop. Evans's ghastly glowing corpse lay before me, his bloated gray-green face almost unrecognizable. Even more pieces were gone from him—not only his foot, but his right forearm and his left buttock, a whole haunch devoured. "You are next," said a woman's voice, but I could not tear my eyes away from Evans's corpse. Suddenly something happened to the face—his eyes opened—they were not alive, could not be alive, yet some deranged animation… He coughed, choked, and made a horrible garbled noise.

"Henry–Henry!" That was Michelle.

I opened my eyes. The room was dim, but I could see certain shapes and forms.

Michelle squeezed my arm again. "It's all right, Henry—you were having a nightmare."

I shivered, the horror of the dream still very much with me. "One of the worst ever."

"What was it?"

"Never mind." I pulled her against me, ran my hand along her shoulder down to her hip. "I don't want to talk about it."

"Poor darling." She began to caress my arm and snuggled closer.

Soon I slept again, and although the worm lurked nearby, nothing like the horror of that earlier dream reoccurred.

As usual, Arabella was still abed when we went down in the morning. Mrs. Troughton greeted us warmly, and we joined Holmes and Diana at the breakfast table. Diana smiled up at us both and asked if we had slept well. I had remarked before that both she and Mrs. Troughton were always in excellent spirits first thing in the morning, but their mood gradually drooped as Arabella's appearance drew nearer.

Michelle had a formidable appetite, and when she was truly hungry, few women could eat more. Luckily, her active nature and natural energy prevented any tendency to corpulence. The food instead seemed to nourish those feminine curves I so treasured. Diana, a rather lackluster eater, watched in some awe as Michelle devoured a huge plate of scrambled eggs and a rasher of bacon.

Shortly after breakfast, Selton arrived. He had driven over with Michelle's bags. It was another beautiful day, and we decided to go down to the beach. Michelle was eager to see the sea. Holmes, however, decided to have a look in the woods and search for some trace of the "worm" from the night before.

We made our way down the path which skirted the high cliffs, and before us was a long, flat expanse of gray shingle and then blue sea, the waves sweeping in gently. The tide was still low, and the sun had dried the small gray pebbles. Only at the edge where the water swept inward did they become black and shiny. A hazy thin band of cloud lay along the horizon, muting the sun slightly, but its rays still lit up the gray-white limestone cliffs. We saw birds perched here and there amongst the rocks, and a gull soared overhead, making its distinctive cry. The air had a salt tang and sharp smell.

Michelle smiled at me, her face radiant. The brim of her big hat cast a shadow over her eyes and nose. A few days here, and I knew she would begin to freckle. I wished Adam and Diana were somewhere else so I could kiss her. Instead I gave her big hand a squeeze, and she squeezed back fiercely.

"Oh Henry, it's perfect!" She turned to Diana. "How I envy you! To be able to come out here whenever you wish, to have all this practically outside your door."

Diana smiled back, unable to resist such enthusiasm. "It is a pleasure. And it has always also been... a sort of solace."

Michelle let go of my hand and seized hers. "Oh, I hope so. Henry has told me about you. You have had a hard time of it. But things will change—you will see." She looked over at Selton, and the right side of her mouth rose in a crooked smile which I knew signified a certain irony. His brow furrowed, and then he stared out at the sea.

"You are very kind," Diana said. A brief smile pulled at her lips. "I wondered what you would be like. I should have known..." She glanced briefly at me.

"Known what?" Michelle asked.

"That you would be a good person."

"How would you know that?"

"Because... of Dr. Vernier. He would not marry someone who was not."

I smiled. "You are kind, too, Diana."

Michelle took on a stern look, then shrugged. "Well, despite his many faults, he is not without a few feeble redeeming qualities." Diana looked dismayed, which made Michelle laugh. "My dear—I'm only teasing! He is one of the least obtuse men I know, which is why I married him. Actually, he is a paragon among men, but he must not be told so. It will go straight to his head."

She turned to Selton, who had been listening to this exchange with an uneasy look. "I might also say something comical about Mr. Selton, but I can see that he is easily flummoxed. After his chivalrous behavior in confronting..." I quickly raised my hand, trying to warn her Holmes didn't want the apparition mentioned, and she went on so smoothly the pause was hardly noticeable. "It was generous of him to accompany me in my walk across the moors, so I will not tease him for at least twenty-four hours. However, tomorrow morning will be a different matter." She said to him, "Is that clearly understood?"

He nodded, but said nothing.

Michelle laughed. "Is he always so taciturn?"

Diana shook her head. "Not when you know him."

"Well, you must tell me about him and about yourself. The men must remain some ten paces behind so they cannot hear the dreadful revelations to come."

I smiled and shook my head. "You are in rare form."

"Ten paces—remember!"

She took Diana's arm, and they strode down the shingle before us. By chance, both of them were wearing blue woolen suits with long skirts and short-waisted jackets. Michelle had had a brilliant purple hat specially made for her with a wide brim to protect her from the sun, while Diana wore something related to a bowler with a few feathers. Michelle had let go of Diana's arm, but her hand rose again to touch her elbow as they talked.

I smiled. "They really might be sisters."

Selton nodded. "Your wife is more like her than her aunt."

"Is she? Michelle has bigger hands and shoulders than Lady Verr or Diana, and her hair is a different shade."

Selton shrugged. "I wasn't thinking so much how they looked, but their... natures."

"Oh."

He glanced at me, a sad sort of smile pulling at his lips. "You are a lucky man, Dr. Vernier." He was wearing his usual worn gray tweed jacket and his cloth cap. His face was bronzed from his time in the outdoors of Yorkshire, something which further set off his striking good looks, the high cheekbones, square jaw and straight nose. We walked slowly, keeping back by the required ten paces.

"I know. But it isn't exactly luck, not entirely. Diana would make a wonderful wife."

He let out a long sigh. "I know."

"Then what's holding you back?" He visibly stiffened. "Is it your father? I'm not sure he would really cut you off financially. Perhaps..."

"It's not a question of *money*." He shook his head. "That means nothing—I'd trade it all for even a single night with Diana. I..." The implications of what he had said suddenly seemed to strike him, and he began to flush, even as he shook his head. "Not the money, no."

"What then?"

He hesitated a long while, and when he spoke his voice was so soft it could barely be heard over the sound of surf coming in. "I can't tell you. Not... yet. Maybe..."

"You said you loved her."

"I do." He turned to me. "*I do.*" He drew in a great breath, almost snapping at the air. "I've loved her for so long, it seems. Not exactly at first sight, but almost. It was the first time she told me about Natty Bumppo and Chingachgook. I was listening to the story—she told it well—but then I saw how beautiful she was, how it was almost in the air around her. I had never met anyone so full of life. I was only a boy when I decided I loved her, and when I grew older... None of the girls I met could ever compare. And she has always been my friend—my best and truest friend."

"That is as it should be. It's the same with Michelle."

He was staring out at the sea, but he turned to me. "Dr. Vernier, is it...? It seems to me... But it's not what my father thinks or any of the other..."

"What are you talking about? Ask it directly. I know you can."

He drew his breath in resolutely. "It seems to me that women, many women, are better than men—certainly better than me. We're supposed to be the strong and brave ones, but they—Diana is afraid of nothing—and she has suffered so much, and yet it has not broken her. While I..." He shook his head.

I laughed softly. "You're right."

He stared at me. "What?"

"It's true. Many men never quite figure it out, but women are better and stronger than we men. Oh, perhaps one cannot really generalize about such things. There are those rare beings like Sherlock Holmes—he is brilliant beyond belief and absolutely fearless as well, even though he sometimes cannot attend to his basic needs like eating and sleeping. Yes, it all has to do with individual men and women, but from nearly the first day I met her, I have felt Michelle was my superior. She is every bit as intelligent as me, but she is braver and more generous. I have to work at courage and kindness and generosity, but they come naturally to her. And the most bloody sight imaginable does not make her falter. She would have been able to stare directly at Evans's corpse, and she would not have felt like fainting."

"Is that true?"

"Yes. I have never told her that, but it is something I figured out early on."

"But all the same—it does not matter. You are happy together, very happy. I can see that."

"She has made me a better man than I ever would have been on my own. Loving her has... weakened that terrible selfishness we all carry around inside ourselves."

His eyes were fixed on mine. At last he shook his head. "If only it were possible…"

"Of course it's possible! You are twenty-one years old and you have your whole life before you–a life with Diana. It's waiting for you. Just reach out your hand and take it."

His eyes had an odd gray-green color, a mere sliver of rings in the bright sun alongside the giant black pupils, and they seemed to suddenly glisten.

"What is it, Adam? Tell me."

He shook his head savagely. "Oh I cannot–I cannot! It is too… Let me be. Just let me be. You have told me enough. Let's–let's talk about something else–anything else." He shook his head, his mouth grimacing. "Oh, it hurts–it hurts so."

"Are you ill?" I asked.

He smiled fiercely. "It is nothing that will kill me outright–unfortunately."

I stared at him incredulously. He could not be physically ill–he simply could not. He was the embodiment of physical perfection, and he had no symptoms of any disease. I had seen him eat and drink, and the large quantities made sense for so big a man.

"Explain yourself."

He swallowed once, then looked away. "I asked you to leave me alone."

I shook my head angrily. "Oh, very well–there is no cure for stupidity, for mindless–"

"Oh please don't be angry with me!"

He seemed so genuinely hurt that my fury dissolved. "All right."

"I shall–I shall tell you. Sometime. When I am ready. When… But not now. Not now."

I shook my head again. "I told Sherlock I hated mysteries, and that was the truth, by God! Life is complicated enough without blasted mysteries." We were silent for a while. "I'm going to hold you to it, you know. I'm not going to just go off and leave you alone and miserable. You and Diana need one another. Think about her."

"I only want what is best for her, I promise you."

"And that doesn't include you?"

He shook his head, unable to speak.

"You are infuriating, but I suspect you also have... a few feeble redeeming qualities. I'm sorry. Let's find another topic. I haven't thanked you for escorting Michelle across the moors last night. You have seen her boldness and determination first hand."

He nodded. "Yes. She is truly... most determined."

I laughed. "That she is."

We walked nearly all the way along the beach to Lesser Hill, then turned and went back, since Adam had left the wagonette at Diana's Grove. At the end of our walk, we could clearly see the effect of the rising tide; there was much less exposed shingle than when we had left.

Diana stared up at the path. "I don't want to go back," she murmured. I suspected she was thinking of Arabella.

"I have monopolized you shamelessly," Michelle said. "Mr. Selton has earned a few minutes with you. Henry and I will start back. You two may take your time. There is no rush."

Adam gave her a grateful smile. "I could walk some more."

Diana nodded. "So could I."

He started forward, and Diana slipped her hand lightly around his arm just above the elbow. Michelle and I watched them for a while. Her hand also touched my arm lightly, and I felt a muted shiver of content work its way along my spine.

"It is so beautiful here," Michelle said.

"Yes."

"They are a handsome couple. But they are so very young. She has no doubts about him, none. She does seem to know his weaknesses. She says something happened two years ago. Something changed with him."

I told her my theory about a bad experience with a prostitute, which his father had basically confirmed.

She shook her head. "How stupid. But surely he must understand that it would be different with someone he loves. And he does love her, doesn't he?"

"Absolutely."

"Then what is the matter with him?"

"I don't know. He wouldn't tell me. But I intend to find out. Sherlock has taken on the case of the White Worm, but he has entrusted me—and you—with solving the riddle of Adam and Diana."

"Has he!" She laughed. "How like him. Well, you have deduced the business with the prostitute. I am sure you will discover some strange dirt on his coat which will completely unravel the mystery."

I laughed. "Certainly."

She took my hand, and we started up the path to the grove. We were nearly at the top when we saw a tall, thin figure standing with his arms folded. I was struck by how much better my cousin looked after a week in Yorkshire. His face had browned and lost a certain weary edge. After a brief greeting, I asked if he had found anything in the woods.

"No. The park is large. A proper search might take days. There is probably a hut where the paraphernalia is stored by a clearing where the production is staged."

"You make it sound like the theater," I said.

"And so it is, exactly. I believe they used something akin to a balloon, a sort of enormous white sleeve of canvas which they filled with hot air, causing it to rise. They probably manipulated it with ropes, making it bob up and down. And the eyes were lanterns with green lenses."

Michelle shook her head. "Why on earth would someone go to all that trouble?"

"Oh, they had their reasons. Believe me, it is no idle jest."

"Sherlock," I asked, "can you make any sense of this whole business?"

His smile had a cold hard edge. "Oh yes, Henry. I have it, nearly all. But there remain a few details. One very glaring detail indeed."

"What is that?"

"A missing person, Henry. To be precise, a missing lover."

"The lover of Lady Verr–the man her husband was so jealous about."

"Exactly."

"How do you know...?" Michelle let her voice die away. Her brows had come together, and she briefly pursed her lips, lost in thought.

"Michelle?" I said. "Know what?"

Her blue eyes stared at me, her forehead creased. "Oh, nothing. Nothing, I think."

Holmes looked at her. "And what do you make of young Selton and Miss Marsh, Michelle?"

"They are a beautiful young couple who would seem to have almost every advantage, and yet..."

"But Selton's father disapproves," Holmes said.

"That makes it all the more enticing," she said.

I laughed. "You may be right. That's not what is holding Adam back. They obviously love one another, and each is obsessed with the other."

Michelle nodded. "She is certainly obsessed with him."

"It is mutual," I said. "But something truly has him worried."

Holmes shrugged. "Perhaps it is only his natural timidity, as well as these ominous letters. Then too, there was the discovery of Evans's corpse, someone he considered almost a friend. Little wonder he is troubled."

"Yes, and the prostitute has left him unsure and fearful. All the same, they do not explain his... despair. There is something else involved, something more he will not yet tell me."

Michelle shook her head. "Men can be such idiots, especially when it comes to women–it always comes back to that. I only hope... I want to like him, but I shall not forgive him if he breaks Diana's heart."

After lunch, Michelle was dragged away for the grand tour of the reptiles, but I was allowed to excuse myself. Later she joined me in the library.

She shook her head, her brow creased. "She is simply a very odd woman. I have never met anyone like her."

"Odd in a good way, or odd in...?"

"In a peculiar way–most peculiar. But 'good'? No, I don't think so."

"And did you see the rabbit swallowed?"

"Yes. Poor dumb creature. She was watching me closely the whole time."

"The rabbit?"

She laughed. "No, no! Arabella, of course. It seemed to be almost some examination, and I believe I passed. She talked incessantly for over an hour, and finally I felt as if I could bear it no longer. Something, too, about her eyes staring at me through those odd green

232

spectacles. I managed to tear myself away, even though I could tell she wanted me to stay. I was so weary of her!"

She was standing beside me, and I reached over and took her hand, then kissed her knuckles. "My poor darling." Her skin was almost white, and I could see the network of blue veins underneath.

She caressed my cheek lightly with her other hand, then touched my mustache, feeling the bristly ends. I opened my mouth to kiss her fingertips. "She seems so determined that we are to be friends. She acts as if... we are already intimate acquaintances. But I do not want to be her friend."

"And you needn't be."

She seemed to realize her fingers had just been in my mouth, and she leaned over to kiss me. It lasted a while but lacked the hungry passion of the night before. "Oh Henry, I do love you." She sighed. "I'm afraid I tire rather easily of women, especially women like her. I hope we don't have to stay here too long. I hope Sherlock figures it all out so we can be done with Diana's Grove and Lady Verr."

"I hope so too. I'm sorry you find her so tiresome. All the same, I am so glad you are here."

"So am I." She took my hand and pulled me to my feet. "Let's go out and walk somewhere, anywhere—just the two of us. Let's escape from everyone for a while and pretend we are alone on a holiday together."

"That is a wonderful idea."

Dinner that night reached another new culinary height, local lobsters with melted butter being the main course accompanied by chilled champagne of an outstanding vintage, and Michelle had noticeably become the latest object of Arabella's charm offensive.

Angela must have labored long over Diana and Arabella's dress and coiffure. Arabella wore a spectacular ivory silk embroidered with gold thread and with gold lace at the neck and cuffs. Gone was the usual necklace with its three smaller stones, replaced by an elaborate golden one with a single enormous green emerald surrounded by a few diamonds. Her red hair was all pinned up, setting off her long thin neck, and a tiny green stone shone in the center of each white earlobe. No one could deny her beauty and splendor, but the spectacles with the octagonal green lenses somewhat spoiled the effect.

Diana wore a green silk which brought out the color of her eyes. Her hair had been elaborately done up, curled and pinned, and someone had put a dab of rouge or powder on each cheek. One wayward brown-orange strand had escaped and fell in a curve across her broad smooth forehead. She and her aunt superficially resembled each other, and their narrow upturned noses were clearly a family trait. However, the two women also seemed fundamentally dissimilar, very *unlike*, and it was not merely the difference in age or the sophistication of one versus the innocence of the other. I was somehow absolutely certain Diana would be nothing like her aunt when she was near forty. I was, of course, prejudiced, but I thought Michelle in her simple electric-blue silk with her hair loosely bound up and no jewels, was by far the most beautiful woman at the table.

Arabella wished to talk about the Continent. She told of her adventures there, but she also wanted to discover more about Holmes's European cases and Michelle's and my time in France. The fact that Michelle and I each had a French father and an English mother fascinated her. All our efforts to direct the conversation elsewhere were turned aside. This meant that Diana, who had spent her entire life in Yorkshire, was left with little to say. Still, Michelle and I struggled to include her in the conversation.

Dessert was a spectacular chocolate cake of four layers. Hamswell's enormous hands in the white gloves set an elegant china plate before each of us. I chewed thoughtfully. "Delicious."

Arabella nodded. "It is good to know one can teach an old dog new tricks. The recipe is a French one for *gâteau au chocolat* which I insisted the cook try. This was not, of course, its maiden voyage, but her third attempt. The results are finally acceptable."

Michelle nodded. "More than acceptable."

Diana had taken a single bite, then set her fork down.

Arabella shook her head. "Oh Diana, you must try more than one bite."

"You know I have never cared for chocolate cake, and this is even more... sour."

Arabella sighed wearily. "What is to be done?" She cut off a small triangle of cake, toyed at it with her silver fork. "We simply must take you abroad, once and for all. The art, the architecture, the food, the music—it is human civilization at its best." She waited for a response, but Diana said nothing. "We have delayed long enough. Perhaps this summer..."

Diana looked up, the tension showing in her forehead and the small muscles around her mouth. "I don't want to go anywhere, and certainly not in the summer."

Arabella again shook her head and looked round the table. "As I said, what is to be done?"

Michelle smiled. "Summertime does seem brief and precious in England. There are advantages to going to Europe in the autumn or even winter."

Diana shrugged. "That would make more sense, but..."

"But what?" Arabella asked.

"I don't want to go anywhere. I want to be here. I... I want to be near Adam."

"*Adam*," Arabella said. "Oh my dear, I am certain he will not run away if you are gone for a month or two. You have had so little formal education. A tour of the Continent would be just the thing. Very broadening."

"You said we needed to save our money, to watch our expenses."

I could see that for once Diana was not going to simply yield to her aunt.

"We need not spend a fortune. Besides, I still have some hopes for Edgar. If they materialize, money will be no problem."

Diana went pale and clutched the handle of her fork tightly. "I'll not go anywhere with him–I'll not be near him! Never–do you understand?"

"I know he is eccentric, Diana, but really, he..."

Diana dropped her fork, stood up and clenched her fists. "Do you understand!"

Arabella sat up very straight. "I suppose I do."

"I am not a child–I am not–and it is time you learned that. My... my patience is not unlimited." Diana sat down, her mouth twisting as she struggled to compose herself. I wanted to applaud.

Michelle reached over and touched her gently on the wrist. "Perhaps if things work out as you wish, you might go with Mr. Selton in the autumn or winter."

Diana stared at her, and you could tell that had not occurred to her before. "Oh I hope so." She gave Michelle that same look of gratitude she had given me. "I–I am very tired, and I have something of a headache coming on. Would you please excuse me?"

We all said our good nights. After Diana had left, Arabella seemed momentarily subdued, but then she turned to Michelle and rolled her eyes upward. "I'll wager that you never languished after some young man when you were her age! You must have already been hard at work with your medical training."

Michelle's lips pulled outward in a characteristic smile. "I had begun my education by then, but you would lose that wager."

"But I thought you and Henry have only been married two or three years?"

"Oh, this was long before Henry." She set her hand on mine. "He was well worth the wait. His predecessors—especially the first one—were all wretched disappointments."

Arabella shook her head. "Adam is a nice enough young man, but I do wish something could be done about this hopeless infatuation with him."

Holmes had been listening carefully, pausing between each mouthful of cake and seeming to savor every bite. "What does it matter, madam? After all, if your dearest hope comes true and you are united in wedded bliss with the inestimable Mr. Caswall, Diana's Grove may be left behind, and you may go your own way." He was smiling, but I could see the restrained anger in his gray eyes. That was rather caustic for him—again I wanted to applaud!

Arabella smiled back. "That may be so, Mr. Holmes, but I do have a sense of familial obligation." She turned to Michelle, and her smile became radiant. "I think you are right about the best time to travel. I had already forgotten how beastly hot August in Italy can be!"

Ten

The next morning, incredibly, Lady Verr appeared before nine a.m.! She already had on her emerald necklace, a white silk dress and a long green coat. She was going to see Edgar Caswall. Hamswell would take her in the dog-cart.

"Things must be settled with Edgar once and for all. I know you can amuse yourselves without my company. I should be back by afternoon. And Diana, I apologize if I seemed rather overbearing last night. You must know that it is only because of my concern, because of my wishes for your well-being. You do understand, don't you?"

Diana smiled weakly and nodded.

"Oh, I hope you do. Good day, then: Mr. Holmes, Henry, Michelle." Three quick nods—her smile seemed to linger on Michelle— and then she was gone.

I shook my head. "I would not have believed it, if I had not seen it."

Diana gave a relieved sigh. "Thank heavens she didn't ask me to come. I think finally she understands."

Michelle and Diana decided to walk along the beach and go to Adam's house, while Holmes and I remained behind. I would have liked to come, but I wanted Michelle to have some time alone with the girl. Michelle paused before the tall doors of the great hall. "We shall bring Mr. Selton back with us," she said.

Diana smiled. "Oh, yes! He can join us for lunch."

I nodded. "Have a pleasant walk."

I stepped back. Angela closed the doors behind them. She wore her well-made black maid's dress, and her black hair was bound up in a tight bun. Her dark eyes caught mine, flashed a sort of brief, hard anger, and then she strode away. I frowned, reflecting that she had seemed curiously out of sorts for the last day or two.

She passed Mrs. Troughton on her way out, and I walked over to the older woman. "What do you make of her?" I asked. "She obviously doesn't like to show her emotions."

Mrs. Troughton nodded. She was so different, her complexion all pink and white, her face full and slightly worn, not olive and slender like Angela's. "She's an odd duck, all right. I don't trust her any more than Lady Verr. The two of them..." She shook her head. "Not like any lady's maid I've ever seen."

"You can hardly fault her for being Italian."

"She puts on airs. She acts as if she was a lady herself, a queen even. She keeps to herself. Can't be bothered with the likes of us commoners. Can't even eat with the rest of us." She shook her head. "I pray to God she and her mistress will go off to crazy Mr. Caswall's and leave us in peace. Do you think that might happen, Dr. Vernier?"

I shrugged. "It would certainly be ideal, but..." I remembered again Caswall's last visit, his curses and fury. "I don't think so."

"Pity—what a pity."

Holmes had settled in the library smoking his pipe, one of the large volumes on British marine life open before him. I sat in a large leather chair with a medical journal on my lap and promptly fell asleep. I had had more nightmares the night before.

Adam returned with the ladies later that morning. We had a long leisurely lunch. I was afraid Lady Verr would return and spoil things, but she was gone until two o'clock. By then Adam had left.

We were all in the library, and she appeared with a triumphant smile on her face, her cheeks flushed. "It went well," she said, "very well." She turned to Diana. "You may not have to put up with me forever, after all." She laughed, then asked if Michelle would join her in attending to her reptile menagerie. I knew this was the last thing Michelle wanted to do, but she was too polite to refuse. Arabella grasped her arm just above the elbow as she guided her toward the door. "Delilah, of course, will not eat again for several days."

The morning fog had lifted, and Holmes and I decided to walk into the woods. We had just stepped outside and advanced a few paces when Selton appeared on the path. He was practically running, his face flushed, but he came to a stop when he saw us, swayed slightly, then came forward.

"Thank God!" he exclaimed. "Mr. Holmes, you must—you must come with me. Please, can you?"

"Certainly, Mr. Selton. But what is wrong?"

Adam turned about and started forward, his long legs taking such strides it was work to keep up with him. "My room," he said. "My room."

"Your bedroom?" Holmes asked.

"Yes. I went there just now, when I got back. The window was open."

"Had you left the window open?"

"No. And there was a note on my desk."

Holmes nodded. "Ah yes, another note. And what did it say?"

"It said, 'The snake is from Diana.'"

Holmes laughed softly, even as he shook his head. "Not terribly original, but rather clever all the same."

"I left at once, Mr. Holmes! I closed the door and told the servants to keep out of my room."

"That was very wise of you, Mr. Selton."

"Do you think…?"

"We shall see. We shall see."

We walked to Lesser Hill in record time. Holmes paused before the oaken door to Adam's bedchamber. He had taken off his hat, but he still had his walking stick in hand. The room was on the ground floor, and someone outside could have easily climbed in. "I shall just have a look." He set his hand on the brass knob.

"I shall come with you," I said.

"As you wish. If we see a snake, keep well back and do not irritate it."

I laughed. "'Irritate it!'"

"I'll… I'll come too." Adam obviously did not want to come too.

"You needn't trouble yourself, Mr. Selton. It isn't necessary."

Holmes opened the door and went in. The room was small and on the spartan side. The bed had a metal frame, but it and the mattress were obviously custom-made, much longer than normal. A braided round wool carpet was by the bed, and there was a wardrobe, a tall dresser and a desk. Holmes went to the desk and lifted a sheet of paper.

"Cheap paper and a rather flowing hand. Doesn't tell us much." His eyes swept the room, seemed to see under and into things. He tapped lightly at the floor with the tip of his stick. "An adder's bite might kill a dog, a child or an elderly person, but we three are too large and healthy to suffer that fate. However, it would be most painful."

I felt something slithery trying to work its way up my spine. "How reassuring." Adam seemed fixed in the doorway.

"There is one most logical place for the snake to be."

Holmes stepped forward, then knelt down on the rug. The bed was set against the wall. Staying well back, Holmes raised the bedspread from the floor with his stick even as he bent over to look underneath. He held the spread up for a few seconds, then lowered it, nodded, and stood up.

"Well?" I asked.

"It is a male adder, quite a beauty, I think, although it was hard to tell because of the shadow. The contrast between the black and silver was striking."

"I have a revolver," Adam said. "We can... we can shoot it."

Holmes laughed. "You would damage your bed, the wall, who knows what else. That is not necessary. Would you please get me a laundry basket and a sheet."

Adam stared at him, his blue eyes opened a little too wide. "What?"

"A wicker laundry basket. If you have the rectangular kind with a top that opens and closes, that would be ideal. We would not have to worry about the handles. And any sort of sheet will do."

Adam nodded, then stepped back. "You're going to try to trap it?"

"Certainly." He stared closely at me. "How are you doing, Henry?"

I laughed. "Snakes are actually one of the things that do not particularly frighten me. Now if it was a giant cockroach, that would be another matter."

"Excellent! You can assist me."

Adam soon returned with the desired laundry basket and a sheet. "You may remain outside, Mr. Selton."

"I can stay if…"

"No need for that, and the fewer people in here, the better. Just close the door behind you."

Holmes opened the basket, then took out his pen knife and cut the leather straps that held the top on, leaving him with an open wicker box. "Help me move the bed. I want it out from the wall only an inch or so. Just slide it, ever so gently." He took one of the metal posts, I another, and we shimmied it out. "Very good. I want you to get onto the bed, then strike at the floor two or three times with the end of my stick. I believe that will flush him out." He had taken the basket and held it upside down.

I climbed up on the bed, which was rather spongy, then took his stick. I raised it up with my right hand, got the end into the space between the wall and the mattress and looked at Holmes. "Wait until I give the word, Henry. You should be safe there. A little further to the left. Lower the stick and feel about the floor before you strike hard. He should still be nearer the other end, but we want to make sure he has not moved."

I slowly lowered the stick and felt about with the end. "Nothing but wall or floor," I said.

Holmes nodded. "Excellent." He squatted slightly, balancing on the balls of his feet, the basket held on either side between his long fingers. "Whenever you are ready."

I raised the stick, brought it down hard. A loud clunk, then another and another. Holmes had stepped back, his gray eyes fixed on the ground—with his beak of a nose and those fierce eyes he truly resembled some bird of prey. He seemed to dance back, even as he almost hurled the basket down. "I have you!" His voice was exultant, and he smiled at me. He ran his fingers back through a lock of black hair which had come loose.

I climbed down off the bed.

"Can I come in?" Adam asked from behind the door.

"Not quite yet." Holmes took the sheet, unfolded it until it was about three feet square. "This will be akin to trapping an insect under a glass with a piece of paper. I will hold down the basket and take one end of the sheet. You take the other, and we shall work it under the basket. We'll be able to tell when we come to the snake, but it should be easy if we keep the sheet taut to keep the cloth under the snake."

He laid out the sheet next to the basket, then bent over, put one hand on the basket and took a corner of the sheet. I took the other corner. We pulled it tight, then started pulling it under the basket. I could tell when we came to the snake, but we kept the cloth tight and soon managed to keep going. Again, I could feel when we had come to the end of the snake. Soon the basket sat with the white sheet forming a neat frame around it.

"Very good, Henry. Now we must turn it over very carefully, making sure the sheet stays tight. We can then just substitute the basket top."

This was the trickiest part, and although I wasn't exactly frightened, I was tense. We each tried to keep the sheet taut on the two sides of the basket we held. I could tell as we moved the basket that the snake must be fairly good-sized! When it was done, Holmes seized the square lid and covered the basket, leaving the sheet in place.

"Bravo!" he said. "Well done, Henry. Mr. Selton, you may come in."

Adam stepped into the room, then glanced down at the basket. "You have him in there?"

"Yes."

"Let's get him out of the house. Then we can dispose of him."

Holmes's brow creased. "We shall take him to the trees and release him."

Adam shook his head. "He should be exterminated. He's venomous!"

Holmes sighed. "As I told you before, adders only bite if provoked–as this one surely was. He is as much the victim as you, Mr. Selton. I must insist that you oblige me in this matter. After all, it is I who have taken care of the serpent for you."

Adam drew in his breath slowly. "All right, Mr. Holmes. I am certainly in your debt. You may do as you please."

Holmes smiled. "Very good! I'm certain the poor beast has had more than enough of bedrooms and wooden floors for the day."

Holmes and I carefully carried the basket outside, each with one hand holding a handle, the other the top. Occasionally I felt the adder moving about. We came out into the sun, then walked across the grass toward the trees.

We set down the basket, then Holmes gestured for me to step back. He bent over, then like some magician, quickly wrenched away the sheet which also sent the wicker top flying. We were in the shade, but I could see the adder curled in the basket's interior, a vivid black and silver-gray, with that distinctive zigzag pattern along its back. The snake's head reared up, it's split tongue flickering out, even as Holmes backed away and kicked over the basket with his boot. The snake slithered out, moving remarkably fast as it swerved away into the trees, soon to be lost amidst the jagged green leaves of a large fern.

Holmes smiled at me. "Very well done, indeed, Henry. A good day's work." He glanced at Adam. "That was certainly better than trying to beat the poor creature to death with a stick."

Adam shrugged, then shook his head. "Who... who is doing this?"

Holmes's smile faded. "I have some idea."

"Tell me–then tell me."

"It is too soon, Mr. Selton. But I am very close. I think I can promise that you will know... by next Monday."

I frowned. "May Day?"

Adam pulled off his hat and ran his fingers through his black hair. "Someone has just tried to kill me."

Holmes shook his head. "No. They only wanted to frighten you."

"But they put a venomous snake in my bedroom!"

"And left you a warning note. If they really wanted to kill you, they would not have left the note. Besides, as I said, an adder bite would be unlikely to kill any of us—especially you given your weight and size."

Adam stared into the trees. "This is all... a nightmare. I..." He drew in his breath. "I must get away—London—Derbyshire, somewhere else. They don't want me in Yorkshire. They don't want me... with Diana."

"If you run away, you will be giving them what they want."

Adam looked at him, his eyes suddenly angry. "Oh, so what? Who cares? I am just weary of this all. Enough is enough!" He turned and started back for the house, his steps gargantuan. "I can spend the night in Whitby—I can take the first train out in the morning."

Holmes followed him. "Wait—wait!" Adam reached the doorway, then turned to face Holmes. "I cannot pretend it is safe here for you, but someone else is actually in much more danger. She is the real target, and she is much likelier to be killed than you."

Adam seemed to freeze for a moment, even as he grew pale. "You cannot mean Diana?"

"I do mean Diana."

"But why would anyone want to hurt her? I don't understand, Mr. Holmes."

"I cannot tell you, Mr. Selton, not yet. You simply have to trust me. Things are coming to a head, and all should be resolved shortly."

"But–but–I shall take Diana with me! I shall protect her."

"You cannot. Our adversary is clever and resourceful. Danger would follow Miss Marsh wherever she goes. The best thing you can do for her is to stay here and pretend nothing has happened. I shall be watching and waiting. I have it all, almost all, but I have no proof. I must catch them in the act. That is the only way."

Adam hurled down his woolen cloth cap, then put both of his huge hands in his curly black hair, clutching at his head. "Oh Lord–*Lord.*"

"It is for Diana, Mr. Selton. Only a little while longer. Help me save her."

He lowered his hands and took in a massive breath that went on and on forever. A brief smile pulled at his lips. "I always said I would do anything for her. I wanted to prove that I loved her. Well, now I have my chance, it seems. This hardly… seems so much. Surely not. I shall stay."

Holmes smiled, then reached out and gripped Adam's upper arm. "Very good, Mr. Selton." He glanced at me. "Come, Henry." He started toward the path that led along the cliffs facing the sea back to Diana's Grove.

I followed silently until we were well away from the house. "It is time you told me a thing or two."

"Surely you must have some idea?"

I gazed briefly at the earth, then the sea: clouds hung over the moors and Castra Regis atop its peak; the deep blue of the waters was broken up by whitecaps. "Arabella. It has to be Arabella."

Holmes laughed softly. "Oh very good, Henry. We shall make a detective of you yet."

"But I don't understand any of it! It is only… I don't like her, and I don't trust her. From the first moment I met her… But I hardly imagined her as a murderer."

"Sometimes our instincts can serve us better than our reason. Or rather, they are the precursor to reason."

"You must explain."

"And so I shall, but not yet, not quite yet. And there is still that one piece. We have to see Edgar Caswall. We have put it off long enough."

"But there is hardly time today."

"Tomorrow then. Tomorrow. Then I shall explain."

When we came through the trees and saw Diana's Grove before us, a tall woman in a blue dress was waiting in the shade before the doorway, her arms folded. Michelle lowered her hands and started forward when she saw us. Her smile was brief, tentative. I reached out to take her hand, and she squeezed tightly.

"There you are at last. I need to talk to you." She glanced at Sherlock, her eyes worried.

"I shall be inside."

"Wait." Michelle's voice was very soft. "I... Let me talk to Henry first, and then... we may want to talk to you."

His gray eyes stared closely at her, then he nodded.

"We won't go far." She took my hand and started down the path Holmes and I had just taken.

"What's the matter? Are you all right? Is Diana all right?"

"Nothing has happened. Everyone is all right."

"Then what's wrong?"

She looked at me, her eyes troubled. "I need to–I need to speak to you about it. Then you can decide if we should tell Sherlock. It seems so... base. Unworthy."

"For God's sake, Michelle, what is wrong?"

She drew in her breath deeply. Her hand still held mine. "It is about Arabella. And Angela."

"What about them?"

She stared closely, her eyes questioning me.

"What about them?" I repeated.

"You haven't noticed anything?"

"Noticed what?"

A quick humorless smile pulled at her lips. "Sherlock said he was looking for a missing piece. A lover, the one who drove Lord Verr to kill himself. A black-haired lover."

I suddenly stopped walking. Michelle and I stared at one another. "What are you saying?"

Again an uncomfortable smile pulled at her mouth. "I am talking about a Sapphic lover, Henry. You do know about... Sapphic lovers?"

I drew my breath in slowly. "Yes. I do."

"Have you never noticed how Angela looks at Arabella? And she is hardly... a typical maid. Oh, perhaps I'm only imagining it, but..."

I gave my head a fierce shake. "No. No, you are not."

"I... I have seen such things before. In high society. Some women are so miserable, their husbands cold and indifferent. It is hardly surprising that they turn elsewhere for love, and women are, perhaps by nature, kinder and more affectionate. I knew a very well-bred lady who also had... feelings for her maid. Feelings which were reciprocated. Oh Henry, should we tell Sherlock? It seems like mere gossip, like malice, like..."

"We have to tell him."

She drew in her breath slowly, then nodded. We turned and went back toward the house. We had not gone far, and he was waiting for us. We three started walking. Michelle turned to me. "You tell him." I was much more direct than Michelle had been.

As he listened, Holmes's steps slowed, became more and more deliberate—briefly he was paralyzed, one foot in the air—then he set it down, clutched at his chin with his long fingers, and raised the other hand to silence me. We were all quiet. Somewhere in the woods a squirrel chattered, and we could hear the faint wind stirring the new green leaves in the trees all around us.

At last a sort of groan of laughter slipped from Holmes's lips. He smiled at us both, his eyes fixed on Michelle. "I am the greatest of all imbeciles. Thank God you have come, Michelle, to save me from my own colossal stupidity. We all have our blind spots. Who, after all, would have thought...? But I should have considered the possibility. It was a failure of the imagination. But it is my job to go beyond what is normal, what is conventional!–to consider all the alternatives."

She stared at him, her eyes troubled. "You think it is true, then?"

"Of course it is true. It accounts for everything–*everything*–including the peculiar behavior of Lady Verr and Angela for the last couple of days." His lips twitched briefly upward, and Michelle's cheek began to redden. "But most of all, it perfectly explains Lord Verr's suicide. Bad enough to discover that your wife has been cheating on you for years–but cheating with her maid under your own roof? What could possibly be more humiliating?"

Michelle seemed to wince, and she looked away.

"Little wonder he shot himself. Of course she was goading him, encouraging him."

I sighed softly. "Poor devil. I can only imagine..."

Michelle clutched for my hand. "Oh Henry, surely..."

"I know, Michelle–I know. I do have my share of unreasonable fears and worries, but that is not something that will ever keep me awake at night. I trust you, my darling–I trust you absolutely."

One side of her mouth rose in a half smile. "As well you should. I feel the same way."

Holmes shook his head. "I could not possibly tell Mr. Selton my suspicions. He would be incapable of hiding anything from anyone–

least of all Lady Verr. I probably should not have said anything even to you, Henry. Regardless, you must both try to pretend nothing has changed, that things are the same as always. You must do this for another day or two at least. Lady Verr came back in good spirits today, but I am certain she is deluding herself about Caswall's intentions."

"How can you know that?" I asked.

"Because she is dealing with a lunatic! A lunatic who seems more interested in the niece than the aunt. There is little time. I must convince Lady Verr of her error about Caswall to flush her out. If she thinks things are finished with him, then she will act, once and for all."

"Act?" I said. "What do you mean."

Holmes's smile was icy. "She will try to kill Miss Marsh. She will offer her as a sacrifice to the White Worm."

Michelle looked dismayed, and I shook my head wildly. "But you said—you said there is no White Worm!"

Holmes shook his head. "I did not say that."

"That thing we saw—you said it was a fake, a fraud!"

"And so it certainly was."

"But then... There is no White Worm," I groaned.

"Do not be so sure of that, Henry. Oh, I do not believe in a prehistoric serpent a hundred feet long living in a hole in the ground. However, something has half-devoured the livestock and Evans."

"For God's sake—what is it?"

"I have some... ideas." He raised his right hand, spreading apart his fingers. "But enough idle speculation. We have all had more than enough to digest for one day!"

By the afternoon of the next day, the weather had changed dramatically. Massive gray clouds had swept in, obliterating the sun, and the temperature had dropped several degrees. Holmes was still resolved to see Caswall, but we decided to take the dog-cart. Better that than lumbering uphill and down on foot in pouring rain.

Arabella gladly gave us her permission to use the cart, but her smile faded when she heard our destination. Holmes explained that we had promised Caswall that we would view his collections of weaponry and dead animals, and our visit was long overdue. Her smile returned, although a more ironic variant. "You must be on your best behavior with Edgar, Mr. Holmes. It is in everyone's interests that our marriage goes forward."

Holmes nodded. "Undoubtedly."

As we took the road uphill, the clouds became blacker still. We had not seen a thunderstorm in Yorkshire yet, but the sky certainly looked threatening enough. The landscape grew bleaker, the few trees smaller, stunted-looking, and the grass and heather brown and squat. These were the high moors of *Wuthering Heights*, the kind of blasted setting where it made sense that you would find elemental forces and troubled spirits like Heathcliff, Catherine–or Edgar Caswall. The tower of Castra Regis with its primitive gray-black stone fitted the mood. Set high against the dramatic stormy sky, we could also see a brownish shape quivering and dancing–Caswall's hawk kite.

"I can't believe he is flying a kite in this kind of weather."

Holmes was wearing his rustic woolen walking hat and a black macintosh. His lips formed the customary sardonic smile. "The sky god is not troubled by storms–to the contrary, he enjoys them. It is well that he is using wire, rather than string. String would never hold in these winds."

A wagonette bearing six people approached us. It could only have come from the castle, and one of the women looked like a maid I had seen there before. We had to pull to the side for them to get around us. "Where are you going?" Holmes shouted to the driver.

"Anywhere away from that bloody lunatic!" The man shook the reins, urging the big draft horse on.

Holmes glanced at me. "I wonder what has happened."

A cold drizzle had begun to fall, and a couple of times I had to grab at my hat to keep it from flying away. The black, dead oak on the ridge seemed to have faded into the dark sky, the contrast much less stark than our last visit when the sky had been a brilliant blue. We reached the main doorway at last, and I waited under the arch while Holmes tied up the horse.

He touched it gently on the neck. "It will be easier going downhill, old fellow." He joined me, then raised the huge brass knocker and thwacked the door twice.

I wanted nothing more than to stand before a blazing fire and dry out some. Surely Caswall would not be outside on his roof with a major storm approaching? But my hopes were immediately dashed by the old butler who told us the master was "up top." Holmes and I plodded after the poor old man up all those winding stone stairs and stepped back out into the elements. The wind hurled cold drizzle in my face, and again I had to grab at my hat.

"This is insanity, all right," I muttered.

Caswall stood a few feet away at the north side enveloped in a heavy black cloak, his back to us. Next to him was the kite hoist, but the wire was hardly visible. Nearby was a small stone shelter with a roof built into the wall, a place where a guard or someone else might stand out of the wind and rain, but Caswall had not taken advantage of it.

Holmes and I went forward, while the servant quickly retreated. With the wind, Caswall could have never heard us coming, but all the same, he turned. His face was very pale against the dark sky and his black garments. The storm blew his black hair all about, and his mono-brow was a long black smear above his nose. He smiled triumphantly and folded his arms, waiting for us subjects to come pay homage.

"Holmes—Watson—you've come at last. I've been expecting you."

"Have you?" Holmes said.

"Oh yes." He opened up his arms, and in one hand was a grotesque little statue of a naked woman carved in white stone, all swollen hips and breasts. "Now that you are here, I can send the last message."

He withdrew a metal disk and connected the tiny statue to it with a piece of wire. He stepped over to the hoist, threaded the disk onto the wire, then stepped back. The little statue danced and bobbed for a few seconds. Since it was stone, I wondered if it might be too heavy to go up, but sure enough, soon it seemed to skip up a notch or two, jerked briefly, then began to hop its way sporadically up along the wire.

"Go and be destroyed, harlot bitch!" Caswall snarled.

Holmes and I looked at each other. Neither of us could think of any appropriate response, so we kept silent. Caswall seemed even more deranged than last time. Again I thought of Caligula and the other mad Roman emperors after Augustus.

"I see a little inclement weather does not bother you," Holmes said.

Caswall shook his head fiercely. "Certainly not."

In the distance, a particularly black cloud briefly lightened. My eyes swept quickly about the top of the tower. "Would the castle happen to have a lightning rod?" I asked.

"Lightning rod!" He glowered at me.

"Yes, it's a device which…"

"I know what a lightning rod is, Watson. I am the master of the sky and the elements, the god of storms and thunder! What need has a being such as I of a lightning rod?" He began to laugh in earnest, and the sound made the back of my neck feel cold.

Holmes set one gloved hand over the brim of his hat to keep it on. "Mr. Caswall, we have come to congratulate you. We have heard something about a marriage with Lady Verr."

Caswall's lips twisted into a sneering smile. "So she thinks."

"Is she mistaken, then?"

Caswall nodded. "Oh yes! Do you think I would willingly put my head in the noose? Let the dirty little whore..." He launched into a series of vicious curses and foul language, which made me draw back slightly. Holmes, however, managed to remain completely impassive before this torrent of abuse directed at Lady Verr.

"Very clever, Mr. Caswall. You tricked her into thinking you were going to marry her."

"She dared to speak of ultimatums—and she takes me for an utter fool." He laughed sharply. "She spoke to me of love, Mr. Holmes, and she again offered herself to me. She is tempting bait, but could any sane man possibly believe that a woman like her could care for anyone but herself? She is utterly and totally selfish."

My mouth twisted into a smile. I looked away, and my mouth formed the words, *You should know.*

"No, no, I am not so easily caught, but I wanted to lure her to complacency so I could have my revenge."

"Revenge? What has she done?" I asked.

He gave me an incredulous stare. "She is a monster, Watson—a monster. She has a dual nature. She is all voluptuousness and honey, all white limbs and curves and tempting flesh, but she is also a monster who would suck the life from a man and consume him entirely. I have finally figured it all out. The old story was true. She *is* the White Worm. She can become the great white serpent which dwells in that dark hole in the ground. She has lived for centuries, taking different forms, sleeping for a while in her lair, but always she returns to her alluring female shape to seek a man to devour. The knight thought he had killed her, but she eventually grew a new head. However, her time has finally come. I am going to eliminate the curse of the White Worm once and for all." His black eyes had an exultant glee.

"And how are you going to do that?" Holmes asked.

"It is quite simple. Modern technology will provide the means to obliterate this ancient threat."

"What are you talking about?" I asked.

"Dynamite, Watson—a vast quantity of dynamite! I shall have it taken to the grove on May Day, to the sacrificial site, and dropped into the creature's lair. When it is ignited, she will be destroyed once and for all, along with her hiding place. Both will be blown to bits—pieces of her stinking bloody flesh hurled across the countryside! Diana's Grove—the Lair of the White Worm—will be gone forever."

Holmes stared at him, a tenuous smile working at his lips. "Not exactly subtle, but that is certainly one way of approaching the problem."

"Once she is gone, there will be no one to interfere with Diana."

I struggled to keep my face neutral.

"How could the old harlot ever imagine I would prefer her over a youthful virgin? No, no, I was willing to take her if she would assist me, but she lied to me. She told me she could make Diana submit, that she would make her understand, but all that time, she was actually doing her best to turn her against me. How else to explain that the girl could resist? No, only Arabella's interference can explain the failure of my powers. She is, indeed, a goddess, but even a goddess can be destroyed by a sufficient amount of dynamite." He smiled and nodded.

Holmes's nostrils flared, and his eyes briefly caught mine. The sky behind Caswall lit up for an instant, and then within a few seconds, a long low rumble followed. "Exactly how much dynamite are we talking about, Mr. Caswall?"

He shrugged. "About a ton. It took two carts to deliver it yesterday."

Holmes drew in his breath slowly. "And where might that dynamite be just now?"

"In a safe place, Mr. Holmes. It is in my tower, at the very top, a large chamber just beneath us."

Holmes drew in his breath. "I see."

A black cloud seemed to be advancing along the ridge toward us. This time I saw the lightning, a jagged, impossibly bright streak of blue-white light flowing out of the clouds down to the brown barren ridge. The crash was almost instantaneous, and I flinched wildly.

Holmes again looked at me, then at Caswall. "Well, sir, this has been most interesting, but I am afraid we must be running along."

"But you have only just arrived! I can finally show you my weapons, I can show you my collections."

"Another time, sir—the storm is—something of an inconvenience, and it reminds me—we have business elsewhere. Henry." He turned and started for the doorway. I quickly followed him. Rain had begun to pour down in earnest.

"You must come back again soon!" Caswall cried behind us.

We practically ran down the stairs and strode into the great hall. Holmes grasped the old butler by the arm. "Who is left here in the castle?"

The old man glanced at an equally tiny old woman all in black standing nearby. "Only me and my wife, sir. The others are gone."

"You must get away—there is dynamite in the tower—the lightning storm may set it off."

The old man shook his head. "We cannot leave the master."

Holmes gave me a wild glance, then drew in his breath resolutely. "We don't have time for this. I shall take him, Henry—you take his wife." With that, he stooped and swung the butler up over his shoulder like a sack of flour. I scooped up the old woman and carried her in my arms. She weighed hardly anything. Neither of them cried out or struggled. They must have been relieved.

We made it through the front door, leaving it open, and Holmes put the old man in the back of the dog-cart, I the old woman. They sagged against one another. Holmes quickly untied the horse while the rain and wind lashed our faces. I sat beside him as he took up the reins. "Surely if the castle has lasted this long…"

Holmes shook his head, even as he took the reins. "The stone tower might take a lightning strike, but no one has ever stored a ton of dynamite up there before."

A great crash of lightning made me bolt upright, and I waited an instant before letting my shoulders sag. "He is certainly absolutely crazy."

We were going downhill, and Holmes let the slope assist us, driving much faster and certainly more recklessly than on the way up. All the same, it seemed painfully slow As we left the castle further and further behind, I felt myself gradually relax. The wind lessened once we reached the base of the ridge, but the rain had soaked our hats and macintoshes. Occasionally the barren brown moors would light up, and the crash of thunder would follow in an instant.

"Maybe he isn't…" I began.

Again the landscape lit up, again the crash—which swelled, which grew and changed—became impossibly loud. The landscape brightened even more, but with a reddish tint, even as a hot wind came howling through the rain. The horse cried out, and Holmes struggled to control it. I turned but the fireball was finished. Black smoke poured forth from where the castle had stood. Something hit my hat, then my hand. I raised my hand, felt something else hit my back, my leg. The deluge of stones lasted only a few seconds, and luckily all were small.

Holmes managed to calm the horse at last. I drew in my breath and shook my head. The cold rain poured down around us. I looked up again at the top of the hill where Castra Regis had stood for so long. The smoke obscured everything, but I doubted much of the structure remained. Caswall would have died instantly. One of the old servants groaned softly.

Holmes shook his head. "I am glad we did not linger."

This set me laughing uncontrollably. I knew it was excessive.

"And we shall not be able to see his collections." This I also found hilarious, and Holmes laughed nervously as well. At last he shook his head. "That certainly settles things for Lady Verr, once and for all. Edgar Caswall's fortune is lost to her."

I had a final look at the smoking ruins against the dark stormy sky. Something was gone, something was missing–the kite, the hawk kite. Holmes shook the reins, and we started down the path through the tall brown grass.

Eleven

&

A t his request, we dropped the sodden old butler and his wife off at a nearby farm where they knew the owner. When we returned to Diana's Grove that afternoon and told the ladies what had happened, Arabella only laughed, convinced this was some bizarre attempt at humor. Holmes and I grimly insisted we were not joking.

Diana's eyes were open wide, revealing the pale blue-green circles of the irises. Her mouth pulled out ever so slightly at the corners. "Remember that terrible crash we heard, the one that was so loud? We thought it was only thunder very near, but…"

Arabella's smile slowly faded. "You say he had a store of dynamite in his tower? For God's sake, why would he have had dynamite?" She looked at me, then at Holmes.

"He wanted to destroy the White Worm, Lady Verr, and he associated you with that mythical creature. He was convinced that its lair was indeed at Diana's Grove, and he planned to drop the dynamite down the pit and blow it to pieces."

An odd pained laugh slipped from Diana's lips, and she immediately covered her mouth with her slender white hand. Michelle stepped nearer and grasped her arm lightly just above the elbow.

Arabella shook her head, even as her hands formed fists. "*That bloody damned stupid fool.*" Her words were full of venom. "I should have…" She laughed once, then again, then louder still in a long rippling melodic run.

Holmes frowned. "Madam?"

"You must be enjoying this, Mr. Holmes. Seeing all my clever plans and stratagems go up in smoke–literally up in smoke–all in an instant."

Holmes gave his head a brusque shake. "Not in the least. Your plans have nothing to do with it. I never enjoy seeing anyone die unnecessarily, even the worst of men, and in Caswall's case, his obvious insanity was a mitigating factor. It's also something of a miracle that none of his servants were killed as well."

"Ah, Edgar–for once he actually had me fooled. And of course, he was deluded to the end, or perhaps merely ignorant to the point of idiocy. One cannot simply dump dynamite into a pit–it must be treated with great care, and in this case, the pit always has water at the bottom which would soak the dynamite, probably rendering it useless. And then to actually store the dynamite at the top of his tower! Such colossal stupidity." She shook her head, then smiled again fiercely. "No more stupid than willingly marrying a madman! I suppose I should be grateful to him for sparing me from my folly."

Holmes stared at her, his brow creased. "Perhaps you should, madam."

Again that rippling laughter. She shook her head. "You must excuse me. I… I need to compose myself." She strode from the room.

Angela had been seated nearby, dressed all in black, silent and impassive as ever, but she rose and quickly followed her mistress. Her dark eyes were carefully neutral, but her full lips curved slightly upward at the corners.

Diana laughed once, a sound different from any I had ever heard her make. Michelle squeezed her arm. "Are you all right, my dear?"

Diana shook her head. "I feel so strange. I did not like Mr. Caswall–I must admit I was afraid of him. I am glad he is gone, but I would not wish such a death on anyone." She shook her head.

I nodded. "I think that is how we all feel, Diana. Crazy as he was... Before today, I had not realized just how much he hated your aunt."

Again she shook her head. "Oh I don't understand–I don't understand at all! Aunt Arabella and Mr. Caswall–how can you talk of love and marriage and actually hate someone! None of this makes any sense to me at all."

"That is because you lack guile or duplicity, Miss Marsh," Holmes said. "And despite what you may sometimes think, innocence is a virtue."

"Dinnertime is at hand," I said, "and I for one could certainly use an aperitif, a particularly strong one."

Holmes nodded. "An excellent suggestion."

We went down to the great hall. Holmes had a whiskey and soda, I a brandy, while Michelle and Diana drank more lady-like pale dry sherry. We spoke no more of Caswall, and a certain normalcy had finally returned, when Adam Selton came striding into the room, his wool cap in his hand, his brown macintosh glistening from the rain.

"Have you heard the news–have you heard about Castra Regis?"

Diana went to him and grasped his upper arms with both her hands, not caring that she was getting her dress wet. "Oh, yes!"

Holmes and I had to explain things all over again. Adam kept shaking his head and saying, "I cannot believe it."

"You must stay for dinner, Adam—you must!" Diana exclaimed.

He smiled. "Gladly."

We went to the dining room. Diana sent Mrs. Troughton to inquire after her aunt, but she soon returned, shaking her head. We all sat down, and Mrs. Troughton served us the soup. Hamswell was nowhere to be seen. The soup plates had been cleared away when Arabella came into the room. She had changed into one of her white silk gowns, set off as usual by her emerald necklace and her green-tinted spectacles.

"I have come to my senses. I am hungry, after all."

I murmured some politeness. We all sat a bit stiffly and silently, while Mrs. Troughton set a large blue-and-white china plate before us each. Adam Selton had a grave look on his face. "Lady Verr, I must offer you my condolences for your loss."

Diana's eyes opened very wide, she looked briefly stricken, but none of us said anything. Arabella's mouth formed a mocking smile which gradually faded away as she stared at Adam. Creases appeared in her forehead. At last she said, "That is very kind of you, Adam." Somehow I felt as if she were truly seeing him for the first time.

"Since we were neighbors, I made an effort to make Caswall's acquaintance, but for some reason he seemed to dislike me. I don't know why. We only met twice." He shrugged. "All the same, what a terrible tragedy." He stared at Sherlock. "Do you know why he had all that dynamite, Mr. Holmes?"

Holmes's gray eyes swept round the table, and he shrugged. "Clearly it was a manifestation of his insanity."

Arabella said nothing. Her eyes were still fixed on Adam Selton.

She was quite subdued during the rest of the meal. Always before she had dominated at the dinner table, actively wielding her beauty, charm and wit. Now she seemed to be the observer, although clearly at times her thoughts turned inward. After the meal she excused herself and thanked Adam again for his thoughtfulness. Those green octagonal lenses shifted to Holmes, even as a brief smile pulled at her lips, and with a curtsy, she was gone. There was something in her stride which revealed this was not a vanquished woman.

We chatted for a while, and then Holmes glanced at me. "Dr. Vernier, I must admit to a craving for the forbidden fruit. I think I shall step outside for a cigarette."

I glanced at Michelle who was talking to Diana and Adam. "Perhaps I shall join you."

The great hall was all darkness and shadow, save for one feeble lamp, and Holmes pushed open the tall entrance doors. I had expected pouring rain or at least drizzle, but the clouds had briefly parted, revealing a swath of black sky with bright stars and the nearly full orb of the moon. Its light shone on the grassy expanse before the house.

Holmes withdrew a cigarette and struck a match against the rough stone by the door. He drew in twice, getting the tip aglow, then exhaled. He stepped forward onto the path and looked up at the moon.

I shook my head. "It is spectacular here. You never see a sky like that in London."

"No."

The wind was stirring the nearby trees ever so gently, and we could also hear the muted roar of the sea.

"It's nice to have a quiet moment. I still cannot... It is difficult to believe that Caswall and that entire castle are gone."

Holmes raised his hand, the cigarette held loosely between thumb and forefinger. "Perhaps, but we practically saw its destruction with our own eyes."

I thought of Caswall buried somewhere beneath the rubble, crushed, obliterated, and the cool air suddenly felt cold. "Is it—is it almost over?"

"Oh yes, Henry. One way or another, it is almost over. Unfortunately, now comes the most dangerous time. Lady Verr is desperate. There is no telling exactly what she will do. She may decide to… improvise." He laughed softly. "Sometimes improvisations are inspired, other times they are foolhardy. I have my suspicions."

"I thought you said she would try to sacrifice Diana."

"That is still likely, but as I said, she may come up with some other scheme."

"Why ever would she want to kill her own niece?"

"Oh Henry, isn't that obvious by now?"

My mind felt leaden, and an odd fear settled in my chest, seeming to slow my thoughts even more. "I suppose so." I suddenly laughed. "That is why it is 'just right'! Why Diana's income is just right. If she dies, Arabella will have Diana's Grove to herself, as well as the money. She is Diana's nearest—her only—living relative. It is not a great fortune, but it would allow her to live comfortably, especially here in Yorkshire." I laughed again. "She and Angela could live happily ever after."

"Very good, Henry."

"And I suppose… Oh, of course. She wanted to scare Adam away. If he married Diana, her estate and money would all go to him, as her husband. Diana's Grove would then be out of Arabella's reach forever. Oh Lord—now I see what you mean. Caswall had a fortune, and if she had married him, then she could have let Diana and Adam go—they would not have mattered anymore."

"You are doing very well, Henry. Very well indeed. Lady Verr was being prudent. She had Caswall as her major objective, but Diana's

Grove was her fallback option. This grand cult of the White Worm must provide a creative and amusing diversion for a woman like her, besides assisting in her plans. Perhaps she once thought she might be able to simply dominate Diana, to control her, but I think it has become clear by now that the young lady has a mind of her own, that she will not be her aunt's minion. No, no–safer by far just to be rid of her."

"Oh Lord," I moaned.

Holmes reached out with his right hand and grasped my wrist firmly. "We will not let that happen, Henry–we will not."

I shook my head. "No."

He stared at me. He wore no hat, and the moon shone on the long expanse of his forehead and the black hair combed back. His thin lips formed a weary smile. "Human iniquity does grow tiresome, does it not?"

"Oh yes."

"I am glad you and Michelle are here." He laughed softly. "Especially her–she saw in an instant the relationship between Lady Verr and Angela. I still feel like a dunderhead. I do know about such things, Henry. There was actually another case where… Regardless, Michelle provided the last piece of the puzzle."

A soft sort of wavering, moaning cry sounded somewhere in the trees, making me start slightly.

"Only a barn owl," Holmes said, "searching for supper."

I drew in my breath slowly. The clouds had again obscured the moon, throwing the grassy expanse before the limestone facade of the dwelling back into shadow. "But it's nearly over? By May Day morning–by Monday, it should all be resolved?"

Holmes took a final draw on his cigarette, then dropped the butt and crushed it under the heel of his boot. "I think so, Henry, but one can never be sure." He gave a brief sharp laugh. "A day or two ago, I could never have predicted Edgar Caswall's fate. The dynamite was a missing unknown. I hope there are no others. All the same... I hope to show Lady Verr that she is not the only one who can improvise."

When we went back inside, we found Diana, Michelle and Adam sipping some port and talking. Angela sat in the big leather chair in the corner working industriously on the usual embroidery.

"It has stopped raining," I announced.

Adam finished the last of his port, then pulled out his watch. "I should be leaving."

Diana leaned over and set her long, slim hand on his brawny forearm, her eyes fixed on his. "Must you?"

"I suppose I might stay a while longer."

Who could reject such an appeal from a beautiful woman? I thought.

"Good." She gave his arm a squeeze, then sat back in the sofa. "There is something I wanted to ask you."

"Yes?"

She looked at him, then took a quick sip of port. "I am trying to decide if I should send Aunt Arabella away."

To my side, I saw Holmes stiffen, then rise up. I realized he must be on the balls of his feet. Gradually he sank down.

"Send her away?"

Michelle frowned, and I could see her eyes shift to the corner where Angela sat.

"This sounds like something you two might best discuss alone," I said. "Perhaps the rest of us should leave."

"It's not a matter of discussion," Diana said. "I just wondered what you think, Adam."

"It seems harsh given that Mr. Caswall has just... passed away."

"Oh, I don't mean this instant—or this week, or next—I just thought... I have been thinking about it a long while, even before Dr.

Vernier mentioned the idea." She glanced up at me. "Remember?"

"Yes," I said.

"Summer is coming, and I would like…" She was staring straight into his face. "Oh, I want to be free—I just want to be free! I want to be myself."

"But her husband left her nothing. She has no money."

"She can have some of mine! I have more than enough to live the way I want to live. I shall gladly give her a monthly sum. So long as she does not try to find lodgings in London, it should not be terribly dear. I don't think she has ever truly been happy at Diana's Grove, and I—neither have I. It would be best for both of us."

Adam had a worried look. "I suppose so."

Diana shook her head, her smile bitter. "Or do you also want me to remain a child forever? Do you want me never to grow up, never to become a woman?"

"I…" He lowered his eyes, then stared thoughtfully at her. His mouth suddenly pulled into a smile. "I like you as a woman."

She laughed, then squeezed his forearm again. "I think that is the nicest thing you have ever said to me."

"You must do what you think is best."

She shook her head. "Don't say that—don't be stupid." She stared at him. "Oh Adam, what is to become of us?" The question was a simple one, but full of anguish.

He looked away. "I don't know."

She bit at her lower lip. "I wish you did."

He swallowed once. "I have to go."

She nodded. "Very well. But will you come back tomorrow? Come for lunch, and if it is nice afterwards we can walk in the woods. We can show the doctors and Mr. Holmes the bluebells and what remains of the daffodils by the old stream. The daffodils are past their peak but still beautiful."

He smiled. "Of course, I'll come." He said his farewells and left.

Holmes glanced at Angela in the distant corner, then at me, and said softly, "Now all the bridges are truly burned."

Arabella appeared at ten the next morning, something which I did not think augured well. She mentioned that Hamswell would be driving her in the dog-cart to Whitby where she had business. As was her custom, she was elegantly dressed in white, and her cheeks had a rosy flush. She seemed in good spirits—certainly she was not mourning for Edgar Caswall!

As usual, both Diana and Mrs. Troughton seemed much happier once she had departed. Diana's spirits were high, obviously in anticipation of Adam's arrival and our afternoon walk in the woods. The weather was cooperating, the clouds and fog having lifted to reveal blue sky and bright sunshine. However, as noon came, then twelve thirty, and finally one, her happiness faded, replaced by discomposure. We finally ate lunch together a little after one.

When we had finished, Michelle reached over and touched her hand. "Come, my dear. Let's get dressed and be off."

"Should we go alone, then?"

Michelle shook her head. "No. Let's go and find out what is keeping that lout."

Diana laughed in spite of herself, and her good spirits returned. We walked along the ridge facing the sea, Michelle and Diana in the lead, Holmes and I a few paces behind. Holmes's face had truly bronzed after two weeks in Yorkshire: gone was that pale, sickly wraith I had found at Baker Street earlier in April. However, he was silent and stern, uninterested in conversation.

We were almost at Lesser Hill when I said, "All right—what is troubling you?"

His gray eyes and his mouth both had a grim set. "I have my suspicions about what Lady Verr might be up to."

"And?"

He shook his head. "I am not truly superstitious, but some things are best left unspoken."

When we reached the house, Mrs. Childes told us her master was out, gone to Whitby. "*Whitby*." Diana's distress was obvious. "But why?"

"He didn't say, miss, nor when he might be back."

"Oh."

"I'll tell 'im you were by as soon as I see 'im, I promise. I'll send 'im straight over."

Diana smiled weakly. "Thank you, Mrs. Childes."

Michelle managed to persuade Diana to take us to the woods to see the flowers anyway, so we started off again.

Holmes stared at me and shook his head. "This is what I feared."

"What is it?"

He shook his head gruffly and would not speak.

We followed the stream of clear water running over rocks and boulders through the old woods, the bluebells flowering everywhere in the grass alongside the path. They were somehow muted, their color and shape slightly past their prime, but still beautiful all the same. The yellow daffodils were wilted and in decline. However, no one seemed in the spirit to admire the flowers except Michelle, who tried singlehandedly to make up for her lackluster and silent companions. When we returned to the house late in the afternoon, Diana smiled weakly, nodded and left us.

Michelle turned to me, an angry glare in her blue eyes. I was glad I was not the object of her fury. "Where can that idiot possibly have gone!"

Holmes smiled once, a brief grimace, shook his head and stalked away. "Oh Lord," I said. "Let's sit on the terrace and be by ourselves for a while."

Michelle shook her head, clearly near tears. "Doesn't he realize what he's doing to her? How this hurts her?"

"I don't know, Michelle. I don't know. Sometimes he seems like a basically good, decent sort of man, if a trifle thick-headed, while other times... We shall have to wait and see."

The afternoon dragged on, and supper came, with still no word from Adam. Arabella had also not returned either. I felt a growing sense of unease, of apprehension, and I knew the others felt the same. Michelle was relentlessly cheerful, but I knew her too well to be taken in. Diana tried to smile and attend to our conversation, but occasionally her smile would slip away even as her eyes stared off blankly into the distance. I tried to tell myself that nothing too dreadful could have happened. Certainly it was not an impossible coincidence that Adam and Arabella could both have business in Whitby. Certainly Arabella could not have dragged him away there to be murdered! Two large glasses of wine did take off the edge, but I knew I would be immensely relieved if Adam did finally show up.

After dinner Michelle and Diana went to the sitting room, while Holmes and I walked about the great hall. He was even more restless and agitated than I, so much so that I said nothing as he smoked three cigarettes and prowled to and fro. His steps echoed faintly high above, and a wood fire burned in the grate at the far end. The sun had set, and the gray twilight showed through the panes of the many mullioned windows. I began to feel cold and went over to the fire.

I was warming my hands when I heard the faint sound of a

woman's laughter. I turned. Lady Verr had appeared at the far end of the hall, the man next to her clearly recognizable even in the dim light because of his height and size. Further behind her was another man who must be the servant Hamswell. I felt a sudden overwhelming dread, the kind that seems to clutch and squeeze within your chest at your heart. *Easy–easy.* I tried to tell myself that Adam was back–that nothing much could be wrong, that I should be relieved, not fearful. I forced myself to walk forward.

"Good evening, Mr. Holmes, Henry." Lady Verr sounded perfectly content. She had her left hand round Adam's arm, and he seemed incapable of walking normally and had to be almost pushed, step by step, into the hall. Hamswell remained near the entrance way. Holmes crossed his arms but said nothing.

"We have some news," Arabella said. "Don't we, Adam?"

While she seemed to be playing some part, he looked simply stunned, almost paralyzed. One of his hands rose awkwardly, swiped once at his forehead.

I had stepped past Holmes, and the single lamp burning in the distance illuminated his thin face. "What might that be, madam?" he asked. His mouth was rigid, but carefully neutral. However, his eyes gave him away–I would not have wanted to be the object of such anger and scorn.

In the dim light you could not see Arabella's eyes behind the green octagonal lenses. "We are engaged to be married."

Adam sucked in his breath, his body going rigid, but he did not speak.

"You must be joking!" I exclaimed.

Arabella tilted her head slightly. "Not at all, Henry. Do you find me so terribly old and repulsive?" She laughed.

I shook my head. "Impossible. Impossible." I stared at Selton. "Adam–is this true?"

The Further Adventures of Sherlock Holmes

He opened his mouth but seemed unable to speak. Arabella jostled his arm slightly, and he managed a feeble nod.

I heard someone draw in their breath sharply. "*Oh, no, no.*" The words echoed off the stones high above. Diana was on the stairs, halfway down, Michelle just behind her. She gripped the railing with one hand, while the other covered her face. She bent over slightly.

While Adam had appeared in a stupor before, now his face contorted, his anguish obvious.

Arabella shook her head. "I know it is sudden, nor did I want or suspect such an honor, but..."

Diana had begun to cry, and Michelle had put her arms around her. Adam also looked ready to weep. Holmes lowered his arms abruptly. "No, madam—*no*. It will not do."

A faint smile pulled at Arabella's lips. "Who are you, sir, to judge? Who are you to attempt to run my life?"

"You have not thought this through, Lady Verr."

Her smile abated somewhat, but the corners of her mouth still curved upward. "Have I not?"

"No, or you would realize the folly of such a union. Mr. Selton's father threatened to cut him off entirely should he marry Miss Marsh. Adam would be penniless until his father dies, and Mr. Selton senior is only in his late forties and in very good health. He could easily live another twenty or thirty years. And do you expect Mr. Selton to be any more welcoming to you as a prospective daughter-in-law? Yes, you have a title, but your past is... questionable."

"Questionable!" Arabella seemed genuinely outraged.

"As I say, madam, you have not thought this through. Not only would Mr. Selton cut off his son, but he would be likely to have you investigated. If you have any of the proverbial skeletons in the closet, they would come tumbling out. Do you really want your late husband's suicide investigated further? Oh, I know you are doubtless innocent, only the victim of the ravings of a madman, but all the same, certain unpleasant allegations might come up. Better to spare yourself such an ordeal."

Lady Verr's smile had gradually vanished, but it returned only for an instant. "Your reputation is not without merit, Mr. Holmes." She stared at him a long while, but she was the first to look away. "Perhaps you are right."

She released Adam's arm, then stepped away. "Oh, I did not want to marry him–I never wanted to marry him!–but it seemed the only way!" Her voice had risen in a great crescendo, and then she lifted one hand and sobbed loudly.

Holmes shook his head, then folded his arms again.

"For God's sake!" I was genuinely outraged. "What are you talking about? What is this!"

She swept toward me, clutched at my arm. "He–he–forced himself upon me! He touched me–he touched me–in a most inappropriate way! What was I to do? I felt I had no other choice." She stepped back and wept loudly.

"Adam–*oh, Adam!*" Diana's cry was the real thing, not the artifice of her aunt.

He staggered and clutched at his hair. "Oh God."

Diana broke free of Michelle and staggered down the stairs. She came up to Adam, a tall, slender figure with her arms outstretched, her hands clenched into fists. "Is this true?" She could hardly get out the words. "Is it?"

Adam could not seem to look at her. His head jerked to the side, even as he closed his eyes. "I... Oh, Diana."

"Is it? Is it?"

Arabella sobbed. "Oh my poor dear girl, my love!" She started forward but I grabbed her by the arm.

"You leave them alone!" I snarled.

"I didn't mean..." Adam said.

"You touched her? You touched *her.*"

"I didn't know what I was doing–I swear it."

She shook her head wildly. "*Adam.*"

"I didn't hurt her–I didn't. I couldn't hurt a woman–I could never hurt a woman."

"*How could you!*" Diana looked at the windows. "I wish I were dead! I wish..." She whirled about and ran toward the doors.

Arabella would have gone after her, but I still had hold of her arm. Michelle was behind Adam, her face ashen. "Follow her, Michelle," Holmes said. "See that she does not harm herself. Bring her back when you have calmed her." Michelle nodded.

"Oh let me go to her!" Arabella cried. "Oh let me console her, I who have also suffered!"

Holmes could not restrain a savage laugh. "Oh very good, madam! You might equal Sarah Bernhardt on the stage. You should have chosen the theatrical arts rather than science as a vocation."

She tried to break free, but I am fairly strong. "Let me go, Henry! It is not like you to be such a brute."

"Henry is behaving quite rationally. The last thing the poor girl needs is more of your histrionics. And you, Mr. Selton–what is this nonsense? How could you let yourself be so manipulated? I can smell the alcohol on your breath, but that is hardly an excuse. You who are so fearful of your manhood–how could you allow...?"

I shook my head. "No, no, Sherlock–that is not the way–nor is it fair. You know him. He has no experience, no knowledge, and she is... a master."

Adam wiped at his right eye. Holmes shook his head. "I suppose you are right. All the same..." He drew in his breath. "Take him aside, Henry. See if you can determine what actually happened. Lady Verr and I shall stroll about the hall. "

She shook her head angrily. "I must go to her—I must." Hamswell had stepped quietly up beside Holmes. "Hamswell, if Henry does not release me, I must ask you to force him to desist. Diana needs me, and I must find her."

Hamswell stepped toward me, but Holmes was faster still, blocked him. "Get out of the way, Mr. Holmes. You heard her." His big hands formed fists.

"I shall say this only once, Mr. Hamswell. Stand aside immediately and stay out of this."

"You heard..."

Holmes had his back to me, but I saw the rapid movement of his left arm. His fist made a healthy thudding sound as it struck Hamswell square on the jaw. The big man dropped like the proverbial felled ox.

Arabella's laugh was exasperated. "Oh, very good, Mr. Holmes. I forgot you were a pugilist. That was one detail that Watson apparently had right."

Holmes said nothing, but stepped nearer and took Arabella by the other arm. "Yes, you and I shall take a little stroll while Henry and Mr. Selton chat, Lady Verr. Surely you would not be so uncouth as to require me to drag you away?"

She laughed again. "Certainly not, Mr. Holmes."

"Come, then."

He led her away, while I took Adam by the arm and walked toward the fireplace. His gait was askew, his balance off. I had not noticed the smell of alcohol, but he did seem inebriated. He coughed once, then gasped, then sobbed. We came to the fireplace, but I had to hold his arm to keep him from shuffling on.

"What happened, Adam? Tell me."

"She will never forgive me. Never. It's finished now, and it's my fault." He could hardly get the words out.

"Perhaps it is over, perhaps it is not. You and Arabella were at Whitby, weren't you? Why did you go there in the first place?"

"A note. A note from Diana telling me to meet her there."

"Yes?" I gave his arm a squeeze.

"She wasn't there. She was supposed to come, but she didn't come. Lady Verr said she would come, that she was delayed."

"So Arabella kept you company?"

"Yes. She felt bad about Mr. Caswall. She kept thanking me for being so kind. She… she squeezed my hand. She was…"

"She was what?"

He shook his head. "I had never exactly noticed that she was beautiful before. Not like Diana, but… somehow… the same, somehow…"

"I suspect that she offered you something to drink, brandy perhaps?"

"Yes." He stared at me. "How did you know?"

"Just a guess."

"She said she didn't want to drink alone. She talked about… how sad love could be… how sad to love and lose…" His breath had slowed, and he was staring into the flames. "She sat closer and touched my hand. And then…" His eyes opened wider, even as a kind of shudder worked its way up to his broad shoulders.

"She kissed you."

He stared at me. "How could you know that!"

I smiled wearily. "Another guess."

"I thought… I thought it was only friendliness. Her mouth was so… warm. I never knew a woman's mouth was hot, exactly, especially their tongue. Although Diana…" He shuddered again.

"Then it became more than friendliness, more than... My eyes were shut, and I remembered when Diana had kissed me that way once, but I had been afraid, but I wasn't afraid this time." He ran his fingers back through his hair. "Oh none of this makes any sense at all!"

I smiled sadly. "Adam, it does make sense. And I suppose... it didn't stop with kissing. Did you... keep your clothes on?"

He stepped back and stared at me in horror. "Of course I kept my clothes on!"

"But there was touching?"

He looked away again.

"Where did you touch her?"

"I–I held her, held her tightly while we were kissing."

I hesitated. "Did she touch you?"

He moaned and looked away.

"She did, didn't she? She touched your... trousers?"

He gave me such a look of desperation as he nodded, that I wanted to laugh at the absurdity of it all, but I could not do that to him.

"And so now I suppose... you felt you had to marry her, although I suspect that was her idea."

He nodded. "She said we had to. After all that had happened. My intentions... were clear from what had happened. I must not... dishonor her. I didn't know what to say, and she poured me more brandy. The brandy helped. I fell asleep on the way back in the dog-cart, and I was only half awake when we got here." His hand shot out and seized my arm, squeezing it so tightly I winced. "Why did Diana have to be here? Why did she have to come down? Oh, whatever can I do? But tell me, Dr. Vernier–*tell me!*"

"Tell you what?"

"Do I have to marry Lady Verr?"

I laughed softly. "No, you do not have to marry Lady Verr.".

"I want to be a gentleman—I want to do the right thing, but I don't want to hurt Diana." He shook his head wildly, his eyes filling with tears. "I have already hurt her so badly."

I grasped his arm. "Look at me, and listen very carefully." I waited until I saw that he was calmer and attentive. "You absolutely do not have to marry Arabella. She tricked you. This was part of a plan. You have behaved foolishly, but you have no obligations toward her—none at all."

His eyes were fixed on mine. "Is this true?"

"Yes."

"Oh thank God—thank God. It is over with Diana, I understand that, but to be pledged to Lady Verr..." Another shudder worked its way up his spine. "Oh I do not feel well. I..." He gasped, and I stepped quickly back. He bent over, retched twice, great gasping sounds as he spewed up some dark chunky liquid onto the fire.

I shook my head. "Oh, Adam."

"Henry—Henry!" Holmes cried.

I turned. He was in the middle of the hall, his hand still grasping Lady Verr's arm tightly. "See what has happened to Michelle and Diana. The girl was desperate. Michelle may need your help."

"Very well." I nodded, then started for the doorway. I had passed Holmes when I heard something behind me. Adam was following, his walk something of a stagger, foul-smelling vomit still on his jacket and his mouth. "Where do you think you are going?"

"Diana—I have to see that she is all right."

"You have done quite enough for one night. Stay here, and I'll bring her back."

He shook his head. "No, no, this is my fault—I have to help—I have to see..."

"Oh Lord." I turned and strode away, hoping he would remain

behind, but when I reached the tall front doors, which stood open, he was still following me.

The moon had risen, but the house hid it, cast a great dark shadow across the lawn. The sky was without a cloud, the stars coming out. "Michelle?" I called. I looked round, but could not see her. "They must be at the back of the house." I started for the far end of the house, and Adam followed quietly.

When I finally rounded the corner, I could hear the sea more loudly, and the wind touched my face. I strode forward. "Michelle! Michelle!"

"Henry!" Michelle's voice was up ahead, near the sea.

I walked faster, almost a run. The moon had risen to the east, a great white swollen orb, only a day away from full, and it glowed upon the lawn and the black sea beyond.

"Henry!" Michelle was upset. I could see her and Diana in the distance silhouetted just at the edge of the lawn near the cliffs.

"Diana?" Adam muttered softly.

I turned suddenly and grasped his arm. "Listen to me, and listen well. I want you to stay by that tree and keep your mouth absolutely shut until I tell you otherwise. You have done a great deal of harm this evening already. You do not want to make things any worse for Diana, do you?"

He shook his head dully.

"Good. Go by that yew, stay out of sight and keep quiet. All right? Promise me?"

He nodded dully. I seized his arm, took him closer to the old yew, then turned and ran toward the women. Michelle was standing a few feet back, but Diana was perched at the very edge, her back to the sea. Despite my vertigo, despite all my fears, I started for her, but she raised her hands. "No—don't come any closer! Don't! I shall jump—I shall just jump—I promise you!"

I stopped. Michelle was next to me. She reached out and grasped my hand, squeezed it fiercely. "Oh Henry—oh thank God you've come. Maybe she will listen to you." We could hear the sound of the waves crashing against the rocks below, then the water sweeping back outward.

"Diana," I said sternly, "what is this nonsense? Come here."

She shook her head. "No. No. Don't you see? I have lost everyone who is dear to me—everyone. They are all dead. Only Adam..." She made a choking sound. "And now he is lost as well. I have no reason to live, not any longer."

"That is foolishness," I said. "You know better. You have had a shock—we have all had a shock, but that is no reason to throw your life away. Come here. You know Michelle and I care for you. Let us help you."

She shook her head. "No one can help me, not now." Her red hair had half come down, and she reached up, pulled at some pin, and then the tresses all fell down round her shoulders. The wind stirred them slightly. "There is a story of my great-aunt throwing herself into the pit at the grove. I could never do that, not that, but the sea is different, and the rocks. The sea is my old friend and companion. It has sung to me all these years. It would welcome me, I know, and I would rather the fish ate me than rot in the ground like my mother and father. Far better."

I shook my head. "Don't talk that way! You would not say that if you had seen Evans. Don't talk nonsense."

She shook her head. "It isn't nonsense." She shuddered, and her teeth clacked slightly.

I smiled, even though I felt horrible. "Remember—remember when you were out on the terrace that afternoon. Your teeth were clacking then. You were cold. Remember?"

She laughed. "Oh yes, I remember."

"I took you inside. I gave you my jacket. I'll give you my jacket now." I took a step forward.

She was shivering uncontrollably. "Would you?"

"Yes." I took another step, even as I slipped off my jacket.

She raised her hands. "No closer! Not this time. Not this time."

"Diana," I moaned.

"Listen to him," Michelle said. "He is your friend. He wants what is best for you. There's no reason for you to die. That is stupidity, vanity, nothing more."

"Is it?" she asked.

"*Please*," I said.

We all stood silently, and I began to tremble myself. Without my jacket, the wind from the sea was freezing.

"Diana–oh Diana." It was Adam Selton.

"That bloody idiot!" I shook my head. "He promised he would stay by the tree."

Diana was staring past me to the left where I had heard Adam's voice. I wondered if he might distract her long enough that I could make a run for her, but she was still a good ten feet away and perched on the very edge.

"You can't hurt yourself because of me–you can't. I couldn't..." He sagged down onto his knees. "I know you'll never believe me–not now–not after... But I love you so much. I know I've lost you–but I love you–I love you." You could hear that he was crying. "If you die, I will die too. If you go off that cliff, I shall follow you–I swear it. And I deserve to die–*I do*–but you do not. You are so beautiful and so good. You must live. I can't have killed you–I can't. Please, Diana–please. I know you can't forgive me–I don't deserve your forgiveness–but promise me you'll live–promise me that much. I don't care what happens to me. I deserve to be miserable and alone, but you deserve to be happy. You deserve to be..." He was sobbing now. "Just say that you will live—*please*..."

Her eyes were fixed on him. "*Adam.*" His name was a long moan. I strode quickly forward and grasped her wrist. She saw me coming, but she did not try to flee. She let me lead her back, away from the cliff. She was still looking at Adam, but then she turned to me. I put my jacket round her shoulders. Her mouth twisted, and then she came into my arms and held me tightly. I felt her begin to cry again. She was so thin and slight compared to Michelle.

I sighed wearily. "Oh Lord."

Michelle looked at me, that crooked lopsided smile pulling at her full mouth. "Well done, Henry. Well done."

Adam was still on his knees muttering "thank God" over and over again.

"What a night," I murmured. I hugged Diana tightly, then patted her twice on the back. "Let Michelle help you. I need to see to Adam. Get inside—you're freezing."

She nodded, and Michelle took her from me. I went over to Adam and extended my hand. "Get up." He drew in a great breath, then wiped at his eyes with the back of his hand. He took my hand and let me help pull him up. He stared at me warily. "Don't worry. I shan't berate you for forgetting your promise and coming over here. In the end, for once you haven't behaved so badly. It was you that she needed."

He shook his head. "I've lost her. I've lost her."

I smiled faintly. "Don't be so sure of that."

Twelve

The moon shone on Adam's face. He took a deep breath. He seemed more secure on his feet than earlier. I started back for the house after Michelle and Diana. I pulled out a handkerchief. "Do wipe your chin, Adam."

Even as we walked, he took the handkerchief, dabbed at the last remnant of vomit, then stuffed the handkerchief into his pocket. The house still cast a shadow across the lawn in front, although it was smaller because the moon had risen higher. The front doors were ajar, a long gap of feeble orange light showing between them.

I turned to Adam. "I think it would be best if you wait out here. 'Quit while you're ahead' is a good maxim. I shall come back when I can."

He nodded. "I'll wait." He drew in his breath. "But I must know about Diana—how she is."

"And I shall tell you. It may be a while, but I'll be back."

I went through the front doors and into the hallway. The fire had died down, but the one lamp was still lit. In the center of the hall, near the furniture alongside the window, Hamswell was sitting on the stone floor, rubbing dully at his jaw. Holmes held Arabella's wrist tightly. There also seemed to be an apparent faceoff between Mrs. Troughton and Angela, both of them in their black garb. I could not see either of their faces, but Mrs. Troughton stood beside Holmes, arms outspread and fists clenched, blocking Angela's way. Angela might be taller, but Mrs. Troughton outweighed her and had broader shoulders and brawnier arms. Michelle and Diana had come in just before me, and Diana had turned away from the others, as if wanting to escape further turmoil. Michelle still had a protective arm about her.

"This is quite enough, Mr. Holmes!" Arabella exclaimed. "Let me go to the poor girl–let me comfort her. I know exactly how she feels."

"All in good time, madam. If I release you, will you give me your word to remain here an instant longer? I promise it will be only two or three minutes at most. I need to confirm with Dr. Doudet Vernier that Miss Marsh is well."

"It is most infuriating, but you have my promise."

"Excellent, and I must point out that should you break that promise, I shall just have to drag you away, something which would ill become both of us." He turned toward me. "Henry, see to Diana for a moment." He crossed the hall very quickly and touched Michelle's shoulder, even as I walked over to Diana.

I hesitated, then grasped her arm tightly. "Are you feeling better?"

She nodded. "Yes. It was–it was the surprise of it all." I felt her shudder.

Holmes said something to Michelle. She answered, he spoke again, then nodded and turned to Arabella. "Very well, Lady Verr. You may see to your niece."

Diana glanced at me, her face showing confusion and dismay.

Lady Verr swept toward us, raising both arms, her long white hands outstretched before her. "Oh my poor darling, come to me–oh Diana."

I stepped back reluctantly, and Arabella embraced her. Holmes's bony fingers sank into my arm, and he drew me back, pulling me around slightly as we walked toward the windows. "Michelle does not think Diana could take a sudden shock like our departure. Do you concur?"

"Yes! We almost lost her. Hopefully she will recover quickly, but we cannot abandon her now."

In the dim light I saw a quick flash of his smile. "But that is what we must do. You must follow my lead, regardless. Now it is my turn to improvise. First, however, you must tell Diana that we shall not truly leave her–that we shall be back in two days at most. Tell her to be friendly with her aunt–no talk of sending her away–and let her know we shall be close at hand. Lord, I hope there is something of the actress in her. Tell her this is for her and for her Adam."

I stared at him. "Tell her when?"

"Momentarily." His voice had been very quick; we had spoken for only a minute. He spun around and stepped nearer to the three women. Michelle was standing with her arms folded, while Arabella was still mouthing consolations and hugging Diana. This went on for a long while.

"I know it's hard to understand, but you'll be better off without him. We both shall be. Oh, I cannot help blaming myself for this, even though I did nothing to encourage him–I promise you! In fact I…"

"Enough of that particular topic, Lady Verr. I have a favor to ask of you, and then we must have our reckoning."

Arabella had her long arm round Diana's back, her hand grasping her shoulder tightly. "A favor? You dare to ask a favor of me after your behavior this evening?"

"It is because of my behavior that I ask it. I fear I may have injured your wrist inadvertently. Would you allow Dr. Doudet Vernier to examine it?"

She laughed. "You have a nerve, sir!"

"Please, indulge me in this. It will take only a moment. Henry can attend to Diana while Michelle has a look under the light. She can also check Hamswell. The blame lies with him, but I would like to be certain he has not been harmed."

Arabella hesitated, but Michelle drew nearer. "Please, Arabella. Let me make sure that none of the ligaments or tendons are injured. Please." Michelle used her most honeyed and coaxing tone.

Arabella smiled. "Oh, very well." She turned again to Sherlock. "Anything to salve your guilty conscience, Mr. Holmes."

Michelle took her by the arm and led her toward the lamp. "Can you open and close your hand without difficulty?"

I stepped nearer to Diana. She stared up gravely at me, her mouth twisting. "I–I feel so odd."

The others had their backs to me, and I stepped forward and gave her a quick embrace. "I'm sure you do!" I drew back, but I grasped her right hand with my own. Her fingers were cold. "Listen, we have only a moment. We are friends, are we not? And you know I only want what is best for you and Adam."

"Adam," she murmured.

"You know that?"

"Yes. Certainly."

"Then trust me. Sherlock would never abandon you–I will not abandon you–but we must pretend to do so. We shall be back in two days at most, I promise. Go along with your aunt–say nothing of sending her away–in fact you must act as if you trust her, not us. But know that she is your enemy–your deadly enemy. Above all, you must not give us away–or yourself. In fact… I'll wager you could easily cry just now?"

Her laugh was almost a moan, and she nodded.

"If you don't know what to say or how to act–just cry. That should work. This is for your safety and for Adam." I drew back. "Can you forgive him?"

Again she stared up at me. "Should I?"

"Yes. It is not so simple as it seems. I shall explain later. Just trust us–and wait for us. All right?" She nodded. "Good girl. I know you can do it." I smiled and hoped with all my heart that she could.

I touched her elbow lightly, and we walked nearer to the others. Michelle was still probing at Arabella's forearm. "Does this hurt? And this? Good, good."

Holmes had turned, and his eyes locked on mine. I gave a quick nod. He swept closer, then his hand shot out and seized Diana's free hand, gave it a quick squeeze. They both appeared startled. His smile was almost a grimace, and then he stepped away. The gesture was an indication of his great concern; normally he would never touch a young woman in that way.

"Henry," he said. "You might attend to Hamswell."

"That's not necessary." Hamswell was on his feet. He approached slowly, a dull anger in his eyes. "I'm perfectly all right. You surprised me. That's all. In a fair fight–"

Holmes laughed. "Believe what pleases you, sir. I am happy you are none the worse for wear. No bump on the head when you fell?"

"None."

"Excellent." He glanced at Michelle. "And Lady Verr has not been harmed?"

Michelle shook her head. "She has full movement, and I don't really see any sign of bruising."

"That is a great relief."

Arabella made a fist with the hand which had just been examined. "Your impudence defies belief, sir! I think you spoke of a reckoning."

Holmes folded his arms sternly. "I did."

"You have outworn my hospitality, Mr. Holmes."

"Odd you should say that–because I have had quite enough of all the lunacy in this neighborhood! First there was that raving madman with his kite whom you were so eagerly pursuing, then there is Sir Nathaniel with his absurd fixation on giant serpents, and now finally there is young Selton. He brought me here because of some ludicrous fear of white worms and the Marsh women, but he has behaved more and more stupidly. I have come to believe he is only the victim of some bizarre, extended practical joke, nothing truly criminal, and I am sick and tired of his unmanly hysterics over such utter nonsense. Today's buffoonery with you is the last straw–he has betrayed my trust. I am done with him, and I am done with you, madam!" Holmes's voice had grown louder and louder.

"Then feel free to leave, sir."

"So I shall!" Holmes roared.

"Mr. Holmes?" Diana said, her brow knitted up.

I watched her closely and wondered if she could pull it off.

"And *you*–you let yourself be led around by the nose by this madwoman with her menageries and ludicrous whims! Send her away at once–this instant, and I might reconsider. Otherwise I am done with you forever. It is your aunt or Sherlock Holmes? You must choose!"

My lips drew back involuntarily, my teeth clenching. I knew it was pretense, but Holmes was most convincing. I hoped Diana understood.

She stared at him, her mouth half open. Arabella moved closer and seized her arm. "Let him go, my darling–let them all go! They do not truly care for you—none of them do. They do not love you as I do. It shall be you and me together, Diana—the last of the Marsh women!"

Diana stared at Holmes, then sobbed and turned away, letting Arabella engulf her in her embrace.

"Excellent—very good!" Holmes shouted. "As you wish. And I—I shall not remain an instant longer in this madhouse! I shall go immediately to Lesser Hill and leave for Whitby in the morning."

"You and your friends may stay the night, Mr. Holmes," Arabella said. "I shall treat you better than you have treated me. It is late, and I shall not send you packing this instant."

"As I said, I'll not stay a moment longer! I shall take my things and leave at once. I can have the wagonette sent over first thing in the morning for Henry and Michelle." He glanced at us, and we both nodded.

"As you wish," Arabella said.

Diana continued to weep in earnest, and Arabella said, "There, there," and patted her back. Arabella looked up. The green spectacle lenses hid her eyes, but her face revealed her sense of triumph. In the set of her beautiful mouth, in that victorious smile, I saw something cruel and malicious. I hoped Diana was only following my advice, but I could not be certain. Holmes whirled about and strode away toward the stairway. Michelle stared uneasily at Diana and Arabella. "Michelle," I murmured softly. She sighed, then came over. I took her hand and started for the stairs. We were halfway up when she squeezed my hand tightly. "I hope Sherlock knows what he is doing."

"I hope so too," I whispered.

He was waiting for us at the top of the stairs. "Come with me while I get my bags ready. I must leave at once."

I started to follow, then stopped. "Adam—I nearly forgot about him! He's waiting for me."

"He can wait a little longer, and then you and I shall both go down." Holmes stepped into his room. He must have foreseen how things might go, because his two full bags were waiting by the bed. "I have a few final things to pack." He went to the bureau and pulled out a drawer.

"Isn't this carrying your outrage a bit far? You could wait until morning."

He shook his head. "No, I cannot. I shall leave with Selton but not stop at Lesser Hill. I am certain he will lend me a horse. I am going on to Whitby."

"Whitby!" I said. "This late?"

"I shall be there around midnight and go straight to see Mr. Pratt." He put a jacket and a small leather case in his bag. "I should be back with two of his men by morning. They will watch the house tomorrow and join us at night for the May Day rites."

Michelle shook her head. "Oh Sherlock, are you certain about this? Diana was truly desperate out there. I think she is ultimately sensible, but to leave her alone in such a state—or worse, to leave her with her aunt! Is there no other way?"

Holmes gave his head a brusque shake. "None. I am absolutely certain Lady Verr plans to kill her niece, but I haven't a shred of real proof. Nor can I prove that she drove her husband to suicide, that she had Evans hurled into the pit, or that she has been trying to frighten away Adam Selton. The only way is to catch her in the act."

"But it is so dangerous!" Michelle exclaimed. "Diana might still try to harm herself—or Arabella might simply murder her tomorrow, during the day!"

"That is why the men will be watching the house, and I also have an inside ally—Mrs. Troughton. I have not told her everything, but I have prepared her. Henry, after I leave, you must let her know that the policemen will be nearby, as she and I discussed, and that if Diana seems in immediate danger, she can go outside and call for assistance."

Michelle stared at him bleakly and shook her head.

A grotesque, agonized smile pulled at Holmes's mouth, something akin to a spasm or tremor. "Besides, Michelle, in general, a human sacrifice requires a living victim."

Michelle groaned. "Oh, I do not like this."

Holmes shook his head violently. "Nor do I, but it seems the only way. I have racked my brains over and over, but it is the best I could come up with."

I bit at my lower lip. "I suppose so."

Holmes scooped up some shoes, stuffed them into one bag, then lifted both bags by their handles. "I must go. You two can keep an eye on Diana tonight. I shall send the wagonette over early for you in the morning. Lady Verr must think she has won, that I am a proud blundering fool, and that we have retreated."

Michelle again shook her head. "How could she possibly think we would just leave Diana?"

Holmes smiled. "She is not like you, Michelle—not at all. She assumes that everyone is ultimately as selfish and vain as she. I think she also believes that I have my eyes fixed on Adam Selton, that I am ignorant of the danger to Diana. I tried to convince her of that with my blustering." He glanced at me. "Let's go, Henry."

The wagonette arrived early the next morning, and Michelle and I left after saying our farewells. Diana looked pale and unhappy. Michelle and I were grave as we embraced her. Lady Verr was probably the only one who had slept well the night before. Her cheeks had a slight flush, and her beautiful mouth still formed that arrogant smile of triumph. She behaved as if we were all still the best of friends and as if nothing the least unusual had happened the evening before.

Michelle and I sat together in the wagonette. We saw Diana and Arabella standing before the tall oaken doors with Angela nearby in the shadows. Arabella wore the usual white dress along with her emerald necklace and green spectacles, Angela her black maid's dress, while Diana was in blue. Diana and Arabella's red hair shone in the light. Angela's full sensual lips formed a slight, bitter smile. Arabella kept waving a long while.

Michelle and I certainly had not slept well. We had been up discussing the situation and our misgivings until around three in the morning. Holmes, of course, had been busy all night long: he had gone to Whitby, talked to Pratt, sought out the two men, slept only a couple of hours, then returned with the policemen well before dawn.

Adam Selton had also slept little. Holmes had told him everything— that Arabella was behind it all—the letters, the White Worm, the threats—and that she planned to kill Diana for her inheritance. The moment he heard Diana was in danger, Adam had immediately turned and started back for Diana's Grove. Holmes had to use a mixture of berating, threats, reasoning and cajoling to get him turned round and pointed back at Lesser Hill. Adam was still pacing about uneasily when we arrived that morning. We had to reassure him that Diana had been perfectly well when we left.

I had hoped to be able to rest after the long night, but Holmes insisted that we must all leave at once for Whitby. He explained that Lady Verr was not such a fool as to take anything at face value. Undoubtedly she had her agents, perhaps members of the White Worm cult, who would be watching. We must be seen to leave Lesser Hill, arrive at Whitby and depart on the train.

"Depart on the train!" I exclaimed.

And so we did, shortly after eleven that morning. On the platform, the three of us spoke with Adam, stepped into the first-class carriage and waved goodbye from the window. Adam's huge forearm and hand swept back and forth in reply. We went a few miles into the nearby valley, and then the train came to a wheezing huffing stop. We disembarked with our bags and found Mr. Pratt waiting with a wagonette. He drove us round Whitby up through the woods and out onto the barren, grassy ridge above the sea.

We headed inland and spent most of the afternoon at a small cottage on the moors where Pratt's sister and her husband lived. Michelle and I did get in a brief nap. Holmes explained that the ceremony would most likely take place around midnight, when the tide was at its highest, but he wanted us all hidden in place early. He tried briefly to convince Michelle to remain safely behind at the cottage, but of course, she would hear none of it. He knew her well enough to yield. He and Pratt departed around five that afternoon. They were going to check in with the two men who were hidden at Diana's Grove watching the house. Michelle and I left with Pratt's brother-in-law, a Mr. Dodd, toward dusk.

By the time we reached Lesser Hill, the color had mostly faded from the scattered clouds along the high moorlands–those pinks, oranges and violet tints–and the stars had begun to appear. Dodd remained behind while Michelle and I started up the path through the grass to the rise overlooking the sea. Silhouetted against the vast sky was Adam Selton, his back to us, his right hand gripping his left wrist.

"Adam?"

He turned. He tried to smile, but his forehead was creased, his eyes worried. He held his cloth cap in his hand, and the breeze off the ocean had ruffled his long curly black hair. That and his sculpted features gave him the look of some wild Byronic hero, a Manfred or Childe Harold, but I knew that he had little in common with those stormy romantic characters.

"It is almost dark," he said. "We are to join Mr. Holmes at the grove."

I nodded. The sea still had a certain muted shimmer, reflecting the color of the dying sky. At the horizon I saw a sudden flash of orange, a sliver of light. "Oh look!" Michelle said. "The moon." We watched a great pale swollen orb with a faint orange flush slowly rise over the dark waters.

"Good Lord," I said. "It looks so big. An illusion, I know."

"It will light our way," Adam said. He shook his head. "Such a beautiful evening for... How I wish this was all over with–how I wish Diana was safe."

We went back down the hill. Dodd joined us as we started along the ridge. No one felt much like talking. Michelle stayed by my side. Once or twice her hand reached out to take mine. I was carrying my medical bag, which paradoxically enough also held Michelle's revolver. Holmes and the policemen would also be armed. There might be perhaps some thirty pagan worshipers, but Holmes and Pratt did not think many would be combative before a display of authority. Some would be women, others, like Sir Nathaniel, were elderly.

As we walked, the moon slowly rose, losing its orange hue and appearing to shrink. When we skirted the ridge, we could see the orb cast a great swath of white across the black waters, a strip which bobbed and danced with the movement of the sea. To our left, our own dark shadows seemed to trudge along with us. Here amidst the absolute darkness and the quiet solitude of Yorkshire, one saw the true power of the moon's luminescence.

Michelle shook her head. "Adam was right. It is so beautiful here, so incredible–and that there should be wickedness, evil... It is just wrong."

I sighed softly. "Tomorrow night this will be all over. One way or another, things will be resolved."

Michelle squeezed my hand fiercely. "For the better," she whispered. "For the better."

Once we reached the woods, the dazzling light was muted by the thick foliage of the trees. I realized how much they had leafed out since my arrival nearly two weeks ago. Adam, however, led the way. Those childhood games with Diana must have made the grove truly familiar to him, and he did act the part of the worthy Natty Bumppo or his Indian friend Chingachgook in leading us to our destination. Dodd had a dark lantern, but we never needed to use its beam.

When we finally came out into the clearing, the change was dramatic. The moon had risen still higher, and the light cast upon the grass, stones and vegetation was intense. One could see some green in the fern leaves. The tall stones were even more dramatic, black monoliths against the sky like giant jagged teeth. My eyes followed the grassy turf, then a ridge of rock and found a black shape which I knew must be the mouth of the pit. I felt a curious emptiness in my chest and looked away at once. We hesitated, somehow not wanting to advance out into the clearing.

"There you are, Henry." It was Holmes's voice; his tall figure had appeared out of nowhere to my left. He was wearing his wool walking hat and a long dark overcoat. "Any trouble making your way?"

"No. Adam was an excellent guide. Did you and Pratt talk to the men?"

"Yes, and as I suspected, nothing out of the ordinary has happened."

"Diana is all right? She has not been harmed?" You could tell from his voice that Adam was on edge.

"Not so far. The man observing the back of the house saw the two Marsh ladies come outside briefly during the afternoon. The day was uneventful. Even now the two men are still watching. I suspect the worshipers will have a procession through the woods, while the others will come from the house."

I frowned. "Sir Nathaniel was certain Arabella was not Corchen. I don't think he was lying. Who do you think she is? Some local woman?"

"Oh, I believe I have that figured out."

"Yes?" I asked.

He laughed softly. "It will be much more dramatic if I show you."

I shook my head. "'Dramatic.'"

Michelle had listened with her arms crossed. "What must be done now, Sherlock?"

"We must practice patience, for there is nothing to do but wait. As I told you, high tide will be at eleven fifty, and I do not expect them to arrive much before midnight. Pratt is waiting by the main path from the road; it is the only way a large group of people could take. One of the men will also come from the house to alert us as soon as anyone leaves from there."

I shook my head. "Three hours or more, then."

The time passed slowly, and the air grew more chill. Michelle and I went round the grove to a spot near the cliffs where we could see the ocean. We remained well back to keep my vertigo in check. I put my hand on her shoulder, drawing her closer. The wind off the sea felt cold. The moon had risen, but its light still shone on the water. The stars were out, but they and the darkness itself were muted by the shining orb.

Suddenly a star streaked sideways, creating a vivid white diagonal line across the sky which faded immediately. I felt Michelle stand straighter and stiffen. "Make a wish," she murmured.

I drew in my breath slowly and thought of Adam Selton, who had remained behind with Holmes. A man who seemed to have everything–money, a certain intelligence, good looks and a beautiful, devoted woman madly in love with him. But he was miserable. *I hope things work out for the great blundering oaf,* I thought to myself. And Diana... But the wish had already been made.

The wind made us feel cold, and we returned to the grove and Holmes. I had begun to yawn compulsively, the lack of sleep catching up with me. Michelle told me to sit by a tree and have a rest, and I actually dozed for a while.

Around eleven thirty, Pratt appeared and said a procession was approaching. Holmes told us to take up positions behind the standing stones and stay hidden until he stepped out. He stared sternly at Adam. "Do you understand? You must not act on impulse. We must wait until the last moment so we have clear proof of Lady Verr's intentions."

Adam nodded, but you could see that he was very uneasy.

"Very well." Holmes started forward, then stopped suddenly. "One other thing: should anyone fall into the pit, it is of the utmost importance that the person be pulled out as quickly as possible. It is a matter of life and death."

"The water is cold," I said, "but if someone can swim, surely..."

"Henry–there is no time now for lengthy explanations or a discussion of various possibilities. Take my word for it: anyone who falls into the water is in terrible danger and must be fished out immediately."

I shrugged and nodded. We started across the grassy turf. A man stepped out from the trees. "They are coming from the house," he whispered loudly. Holmes nodded. Michelle and I took up a place behind one stone, Adam and Holmes behind another, Pratt and one of his men behind a third, Dodd and the other man behind the fourth. Pratt and his men were all carrying dark lanterns which had been lit and were ready to illuminate the grove once their square shields were raised. The sea and the cold wind were at our backs, and we could hear the low rumble of the surf.

Soon another sound could be heard, a choir chanting softly. I stared out from behind the massive lichen-crusted stone face, careful to conceal as much of myself as possible. Orange light danced about within the trees, and two of the figures in white robes bearing torches came out into the grove. The bearers were tall, but their cowls hid much of their faces from the twisting yellow-orange flames. The group slowly advanced, still chanting, and you could hear both male and female voices. The bulky white robes and cowls hid their sex, their shapes and identities, but one figure was clearly stooped and used a cane-like stick. It had to be Sir Nathaniel. They gathered before the pit, still chanting some words I could not make out, probably some variant of Gaelic or Welsh fitting for the followers of Druids. Six of them held smoking torches, which were unnecessary under the dazzling moon.

I wondered how many times over the past millennia men had trekked to this grove and gathered under the full moon for some ritual sacrifice. A shudder worked its way up from the base of my spine. So little was really known about the Druids and Celts. Surely they had not worn such uniform and neatly made white robes! One could hope… perhaps they gathered to wonder at the moon, the stars and the seas. Perhaps these monoliths were here only to mark the motion of the heavens.

The chanting suddenly ceased. I looked about the grove and saw that others had come out of the trees: two women all in white, and Hamswell carrying Diana draped across his arms. My lips formed the word *damn.* It was one thing to conjecture Diana being sacrificed, another to actually see it begin to unfold. Holmes must be holding Adam back.

Slowly the women approached. Diana wore only a white gown. She appeared slack and lifeless, but I told myself Holmes was right: she had to be alive for the sacrifice. Most likely she had been drugged. Arabella was the scientist. She would know about chloroform or ether. I hoped to God she had used ether—chloroform was far more dangerous.

As they came closer, I still did not recognize either of the women. One was tall with an incredible long curling mane, its reddish color muted but visible by moonlight. Her face was so pale and white, it almost glowed. This must be Corchen. Just behind her was a shorter woman with similarly abundant and curling tresses, only black. Her complexion was much darker, so much so I wondered if she might be a mulatto.

Corchen stopped some ten feet from the others and raised her hands; the white sleeves fell, revealing her slender arms. Around her right wrist was an elaborate silver bracelet shaped like a snake. "Welcome, followers of the great goddess—welcome! I, your Druidess and the servant of the White Worm, greet you."

I frowned slightly. The voice was oddly familiar. There was a slight hint of some accent I could not place, one which went well with her part.

"Tonight is the night long awaited. The celestial spheres are all aligned: the stars, the moon and the planets. The moon waxes full, midnight brings the first of May, and the waters rise within the pit, even as I speak. The time long preordained cometh: our goddess demands a special sacrifice—not mere cattle or sheep—but a young virgin!"

A murmur went up in the group. Some obviously found this troubling.

"I have warned that this day would come. To bring forth our mighty goddess at last and satisfy her, we must offer up a worthy victim. This girl, last of the wretched line of the Marshes who have so long warred against our goddess, must be given to the worm. If there are any of you who do not want to join in this offering, go now and never return."

She sternly looked at the group. One figure came forward, pulled down her cowl, and shook her head. It was an old woman. "It's wrong."

Corchen raised her arm with her forefinger thrust forward. "Do not presume to judge the mighty goddess! Go, but remain silent if you would live."

The woman shook her head again, then turned and slowly walked away. Corchen stared at the others a long while, then stepped nearer to the pit and raised her arms again. "Oh, great goddess, hear your humble priestess and servant. You are mighty and immortal, you have existed through the centuries, dwelling within the earth and sea. We, your followers, beg you to return to us, and we offer you as a gift this young virgin. Take her, goddess–devour her!–and then rise again! Come to us, oh goddess!" Her voice had grown louder and louder. It certainly was not Arabella, but whoever she was, she was quite an actress. "Bring forth the sacrifice–cast her into the pit!"

Hamswell started forward. A beam of light suddenly shone on the priestess and the crowd, and then other beams flashed into the clearing. "Halt!" Holmes cried. "Not another step or I shoot!" I had stepped out past the stone, and Michelle was at my side. The wind had shifted, and I caught a whiff of ether. Hamswell must have a rag soaked in it. Pratt and his men started forward.

Hamswell turned and started toward the pit, Diana still in his arms. Holmes did not hesitate, but fired two shots. Hamswell screamed and staggered, one hand swatting automatically at his leg, then went down. Diana seemed to half stand rather than fall, then stumbled forward and disappeared over the edge into the pit.

"Diana!" Adam cried.

"Blast it!" Holmes snarled. He dropped his revolver and tore off his hat, overcoat and jacket even as he ran forward. "Watch the two women, Pratt–don't let them escape!" He reached the edge of the pit even before Adam. "Wait–just wait!" I had also run forward. Holmes seized Adam's arm. "The ledge–get down on the ledge–you can pull us out."

In the moonlight, Adam's face was contorted, his eyes wild. His hat had come off. He nodded. Holmes wrenched off his boots, then leaped into the pit, making a great splash. I reached the edge along with one of the policemen, and he shone his dark lantern into the opening. The light danced on the undulating surface. Holmes was in the water, bobbing about–along with Diana.

"Thank God," I muttered. I had feared that she might be so anesthetized she would sink and drown. Instead the shock must have revived her. I could not believe how high the water had risen compared to last time Holmes had gone into the pit.

Adam swung round, dropped his right leg and eased himself down to the small sloping rocky ledge some six feet below. The water was only two or three feet further down. Holmes had his arm about Diana, and he managed to get them both closer to the ledge. "Take her–take her!" he cried. Adam lowered his enormous hand, grabbed her wrist, and pulled her upward as if she were only some rag doll. He had her halfway out of the water in an instant.

"Diana!" he cried.

"Adam–oh, Adam."

He set her onto the ledge. "Get her out!" Holmes cried. Adam hesitated, then put his hands about her waist and lifted her. Dodd and the other men quickly pulled her up and out. Adam turned and lowered his hand again, then effortlessly plucked Holmes out of the water. Holmes scrambled wildly with one leg, then got himself up onto the ledge. I could hear him panting deeply. "Oh thank God," he moaned. "Go on—get up there." Adam hoisted himself up using his arms, then brought one leg around and climbed out. He reached down again and helped Holmes up.

Holmes was soaked. The moonlight showed on the dome of his long forehead and his thin face, all nose now with his wet black hair plastered back. He managed to smile at me, then his shoulders rose as he shuddered. I grasped his arm. He was trembling uncontrollably.

"You're freezing," I said.

He nodded. "I am cold." His teeth clenched involuntarily. "But it is not just that—I am afraid." He laughed once. "Terrified, actually."

I stared at him incredulously. I could not recall ever seeing him truly afraid of anything.

Michelle had his jacket and his coat. "Put these on. It will help."

"Gladly." He slipped into both and also found his boots. He pulled off his wet stockings before putting them on. He turned to Diana. "Are you all right, Miss Marsh?"

Adam had taken off his overcoat, put it over Diana, and now his big arm clasped her tightly to him. The moon shone on her bony white feet. She nodded. "Yes. Still a little dizzy. Thank you, Mr. Holmes—oh, thank you."

"You're quite welcome, my dear young lady." He glanced at Pratt who was watching the two women, revolver in hand. "It's done, Lady Verr. It is over. You have lost, and now you shall pay for your crimes."

My forehead creased. "What?"

Neither of the women spoke but only regarded Holmes warily. He drew in a long deep breath, then stepped forward, grasped the hair of the shorter woman and pulled hard. The black wig came off, revealing red hair. The woman smiled. "Very good, Mr. Holmes. Bravo."

He turned to the other woman. "You might as well take yours off as well."

She hesitated only a second, then used her long slender hands to remove the red wig. Her hair was black. She smiled proudly.

"Oh Lord," I whispered. "Angela. Of course." Arabella with a black wig and dark makeup, Angela with a red wig and pale makeup–how obvious now! And Angela's pathetic "I no speak-a de English" had only been an act.

"Your English is most impressive, madam," Holmes said. "Those cadences were positively biblical in their grandeur."

I looked round me. The group of worshipers had shrunk, many of the younger and more spry ones disappearing into the woods. These were mostly older women, or the more devout. Sir Nathaniel had thrown back his hood; he appeared frustrated. The policemen had their dark lanterns and revolvers in hand.

Pratt shook his head. "An incredible business, this."

Hamswell was moaning. "Help me–someone help me." Michelle and I glanced at one another, then she took her bag, went over and stooped down beside him. After a moment she looked over at us. "He's in no danger. One bullet is buried in muscle, the other went cleanly through the outer thigh, with little real bleeding. He will have trouble sitting for a while." She took out a roll of bandage and wrapped it round his leg several times. "Henry and I can tend to him, but that can wait for a few minutes." She rose.

"We should have known we could never fool you, Mr. Holmes," Arabella said.

Holmes's forehead creased. "We?"

Arabella took a step back, in the direction of the pit, then another.

"You thought you were so clever, but you see, it was never my idea."

Angela stood up very straight. Her arms stiffened even as her fingers spread apart slightly. "Arabella?"

"I met her in Italy, of course. It was a crazed infatuation. I knew it was foolish, but I could not resist her. I loved her you see. I did not want to hurt Diana–I never wanted to hurt her. But she said it was the only way, the only way we could be together."

Angela drew in her breath sharply, a noise almost like a hiss.

"She planned everything! The Worm–the human sacrifice–it was all her idea, all her…"

Angela moved so quickly I don't think anyone could have stopped her, even if they had suspected what she might do. She extended both arms, cried "*Traditore!*" and struck Arabella, knocking her backwards into the pit. The splash was almost instantaneous, followed by a pause, then a scream. "Oh get me out–get me out–for the love of God!"

Again we rushed to the edge, and the beams of the lanterns showed the black water and Arabella's head bobbing about. Her white hands clawed futilely at the wall.

Adam would have climbed down to the ledge, but Holmes grasped his arm. "Not this time–it is too dangerous." He looked at Pratt. "Get the rope–quickly!" He stared down at Arabella. "Hardly very original trying to blame another, madam. By now you should have learned that your efforts at improvisation can end badly."

"Get me out! Please–oh, please! I did it–I admit it all–but get me out! Please, Mr. Holmes. *I beg of you.*" Her terror was evident, her voice harsh and completely changed.

"It is your pet, isn't it? Just like Delilah or those others in your menagerie, only this one I suspect goes back almost to your childhood."

"Yes–yes–but hurry! For God's sake hurry!"

Pratt arrived with the rope, and threw it into the pit. "The rest can wait, madam. I need not tell you to make haste." Holmes and Pratt both had hold of the rope. "Wrap it round your wrists, so you cannot lose your grasp."

Arabella wound it round her wrists twice, then grasped it with both hands. "*Pull–pull–hurry–hurry.*"

They hoisted away, and by the time her torso came up out of the water, I felt somehow relieved myself. I could not understand her obvious terror, but it was contagious. They pulled again, even as the beams danced about on the shimmering surface and the stony side of the pit. Something appeared in the black water, something long and white and slender, snake-like, moving very fast, disappearing, appearing, then one end rose and became a rounded sort of head with jaws which opened even as it shot upward. Arabella gave a howl of pain and terror, and she immediately plunged back into the water. Holmes and Pratt had not been able to hold onto the rope.

Holmes grabbed it again. "Quickly, or she is lost!" He tried to pull, but could not budge it. "Selton—all of you—help me!" he cried. Adam grabbed at the rope and Pratt, Dodd and the others soon joined him. They managed to slowly hoist Arabella out of the water. She was screaming and screaming; if the rope were not wound round her wrists, she could never have held on. As she rose, the thing came with her, a terrible weight, its jaw obviously clamped to her upper leg.

"The worm!" Sir Nathaniel cried, his arm gripping mine fiercely. "A little one! A babe!"

"Dear Lord," I muttered.

They kept pulling, and Arabella slowly ascended, but there seemed no end to the pale serpentine form which had her in its grip. Arabella's cries were more like moans now. There must have been seven or eight feet of the monster out of the water, but still no diminution.

"For God's sake," I cried. "What is that thing?"

Arabella made a choking gasping noise. "Help me—help me."

Holmes had let go of the rope, and he took a long walking stick in his hand. He knelt down at the edge, held the end with both hands, then bent over and swung it round in a great arc, striking the creature on the head. A quaver shimmered down along its serpentine shape. He struck it again. Arabella screamed and swayed. The beast let go at last, plunging back down into the black waters, and Arabella almost shot up and out of the pit as the men holding the rope staggered backward, the greater part of the burden suddenly gone. Arabella lay on her side gasping and moaning. I glanced a last time at the waters. I saw the gray-white head and the slightly parted jaw and sharp teeth, then the creature submerged for the last time and vanished with a final flash of its pale back.

"I don't understand," Michelle moaned. "I do not."

We both went to Arabella's side. She looked ghastly. The makeup was partly gone, leaving her face a blotchy white and gray. A huge dark stain was blossoming on her torn white robes and her leg. I wondered if one or both of her wrists had been broken by the rope wound around them and the great weight pulling at her.

Michelle bent over and tried to staunch the bleeding with her hands. "Oh no, no," she muttered.

Arabella let her head roll sideways and drew in a great shuddery breath, her face staring up at Holmes. She tried for a smile but could not manage it. "Hoist on my own petard, Mr. Holmes. Fitting enough, yes?" Her voice was hoarse.

"Do not try to speak—not now."

"It's probably my last chance. It hurts, but it is not like... Oh, I don't care, so long as I am out of the water. I didn't want to end up in the pit, not that way. And you were right about improvising. It was all utter nonsense. Angela could have never dreamed it up. And she hates reptiles and fish."

"Hush," Michelle said. "Hush."

She had raised the rope and was looping some around Arabella's bare thigh, no doubt to act as a tourniquet. Blood was spurting out. I shook my head. "Can I help?" I asked.

"No." She looked up at me and gave her head a quick shake. "It's bad."

"Petard," Arabella muttered. "Poetic justice. Clever that." She was shivering. "I'm so cold." I took off my overcoat and put it over her. "Dr. Henry Vernier, always the gentleman, always the guardian of the fair sex... always..." Her eyes rose upwards even as her mouth stiffened.

Michelle shook her head. "She has lost so much blood. That thing must have severed the femoral artery. Even a tourniquet... Arabella!" She drew in her breath. "Arabella?" One hand still held the rope, but she touched Arabella's throat with her fingertips, probed gently. At last she drew in her breath and shook her head. She let go of the rope and slowly stood up.

I had begun to shiver myself and not merely from cold. I stared at Holmes. "For God's sake—now you can explain? What was that thing in the water?"

"The worm," Sir Nathaniel cried jubilantly. "It was..." The rest of the worshipers watched silently.

"Nonsense!" Holmes exclaimed. "That was no White Worm, not even a serpent. It was a conger eel, nothing more."

"An eel?" I muttered, thinking of its smaller brethren who could be purchased chopped and stewed from many a London street vendor.

"Yes, an ocean-going variety, technically a fish, and the largest of its race. They can grow to some twelve feet and weigh nearly five hundred pounds."

Pratt nodded. "I saw a big one hung up by the dock at Whitby two years ago, the same sort of ugly brute. It was ten feet long and three hundred or so pounds, but only a babe compared to that thing!"

"The females are larger than the males," Holmes said. "They can also live as long as a man, sixty years or more. Lady Verr must have encountered that creature in the pit at high tide when she was a girl. She trained it to come for food. Perhaps she offered it rabbits. She was gone for many years, but when she returned last year and put out some bait, amazingly enough the creature reappeared. She began to feed it again. This was the foundation of her cult and the animal sacrifices. It must have amused her greatly."

Sir Nathaniel shook his head and moaned. "No, no. It was the worm, a juvenile variant."

Holmes stared at him. "You call yourself a naturalist, sir! Ask any fisherman about conger eels. They can tell you that they are very fierce, a difficult catch indeed, and that they can grow to immense size, as Pratt has just noted." He drew in his breath, then looked at Angela. She had seemed dismayed earlier, but now she stood wearily, her arms folded. Dodd was next to her, his revolver in hand. "Was my surmise correct, madam?"

She nodded twice. "Certainly, Mr. Holmes. And you realized, of course, that with that lunatic Caswall gone, she had resolved to kill her niece for her money and for the estate. She said we would do well enough then, but given her extravagances, we would have been bankrupt and in debt within a year or two at most. She seemed to think this was all a game between the two of you, a kind of chess match. I tried to warn her, tried to persuade her…" She drew in her breath and let out a long sigh. "In the end, I have come to understand that she was… a sort of monster, a cold, unfeeling beast like her reptiles or that creature in the pit, and yet I loved her. I loved her from the first moment I saw her. But she–she could not love! She could not. She could pretend well enough, and she had her brief infatuations, but real passion–true love–no. I finally understand that, but too late. And that she should try to betray me after all I had done for her, all I had endured! No, no–impossible! All the same, I did not truly want to kill her. I swear it. After all, you had survived the pit without harm."

Holmes nodded. "I believe you. It was as I said. She was not good at improvisation. That business with Adam was pathetically inept. She had not thought things through."

"And she did not think things through tonight! She turned on me–I who had loved her and served her so long and faithfully!" Again Angela shook her head, then she stood upright proudly. "Do you know opera, Mr. Holmes, Italian opera?"

He stared warily at her. His hair was still wet and black under the moonlight. "Yes, certainly. Which one?"

"Do you know *Norma* of Bellini?"

Holmes laughed softly. "Yes, of course. The story of a high-priestess of the Druids. She loved a Roman. She and her lover go together to the sacrificial pyre at the end."

Angela smiled fiercely. "Very good, *signore*. This grove, this whole business–it is all like *Norma*. I did help her plan everything, and of course, I was Corchen! I was the high-priestess of the snake goddess, the mighty White Worm. I played my part well, even if I do say so."

Holmes nodded. "Very well indeed. Most impressive."

"Norma was a priestess and a mother. She felt real love for Pollione, who was an unfaithful cur. She was not like Arabella, who could not love. She was not a fake. She was not empty inside, capable only of lies and deceit, even to the one who most..." She drew in her breath, struggling for control. The white makeup still covered her face, and its pallor seemed appropriate. "The pit—she was right about the pit. I cannot face the pit either. But there is an alternative—something worthy of Bellini, something worthy of Norma, something truly... operatic."

She smiled fiercely at Holmes, then whirled about and ran straight for the cliff. She had surprised us all, she had a head start, and she was very fast. I stopped well before the edge, but I saw the figure in white go over without hesitating in the least. Holmes and the others paused to stare down at the rocks and the sea far below. I could see their silhouettes framed against the bright starry sky. At last they turned and walked back toward me.

Holmes shook his head. "Lady Verr was not worth it—not worth it at all." Adam and Diana had remained behind. She was crying, her face hidden against his massive chest. "Well, Mr. Selton, you needn't worry any more about White Worms or curses on the Marsh daughters."

The few worshipers who remained were absolutely silent. Most had lowered their cowls. They looked stunned or dismayed. Pratt glanced at Holmes. "Any reason to keep the lot, sir?"

"No, except for Hamswell. Once one of the doctors has had a look at him, you'll want to take him into custody. I am certain he was involved in Evans's murder. That, unfortunately, will be difficult to prove, but we all saw him attempt to murder Miss Marsh. Perhaps he can lead us to the apparatus used to create the worm at night."

Pratt folded his arms and looked around at the hapless worshipers. "All right, this business is finished once and for all, done with. Go home and consider yourselves lucky. I hope you've all learned your lesson."

Sir Nathaniel's face formed a sorrowful grimace. "Only a conger eel," he moaned.

Thirteen

Michelle and I took care of Hamswell, using the back of the wagonette as an operating table. He actually still had a bottle of ether in his pocket, but we used our own. Michelle muttered something darkly about dispensing with an anesthetic, which did worry Hamswell, but I knew it was an idle threat. Once he was under, she probed about and had the bullet out of his haunch within two or three minutes. She was remarkably fast. Meanwhile I was scouring out the other wound through the leg with carbolic acid. He stirred even under ether. After some stitching and bandaging were complete, his trousers finally came back up, much to our relief and that of the two policemen who had been shining the beams from their dark lanterns onto his posterior.

Holmes had been talking with Pratt and Sir Nathaniel. Pratt and all his men soon left in the wagonette, along with the still unconscious Hamswell. Diana and Adam sat quietly on a rock. She was completely engulfed in his woolen overcoat, her head leaning against his shoulder. Neither of them said a word, but they looked very happy. Since Diana had no shoes, Adam insisted on carrying her back. He held her in his extended forearms, and it didn't slow him down at all, although he had to turn her occasionally to dodge a tree trunk.

When we finally entered the great hall of Diana's Grove, we found Mrs. Troughton bound to a chair. She was greatly relieved to see us, especially Diana, and once she had been untied, she embraced the girl fiercely. Her jaw was thrust forward slightly, her eyes stern, as she heard what had happened to Arabella and Angela.

"I suppose as a Christian I mustn't exult in their terrible end, but they had their just deserts, all the same."

Diana sighed wearily. She was standing next to Adam, and he still had his arm around her. He hadn't left her side for an instant since getting her out of the water. "I still can't believe it all. I do... I do feel sorry for her. In fact..." Her eyes had filled with tears, and she could not continue.

"I am not certain I exactly believe in the theory of just deserts," Holmes said. "Lady Verr was vain, selfish, and as Angela realized at last, she was incapable of love. Still, I would not have wished such a fate upon her. 'Poetic justice,' as she called it, is rarely so swift or bloody. Nor was there anything the least poetical about that monster."

Michelle sighed. "It was very fast. I don't think she suffered much, not once she was out of the water."

Mrs. Troughton shook her head. "Such wickedness." She suddenly made a terrible face. "Whatever are we going to do with all those beasts?" She and Diana stared at one another. I'm not sure who started first, but both began to laugh. Diana's laughter had a certain hysterical edge.

"You might try the London Zoo," I said.

Diana was smiling, but her face was pale and strained. "I cannot believe she's really gone. I wanted her to leave, but…" She bit at her lower lip, then turned. "Will you stay with me, Adam—will you please stay with me?"

His black eyebrows sank inward over his nose, and his lips parted. I could see the fear slowly appear in his eyes. "Diana," he whispered.

She touched his face. "I would have forgiven you, anyway. You know that. I would have forgiven you because I love you, but you saved my life. You and Mr. Holmes. You pulled me out of the water. Aunt Arabella deceived us both. She was wicked. She wanted your money, but I think she also wanted to hurt me. She's gone. There's nothing to keep us apart now—nothing."

He seemed frozen, unable to speak, and the look in his eyes simply made no sense to me. "Adam?" I said softly.

He lowered his gaze. "Diana, I… I love you, but… but…"

"But what!" she cried.

"I… I cannot be a fit husband for you."

"What are you talking about? Let me be the judge of that!"

"There is nothing…" He clenched his teeth, then shook his head. "If only it could be."

She let go of his arm and stepped back. She was still wearing his overcoat, her bare white feet showing beneath it. "So you won't have me, is that it?"

"Not won't—*can't.*" He would not meet her gaze.

"Oh I don't understand—I don't."

Michelle shook her head and stepped nearer. "We are all out of sorts. This is not the time."

Diana stared at her. "It's never the time—never the time with him— oh, I give up. I give up! It's hopeless."

She began to cry and let Michelle take her in her arms. Michelle held her tightly and glared at Adam. "I… I'm sorry," he said.

"Sorry!" Michelle exclaimed. "Oh my dear, let's get some dry clothes on you. You must be freezing."

"Yes, yes," Mrs. Troughton exclaimed. She gave Adam a venomous gaze. The two women led her toward the stairway.

Holmes shook his head. "Incredible. Simply incredible. Even I with all my peccadillos find this utterly incomprehensible. Sir, this has gone on long enough." He looked at me. "Henry, can you put some sense into this great buffoon? Perhaps you can get through that incredibly thick and dense skull of his. In the meantime, I shall finally get into some dry clothes myself."

I nodded brusquely, then seized Adam by the arm. "Come with me." He followed docilely as I led him to the drawing room. I turned up the lamp, then poured us each a brandy. "Sit down."

He sagged into one end of the sofa, I into the other. I took a big swallow, felt the warmth slip down my throat and into my stomach. "That creature—that fish—was incredible. I don't think any actual snake could have been half so frightening."

Adam stared at me curiously. "I didn't find it exactly frightening."

"You didn't?" I sipped at my brandy. Adam hadn't touched his. "Drink."

He took a swallow, then sighed. "Now everyone hates me."

My laugh was a moan. "Adam, no one hates you—least of all Diana." I drew in my breath slowly. "This has already lasted far too long. Can you explain to me what is going on?"

He swallowed the brandy. One hand fumbled awkwardly at a lock of his black hair. "I'm ashamed," he whispered.

"Ashamed." My brow knotted up. All right, he didn't think he could be a proper husband. He was probably worried about conjugal "duties". That must go back to the problem with the prostitute, but something more seemed to be involved, some… mystery. Could he have some actual physical defect which would make the sexual act impossible for him? And how would he know that? Of course, if he were normal, he would know well enough whether he was capable or not. I hesitated. "Adam, do you know what onanism is?"

This time he truly froze–he had the glass almost to his lips–and it hung suspended two inches below his mouth. He seemed to have forgotten to breathe, but then he sucked in air. At last he lowered the glass.

"Well?" I asked.

He let out a long shuddery sigh. "Yes–to my shame! Now…" He looked up at me, and his eyes had gone liquid. "Now you must understand."

I stared at him. "I do?"

"Yes–*yes*. I have squandered my manhood, wasted… wasted…" He looked away, then took a huge swallow of brandy.

Idiot, I thought. *Dunce*. I was not berating Adam, but myself. Even respectable physicians of a certain age still believed that every sexual act weakened the body, and of course school masters and vicars constantly warned young men about the dreadful consequences of masturbation. My laugh this time was brief and bitter. Could it really be so terribly simple, so inane, so stupid?

"I suppose someone at school warned you about the consequences of onanism?"

He nodded. "Yes, yes. Old Master Herbert warned us again and again. He told us what would eventually happen. Some of the boys thought it was funny. They even laughed afterwards, but not me. I knew it was wrong and what it would do to me! Oh I tried–I swear I did–but I simply could not help myself. I prayed and prayed, but that didn't help. I still… I still don't understand… why it should be so difficult to be pure."

I shook my head. "Oh, Adam. And I suppose the episode with the prostitute convinced you that the worst had already happened."

He sat upright. "Who told you about that? Surely not my father!"

"No, no—I figured it out on my own. I have seen other men who have had a similar experience. It proves nothing—nothing at all. It does not mean you are not a man. It means you are not an animal who can copulate at will with any female. Nor does it mean there is anything physically wrong with you. In fact I am certain…" I smiled gently. "I am certain your manhood is completely… viable. It might take a little while, but should you marry Diana you will absolutely be a proper husband to her."

Again he seemed to freeze, the glass in mid-air, this time hovering over his knees. His eyes were locked on mine. "You are serious? You are not just trying to keep me from despair?"

"I am trying to keep you from despair, yes—because there is simply no reason for despair. There is nothing wrong with you."

"But I thought…"

"Yes, I know what you thought. It is an old idea—it is medieval medicine. 'Each sexual act drains some vital essence, shortening one's life. You only have so much essence, and if you squander it, you gradually become a drooling sort of idiot, pale and weak, like Uriah Heep.' That is nonsense, Adam! Modern doctors no longer believe that."

"Can this be true?"

"Yes—*yes*. Listen, I think I can demonstrate to you the absurdity of this whole theory. According to it, you should grow weaker over time as your vitality drains away. That is true, is it not? Well, then, your desire should also lessen and your ability to squander that essence. Now you tell me—I suspect you began as a boy. How old were you when you first discovered the act?"

"Fifteen."

"So that was some six years ago. Has your desire waned over those six years?" He shook his head. "In fact, I'll wager the frequency has not gone down, but quite the opposite."

His eyes were still locked on mine. "Yes. It's gotten worse and worse. And when I'm around Diana... I can't seem to help myself." He shook his head. "It's always her–always her that I..." He looked away. "It is shameful–*it is*. I can't stop thinking about her, thinking about her naked and..."

I leaned over and seized his arm, squeezed it tightly. "Look at me." He swung his head round. "It is not shameful–it is not. It means that you desire her. That's what happens when men and women love one another. It is not all pure and idyllic and soulful–it is carnal and fleshly as well–and it is all one, all part of love. You can love Diana, Adam. I know you can. You will not fail her, and you must know she will never fail you."

He stared at me a long while, then sank back into the chair. He stared briefly at the brandy, downed the glass in a single swallow, then covered his mouth with his big hand. "You would not lie to me, I know. You are my friend."

"Yes."

He lowered his hand, and an odd smile pulled at his lips, even as he shook his head. "What you must think of me. I must have seemed truly mad to you."

I laughed. "Yes."

He suddenly stood. "But Diana! How many times I have hurt her. Oh I must tell her–I must tell her at once."

I swallowed the last of my brandy and stood. "That would be a good idea. I think she would be most relieved."

"You don't think it's too late?"

"I *know* it is not too late."

He strode out of the room and into the hallway, shouted, "Diana! Diana!" The door to her room was ajar, light streaming into the hall. He went in first. Diana stood up. She and Michelle had been sitting on a small sort of sofa. She had put on a blue woolen robe, dried and brushed out her long red hair. Her face, her eyes, still seemed wary, but she could not restrain a smile.

"Oh, Diana." He crossed the room in three huge steps, seized her hand. "I have been so stupid. I thought–I thought I was sick. I thought I could not–but Henry says there is nothing wrong with me. Nothing. I…" He raised her hand and kissed her knuckles. "I'm sorry, so sorry for all my foolishness. I do love you. I swear I do."

Her face had been so pale, but a flush had appeared at each cheek, spread slowly outward. "Do you?"

"Yes."

"And you'll stay with me? You'll–"

"*Forever.*" He kissed her hand again. She stared at him. He let go of her hand, then put his enormous hands on either side of her slender face. He hesitated only an instant, then bent his head and touched his lips to hers. Her long fingers gripped his arms just above the elbows and slowly tightened. She let go, then slipped her arms round him, even as he lowered his hands and embraced her. They were still kissing. Michelle was behind them, and she raised one eyebrow and gave me that crooked, one-sided smile. I noticed that Diana's feet had left the ground. Her right calf and bare foot rose involuntarily as she tried to caress Adam's leg.

Michelle quietly stepped around them. Their heads had tilted slightly, their mouths opening wider. Michelle took my hand and we stepped outside into the hallway. "What on earth did you do, Henry?" she whispered. "Talk about a miracle cure!"

"I should have figured it out a long time ago. It goes back to his school days and some stern half-crazed master. Adam has long been guilty of the frightful crime of onanism, and he thought it had drained him of all his manly essence and rendered him unfit for marriage."

She looked closely at me. "Are you serious?"

"Oh yes."

"Oh for God's sake! I cannot believe it. Although... when I was a girl, the sisters often told us about the great treasure of our virginity and the frightful consequences should we yield it up." She drew in her breath slowly, then leaned over and kissed me lightly on the lips. "Very good, Dr. Vernier. A masterful diagnosis."

We heard a long kind of moan, and then Diana said, "Oh Adam," in that sort of voice one only hears in bedrooms. I reached over and closed the door as quietly as I could, leaving us almost in darkness. Another door down the hall was still open with the lamp lit. "I think any doubts about his manhood may soon be resolved once and for all."

Michelle reached up and grasped my arms just above the elbows, then pushed me back against the wall. "Henry," she whispered. She turned her head to kiss me. Our arms came round one another even as our mouths opened wider. Her body and her mouth were so familiar to me, but familiarity had not bred contempt, but instead immediate passion, warmth and comfort. Her kiss was playful at the end, something about the way she moved her jaw. She backed away and slowly drew in her breath. "We could still teach these youngsters a thing or two," she said.

"Oh, but the fun is in discovering for yourselves."

"I suppose you're right. I do love you, you know, especially when you make wonderful things happen."

"And I love you. Let's get to bed."

She laughed. "Forward man! Yes, let's." She took my hand. Behind the door came an odd cry, whether from Adam or Diana I could not tell.

"Oh wait–I must speak to Sherlock. He will want to know." I squeezed her hand. "I won't be long, I promise."

"Very well. I'll warm up the bed for you." She went one way down the hall, I the other.

I paused at the top of the stairs. Holmes stood before the distant fireplace, a tall thin figure holding a cigarette in hand. Mrs. Troughton sat in a nearby chair talking. He turned round and saw me, then raised his other hand. I slowly descended. A heavy silence had settled over the huge room, and the air was cold until I was near the fire. I pulled out my watch and saw that it was one thirty a.m. Little wonder I suddenly felt exhausted.

Mrs. Troughton rose. "It's long after midnight. I'll be off to bed, gentlemen. I'll sleep well tonight, I know, and I'll give a prayer of thanks that the mistress is safe at last."

Holmes nodded. "Good night, madam. And thank you for your assistance in this business."

"It was the least I could do. And thank you, Mr. Holmes, for saving Diana's life." She nodded, smiled briefly at me, then walked away.

Holmes's drew on the cigarette. "Any luck with our reprobate, Henry?"

"Oh yes." I explained briefly what had happened.

Holmes brow creased as he listened, then his mouth twitched once, twice, in and out of a smile. He shook his head at last. "Incredible. I am glad I entrusted the matter to you. It is a case I could have never solved, that sort of grand muddled tangle of the human psyche. Perhaps I should assume the role of Watson and write up your adventures, Henry. I could call this one 'The Case of the Befuddled

Bachelor.' Surely the *Strand* would be interested in the story."

I laughed. "I suspect it would be somewhat too controversial."

"I suppose so. All the same, well done indeed. I only wish... It is a pity young men at school are subjected to school masters like Herbert rather than men like you. The educational establishment of Great Britain depends too much on dried-up old bachelor prudes." Again that grimace of a smile. "Men like myself."

I stared at him. "Don't be ridiculous. You know better."

He sighed, took a final draw on the cigarette, then tossed the butt in the fire. "I hope so. 'Know better.' Hard to be sure. Was it wisdom or foolishness...?" His gray eyes were fixed on mine. "I mean what passed with Mrs. Wheelwright. With Violet."

I hesitated. "It was neither, exactly. The brain deals in wisdom and foolishness, but the heart is another matter. We think that our brain reigns supreme, but the heart sometimes wields its own power and will not be denied."

Holmes shrugged. "It is far too late for philosophy, Henry. I shall smoke another cigarette, and I suspect Michelle must be waiting for you." He smiled, and I knew that it had not required some labored deduction of that phenomenal brain for him to know why she was waiting.

I covered my mouth to stifle a yawn. "I am tired. All the same, if you had not dealt with Arabella, Diana might well be dead by now. She and Adam would not have had their chance. You are the true hero of the hour, as always. And the way you dealt with that monstrous creature! I could not understand why you were shaking so earlier when you came out of the water."

He nodded. "It is true. I cannot remember when I last felt such fear. Momentum drove me into the water, the need to act, but once I was bobbing about there with Diana I had time to reflect! I did not know how long I might have or what the real odds were. It was only a sort of dumb luck, Henry, that the eel appeared a few minutes later when Lady Verr was in the pit, rather than earlier."

I smiled. "So you truly don't believe in poetic justice, then?" He only shrugged. I sighed. "I am an agnostic, as you know, but in this case... I prefer to think that God had something to do with it."

Holmes had withdrawn his cigarette case and taken out another cigarette. "I hope so, Henry. I hope so."

I stared down at the flames, then suddenly noticed Holmes's bare feet. His boots were nearby. He must finally be warming his feet after that icy plunge into the pit and all our time outside. They were white and bony, the long toes clear brethren to his thin fingers. Everyone had been solicitous of Diana, but no one had thought to look after him.

"Go on, get to bed," Holmes said. "I shall just go up after this last cigarette."

"Oh, I'll stay with you that long. It is nice here by the fire. And I must make certain you limit yourself to only one more!" He smiled. I covered my mouth and yawned again. The tension of the long day had mostly dissipated. "You know, this time I do feel that I actually helped out somewhat, rather than just being a witless observer—helped with Adam, anyway, that is."

"You have always helped out, Henry. You have never been merely a witless observer. You have a way, especially, with these young women that I can never match."

"Well, your courage is incomprehensible to me. Yours and Michelle's both."

He shrugged. "We all have our strengths. And our weaknesses." He held the cigarette between thumb and forefinger and slowly drew in. The log on the grate made a crackling noise and spat out some sparks.

* * *

Holmes, Michelle and I were having a late breakfast around ten a.m. the next morning, when Diana and Adam finally appeared. They were dressed, but their hair was still somewhat astray. Hers was bound up, but a wispy red strand came down past her white ear, and another drooped over her forehead. Both also had a flush akin to a glowing coal, a warm radiance, which I recognized only too well. They appeared dazed and sleepy, but beautiful and very happy. Adam, in particular, was so transformed as to be almost unrecognizable. I realized that never before, in all the time I had known him, had I truly seen him happy.

He stepped up to the table, Diana's slender fingers clasped in his enormous hand, and smiled down at us all. "Mr. Holmes, Diana and I must be married!"

Holmes regarded him thoughtfully, a certain humor showing in the antics of his mouth. "Yes, I suppose you must, and as soon as possible, I think. Best to present your father with a *fait accompli*." They nodded. "Very well, then. You have both been dwelling in the parish longer than the required fifteen days, so you may dispense with the banns and purchase a license today from the Reverend Sloap. You can be married sometime tomorrow in the morning, as is customary. I know the vicar will be happy to perform the ceremony. Henry can serve as best man."

Adam nodded and his powerful fingers gripped my shoulder. "Oh yes–yes."

"Michelle can act as maid of honor. And as for myself... In my long career there is one duty I have never performed, nor is the opportunity ever likely to arise again." He stared up at Diana, his eyes suddenly wary. "Miss Marsh, would I be presuming too much, or might I have the great honor of giving away the bride?"

"Oh, Mr. Holmes–the honor is all mine!" She did not hesitate, but touched his cheek with the fingertips of her free hand. "There could be no one more worthy than you." Her smile brought out the dimple by her mouth.

For once Sherlock Holmes seemed at a loss for words.

About the Author

Sam Siciliano is the author of several novels, including the Titan Sherlock Holmes titles *The Angel of the Opera*, *The Web Weaver* and *The Grimswell Curse*. He lives in Vancouver, Washington.

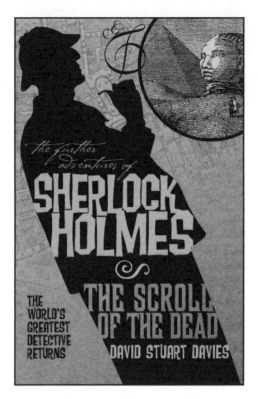

THE FURTHER ADVENTURES
OF SHERLOCK HOLMES

THE SCROLL OF THE DEAD

David Stuart Davies

In this fast-paced adventure, Sherlock Holmes attends a seance to unmask
an impostor posing as a medium. His foe, Sebastian Melmoth is a man hell-
bent on discovering a mysterious Egyptian papyrus that may hold the key
to immortality. It is up to Holmes and Watson to use their deductive skills
to stop him or face disaster.

ISBN: 9781848564930

AVAILABLE NOW!

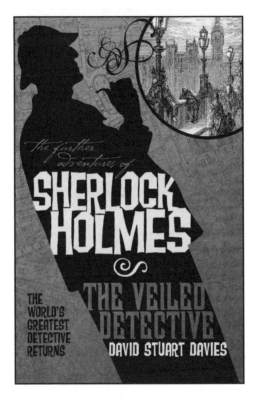

THE FURTHER ADVENTURES
OF SHERLOCK HOLMES

THE VEILED DETECTIVE

David Stuart Davies

It is 1880, and a young Sherlock Holmes arrives in London to pursue a
career as a private detective. He soon attracts the attention of criminal
mastermind Professor James Moriarty, who is driven by his desire to
control this fledgling genius. Enter Dr John H. Watson, soon to make
history as Holmes' famous companion.

ISBN: 9781848564909

AVAILABLE NOW!

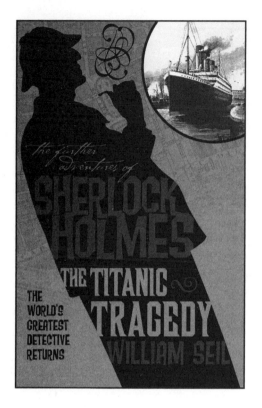

THE FURTHER ADVENTURES
OF SHERLOCK HOLMES

THE TITANIC TRAGEDY

William Seil

Holmes and Watson board the Titanic in 1912, where Holmes is to carry
out a secret government mission. Soon after departure, highly important
submarine plans for the U.S. navy are stolen. Holmes and Watson work
through a list of suspects which includes Colonel James Moriarty, brother
to the late Professor Moriarty—will they find the culprit before tragedy
strikes?

ISBN: 9780857687104
AVAILABLE NOW!

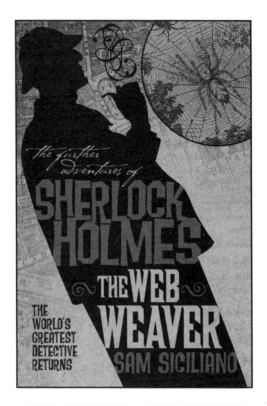

THE FURTHER ADVENTURES
OF SHERLOCK HOLMES

THE WEB WEAVER

Sam Siciliano

A mysterious gypsy places a cruel curse on the guests at a ball. When
a series of terrible misfortunes affects those who attended, Mr. Donald
Wheelwright engages Sherlock Holmes to find out what really happened
that night. Can he save Wheelwright and his beautiful wife Violet from
the devastating curse?

ISBN: 9780857686985

AVAILABLE NOW!

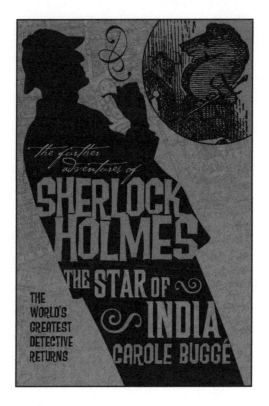

THE FURTHER ADVENTURES
OF SHERLOCK HOLMES

THE STAR OF INDIA

Carole Buggé

Holmes and Watson find themselves caught up in a complex chessboard
of a problem, involving a clandestine love affair and the disappearance
of a priceless sapphire. Professor James Moriarty is back to tease and
torment, leading the duo on a chase through the dark and dangerous
back streets of London and beyond.

ISBN: 9780857681218

AVAILABLE NOW!

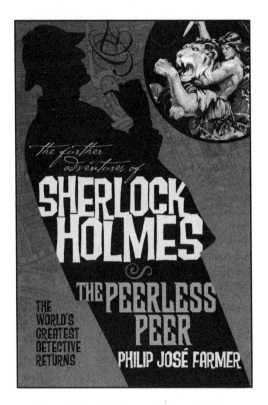

THE FURTHER ADVENTURES
OF SHERLOCK HOLMES

THE PEERLESS PEER

Philip José Farmer

During the Second World War, Mycroft Holmes dispatches his
brother, Sherlock, and Dr. Watson to recover a stolen formula. During
their perilous journey, they are captured by a German zeppelin.
Subsequently forced to abandon ship, the pair parachute into the dark
African jungle where they encounter the lord of the jungle himself...

ISBN: 9780857681201

AVAILABLE NOW!

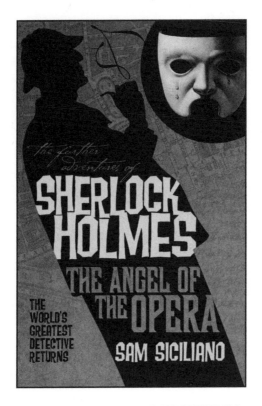

THE FURTHER ADVENTURES
OF SHERLOCK HOLMES

THE ANGEL OF THE OPERA

Sam Siciliano

Paris 1890. Sherlock Holmes is summoned across the English Channel
to the famous Opera House. Once there, he is challenged to discover
the true motivations and secrets of the notorious phantom, who rules its
depths with passion and defiance.

ISBN: 9781848568617

AVAILABLE NOW!

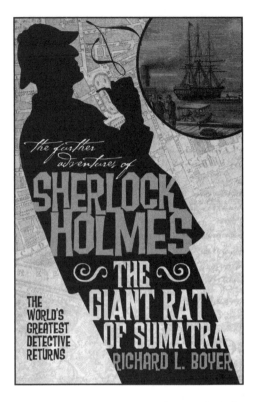

THE FURTHER ADVENTURES
OF SHERLOCK HOLMES

THE GIANT RAT OF SUMATRA

Richard L. Boyer

For many years, Dr. Watson kept the tale of The Giant Rat of
Sumatra a secret. However, before he died, he arranged that
the strange story of the giant rat should be held in the vaults of
a London bank until all the protagonists were dead...

ISBN: 9781848568600

AVAILABLE NOW!

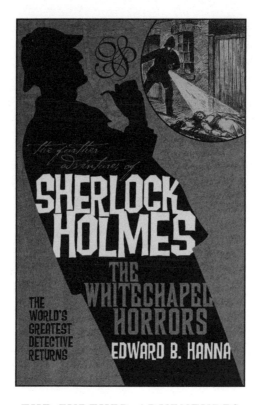

THE FURTHER ADVENTURES
OF SHERLOCK HOLMES

THE WHITECHAPEL HORRORS

Edward B. Hanna

Grotesque murders are being committed on the streets of Whitechapel.
Sherlock Holmes believes he knows the identity of the killer–Jack the
Ripper. But as he delves deeper, Holmes realizes that revealing the
murderer puts much more at stake than just catching a killer…

ISBN: 9781848567498

AVAILABLE NOW!